PICTURE

Praise for *Picture Me Gone*

'Nobody describes the strengths and pain of being young quite like Meg Rosoff . . . she excels at blending tragic events, comedy, philosophical concepts and love into unexpected and engaging fictions' – *The Times*

'The only predictable thing about Meg Rosoff is that each book will be entirely different from the last . . . *Picture Me Gone* is a delightfully authentic slice of life' – *Daily Mail*

'*Picture Me Gone* charts the tiny shifts in allegiance and unexpected situations through which the heroine discovers that the stories she lives by will not be enough for the pitiless, messy, adult world. In this finely tuned minimalist work, every detail counts' – *Guardian*

'Thought-provoking coming-of-age story . . . Mila's sharp observations of the people she meets and the winter landscape add a fresh, poetic aura to her discoveries and the novel as a whole' – *Publishers' Weekly*

'Printz Award-winning author Meg Rosoff's latest novel is a gorgeous and unforgettable page-turner about the relationship between parents and children, love and loss' – goodreads.com

'A great read' – *Mizz*

'Rosoff's talent is in writing believable, many-layered characters, and *Picture Me Gone* is a neat, beautiful little novel that unravels the ties that bind' – *Stylist* (*Stylist's* Top 10 Must-Reads)

'*Picture Me Gone* is completely, completely wonderful – beautiful, sad, funny and true, with a heroine who lodges herself in your mind and in your heart as she pieces together the million tiny clues we leave in life about who and what we are'
– Lucy Mangan, *Stylist* and *Guardian* columnist

'A memorable portrait – touching, alarming and funny by turns – of that time in your life when you first realize how badly adults can mess things up' – *Reader's Digest*

'Compelli~ ~~~ ~~~ ~~~~~ ~~~~~ complicated
relati ~~~~ ~~~ ~~~~ *Magazine*

'In Meg ~~~~ ~~~~ ~~~ wonderful
chara ~~~~ ~~~~ ~~~ *okseller*

MEG ROSOFF became a publishing sensation with her first novel, *How I Live Now*, which won the Guardian Children's Fiction Prize.

Her second novel, *Just In Case*, won the Carnegie Medal, and her novels have won or been shortlisted for nineteen international literary prizes.

Meg lives in London with her husband and daughter.

meg rosoff

PENGUIN BOOKS

PENGUIN BOOKS

Published by the Penguin Group
Penguin Books Ltd, 80 Strand, London WC2R ORL, England
Penguin Group (USA) Inc., 375 Hudson Street, New York, New York 10014, USA
Penguin Group (Canada), 90 Eglinton Avenue East, Suite 700, Toronto, Ontario,
Canada M4P 2Y3 (a division of Pearson Penguin Canada Inc.)
Penguin Ireland, 25 St Stephen's Green, Dublin 2, Ireland (a division of Penguin Books Ltd)
Penguin Group (Australia), 707 Collins Street, Melbourne, Victoria 3008, Australia
(a division of Pearson Australia Group Pty Ltd)
Penguin Books India Pvt Ltd, 11 Community Centre, Panchsheel Park,
New Delhi – 110 017, India
Penguin Group (NZ), 67 Apollo Drive, Rosedale, Auckland 0632, New Zealand
(a division of Pearson New Zealand Ltd)
Penguin Books (South Africa) (Pty) Ltd, Block D, Rosebank Office Park,
181 Jan Smuts Avenue, Parktown North, Gauteng 2193, South Africa

Penguin Books Ltd, Registered Offices: 80 Strand, London WC2R ORL, England

penguin.com

Published 2013
This edition published 2014
001

Text copyright © Meg Rosoff, 2013
All rights reserved

The moral right of the author has been asserted

Set in Sabon LT Std
Printed in Great Britain by Clays Ltd, St Ives plc

British Library Cataloguing in Publication Data
A CIP catalogue record for this book is available from the British Library

ISBN: 978-0-141-34406-5

www.greenpenguin.co.uk

For Brenda

1

The first Mila was a dog. A Bedlington terrier. It helps if you know these things. I'm not at all resentful at being named after a dog. In fact, I can imagine the scene exactly. *Mila*, my father would have said, that's a nice name. Forgetting where he'd heard it. And then my mother would remember the dog and ask if he was absolutely sure, and when he didn't answer, she would say, OK, then. Mila. And then looking at me think, Mila, my Mila.

I don't believe in reincarnation. It seems unlikely that I've inherited the soul of my grandfather's long-dead dog. But certain traits make me wonder. Was it entirely coincidence that Mila entered my father's head on the morning of my birth? Observing his daughter, one minute old, he thought first of the dog, Mila? Why?

My father and I are preparing for a journey to New York, to visit his oldest friend. But yesterday things changed. His friend's wife phoned to say he'd left home.

Left home? Gil asks. What on earth do you mean?

Disappeared, she says. No note. Nothing.

Gil looks confused. Nothing?

You'll still come? says the wife.

And when Gil is silent for a moment, thinking it through, she says, Please.

Yes, of course, Gil says, and slowly replaces the phone in its cradle.

He'll be back, Gil tells Marieka. He's just gone off by himself to think for a while. You know what he's like.

But why now? My mother is puzzled. When he knew you were coming? The timing is . . . peculiar.

Gil shrugs. By this time tomorrow he'll be back. I'm certain he will.

Marieka makes a doubtful noise but from where I'm crouched I can't see her face. What about Mila? she says.

A few things I know: It is Easter holiday and I am out of school. My mother is working all week in Holland and I cannot stay at home alone. My father lives inside his head and it is better for him to have company when he travels, to keep him on track. The tickets were bought two months ago.

We will both still go.

I enjoy my father's company and we make a good pair. Like my namesake, Mila the dog, I have a keen awareness of where I am and what I'm doing at all times. I am not given to dreaminess, have something of a terrier's determination. If there is something to notice, I will notice it first.

I am good at solving puzzles.

My packing is nearly finished when Marieka comes to say that she and Gil have decided I should still go. I am already arranging clues in my head, thinking through the possibilities, looking for a theory.

I have met my father's friend sometime in the distant past but I don't remember him. He is a legend in our family for once saving Gil's life. Without Matthew there would be no me. For this, I would like to thank him, though I never really get the chance.

It seems so long ago that we left London. Back then I was a child.

I am still, technically speaking, a child.

2

I know very little about Mila the dog. She belonged to my grandfather when he was a boy growing up in Lancashire and dogs like Mila were kept for ratting not pets. I found a dusty old photo of her in an album my father kept from childhood. Mostly it contains pictures of people I don't know. In the photo, the dog has a crouchy stance, as if she'd rather be running flat out. The person on the other side of the camera interests me greatly. Perhaps it is my grandfather, a boy who took enough pride in his ratting dog to keep a photo of her. Lots of people take pictures of their dogs now, but did they then? The dog is looking straight ahead. If it were his dog, wouldn't it turn to look?

This picture fills me with a deep sense of longing. *Saudade*, Gil would say. Portuguese. The longing for something loved and lost, something gone or unattainable.

I cannot explain the feeling of sadness I have looking at this picture. Mila the dog has been dead for eighty years.

Everyone calls my father Gil. Gil's childhood friend has walked out of the house he shared with his wife and baby. No one knows where he went or why. Matthew's wife phoned Gil, in case he wanted to change our plans. In case he'd heard something.

He hadn't. Not then.

We will take the train to the airport and it is important to remember our passports. Marieka tells me to take good care of myself and kisses me. She smiles and asks if I will be OK and I nod, because I will. She looks in Gil's direction and says, Take care of your father. She knows I will take care of him as best I can. Age is not always the best judge of competence.

The train doors close and we wave goodbye. I settle down against my father and breathe the smell of his jacket. He smells of books, ink, old coffee pushed to the back of the desk and wool, plus a hint of the cologne Marieka used to buy him; one he hasn't worn in years. The smell of his skin is too familiar to describe. It surprised me to discover that not everyone can identify people by their smell. Marieka says this makes me half dog at least.

I've seen the way dogs sniff people and other dogs on the street or when they return from another place. They want to put a picture together based on clues: Where have you been? Were there cats there? Did you eat meat? So. A wood fire. Mud. Lemons.

If I were a dog and smelled books, coffee and ink in a slightly tweedy wool jacket, I don't know whether I'd think, *That man translates books*. But that is what he does.

I've always wondered why humans developed so many languages. It complicates things. *Makes things interesting*, says Gil.

Today, we are going to America, where we won't need any extra languages. Gil ruffles my hair but doesn't actually notice that I'm sitting beside him. He is deep in a book translated by a colleague. Occasionally he nods.

My mother plays the violin in an orchestra. Scrape scrape scrape, she says when it's time to practise, and closes the door. Tomorrow she will set off to Holland.

I narrow my eyes and focus on a point in the distance. I am subtle, quick and loyal. I would have made a good ratter.

Saudade. I wonder if Gil is feeling that now for his lost friend. If he is, he is not showing any sign of it.

3

Marieka is from Sweden. Gil's mother was Portuguese-French. I need diagrams to keep track of all the nationalities in my family but I don't mind. Mongrels are wily and healthy and don't suffer displaced hips or premature madness.

My parents were over forty when they had me but I don't think of them as old, any more than they think of me as young. We are just us.

The fact that Gil's friend left home exactly when we were coming to visit is hard to understand. The police don't believe he's been murdered or kidnapped. I can imagine Gil wandering out the door and forgetting for a while to come back, but ties to Marieka and me would draw him home. Perhaps Matthew's ties are looser.

Despite being best friends, Gil and Matthew haven't seen each other in eight years. This makes the timing of his disappearance quite strange. Impolite, at the very least.

I look forward to seeing his wife and starting to understand what happened. Perhaps that's why Gil decided to take me along. Did I mention that I'm good at puzzles?

There is no need to double-check the passports; they are zipped into the inner pocket of my bag, safe, ready to be presented at check-in. Gil has put his book down and is gazing at something inside his head.

Where do you think Matthew went? I ask him.

It takes him a few seconds to return to me. He sighs and places his hand on my knee. I don't know, sweetheart.

Do you think we'll find him?

He looks thoughtful and says, Matthew was a wanderer, even as a child.

I wait to hear what he says next about his friend, but he says nothing. Inside his head he is still talking. Whole sentences flash across his eyes. I can't read them.

What? I say.

What, what? But he smiles.

What are you thinking?

Nothing important. About my childhood. I knew Matthew as well as I knew myself. When I think of him he still looks like a boy, even though he's quite old.

He's the same age as you I say, a little huffily.

Yes. He laughs, and pulls me close.

Here is the story from Gil's past:

He and Matthew are twenty-two, hitch-hiking to France in the back of a lorry with hardly any money. Then across France to Switzerland, to climb the Lauteraarhorn. Of the two, Matthew is the serious climber. It all goes according to plan until, on the second day, the temperature begins to rise. Avalanche weather. They watch the snow and ice thunder down around them. Mist descends towards evening, wrapping the mountain like a cloak. They burrow in, hoping the weather will change. Around midnight, the wind picks up and the rain turns to snow.

I've tried to imagine the scene hundreds of times. The first problem – exposure; the second – altitude. In the dead of night, in the dark and cold and wind and snow, Matthew notices the first signs of sickness in his friend and insists they descend. Gil refuses. Time passes. Head pounding, dizzy and irrational, Gil shouts, pushes Matthew off him. When at last he slumps, exhausted by the effort and the thin air, all he wants is to sit down and sleep in the snow. To die.

Over the next eleven hours, Matthew cajoles and drags and walks and talks him down the mountain. Over and over he tells Gil that you don't lie down in the snow. You keep going, no matter what.

They reach safety and Gil swears never to climb again.

And Matthew?

He was in love with it, says Gil.

He saved your life.

Gil nods.

We both fall silent, and I think, *and yet*.

And yet. Gil's life would not have needed saving if it hadn't been for Matthew.

The risk-taker and his riskee.

When I think of the way this trip has turned out, I wonder if we've been summoned for some sort of cosmic levelling, to help Matthew this time, the one who has never before required saving.

Perhaps we have been called in to balance the flow of energy in the universe.

We reach the airport. Gil picks up my bag and his, and we heave ourselves off the train. As the escalator carries us up, a text pings on to his phone.

My father is no good at texts, so he hands it to me and I show him: **Still nothing** it says, and is signed **Suzanne**. Matthew's wife.

We look at each other.

Come on, he says, piling our bags on to a trolley, and off we trot for what feels like miles to the terminal. At the check-in I ask for a window seat. Gil isn't fussy. We answer the questions about bombs and sharp objects, rummage through our carry-on bags for liquids, take our boarding passes and join the long snake through international departures. I pass the time watching other people, guessing their nationalities and relationships. American faces, I note, look unguarded. Does this make them more, or less approachable? I don't know yet.

Gil buys a newspaper and a bottle of whisky from duty-free and we go to the gate. As we board the plane I'm still thinking about that night on the mountain. What does it take to half drag, half carry a disorientated man the size of Gil, hour after hour, through freezing snow and darkness?

He may have other faults, this friend of Gil's, but he is not short of determination.

4

Suzanne meets us at international arrivals in New York. We are tired and crumpled. She spots Gil while he is trying to get his phone to work, and I nudge him and point. She's not old but looks pinched, as if someone's forgotten to water her. There is a buggy beside her and in it a child sleeps, despite all the bustle and noise. His arms stick out sideways in his padded suit. He wears a blue striped hat.

Gil kisses her and says, It's been too long. He peers down at the child. Hello, he says.

This is Gabriel, says Suzanne.

Hello, Gabriel, Gil says.

Gabriel squeezes his eyes together but doesn't wake up.

And, Mila, says Suzanne. You've changed so much.

She means that I've changed since I was four years old, when we last came to visit. That's when I met Gabriel's older brother, Owen. He was seven and I don't remember much about him, though we are holding hands in the one photo Gil has of us.

I touch the side of my finger to Gabriel's fist and he opens it and grabs on to me, still asleep. His grip is strong.

I'm sorry it's turned out like this, she says, and shakes her head. Not much fun for you. She turns to Gil. Come on. We can talk in the car.

The car is noisy and they speak in low voices so I can't catch most of what they're saying. Gabriel's in the back with me, fast asleep in his car seat. Occasionally he opens his eyes or stretches out a hand or kicks his feet, but he doesn't wake up. I make him grab on to my finger again and hear Suzanne say, Well, I hope you've made the right decision. She says it in a way that suggests he hasn't made the right decision at all, and I'm sure she's talking about bringing me along.

It has started to rain.

I fall asleep in the car to the rhythmic whoosh of windscreen wipers and the low buzz of Gil and Suzanne talking. Normally I'd be tuning in to hear what they're saying, but I'm too tired to care. Gabriel still hangs on to my finger.

When I awake it's dark. The road is narrow and quiet, nearly deserted; the rain has stopped. I say nothing at all, just look out of the window at the woods hoping to see a deer or a bear peering at me. Gil and Suzanne have stopped talking and the car is filled with private thoughts. Suzanne's are surprisingly clear; Gil's muffled and soft. Gil will be thinking about Matthew. It's a puzzle in his head and Suzanne's and mine. Where has Matthew gone? And why?

Suzanne's thoughts sound like a CD skipping. *Damn damn damn damn damn.*

What I know already is that Matthew and Suzanne both teach at the university in town. Matthew disappeared five days ago, eight months into the academic year, fourteen months after Gabriel was born. He took nothing with him, not a change of clothing or a passport or any money. Just left for work in the morning, said goodbye as usual and never showed up to teach his class.

The actual running away does not strike me as particularly strange. Most of us are held in place by a kind of centrifugal force. If for some reason the force stopped, we might all fly off in different directions. But what about the not coming back? Staying away is frightening and painful. And who would leave a baby? Even to me this seems extreme, a failure of love.

I think hard. What would make it feel like the only thing to do?

Here are the things I come up with:

(A) Desperation (about what?)
(B) Fear (of what?)
(C) Anger (why?)

I know hardly anything about Matthew and Suzanne. I will try to find out what is what when we arrive. There are always answers. Sometimes the right answer turns out to be

(D) All of the above.

5

When Gil told me that Matthew and Suzanne lived in a wooden house in upstate New York, I pictured an old-fashioned log cabin with smoke curling out of a stone chimney, a rocking chair on the portch and hens pecking around. Their house is nothing like this. I tried to hold the original image in my head for as long as possible but it slipped away once I saw the real thing. The real thing is nothing at all like a normal house and nothing at all like a log cabin. Picture a big cube with each flat side divided into four glass squares. The roof is a big square of wood laid at an angle so the snow and rain slip off.

It is set in trees with no other houses in sight and Suzanne left the lights on when she left. When we park the car it looks like a beautiful spaceship that just happened to land in a clearing. It shimmers in the black night. In my whole life, I never saw such a beautiful house. My first thought when Suzanne turns the car engine off is that I would never run away from a house like this.

Suzanne unlocks the front door. Lying across the room is a large white Alsatian that lifts its head when we come in. Suzanne doesn't greet it. She walks straight through as if the dog does not exist. The dog seems accustomed to this and stands to move out of her way. I approach the dog and she stands perfectly still while I kneel to pat her. She has beautiful brown eyes. Loneliness flows off her in waves.

So she is Matthew's dog. The name on her tag is Honey.

Inside the house, bookcases line most of the walls and there is a huge glass-fronted stove with 'eco-burner' etched on the glass. It burns the smoke too, says Suzanne.

I wonder how it does that.

All of the bookcases have tiny lights built in, and all of the walls and ceilings too, so the house seems to twinkle.

It's so beautiful, I say to Suzanne, who is lifting Gabriel out of his padded suit. He's awake now, staring like a baby owl. He waves his hands at Honey, who watches him gravely. Suzanne points at the door. Out, she says, and Honey walks out of the room.

It was built by an architect who ran out of money, Suzanne says. It made him famous though, and now he's built another just like it, only bigger, for himself. It's called The Box House.

As we walk through the house, I collect images like a camera clicking away. I can barely remember what Matthew looks like and there are no pictures of him to remind me. No picture of him and Suzanne on their wedding day or him with Gabriel. Or just him.

Click.

Other details leap out at me: A pair of muddy shoes. A stack of bills. A cracked window. A closed door. A pile of clothes. A skateboard. A dog. *Click click click*.

First impressions? This is not a happy house.

6

My best friend in London is called Catlin. She has hair like straw and thin arms and legs, and starting from when we were seven or eight we always went to her house after school, partly because it was on the way to mine and partly because the top floor has a hidden passageway under the roof through a door at the back of an old cupboard. Perfect for a clubhouse.

We designed code books and stashed our pocket money in a box under the floorboards, making plans to hide out when the enemy invaded Camden. Catlin was big on logistics so we spent days drawing maps of underground escape tunnels running all through London, connecting to sewers and ghost tube stations.

All the people we knew were rated according to how much of a security risk they'd turn out to be when things turned bad. Cat and I had top security clearance and were Head of State and Head of Security respectively. Gil was Senior Codebreaker with four-star clearance. Marieka would be Chief of Operations. Five star.

Catlin's parents were more of a problem. Her father shouted a lot, worked most of the time and was best avoided on the occasions he appeared at home. He and her mother rarely spoke. We made them Protocol Officers, a mysterious title, with only three-star clearance. I thought Cat might be offended that her parents had less trustworthy rankings than mine but she didn't seem to mind.

One day on the way to school Catlin said in her casual voice, My parents don't like each other. She looked at me, watching my reaction.

Lots of parents don't, I said, because I didn't want to hurt her feelings.

They're probably getting a divorce, she said.

I thought she might be crying because she sounded strange, but when I turned to look she was crouching down with an insane grin on her face and then she launched herself straight up into the air like a spring, shouting, I HATE THEM! with something like glee.

For a smallish person she has a very loud voice.

Shouting seemed to make her feel better, though I doubted what she said was true. Most people don't actually hate their parents, even if they are horrible. Her mother, at least, isn't horrible. She always brought biscuits and drinks on a tray up to the top floor where we were planning for the invasion. She never knocked, just quietly left it next to the cupboard door. I liked her for that, though she always seemed a bit sleepwalkerish. The house as a whole felt dulled, as if someone had sucked all the colour out with a straw. I wondered if Catlin noticed that it was different from other houses or whether it just looked normal to her.

This year, for the first time, Catlin and I stopped being in the same class together. She was suddenly wild and loud – rolling her school skirt up short and hanging out with older boys, the ones who scare old people on buses by swearing and smoking cigarettes. It was weird not to walk home with her every day but eventually I got used to it. Sometimes, walking past her house, I had to stop myself turning up the path out of habit.

It wasn't exactly like we avoided each other, and I didn't exactly miss her because she seemed like someone I no longer knew. But every single day I missed the person who used to be my friend. The worst was once when our eyes met by accident and she looked away.

Then, on the last day of spring term, she ran up behind me and shouted *Boom!* like in the old days and we ended up walking home together, pretending everything was normal.

Oh my god, Catlin said, eyes huge. Did you see Miss Evans as the Easter bunny?

Miss Evans is one of our PE teachers. She's a genuine freak, never missing a chance to dress up as Father Christmas or Karl Marx or Harry Potter.

Très awkward, I said.

Très très awkward!! She danced around me, hands fluttering like a joke ballerina.

We fell back in step again.

Are you around over Easter? Her tone was casual, her head almost in her schoolbag as she rummaged around for a lipstick.

The question was surprising because what about her new gang of cool friends? I have to go to New York, I told her. We're visiting an old friend of my dad's.

She didn't answer and it made me feel like apologizing

for going away, which was ridiculous as she'd barely spoken to me for months.

We got to her house and she didn't even say goodbye, just turned and ran up the path like she was angry, and I wondered if it was because I was going away and she wasn't, or because maybe she wanted to be friends again when it wasn't a convenient time for me.

Hey, Cat! I called after her. I'll let you know what America's like! But she was halfway through the door and didn't even turn round.

I stared at the door as it slammed and just as I was leaving I saw her disembodied face peering back at me through the window. Then both her hands crept up into the window like they belonged to someone else and she made a horrible face and started strangling herself, stuck out her tongue, went cross-eyed and disappeared down the bottom of the window.

Bye! I shouted again and waved.

A minute later I got a text from her. It said: **bring me back an American Easter egg**

And I answered: **save me a London one**

And she wrote back: **OK**

And I wrote back: **OK**

And she wrote back: **make it a big one**

And I wrote back: **ditto**

And we both felt better.

7

I am dizzy and a little sick with jet lag. Suzanne puts me in a small room off the study with a built-in bed. One end of my bed is a glass wall that faces out into the woods. She shows me how to use the blinds but I leave them open. I am so tired that I don't remember falling asleep, and a minute later it is noon the next day. Trees break the light up into fragments; above them, the sky is blue and clear. It couldn't be more different from our view in London, which is mainly of other houses.

Gil brings me milky coffee in bed. He smiles but looks distracted. Now that I am fully awake I scan the room – a small desk, a metal swivel chair, two pairs of trainers neatly placed in a corner. A bookshelf holds the *Guinness Book of Records* from a few years ago, a US Army Survival Manual, an ancient copy of *Treasure Island* with a worn leather cover, a tall pile of school notebooks and sports magazines. Just above is a shelf on which silver swimming trophies stand side by side and I realize with a start that this is Owen's room. There's a picture of him with Suzanne in a silver frame. He's got his arm round her shoulders and is already a few inches taller. The room has been tidied and dusted, but a set of keys, a birthday card and a bowl of coins still sit on the dresser as if he will come along any minute to claim them.

Gil clocks the direction of my gaze. Come and have breakfast when you're ready, he says. Did you sleep well?

I nod. Did you?

He shrugs. Honey appears round the corner, silent as a ghost. I put out my hand and she licks it.

No news? I ask, and he shakes his head.

Are we going to look for him?

I have to think, Gil says. Possibly.

I want to say, What if he's been murdered? Or jumped in front of a train? But I don't. Gil would have thought of that, anyway. He must think it hasn't happened. I suppose he might be keeping up appearances, pretending he thinks his friend is still alive so as not to upset me, but I doubt it. My father's faults involve excessive honesty. And absent-mindedness, of course.

Where do you think he went? What if we can't find him? Will he let us know he's OK?

Perguntadora. My father pronounces the word with a slight smile. It is Portuguese for someone who asks too many questions, and he's used the word as a nickname for me for as long as I can remember. First things first, he says. Drink your coffee. Have a shower. Get dressed. Come down to breakfast – He looks at his watch – lunch. We'll talk to Suzanne and make a plan. OK?

OK. I dig clean clothes out of my suitcase and take the towel from beside my bed. Honey watches me gravely. She is like a lost dog only she's not the one who's lost.

I take out my phone, snap a picture and text it to Catlin. **Lots of trees in New York.**

And she texts back: **Shd be tall buildings. Sure ur in the right place?**

It's called upstate I tell her.

There's a pause, then another bleep.

Got my egg yet?

Not yet I text back.

ok.

I put my phone down on a shelf in the shower room, which is black slate – walls, ceiling and floor. Once I figure out how it works, I want to stand under the hot water all day. The soap Suzanne put out for me is also black, and smells of coconut. I make a thick lather and watch it slide down the drain. When I turn the water off, the room is so full of steam it's like standing in a cloud. I wrap myself in the dark-green towel, pine green, the same colour as the trees outside the house. Despite the seriousness of our mission, I am, for this moment, perfectly content.

There is toast for breakfast, and no sign of Suzanne. Gil says she's gone to work for an hour or so, and we can make ourselves at home till she comes back. Gabriel's babysitter has taken him to playgroup.

What do you think? he asks, looking at me carefully.

Sometimes I observe things I can't interpret. Like two people smiling and holding hands when actually they hate each other. This confuses me, and Gil says that's because it is, in actual fact, confusing. It's the same with being a translator. Some things can't be translated because the words don't exist in the other language, or the meaning is so entirely

22

specific to one place or one way of speaking that it disappears in translation.

But sometimes there are clues.

The house, I say a little tentatively, is beautiful.

And?

I take a deep breath. Suzanne is a very tidy person. All her things and Gabriel's are put away. But she hasn't touched *his* things. Look . . .

Gil looks.

A sweater crumpled on the floor. Muddy boots, shoved in a corner. A pile of mail, stacked on a table. It's almost –

He waits.

– as if they live in two separate houses that don't touch. Like . . . only one of them is vegetarian, I say, pointing to the shelf of cookbooks.

That's not uncommon.

I look at him, not knowing whether it's common or uncommon. I just know what a family in which everyone gets along feels like, with all the edges of things blurred and overlapping. What I feel in this house is containment. Suzanne containing her things so they don't touch his. Even the baby doesn't seem to cross over, his toys and clothes and equipment all tidy and stacked up on her plane.

And she hates his dog.

I don't say it, but I've felt other things. Owen, for instance. I can feel him all through the house. They pretend he's gone, but he's everywhere, like a restless soul.

There's someone else. A smoker. Suzanne has a friend who smokes. There are traces of smoke in her clothes, in her hair. And more. I can smell it in certain parts of the house, which

23

suggests it's not just someone she knows, but someone who spends time here. And it's definitely a man. Women smell of things other than themselves – hair stuff, shampoo, soap – even if they don't wear perfume.

Does Matthew smoke? I ask.

Never, Gil says, looking puzzled. Couldn't stand the idea. Why?

I shrug.

Gil sips his coffee. Suzanne says Matthew has a camp near the Canadian border.

When I look puzzled, he says, A little house. Like a shack. *Matthew has a camp*. Not *we* have a camp.

She wonders if he's gone there. Gil looks at me over the rim of his cup. It's quite isolated. In the woods. The sort of place used by hunters.

Hunters?

Gil smiles. Matthew doesn't hunt. But maybe we should go and have a look. It's the obvious place for him to hide. Suzanne says she'll stay here with Gabriel in case he comes back.

I think for a minute. Is it normal for people just to disappear? I ask.

Normal? Gil raises an eyebrow. Not really. No such thing as normal, Perguntadora.

No such thing as normal. Gil's favourite line. I finish my toast and look out at the trees, just coming into leaf. I have learned normal as a word with no real meaning in our language, but sometimes I wonder what it would feel like.

What time is it in Holland? I ask him. Can we phone Marieka?

24

Yes, Gil says, and we do, but she's out so we leave a message. I flop down on the comfortable sofa and when I open my eyes Honey is standing a few inches away just looking at me. I sigh, get up and find her lead, and we go out together for a walk in the woods behind the house. I don't go far because I don't want to get lost.

Matthew's dog is a watcher, like me. Her eyes have a sadness that is almost human. She wants to know who I am. She follows me and pricks her ears to listen when I speak. Perhaps she is hoping I will explain things to her, where Matthew went and when he will be back, but I do not know the answers to these questions, and besides, I do not speak dog.

Honey is intelligent and loyal.

I wonder how Suzanne can hate such a dog.

8

You'd never think of matching Catlin and me up as friends. She's loud, skinny as a twig and pretty much bonkers. I'm quiet, solid and think things through. Cat always jumps first, before she has time to be swayed by facts. While I'm cautious. But I love how bright and daring she is, like a shooting star. She's not like anyone else I've ever met, and sometimes I wonder why she's friends with me.

Once she dragged me upstairs to our clubhouse to look at a cardboard box. Inside were two rats.

I stared at her.

Two rats had gone missing from the school science lab the week before and everyone was hysterical because they were at large. Some people wouldn't even use the school toilets in case they bobbed up in the water underneath them, which apparently happens.

You're a *rat-napper*? I was appalled. How'd you get them out of the building?

Cat pointed at her feet, grinning.

What? I said. You stuffed them in your *shoes*?

Almost. And then she reached down and picked up one of the rats and slipped her hand and the rat into a sock, removed her hand, tied the sock loosely at the end, and voilà, it was the perfect rat carrier. Being schoolroom rats, they were overfed and a bit dopey and docile from being passed around, so inside the dark sock they just curled up and dozed.

Where'd you learn that trick?

Made it up, she said, which figured. Most of what Cat tells me she makes up, but she's so entertaining, it doesn't matter. I prefer her explanations to the real ones anyway.

Her plan was for us to train the rats to carry messages through the sewers – though what messages and to whom was kind of up for grabs.

We weren't allowed to name them, she said, because then we'd get attached, which was extremely unprofessional. So they became Rat One and Rat Two. The first time I picked up Rat One, he scooted up my arm and scrambled down into my shirt.

The next day when two girls jumped up on chairs in the science lab screaming that they'd seen a rat, I didn't even turn round, just said not to bother, there were no rats. Everyone stared at me suspiciously, thinking, *How does she know?*

Anyway, on Tuesday we fed the rats cheese and biscuits and bits of sausage and grass, but by the time we got home from school on Wednesday they had chewed through the cardboard box and were gone.

We never saw them again. Catlin's mum kept complaining that she heard chewing in the cupboards at night, and her dad said, Don't be stupid you must be imagining things, and apparently there were big fights, though in that family there were always big fights. Cat said she thought the escaped rats were the straw that broke the camel's back between her parents, i.e., they ruined their marriage once and for all. There was no way I could tell her that she was wrong, that it was obvious from the first time you met her parents that they just didn't like each other and would have got divorced sooner or later, rats or no rats.

It must be horrible to realize that you come from two people who never should have got together in the first place.

After the rat incident, we started spending more time at my house where everyone got along and there was no shouting. Looking back, I wonder if that was one of the reasons we stopped being friends.

One time when we had to go back to her house after school, we found her mum out and everything perfectly tidy and all the windows in the house closed up tight, despite the fact that it was a beautiful spring day. It was cold and grey inside, like no one had told the house that winter was over. And outside, trees floated with blossom and birds sang.

We picked up our code books from the clubhouse even though we didn't play spies much any more, and we didn't even bother checking the fridge. We just wanted to get out of there.

Mum doesn't hear rats any more, Cat said. They've deserted us, like a sinking ship.

She looked downcast, so I squeaked *Avast ye hearties!* and *Mizzen ye swarthy poop deck!* and we slammed the door and ran back to mine, shouting in pig-pirate all the way. And when we arrived, Gil called hello from his study, Marieka showed up with bunches of asparagus, and you could smell hyacinths through the windows. At the time I thought it was nice but maybe Cat hated it.

The following year, when we weren't speaking, it occurred to me that her new personality actually made sense – that kissing boys and smoking weed and stomping out of class and insulting teachers and generally acting about a hundred times worse and louder than you really are is what you might do in order not to think about having to go home to sleep in that sad grey house.

9

Translating books is an odd way to make a living. It is customary to translate from your second language into your first, but among my father's many friends and colleagues, every possible combination of language and direction is represented.

Gil translates from Portuguese into English. Most translators grow up speaking two or three languages but some speak a ridiculous number; the most I've heard is twelve. They say it gets easier after the first three or four.

The people I find disturbing are those with no native language at all. Gil's friend Nicholas had a French mother and a Dutch father. At home he spoke French, Dutch and English but he grew up in Switzerland speaking Italian and German at school. When I ask him which language he thinks in, he says, Depends what I'm thinking about.

The idea of having no native language worries me. Would you feel like a nomad inside your own head? I can't imagine having no words that are home. A language orphan.

Perhaps this worries me because it is not a million miles away from my reality. Marieka grew up speaking Swedish first, then English; Gil learned Portuguese, French and

English as a child. I can understand conversations in most of these languages, but the only one I speak properly is my own.

Marieka rolls her eyes when Gil tries to explain syntactic semiotics or tells us his theory of typologies over breakfast. His grandad was a miner, his father became a teacher, but Gil trumped them all with a PhD in applied linguistics. Remember your roots, Mum says, and hmphs. Semiotics!

I love to hear Gil talk but don't always pay attention to the words. When I do listen, I rarely know what he's talking about, but neither of us really minds. Sometimes it puzzles me that he's my father, given how differently our minds work. Perhaps I was switched at birth and my real father is Hercule Poirot.

Marieka's mother was Swedish-Sudanese and though she's fair-skinned like her father, she has beautiful red and gold hair, like a shrub on fire. Gil says he was first attracted to Mum's hair and only afterwards listened to her playing. It was a concert his friend dragged him to and he spent the first half thinking about a paper he was writing and only looked up after the interval to see this woman with wild curls playing the violin.

Marieka couldn't believe anyone would come backstage and appear not even to have noticed the music. She's used to it now, but at the time thought he was eccentric, possibly mad.

I once asked my parents why they didn't live together for the first eight years and Gil just said, We were happy as we were.

He says he never thought of another woman, not even

once, after he met Marieka, and then in the same sentence says, Do you think I'll need my grey suit in Geneva? and Marieka smiles and says, Yes, my darling, you'll probably need it.

Marieka notices the world in what she calls a Scandinavian way, which means without a lot of drama. I register every emotion, every relationship, every subtext. If someone is angry or sad or disappointed, I see it like a neon sign. There's no way to explain how, I just do. For a long time I thought everyone did.

That poor man, I'd say, and Marieka would look puzzled.

Look! I'd say. Look how he stands, the way his mouth twists, how his eyes move around the room. Look at his shoulders, the way his jacket fits, how he clutches his book. Look at his shoes. The way he licks his lips.

The impression was so clear – a great drift of hovering facts – it amazed me that she couldn't see it. But Gil says human capacities are vast and varied. He doesn't understand how people can speak just one language. Certain combinations of chords make Marieka wince. I peer into souls.

Of course, most people don't pay attention. They barge into a situation and start asking questions when the answers are already there.

Where's Marieka? for instance. Gil's favourite.

I look at him. What day is it? Which fiddle has she taken? Which shoes?

Three simple observations tell me instantly where she is and how long she'll be gone. But Gil always asks. Flat shoes, I tell him. Because of the stairs. There are five flights of stairs up to the place where she practises quartets. Otherwise she nearly always wears heels because she likes to be tall. And if you manage to miss the shoes, the baroque violin is gone.

Sometimes I go along with Marieka because they rehearse in the viola player's tiny flat at the top of an old building in Covent Garden, with long windows looking out across London. If I lie on the floor and rest my chin on my hands, my eyes reach just over the narrow skirting board and I can pretend I'm in a balloon floating over Covent Garden. I took Catlin along once but she couldn't keep quiet.

When we first heard that Matthew had disappeared, Marieka and Gil had a long conversation about what to do.

What if it's *not* fairly straightforward? Marieka asked. And Gil answered in a murmuring voice that I couldn't hear.

I don't want Mila mixed up with that mumblemumble family and you know what I buzzbuzz about Suzanne.

Well, I do happen to know what she buzzbuzzes about Suzanne. She doesn't much like her, though she also says it's hard to be likeable when you're so unhappy. But Marieka knew Suzanne before Owen died, and says that even then she never seemed to be telling the truth. I wonder why I haven't seen Suzanne since I was four. Gil says he and Matthew are like brothers, but when did they last meet? Are they like brothers who have grown apart?

What do you think? asks Marieka. I can't hear the answer, but I know my father well enough to imagine what he'd say. Matthew just gets like this sometimes. I'm sure it's nothing serious. We'll go over as planned. He'll be home by the time we arrive. He *is* my oldest friend. And in any case, it's been much too long since I've seen him. Perhaps I can mumble bumble fumble tumble humph.

I have heard stories of the two of them as boys hanging out in the cemetery behind their school, talking about girls and drinking themselves unconscious on cider. I've seen pictures, long before Gil and Marieka met, of the two young men brown from the sun and grinning in Spain, Scotland, the Alps. In pictures they look handsome and young, their friendship tested only briefly by a girl they both loved. In one photo both of them have an arm round her but her head is turned and she's smiling at Matthew, who looks straight into the camera. Gil's face is in shadow.

Once when his mother was ill, Matthew lived with Gil's family for a whole year. He and Gil shared a room, staying up half the night reading comics Matthew stole from the local shop.

Stole?

Matthew, Gil says, not me.

What happened to his mother?

She died, Perguntadora. The summer he was fifteen.

I would like to have known them back then, though I suspect that Gil young wouldn't be all that different from Gil not-young. I have heard how they sat next to each other during the eleven-plus and later their A-levels – Matthew clever at history, Gil at languages, both offered places at Cambridge.

Two grammar school boys from the fag end of Preston, Gil says. On the day the news came we felt like gods.

Gil used summers to study and write. Matthew hitch-hiked round the Black Sea, climbed Annapurna, taught English in East Africa.

*

Marieka phones back. She sounds the same as always on the phone.

Hmm, is what she says now, when I tell her about cute baby Gabriel and Honey and the feeling in the beautiful glass house. And then she sighs, and says, Do be careful, my darling, families can be so complicated.

I tell her I will be careful, and that I love her, and then I give the phone to Gil. His whole body uncurls when he speaks to her.

For a minute I feel like crying because I miss Marieka, but then I see her in my head saying, Do you imagine I'm not with you, silly?

We are three. Even when we are just two, we are three.

10

Catlin always talked about running away, but not in the usual way where you seek out your real parents who are rich and glamorous and gave you up for adoption by mistake and have regretted it ever since.

She wanted to run away to Brussels or Washington DC and head up an international spy ring that would save the world from mass destruction, preferably at the very last second. This she would accomplish by writing an impossibly elaborate computer program involving twenty-eight prime numbers coded into one uniquely high-spec iPhone. I tend to drift off when she talks tech.

All of our spy games involved threats to the free world and invasion by evil enemies while we plotted routes through underground tunnels known to no one but us thanks to a map Cat discovered in the catacombs under the British Museum in an ancient box sealed with a curse.

Untouched for two hundred years, Cat said. Feast your eyes, matey.

I feasted my eyes on an ancient-looking folder, scarred and burnt round the edges, and even though I knew she'd used an old iron to burn the edges and make a bit of ordinary bit of card look antique, I was impressed. It did look old.

Wow, I said, reaching for it. But she pushed my hand away and made me put on bright blue washing-up gloves, which had a satisfying forensic appearance when used out of context. With my gloves on, I was allowed to hold the file while Cat dusted it with baby powder for fingerprints.

Just as I thought, she said with a mad gleam in her eye. Last handled by foreign operatives.

Really? How can you tell? I was genuinely curious.

Look closely, she whispered. See how the fingerprint whirlygigs go backwards? That's foreign.

I must have looked sceptical because Cat bristled. Fine, don't believe me. You think I care?

I believe you, I said.

As you should, young Mila. As you should.

And the date? I asked. I didn't want to piss her off again.

She held one of the pieces of burnt paper from the file up to the bare light bulb in the clubhouse. As I thought, she said. It's ninety per cent linen, distinct greenish hue (that was from the walls in the clubhouse, which were painted green and gave us a greenish hue too), made in Czechoslovakia between . . . hmm . . . 1918 and 1920.

You had to give the girl credit.

And then she carefully looked at all the information in our file, while I drew an approximation of a stencil in red pencil at the top of every page:

TOP SECRET

If we'd managed to hang on to the rats, we could have tied coded notes to their legs, but instead we worked on innocuous-sounding phrases for our code books that would allow us to exchange vital information in public. When I say we worked on phrases, what I mean is that Cat made them up and I said they were good. Here are some examples:

Take an umbrella = TRUST NO ONE
I'm thirsty = I HAVE NEWS
What's for dinner? = WE'VE BEEN BETRAYED
Nice curtains = WE'RE DOOMED

If I ever suggested a phrase, Cat would think of a reason why it wasn't quite right, so after a while I stopped bothering. I didn't mind though, just continued on with my TOP SECRET lettering, which got more and more professional-looking until you might have thought we had a real stamp.

Are you getting a picture of our relationship? The thing is, I could have chosen a more straightforward friend, but I didn't. It never really occurred to me that the friends you choose reveal you. Take Matthew and Gil. Gil required a leader and Matthew a follower. With Cat and me, I was the anchor. I would never, for instance, stuff rats into socks. But Cat was the spark.

It was all good fun, except that I never got to be the one who made the twenty-eight digit prime number code to save the world, despite understanding prime numbers far better than Cat did. She thought you could just have a mystical feeling about a number, no matter how many times I told her that 'prime' meant not being divisible by anything. To Catlin, thirty-nine was a prime number because it looked sinister. Despite it totally not being one.

As for her elaborate save-the-world fantasy – well, maybe it wasn't a random choice. I would rather have played something else occasionally, like orphans or explorers or hospitals. But if my family had been like hers, I might have been equally desperate to come up with the right combination of prime numbers to make the world safe again.

11

Gabriel and his babysitter are back from playgroup. Her name is Caryn, C-a-r-y-n in case we were thinking of going with the usual spelling, and she looks uneasy when we tell her that Suzanne isn't home yet but it's all right, she can go. She says, No, it's OK, I'll just fix his boddle in case Mommy's delayed.

But Mommy isn't delayed, she's back, still looking stressed, but happy to see Gabriel and also – though somewhat less so – us. She asks if I like DVDs and gives me a choice of *Titanic* or *Amélie*. I don't really care, but choose *Amélie*. I start to watch the movie and it's fine, but I want to know what Suzanne and Gil are talking about more than I want to watch Amélie save the world.

Gil says, What else? And Suzanne answers with a sigh.

Maybe he's having an affair with one of his students. I don't know.

And then I am inside the head of a person with a young child whose husband has gone missing and I am much more upset and panicked than Suzanne. What if he's *dead*? screams this person with a child. What if I *never see him again*?

But nothing about Suzanne is screaming. When I say this

to Gil, he nods as if he's noticed the same thing. I suspect there's more to this marriage than we know, he says. And of course Owen changed everything. Most couples who lose a child don't stay together.

I've been thinking about the connection between language and thought. Languages that read from left to right picture the passage of time moving left to right. If a French speaker tells the story of a cat catching a mouse, time starts at the left and moves to the right. Hebrew and Arabic speakers start with the cat and the mouse on the right and time passes to the left. So it's not just a question of words.

I try to remember this when I talk to Suzanne, and wonder how time moves in her brain. Maybe it stopped when Owen died. Or got dammed up like logs in a stream. Or just goes round and round like the clock icon on a computer. Whatever it is, she seems like a person made of glass. Tap her and she'll shatter into a billion pieces.

It is difficult having a conversation with a glass person but she watches patiently when I hold Gabriel and feed him his boddle, even though I can tell she wants him back. Honey desperately wants to protect the baby. She makes a faint noise in her throat and Suzanne shoos her away. Suzanne is not a horrible person masquerading as a nice one, just an angry one pretending to be normal.

Perhaps she is the sort of person who says nothing for fear of exploding with words. In my presence, at least, she doesn't ever mention Matthew. The language that structures her thoughts seems to be one that no one else speaks. And she avoids the only other creature who shares her loss. I think the dog's unhappiness frightens her.

Gabriel is too young to notice. I play a game with him where I lower a toy mouse on a string over his face and jerk it up again. He laughs and laughs and then out of nowhere his face collapses and he starts to howl. Suzanne swoops in and picks him up, saying, Mommy's here. Gil looks at me.

I walk over to the thousands of books displayed on the walls, run my hand along them and pick one out; *Caravanserai*, it's called. Camels. Women draped in black. Men squatting, drinking tiny cups of tea. Low square buildings decorated with inscriptions I can't read. It looks hot and quiet and slow.

Between jet lag and the oddness of being without street noise and other people, the afternoon passes.

Suzanne is going into town for a few things and asks if I'd like to come. Yes, please, I say, and we take Gabriel along too. Gil stays put. He'll work.

On the fifteen-minute drive Suzanne asks me all the usual questions about how I like school and how is my mother, and where is she performing these days, etc. It is polite adult talk and only just lacks the genuine curiosity that connects people.

Suzanne apologizes for the supermarket being boring but I don't find it boring at all. To me it's almost as exotic as *Caravanserai*. She says to tell her if I see anything I'd like to buy.

I see lots of things I'd like to buy: macaroni and cheese in a box, plasters with cartoons of superheroes on them, peanut butter and marshmallow swirled round in a huge plastic jar. In the bakery department there are cakes with talking clown heads and musical merry-go-round ponies in bright colours. The breakfast cereal section goes on for half a mile and I wonder how anyone ever chooses. I'm looking for Easter eggs but the ones I find are all too ugly or too childish or too similar to the ones I could buy at home. When at last I catch up with Suzanne she's talking on the phone. Her face looks different from the one Gil and I have seen. It's younger, suddenly, and her smile is one she has not shown us.

I approach her through the fruit section, where watermelons, apples and bananas all look twice the size of the ones in England. How can this be?

When she sees me she says, I have to go, and clicks off. Her smile has gone all pink and sugary like the clown head on the cake. A friend from book club, she explains, unnecessarily.

A friend? I don't hate Suzanne but I can't bring myself to like her either. She's one of those people who thinks that because I'm young I'm blind to what's true and what's not. I see her far more clearly than she sees me, perhaps more clearly than she sees herself.

Suzanne has to go to the dry-cleaner and the post office, so we pile the groceries into the back of the car and she says, If you'd like to walk around a bit on your own, feel free. Just meet us here in half an hour.

I wander off to a sports shop and browse the T-shirts, but there's nothing I want to buy and anyway I don't have any dollars. Across the road there's a bench catching the last bit of sun and I sit down.

Hey Cat, I text. **Wish u wuz here.**

I wait for a while but Catlin doesn't answer. In the meantime, everyone's running around like crazy, and it's funny to think that rush hour exists in a town the size of a peanut as well as at home. I sit as still as humanly possible, making myself invisible so I can watch what's going on without being seen. It works. No one looks.

The only thing worth watching is a man who backs his 4x4 much too fast into a parking spot and smashes the car behind him by mistake. He shouts at his kid, who's maybe sixteen, for distracting him, and the kid gets out of the car, slams the door and storms off while the guy gets down on his knees to examine the dent in the other car.

Catlin texts back. **Me too. It rains.** Attached is what I think might be a photo of a puddle. It's hard to tell.

I tear myself away from the local five-star entertainment to meet Suzanne at the car. Gabriel stares at me intently and when I smile at him his entire face lights up.

We drive back to the house without saying much. Suzanne talks to Gabriel, who's grizzling in the back seat. Who's Mommy's tired boy, she says, and then glances over at me like we're in a conspiracy. Being with her makes me tired. Then I remember Owen and feel ashamed.

Dinner is risotto with peas and Parmesan cheese. It tastes nice but halfway through the meal I excuse myself to lie on the sofa. Honey is beside me on the floor. I close my eyes and rest one hand on her back, feeling the rise and fall of her slow breathing. Gil covers me with a blanket. He thinks I'm asleep.

So, he says in a low voice, sitting back down at the table. What are we going to do?

Suzanne doesn't answer right away. Eventually she says, I can't leave. Surely you can see that. I can't leave Gabriel and my students and . . . everything.

I hear Gil sigh. Suzanne, tell me please. There must be more.

There is a silence. I can almost hear the fizzing of Suzanne's nerves.

Tell me, he says.

She begins to speak, quietly, so I have to strain to hear. I don't know, she says. He says he's fine but he's not. He blames himself for Owen. Her laugh is bitter. I blame him too. I hoped Gabriel might make it better, but surprise, surprise, it's worse. So it's true what everyone says about save-the-marriage babies. Who'd have guessed?

Gil says my name. He was not born yesterday. I make a noise like a sleeping person, a kind of grumbly sigh. It works. I was not born yesterday either.

And?

Who the hell knows? He doesn't speak much, your friend.

My father doesn't speak much either. He uses words sparingly, as if they're rationed. It's what comes, I think, of knowing so many words in so many languages. Too much choice.

You knew that when you married him. Gil speaks gently, without reproach.

Yes, of course. But knowing it, and then living for sixteen years with a man who doesn't speak . . . it's different, surely?

There is an edge to her voice, like a knife. For the first time I realize how much older Matthew must be than Suzanne. If Matthew is Gil's age, he's nearing sixty. And if Suzanne's just had a baby, can she be much more than forty?

Marieka always says fondly that she has to read Gil's mind. I've become very good at it, says she. And then she kisses him on the back of the neck if he is bent over his work, and he reaches up one hand and buries his fingers in her thick hair and she turns her head and kisses his wrist. There is something in this gesture that makes me feel completely safe. Despite the fact that the scene does not include me, it does not exclude me either.

I feel a sudden rush of pity for Gabriel with his glass mother, his glass house, his baby smile.

Take the car, please, Suzanne is saying. I don't need it. I have a friend nearby; she can take me to college.

She? I think. Whoever visits isn't a she.

I close my eyes once more and when I open them again I realize that time has passed and the conversation has moved on. *What have I missed?*

It's late, Gil says. Goodnight, Suzanne.

I don't have to pretend to be woozy now. I lean on Gil till we get to my room and he folds back the covers of my bed. That's all I remember.

12

In the morning, Gil says we're going on a road trip. He says it almost gaily; we are both keen to move on. There doesn't seem to be enough air in this house, though I don't know how that can be.

I'll miss Gabriel. He claps his hands now when he sees me or I call his name, and he snuggles into my shoulder when I pick him up. I like the feel of him, compact and much heavier than he looks. Like a bundle. I've never known a baby as a person and now I can see why people like them. When he looks at me and smiles I feel chosen.

Gabriel B-B-Billington, I sing. Gabriel B-B-Billington! Gabriel giggles and waves his hands. Do you think he knows his name? I ask Suzanne.

Of course. She smiles. He'll miss you when you go.

Do you think he misses his dad? I look at her.

Suzanne's mouth pulls up tighter than ever. Does his dad miss him? That would be my question.

I must look a little shocked because she reaches out and touches my elbow softly. Don't worry, Mila. Everything will work out in the end. She pushes her hair back off her face with a tired gesture and I think, what end? The end of time?

After a minute I say, Do you want Matthew to come back?

Suzanne frowns. Yes, of course I want him to come back. She glances at Gabriel, then back at me. How could I not?

As answers go, this is not the same as saying, Oh my, yes, if only god would send him home tomorrow I would die happy. It's closer to: Do I want him back? Not especially. But if he happened to come home I'd certainly be happy for Gabriel.

Gabriel's much too little to understand any of this. I guess he'll get the picture someday, but I hope it's not soon. I've only known him for one day but already I feel protective of him. If you could see his big fat smiley face and his little pursed-up birdie mouth, you'd feel the same. I find it hard to believe that a person could walk away from that face.

Suzanne's phone rings and I carry Gabriel into the living room and plunk him on the sofa. I throw a squashy yellow ball at him and he flaps at it with his hands. Flap flap flap. He's no good at catching but I don't want to make him feel bad so I take the ball and throw it again. Flap flap flap flap-flapflap!!! He makes a high squeaking noise like a bat. Gil is standing behind me, watching.

He's very endearing.

He is, I say. He makes you love him. I throw the ball again and he flips and flaps but I can see that his face is starting to screw up like last time so we stop playing ball and I snuggle him into the corner of the squashy sofa on my lap and jiggle him and sing him a song and he calms down and doesn't scream again.

I wouldn't leave him, I say.

48

Gil shrugs a little and frowns and doesn't say *There's nowt so queer as folk*, which is another of his favourite expressions and probably one he doesn't particularly want to apply to his oldest friend, it being not very flattering. He doesn't look happy.

What are the possibilities? I speak quietly because I can still hear Suzanne on the phone in the next room. She has quite a bright voice on – maybe it's someone at the university or a neighbour she doesn't know very well. She even laughs a little to show that she's OK, but it doesn't have that effect.

I suppose he might have got mixed up in something he shouldn't have.

Like?

Like bad company.

What sort of bad company? For an instant I imagine something like the gas company, only full of villains.

Gil shrugs again. Drugs? Gambling? He raises an eyebrow. Smuggling, prostitution, contraband, arms trading, money laundering.

My expression makes him laugh.

Well, you asked. And no, I don't actually think Matt is running a prostitution ring. Not his style. Or at least it never was before. People do change, I suppose. Or something happens so you don't recognize them any more. It happens.

A wave of anxiety chokes me and I think of Catlin. I know it happens. The possibility that someone I know well can all of a sudden change makes me feel sick. I pull Gabriel close and kiss him so Gil won't see how I feel.

Though more usually it's the other way round, Gil continues. More usually you don't see someone for thirty years and when you meet up again it's exactly the way it was back then.

He thinks for a minute, and then says, Matt's had a bad time. It probably goes back to Owen, but what do I know? Maybe it's not that at all. Maybe he's gay and living a lie. I've known him a very long time, he says. But you never really know what's going on in someone else's head. There's nowt so queer as folk, he says.

I manage a smile and Gil looks up and blinks, as if he's forgotten I'm here. And that's the end of today's lecture, he says, as Suzanne comes back in, staring at her phone accusingly.

What lecture? she asks, but it sounds more automatic than curious.

I'm still snuggled up with Gabriel but when he sees his mum he begins flapping his hands and making his high-pitched bat noise. Suzanne's phone rings again. She looks at the number, answers it, and her voice changes once more. Let me phone you back, she says, and turns her attention to Gabriel, sweeping him up out of my lap.

Pooh! she says, giving an exaggerated sniff. Smelly boy! And she's off to change his nappy.

I have the nose of a bloodhound and he didn't smell of anything but baby.

Let's hit the road, Dad says. It's getting late.

13

Fluency in two languages does not make you a translator. And translators from French to German (for instance) rarely translate from German back to French. It's a one-way process, Gil says.

He also says the trick is to visualize the rhythms and idiom of Language One in Language Two – to find the connections between, say, a German mind and a French mind, so that the peculiarities of one voice can be teased into the other without a *calamitous loss of meaning*. Which he always says in italics.

Today, I will be translating from American to English and back again, which should be just about manageable.

We set off at last, after Suzanne phones the insurance company twice to check that her policy covers any driver, including a foreign one. She spends a long time talking to Gil about the cabin Matthew owns near the Canadian border. No phone, no electricity, no running water. No Internet. She gives us a map with the route and our destination marked in red pen. We have GPS, she says, but it gets blinky up there. Best to have the map. Matt doesn't believe in GPS, she adds, as if he'll be with us on the way, disapproving of our methods.

On the other side of the map is a list of phone numbers, including hers, Matthew's mobile and the Automobile Association of America in case of an accident. She's a very organized person, is Suzanne.

The cabin, she says, is the only place I can imagine him going. Not that my imagination is anything to go by. The drive should take about seven hours. Depends on traffic. Crazy to do it in one day, and what if you get all the way there and it's shut up and empty? This route, she says, running her finger up along a long thin lake, won't add much to your journey but is nicer.

So we're hunting down a missing person via the scenic route? Tempting though it is, I don't say this out loud.

You've come all this way, she says. At least don't spend your entire time on the thruway.

OK, Gil says. Don't worry about us. We're good at maps.

The expression on Suzanne's face makes me think she's anxious, but not about us and maybe not about Matthew. What does that leave?

I kiss Gabriel and he beams at me and waves his hands and kicks his feet so I pick him up and hug him close. So far this trip has been useful if only to let me know that I like babies. Or maybe just this one. I don't want to put him down but I do and he turns his attention to the wooden seagull that flaps over his high chair. As we leave I don't dare look back in case he is waving his hands and feet at me.

I'm outside dragging my bag to the car when I feel a feather-light tap on my calf. It's Honey nudging me with her nose. Her eyes are lowered.

I glance at Gil but Suzanne is too quick for us. Take her

along, she says. Please. It's not fair to leave her here on her own all day. And I can't stand it, frankly. She's his dog. If you do find him, at least she'll be overjoyed.

I'll ride in the back with her, I tell Gil, just till she gets used to us.

Sit in front, Suzanne says with surprising force. She'll be fine on her own.

Gil looks like a man trapped in a revolving door.

But what about motels, he asks, will they allow dogs?

Just a minute, calls Suzanne, who has already dashed back into the house. When she returns, it's with a slim paperback called *Driving With Dogs*, and there are pages and pages of dog-friendly motels.

Gil is stuck and I am overjoyed. Suzanne disappears once more and reappears with a brown leather lead, a bed, a bag of dry dog food and two bowls. I feel a sudden pang of empathy for Matthew. It's hard to imagine that Suzanne doesn't always get her own way.

I stand by the front of the car while Honey sniffs the open door and the inside, and only then steps up carefully into the back. She drops her hindquarters into a graceful sit, waiting quietly.

He took her everywhere, says Suzanne, her voice sharp as glass. I avoid looking at Gil, but I can feel the expression on his face. Like me, he has begun to side with Matthew against Suzanne, if such a side exists.

Suzanne looks everywhere but at us. She runs one hand over a scrape in the front bumper. I hope you're not as bad a driver as your friend, she says.

All three of us are thinking of Owen and pretending we're

not, but the truth is that Gil is not the world's best driver. Suzanne would have a nervous breakdown if she saw the state of our London car.

We wave goodbye. Suzanne holds Gabriel's hand and makes him wave back, but she looks as if she's forgotten us already.

It's only a few miles to the motorway and though Gil seems a little hesitant at first, he relaxes once we're driving in straight lines. There are two lanes in each direction, and for a while the road is lined with fast-food joints and shops with names like Garden Furniture World and Christmas Pavilion.

Honey has the resigned air of a seasoned traveller. She seems happier in the car than in the house, though it's hard to imagine she guesses our mission. I would like to sit in the back with her. I have always wanted a dog.

Jet lag makes me hungry at funny times and I didn't eat much breakfast so now I'm starving, and when I see a sign for DINAH'S DINER NEXT RIGHT, I make Gil risk our lives to swerve across the outside lane for the slip road but it's worth it for the most beautiful silver and glass diner with metallic blue trim. Gil parks and I open the windows partway and tell Honey we'll be back. She lays her head on her paws and doesn't look at me.

Inside, the man at the till waves at us to take any booth and then brings us menus in huge padded red leatherette folders. It's translation time.

I could have Three Eggs Any Style, pancakes, hash browns, bacon, sausage patty or corned beef hash, and toast (white-wholewheat-rye-sourdough), eggs over easy, hard or sunnyside up, coffee *regular*. Regular what?

I go for two eggs sunnyside up with toast (rye), plus fresh-squeezed orange juice and at the last minute add pancakes out of greed. Gil orders the bottomless cup of coffee and French toast, which seems to come only seconds after we've ordered – big thick slices of bread all browned in egg and butter and served with icing sugar round the edges and a glass jug of maple syrup. I look at his plate and wish I'd ordered that.

Our waitress has a brown and white uniform with a green plastic badge that says her name is Merilynne. She's nice and friendly and asks where us folks are from. I just love your accent, she says to me, and then tells us she has folks on her father's side living in Lincolnshire (Lincoln-shy-er), England, who she keeps on meaning to look up and maybe drop in on someday?

I wonder if she thinks Lincolnshire is somehow connected to Abraham Lincoln, and therefore partly American.

Merilynne looks tired to me, and when she comes back carrying a tray, I'm pretty sure I know why.

This might be the largest meal I've ever eaten. I can't possibly finish the enormous pancakes, so I ask if we can take the leftovers with us, explaining that we have a dog. Makes no difference to me, says Merilynne, but not in a mean way.

Gil pays and as we go back to our car, we see Merilynne outside the diner, sitting on a step smoking a cigarette. I wonder if she'd smoke if she knew she was pregnant. I guess she'll find out soon enough.

We set off again up the highway towards Canada.

In the car, I sit in the back and open the doggy bag for Honey and find that Merilynne didn't just empty the French toast and pancake leftovers into a bag, but instead packed four pieces of bacon with about a cup of corned beef hash. *For your dog*, says a handwritten note with a smiley face after it, and it's signed *Your server Merilynne*.

Honey sniffs the bag. There are far more clues in the world for her than for any human; her sense of smell is hundreds of times keener than mine and paints whole pictures of places she hasn't been. I nibble the end of a piece of bacon and give her the rest, then put the aluminium tray on the seat of the car and she wolfs it all down in seconds. She's a tidy dog, clearing up crumbs with her neat pink tongue before settling down beside me with a sigh.

My job (other than map reading) is the radio. I lean forward between the two front seats and press the scan button to find something we both want to listen to. Mostly I can find one song we like in a row and that's it. Then there's news. Something about Washington. Something about a church scandal. Nothing about a middle-aged man who ran away from home for no reason in the middle of the day with a class to teach on the English Civil War, leaving his dog and baby and wife without even a note or a forwarding address. After a while I reach through the seats and turn it off. The feeling of trying to tune the radio matches the feeling of trying to tune in to what's happened to Matthew. No matter how much the scanner scans a few millimetres this way or that, the story won't come into focus.

The road here isn't at all like England. Most of the time it has trees on both sides, dense as a fairytale forest and seeming to go on forever. You think you're in a kind of wilderness and then suddenly the road flattens out and becomes a town, and all around are big square buildings called MAXVALUE and SUPERTREAD and WORLD OF RIBS. We are passing through one of these stretches when Gil pulls off the road in front of PHONE UNIVERSE.

We'll get you a cheap pay-as-you-go, he says, so you don't have to phone Mum by way of London.

What about you?

I've got my laptop, he says, and I smile. My father hates phones.

I'm feeling homesick. I look at Honey and bury my head in the loose folds of fur at her neck and try to love her enough to make up for what she has lost. She responds politely, gazing at me without any particular warmth.

I take her out for a walk, then put her back in the car and join Gil, who is staring at a phone that's hopelessly wrong while the girl behind the counter recites all the reasons he should buy it. Spotting the simplest and cheapest phone, I say, We'll have this one. The girl looks about seventeen. She's chewing gum, wears too much make-up and is annoyed that I have chosen such a rubbish phone when she was recommending the newest most expensive thing. All our texts are free, but not to England or Holland. The girl looks it up in a book and it turns out they're not insanely expensive, unless you go crazy and start sending texts to everyone you've ever met.

We set off again. I'm putting Suzanne and Matthew's numbers into the phone and following our progress on the map. Now that there's just one lane in each direction it's fairly slow. Mostly because of Gil's driving, which is not exactly expert and also a little bit wandery. He doesn't notice the cars piling up behind us, looking more and more annoyed. Whenever there's a straight stretch of road and the broken passing line appears, cars pull out and flash past at twice our speed. Gil doesn't look, just drives with his eyes straight ahead, his shoulders hunched over the wheel. He has to concentrate very hard because driving is not one of his natural skills. I've turned off the satnav because it jabbers constantly and annoys us both.

From the back of the map where Suzanne wrote it, the Automobile Association of America number gets added to my numbers, so that makes three people to text in America. For an instant I consider sending the AAA a text reassuring them that we're doing just fine and they don't have to worry about coming to tow us out of a ditch at the side of the road.

What I do is send Matthew a text.

Hi Matthew. It's Mila. Gil's daughter from London. We're in America looking for you. Honey's with us. She's missing you. Please tell us where you are.

I wonder if saying that Honey misses him is horrible, suggesting that none of us cares about him as much as she does. But in the end I send it, thinking he should know the truth. Then I wait. But there's no reply.

Gil and I talk a little bit about what we see, but mostly we drive in silence.

Where shall we stop for lunch? Gil asks eventually. Food becomes a big subject when you're driving.

Let's keep going till we see a restaurant we like.

So we do. We drive through a village full of big Victorian houses. Some of them look all newly painted and some look incredibly run-down. Occasionally we pass a shack that could be right out of a cartoon – windows all different sizes like someone's found them in skips, walls held together with bits of nailed wood and gaffer tape, an ancient rusted car with no wheels up on bricks, broken toys and a scraggy dog by the front porch.

This area was popular as a summer resort for rich people at the turn of the century, says Gil. Nowadays it's full of hippies and drop-outs – and probably survivalists and other scary types, he says, as we pass a tattoo parlour set in the grounds of one of the big Victorian houses.

I squint at him. Since when are you an expert?

He reaches into the side pocket of the door, hands me a fat guidebook (*Frommer's New York State*), and says, Do you think Suzanne would send us off without reference books?

I leaf through it for a minute and then go back to watching the road. How about there, I say, pointing at a white wooden house with green shutters and a wide porch. It has a hand-painted sign that says LENA'S CURIOSITIES AND CAFÉ.

At the same pace that he drives, Gil pulls off the road and glides to a stop.

The menu is nailed to a post on the big wide porch. 'Try some soup and sandwiches on Lena's homemade bread' reads the line across the top. But it's the curiosities that I'm curious about. And when we push through the door, it's clear that they're the main act.

All over the walls are stuffed heads, about fifty of them. There's a large carved eagle painted black, a stuffed fish, an etching of a herd of buffalo, an entire snake skeleton in a glass display box and a faded Japanese kimono hung on the wall. There's a big turtle shell made into a bowl and a fish tank full of crab shells. Also a pair of wooden skis with leather bindings nailed to the wall and beside them some snowshoes. They look very old. A painting in a big gold frame of an Indian squaw kneeling by a fire needs dusting. There are candles in wine bottles on every table. A pigeon I think might be stuffed turns out to be real. Behind the till is a weasel with a rat in its mouth. It's missing one glass eye. Not everyone would want to eat in these surroundings.

Can our dog come in?

It's against the law, says the woman, but she looks at Honey and nods. As long as she's quiet and doesn't mind cats.

Well, she's quiet, obviously, but I don't know what she thinks of cats. Not much, it seems, because she ignores the big grey one staring at us from her perch on the window sill and lies down under the table. For a big dog, she's good at slipping into a small space.

You folks from England? the woman asks, and Gil says, Yes.

I like your accent, she says, looking at me, and I don't know whether to say thank you.

We order bacon-lettuce-and-tomato sandwiches. I ask for root beer because I've never tried it. The person we guess is Lena brings Gil coffee without him asking. When he looks surprised, she frowns.

You don't want it?

No, he says, flustered, I mean, yes. I do.

So, what's the problem? Her face is stern.

Gil accepts the coffee.

You staying in Saratoga Springs? Racing fans?

Not really, I tell her. Not at all, in fact.

Well, that's good cos it's the wrong season, she says. You're either much too late or much too early. I went there once with my husband. Long time ago. She cackles a little and then goes off to the kitchen and comes out again with our sandwiches and sits herself down in a big comfortable chair by the door, adding up till receipts while we eat. She's a genuine one-man band, is Lena.

When we come up to pay, she and Gil chat about racing. It's a short chat. As far as I know, the sum total of Gil's knowledge about racing is Red Rum and maybe Frankie Dettori, the jockey who dismounts by leaping up in the air.

Where'd you say you folks are off to? asks Lena when the conversation fades. Gil tells her the name of the town that's closest to Matthew's cabin and she says, Still a long way to go.

And I think, You can say that again.

14

Have you ever seen a terrier at work? It stands stock-still, quivering all over with anticipation, waiting for the moment the slip collar comes off. Then there's a fraction of a second where it seems to explode, launching itself forward at its prey. And a terrible snarling and growling and shaking and squeaking as it gets to grips, quite literally, with the rat. It's not nice, but it is impressive. And quick.

It is not a sense of responsibility or a desire to please that makes a dog do this. It's what they're bred to do. They can't help it. If I were a dog, I'd be part terrier.

The rational part of me makes a flow chart with two columns, headed MATTHEW IS DEAD and MATTHEW IS ALIVE.

If Matthew is dead, there are four possibilities:

(A) Murder
(B) Suicide
(C) Accidental death
(D) Illness – stroke or heart attack

At Suzanne's, I Googled cases of people who suddenly walk away from their homes and families. Some of the reasons are:

(A) Madness
(B) Amnesia
(C) Money problems
(D) Marital woes
(E) Secret second family
(F) Depression
(G) Fired from job but hasn't told wife
(H) Crisis of religious faith or near-death experience
(I) Terrible secret
(J) Kidnapping
(K) Mental illness
(L) Doesn't know why

Many of these reasons are confusing. Why wouldn't you tell your wife if you lost your job? What's so bad about a crisis of faith? What sort of secret? Someday I'll understand more of these things. At the moment I just have to think them through. Not everything you want to know is explained properly on Google.

To be thorough, I have to take into account the possibility that Matthew was kidnapped. But why would someone kidnap a middle-aged professor of British history? I have no idea. For all I know he has links to the Chinese underworld, about which I know less than nothing, except what I once saw in a TV movie.

Despite the fact that I can sweep a crime scene for rats like a terrier, I frequently have trouble putting clues together due to gaps in my knowledge of the world. I could do with a middle-aged accomplice. Gil is not the person for this job. Miss Marple would be better.

Take marriage. Marieka and Gil have been together for twenty years but have never married. Marieka says it's because where she grew up, women were independent and didn't want to have some man put a ring on their finger and tell them to do the washing-up.

This makes me laugh. I can't imagine either of my parents acting like that. When I asked Gil why he and Marieka never married, he said, I wouldn't dream of presuming.

Presuming what? I asked.

I don't remember if he answered.

Matthew had lots of girlfriends but didn't get married till he met Suzanne. He was forty-two. This tells me something too, but I'm not sure what. Whenever I imagine him, it's on a mountain with a frozen beard. Not the sort of person you imagine getting married.

Most of my friends at school have parents who look like married people are supposed to look – women in dresses, men in ties. Catlin's mum trained as a teacher but stays home each day while Catlin's dad goes to work for a software company. Every time I see her, I think she looks out of place in her house as if she doesn't know where to sit.

Gil glances away from the road for the briefest of seconds and asks what I'm doing and I tell him I'm thinking as hard as I can, in circles and retrogrades and whatever else I can drum up. I ask him the same question and he says he's driving Matthew's wife's car up towards Canada. I know that, I answer. But what else?

I'm thinking too, he says. I'm thinking about my fool of a friend.

What have you concluded? I ask, ignoring the comment about the fool.

Nothing, Gil says. What about you?

I'm trying to be methodical, I say – slightly pointedly, because he never is. I'm trying to organize the possibilities. Once we've done that, it will make our job a little easier.

Oh, you think so?

Yes, I do. I look over at him. He's facing forward because he's driving, but he swivels an eye on me.

Look, I say. You can't just let your thoughts float around in the ether and hope eventually they'll connect with something. It's absurd.

No it's not, Gil says. Lots of good things happen that way. Penicillin. Teflon. Smart dust. Something happens that you weren't expecting and it shifts the outcome completely. You have to be open to it.

When I open my brain, I tell him, things bounce around and fall out. They don't connect with anything. Maybe I haven't got enough points of reference stored up yet.

You're young, he says, that's probably it. When I let *my* thoughts float around, I trust that they'll latch on to something useful in the end or make an association I wouldn't necessarily have predicted. I'm trusting that they'll find the right thought to complete, all by themselves. The right bit of fact to go *ping*. You have to trust your brain sometimes.

Maybe, I'm thinking. But so far I only trust my brain up

to a point. Without guidance it could skew off in any crazy direction or just wander into a cul de sac for a snooze. That's why I make charts. Anyway, I say to Gil, I hope it happens. I really do. Because my flow chart hasn't got me anywhere useful.

Gil smiles without taking his eyes off the road. We'll get there.

You think so? Privately I'm feeling doubtful, but I don't say so.

Yes. One way or another, we will.

OK, I say, and then I stop making a flow chart, reach back and pat Honey, who's dozing, and look out of the window for a while. But it's hard to stop my brain from thinking.

Tell me everything you know about the accident, I say to Gil.

Which accident?

The one that killed Owen.

He glances at me. Is that relevant?

Of course it's relevant. How can I understand Matthew without all the facts? You never know which ones will turn out to be important.

OK, Gil says. OK. But I'm not sure I remember everything.

I sit very still and wait.

So. Matt picked Owen up after a swimming practice, says Gil. It was evening. Winter. Dark. They had to take the highway for a short distance, just long enough for one of those big articulated lorries to skid and crash into the back of their car. It was crushed.

The whole car?

The back of the car.

And what about Matthew?

He was uninjured. Bruised a bit.

Wait . . . Owen was sitting in the back?

Yes.

That's strange.

I don't know, Perguntadora. Maybe American kids have to sit in the back, because it's safer or something.

Little kids. He was taller than Suzanne.

Maybe they'd just dropped someone off or he wanted to stretch out. Maybe there was shopping in the front. Sports kit.

Maybe. And then?

They were in the fast lane. An ambulance came. Police. I remember Suzanne telling Marieka at the time that Matthew was completely exonerated by the police.

Exonerated? I'm frowning, confused.

Found not guilty.

Not guilty of what? Was he a suspect?

I don't think so. It's just normal, I guess. Make sure he didn't fall asleep at the wheel or was on drugs or anything.

I think about this. Exonerated? The grieving father? I try to picture the scene. Once more I look at Gil. What about the lorry? I ask.

It was coming up behind them. The driver tried to swerve and flipped over the centre strip. The back of the lorry must have swung round and smashed Matt's car.

And the lorry driver?

I guess he died too.

You *guess* he died?

He died.

A moving picture takes shape in my brain. Matthew and Owen in the fast lane, far left. The lorry coming up behind them. Not in the same lane, presumably, not in the fast lane. One lane to the right. What causes a huge lorry to skid?

Are you sure he tried to swerve, or are you just making that up?

Gil thinks. Pretty sure. Most of my information came from Marieka, he says. I never had the heart to ask for more details. Why?

Well, if you're going to crash into someone, especially when you're coming up from behind, you don't skid first. Do you?

Maybe it was icy. Maybe he was pulling over into Matt's lane and didn't see him.

Those guys drive for a living. Would they make a mistake like that? And how often have you seen one of those huge lorries in the fast lane? And even if he *did* pull into Matthew's lane, the lorry driver would have been fine. Matt would have spun and crashed, not the truck. Can't you see it in your head?

Despite a thorough understanding of my father's limitations, I feel impatient.

Not really, he says. What about ice?

Maybe.

Or maybe he was tired.

Tired or not, I can't see how it was the lorry driver's fault. The picture in my head is clear now. I can see Matthew's car brake or drift out of lane or do something that causes the lorry behind him to brake so hard, he skids and flips over the central reservation, crushing the back of Matthew's car with the fishtail. If Owen had been sitting in the front, he'd have survived.

Strictly speaking, there's nothing so strange about sitting in the back seat of a car when it's just you and your father. But if you were having a fight, would you sit in the back? Wouldn't you just hunch in the corner of the front seat staring out of the window, feeling wronged? And if you were tired, wouldn't you also just slouch down in the front? Maybe Owen liked sitting in the back, or he'd hurt his leg in practice and wanted to stretch out, or there was a big bag of shopping in the front seat.

I store the question in a file in my head marked M for maybe.

15

The sign reads SCENIC DRIVE and points off to the right. Gil turns. I guess we may as well enjoy the view, he says, having come this far.

I thought we were on a mission. Life and death.

We are, Gil says. But Suzanne said it's really beautiful.

Am I imagining things or is everyone treating this trip like some kind of half-hearted holiday thing, like a treasure hunt to keep us occupied as long as we just happen to be in America anyway?

I look at Gil. Seriously? The scenic route?

He looks back. Would you rather stick to the motorway?

OK. OK. I check the map. There appears to be a big long lake coming up on the right and lo and behold, the dense trees all at once give way to long views across a narrow bright-blue stretch of water with mountains beyond.

Look! I say, and then regret it as Gil slows even more and in the mirror I can see the driver behind us, fuming. On the next clear stretch the guy passes us with a huge roar of his engine. From the cab of his insanely large pick-up, he shoots us a contemptuous look. There are guns on a rack in the back seat. *Guns?*

Did you see that?

Gil nods. They must be for decoration, he says. Hunting season's October.

I stare at him. Did you memorize the guidebook or what?

You can't shoot animals who've just given birth or are pregnant. Even in America. So, it's autumn for slaughter, just like at home.

Great. Now I'm scanning the edges of the woods for bears and deer with offspring. Doomed, yes. But not right away.

A couple of miles later, the view breaks off and we're driving through a pretty little town balanced on the edge of the lake and the sun makes hard reflections on the water. We drive past a boat-builder and a couple of big elegant old Victorian houses. Gil pulls in at an ice-cream place.

Without asking, he orders tall spirals of ice creams for us both, vanilla and chocolate mixed, and a cup of coffee for himself. We sit outside at a wooden picnic table. The air is cool and the sun warm enough to induce sleep. Neither of us feels any rush to get back on the road.

Gil picks up a local paper that someone's left behind and he's reading it back to front, studying the classifieds. I break the bottom off my cone and feed it to Honey and then she and I head down to the water with my ice cream dripping down my hand. I sit on the grass and stare at the lake and the mountains with the sun on the back of my neck. Honey's beside me. I give her my ice cream to finish. According to Gil, Red Indians once lived here. You can see why they chose it.

We circle back to Gil. Look, he says, we could buy an above-ground swimming pool for just four hundred bucks. Or a Nearly New Weed-Whacker. He flips pages and I look over his shoulder at a picture of a raccoon family caught on someone's CCTV. They look furtive, like raccoon criminals.

Honey positions herself in the sun and lowers herself down, head across her paws. She is a beautiful creature with a noble head, but I can see that under her thick white coat her body is gaunt. She is old. About twelve, Gil thinks. My age.

Ninety miles to go. On these roads that's at least two hours, he says, and I suddenly wish we were making this journey for pleasure. I would prefer to be meandering at no pace at all, stopping and going just on the whim of the moment. But even the scenic route can't stop me thinking about Matthew and the pieces missing from the jigsaw. Most of the pieces. All I've got so far is sky.

Think, I think. Think of the facts: Owen died three years ago. In a collision with a lorry. It wasn't Matthew's fault. He was completely exonerated by the police.

When you're looking for answers, it's the things that nag at your brain that count.

Exonerated?

Gil flips over to the front page, where there's a large picture of the winners of the local ten-mile Fun Run. It's mostly women with their arms around each other, grinning. At the bottom there's a notice about hunting licences and a list of regulations, with a big jolly headline that says HUNTING SEASON'S COMING SOON.

I read more. The notice says you must be over the age of twelve to apply for a licence, and a ten-hour safety course is required for new applicants. It also says that 189,000 deer were shot last year in New York State with only twenty-nine injuries to humans, none fatal. One hundred and eighty-nine thousand deer. And three hundred and eighteen bears. Who would want to kill a bear? You can't even eat them. The thought of all those dead animals depresses me. A picture that goes with the article shows a happy guy holding up the lolling head of a dead deer. The caption says '*Steve Wilson and a nice ten-pointer*'.

What sort of place is this?

We flop back into the car. It's hot, and once we get going I turn the air conditioning on. Honey pants a little in the back. We've lingered and dawdled and it's late afternoon before we finally leave the highway for a smaller road. Gil stops for petrol. He pays and returns to the car, but instead of driving off, he sits back, hands resting on the steering wheel, and turns to me.

What should we do now? he asks. We can get there tonight if we drive straight through.

Let's not, I say.

It may just be nerves but I don't like the idea of confronting anything in the half-dark, whether it's Matthew or not-Matthew. Plus, I don't want our journey to be over so soon. What if we find Matthew and he's furious that we've chased him all the way up to the Canadian border after he and Suzanne had a fight and decided to be apart for a while? Or what if we find him with a new girlfriend? Or some kind of contraband? Twenty-eight kilos of cocaine. What if he hates us for coming all this way after him like he's some sort of criminal? What if he *is* some sort of criminal?

I don't say all this, but Gil nods anyway. Maybe he's thinking the same thing.

OK.

I'm staring at the map. We could go to Lake Placid. It looks quite big on the map. What's there?

The 1980 Winter Olympics, Gil says, and passes me the guidebook. Have a look.

I read the entry, which reports that Lake Placid is a charming town with a delightful mix of restaurants, retail facilities (retail *facilities*?), antique shops and sporting goods outlets. '*You'll find something for everyone in Lake Placid!*' says the book in a grammatically annoying way, and with all that stuff going on and all those retail facilities I'm finding it hard to imagine that Lake Placid is actually very placid.

I read some more and then look at Gil. Could we stay there tonight?

They'll have plenty of motels, anyway, he says, and pulls off the road to look at the map. Over his shoulder I see a picture of the ski jump built for the old Olympics.

Christ, it's terrifying, he says, following the direction of my gaze. It's hard to imagine anyone actually skiing down that thing.

I close my eyes for a few seconds and think what it would feel like to drop on to that near-vertical slope, fly down in the crouch position, then explode off the lip of the jump at two hundred miles an hour. I would land on the ice with a splat like a blood pie.

Half an hour later, we pass the real thing. We pull over and get out to look at it. Gil stares. Never in a million years, he says, and sounds like he means it. But at least it has a lift to the top. Not like a mountain. What about you?

Me? I shake my head. No way. Do you miss those days? I ask, thinking of mountain climbing.

Gil shakes his head. No.

Why did you do it?

I don't know, Mila. I was young. And Matt was so convincing. If he said climbing was the thing, we climbed.

God knows where they'd have ended up if they'd lived in different times. I'm imagining my father and Matt as highwaymen or in the French resistance, taking terrible risks. As Hitler Youth.

Would Matthew ski down that?

Gil smiles. He'd probably try.

Didn't you like climbing at all?

I don't know, Gil says. Of course I did. I don't think I'd have started on my own, but I got addicted to the kick.

Adrenalin, I suggest, and he nods.

We climb back into the car, drive into town and park. It's pretty and well-tended, and though I've never been to Switzerland, it looks like my idea of Switzerland – quaint little wooden shops and restaurants facing the lake with the mountains beyond. Minus the guys in lederhosen. And the mountains aren't very big, not like the Alps.

While Gil looks for a real newspaper, I try texting again.

Matthew. It's Gil's daughter Mila again. We need to find you. Pls txt me when you get this message.

After some consideration, I take out the line about needing to find him. And the Gil's daughter bit too. The world is not filled with people called Mila.

Matthew. It's Mila. Txt me when you get this.

I wait for some time but there's no reply so I text Marieka just to say hi and then Catlin. Neither of them answers either.

We shop around town for a while, looking at things in windows. There's an old wooden sleigh in the antique shop with some blue-and-white jugs, and a bookshop with a beautiful view of the lake.

And then, in the window of the deli, I find the Easter egg of my dreams. The pattern on it is cowboys – cowboys with lassos, cowboys riding cow ponies and bucking broncos, cowboys herding cows, cowboys with cowgirls. It's such an incongruous theme for an Easter egg that I burst out laughing. And to top it off, it's enormous.

Oh my god, it's perfect! Catlin will die of happiness, I say, and Gil rolls his eyes, no doubt thinking of the price.

But when we go in and ask how much it is, the deli man says it's not for sale.

I can't sell it in all good faith, he says. It's left over from two years ago so it'll be stale. Lots of people have asked to buy it, but I'm afraid it's staying right here. Hi ho, Silver!

I can understand his point but I want this egg so badly I'm running a whole series of silent scenarios that include breaking into his shop in the dead of night and stealing it.

I don't suppose there's another one?

He shakes his head.

Does it bring in more business for the other eggs? I ask, determined to blind him with the logic of getting rid of it.

He shakes his head again, mournfully this time. I have no

idea. It's kind of a folly, he says. But it looks good in the window, don't you think? Lured you in, anyway.

The other salesperson laughs.

See? he says. They all laugh at me. But everyone loves my cowboy egg. Hi ho, Silver!

I'm wondering what's with the Hi ho, Silver, but what I say is, Please could you at least consider selling it? I have a friend at home whose parents are getting divorced and she's really upset and depressed and this egg would definitely cheer her up. I sneak a peek at him to see if my story is working. She's desperate, I say in my saddest, lowest voice.

Well, he says slowly, shaking his head. That's a pretty sad story. But I'm afraid it's out of the question. It's not for sale. And besides, it's two years old. It won't even taste good.

I think of Catlin. She wouldn't care what it tasted like. It's something else she wants, from me. A sign. This egg is a great big blinking sign that says, We are friends forever and we laugh at the same things.

You'd be asking me to disappoint a whole town, says the child-hating deli guy. Maybe next year.

I know it's only an egg but I feel like crying. Maybe another amazing egg will appear somewhere on our journey. Maybe America is full of them. But in my heart I know it isn't. And then I try to convince myself that the perfect Easter egg doesn't matter, especially when Matthew might be dead, and how on earth would I have managed to get it home anyway? But the egg would matter to Catlin. I know it would. It would make her happy, even just for a minute.

Dad buys a bottle of local organic hand-squeezed artisan

apple juice and I glare at him because I hate the idea of giving this man any of our money.

A collar of reindeer bells on the door rings as we go out. Hi ho, Silver! the man calls, but I don't look back.

16

It's starting to get dark so we park at one of the motels, and the receptionist tells us they're full because of Easter vacation. Try the Mountain View Motor Inn, she says, it's a half-mile down the road.

We get back in the car and because the road is so curly, it seems a long way till we find it. But there's a little dog symbol next to the credit-card stickers on the office window, so we're in luck. I tell the guy behind the desk that my dad is parking the car and he says he likes my accent, am I Australian? When Gil comes in he offers us a family room for no more than a regular double.

So now I have my own room attached to his with my own TV. I like this. Private but connected. There's a snug corner in my bit that's perfect for Honey's bed and she curls up there like it's where she's always lived.

She doesn't need much exercise at her age, Gil says, and I think how strange it is that at twelve she's old and I'm young. He takes her out anyway and I text Catlin.

No sign of our missing guy I write.

Boo bloody hoo comes the text in return, and I'm shocked and upset because I thought we were friends again. But the phone bleeps a second later.

Dad's moved out. Mum cries all day.

Oh. I've known Catlin long enough and can hear her voice, small and furious.

Oh Cat, I text back, **I'm REALLY sorry xxxxxxx**

It takes a while for the next one but I know what it's going to say before it arrives.

I don't give a shit.

Which is more or less definite proof that she does.

Love you loads I text back, but she doesn't answer.

Gil returns with Honey. Temperature's dropping, he says, then gives her one of the dog chews Suzanne packed and pours some dinner for her out of the box. She sniffs it and turns away. No left-over bacon, no French toast, no ice cream, no deal.

We leave Honey and walk next door to a big square restaurant done up to look like a cartoon version of Thailand with huge carved pillars and a pointy roof painted all over red and gold. My Thai, it's called, and it's nearly empty. The waitress says to sit anywhere and we do, and then when she comes over again we order Pad Thai and green curry and she says she likes my accent which I never know quite how to answer. I get up to look at the big orange fish in the tank near the till while we wait for the food to come. I'm really hoping that any fish in our meal don't come from that tank.

The food arrives and it's not too bad, though the Pad Thai is quite sticky. Gil orders a Thai beer, drinks it and asks for another.

What will we do if we find Matthew at the cabin? I ask.

I guess we'll talk to him, Gil says.

What will we do if we don't find him?

Gil shrugs. One step at a time. At least we'll have had a genuine American experience on the way, eh, Perguntadora?

As we eat, the restaurant fills up and I can't help gathering facts about the people who eat here. Tourists, mainly. Some speak a weird-sounding French, which Gil says is French-Canadian. The American families don't talk to each other much, though some of them shout at their children. One father I catch saying grace before they start to eat while his teenage son looks around, mortified. One man knows the waitress. He's either related to her or a friend or he comes here a lot. A few people don't bother with the menu. They know what they want. Two boys come in and when they order beers the waitress asks for ID, which they don't have. But she's nice, acts like it's no big deal and brings them Cokes instead. People order huge plates of food and if there's anything left over, they ask for doggy bags. I wouldn't give this food to Honey; it's not healthy.

At last we go back to our hotel room and I watch TV with the sound turned off while Gil reads, but it's mostly ads for losing weight or gigantic pizzas. As usual I don't remember

81

falling asleep but wake up in the middle of the night with the TV off and the neon glow of the motel sign seeping in through the blinds. In Gil's room, the reading light is still on.

A girl at school told everyone the story of a murderer who hid the body of a dead woman inside the box mattress in a motel. For ten days, people slept in the bed and the body wasn't discovered until the hotel investigated complaints about a foul smell in the room.

The idea of all those people sleeping on top of a dead woman scared me so much that I didn't sleep for a week. The girl knew it would have that effect. You'd have to be either super- or sub-human to get that picture out of your head.

This is something I've considered before: the story that ends up in your head unasked-for, or that gets deposited by someone like that girl. I have a file of horrible images, but I won't share them with you. What if I stuck one here, in the middle of a paragraph you happen to be reading, like a landmine? You'd never be able to forget it; it would be part of you forever, like a bit of shrapnel in your brain. It's bad enough I told the one about the body in the mattress.

I feel lonely all of a sudden for Marieka.

Hi Mum. We're hot on the trail but is it the right one? I don't think we're very good detectives. Defectives more like. Haha. How are u? Miss u tons. Love Mila

Gil looks up from his book and asks why I'm still awake. I shrug, and get a text back.

**What are you doing up at this hour? Bet you and Dad
are great detectives. I love you. XOXO Mum**

This makes me feel better. I get up and climb into bed with
Gil for a while and he puts his book away so we can watch
a nature programme on fish who live in the abyss, the deep-
est part of the ocean. Dad's got his arm around me. Being
in such a strange room with only the television for light
makes me feel sad and lost in a deep place like the abyss. I
push my nose up against Gil's shirt and close my eyes and
can smell home, which makes me feel better.

I know Gil wishes I would read more but I prefer watching TV, preferably with the sound turned off. Just the
pictures. If there's a crime drama on, it's obvious whodunnit from practically the first frame; particularly with
no sound. The minute an actor knows he's the bad guy,
you can see it in his face, the way he walks. If I were a
director I wouldn't tell the cast whodunnit till the very last
minute.

I heard of a famous detective writer who never knew who
the murderer was in his books till he got to the end. Personally,
I wouldn't leave such an important decision to a bunch of
invented characters.

After a while I go back to my own room and drag Honey's
bed up to my end. She stands while I do it, then pads over
and lies down so I can reach out and pat her. I close my eyes
but, no matter what I do, the possibility of a dead body
stuffed through a slit in the mattress haunts me like an evil
smell in the air. I text Matthew.

Don't you care about making everyone worry? Txt back when you get this.

I don't bother signing it.

Gil is still awake. Gil, I whisper loudly.

Hmmm? he answers.

Let's call Marieka.

It's not even seven a.m. in Holland.

I'd forgotten about the time difference. She was awake a while ago, I tell him. My voice sounds small, even to me.

We don't have much credit on the phone, Gil says, but he nods. Marieka picks up on the first ring.

Are you OK? She says she'll phone back, and does. Why are you still awake? She sounds concerned. Where's Gil?

He's right here, I say. I'm sorry to call. I couldn't help it. It's fine, sweetheart. Where are you?

We're at a motel. Near Lake Placid. We're going to Matthew's cabin tomorrow. Today.

I guess nobody's heard anything from him, she says, but doesn't wait for an answer. She knows that any hearing from him would have been the first thing reported. How are you, my darling? Are you lonely?

A little, I say. Though at this moment it would be more honest to say a lot.

Well, she says, I guess you'll either find him or you won't.

That narrows it down. I laugh. Her voice reassures me. How are your concerts going?

Just rehearsals, she says. First one's tomorrow. No surprises so far. How's your father? Why can't you sleep?

Dad's fine, I say. But we miss you. Do you want to talk to

84

him? I pass the phone over and Gil blinks. Without his glasses he looks like a slightly different person.

We'll just take it as it comes, he says after a minute. And then, Of course, with a serious expression. Though she's perfectly capable of taking care of herself. Another pause. I know. I'll try to remember that. He throws me a kiss. That's from Marieka, he says to me, and then to her, I love you too, my darling. Play well. And hangs up.

He looks at me critically. Your mum says you're only young and need your sleep.

You're only middle-aged and need your sleep too.

Good point, he says. And then, OK. We'll both go to sleep. We'll need our wits about us tomorrow.

I say goodnight to Gil and go back to my own bed but too many questions are keeping me awake. I send another text from under the covers.

Matthew where are you?

I don't expect an answer so am not surprised when one doesn't come.

Sometime later, the bleep of the phone wakes me from a deep sleep.

I'm nowhere says the message.

It's from Matthew.

17

Gil once told me about a play in which a man falls in love with a goat.

I laughed. In *love*, in love? And he nodded.

But surely . . . not in *that way*, I said, and he smiled and nodded again. *There's nowt so queer as folk.*

And I remember thinking: that's for damned sure.

When I told her, Catlin said, Well, that's just plain sick, unless it was one really hot goat. And then she made a face and skipped off to smoke a fag and eat horrible chicken and chips from a cardboard box with her new best friends who didn't seem to see me when we passed on the street. Or maybe they were too busy laughing at jokes only they understood.

Gil explained that the goat story is a metaphor for some uncontrollable form of passion, like being a child molester or falling in love with your sister. The mystery of the whole Matthew situation makes me wonder if he carries a secret so devastating that the world would tilt if it found out. Or is it only devastating in his head?

What did Matthew mean, *I'm nowhere*?

I am about to wake Gil and tell him that I've heard from Matthew. Gil, look, a message! He's not dead after all.

But I don't.

Then it's morning and I'm packing my suitcase while Gil shaves. And again I am about to tell Gil about the text.

But still I don't.

We will almost certainly be meeting Matthew at the cabin today. And I know the message would upset Gil.

And yet. He's the adult and I'm the child. I'm worried by the message, but feel protective of my fifty-eight-year-old father. Is it my job to shield him from the icy chill in Matthew's message?

In the blink of an eye, the world has turned upside down. Come along, I could say to him now, don't dawdle, and have you brushed your teeth?

By the time I find a grassy spot to walk Honey and Gil pays the bill, it's nearly eleven. We go back into town and find a place for breakfast on the main street. I have waffles and Gil has scrambled eggs with a large side order of sausages to replace the boring food Honey will no longer eat.

When Gil offers the foil tray of sausages, Honey swallows them down in big chomps. I open the door to the back seat and she hops in and stretches out, licking her chops. Gil and I glance at each other, a little guiltily. We are not responsible dog parents.

So far, we've been following decent-size roads, but they get smaller as we drive north, till at last we're bumping along an unpaved road through dense trees. Honey stands now, both front paws on the armrest between the front seats, her nose pointing through the windscreen, ears pricked. Has she been here before? Does she remember the road? The map shows that there's a lake nearby but we can't see it. Yellow STRICTLY NO HUNTING notices are nailed to trees along one stretch of land. There's something wild about the woods here. I hope the bears remain hidden in case some lunatic with a gun decides to ignore the signs.

Every few minutes another spindly dirt road branches off from the one we're on, sometimes marked with a name or a postbox, sometimes with a number, sometimes with nothing at all. Gil looks anxious, squinting at his map.

We're almost there, he says. It should be just at the end of this road. He turns over the paper with Suzanne's directions on it, as if looking for more information about what we might find there.

Abruptly, the road ends. It turns into a footpath through trees, not wide enough for a car.

There is no building in sight.

Come on, says Gil. This must be it.

We step out of the car.

It's a beautiful morning, much colder than yesterday. Sunshine floats down through the trees. There's a breeze, which makes the leaves rustle and the branches creak. I can hear things scurrying in the underbrush. Small things. I picture them, greyish, brownish, darting rodents with sharp bright frightened little eyes and sharp little feet, tiny and unsettled by our presence.

I squint deep into the woods, hoping to catch a glimpse

of a moose, but all I can see are more trees. The floor of the woods is covered with pine needles and fallen twigs; years of decay make the path soft underfoot. Honey stands very still, quivering a little, her nose in the air. Does she remember being here with Matthew? Does she smell him? Is he here? She's sniffing the ground now and my heart races as she takes off down the path. He must be here. He must be.

We follow.

Gil stops at a clearing. The cabin is made of wood, painted but weathered and peeling. Windows circle the little house and are all shut. The front door is painted green, shut tight, but there's an outer screen door that doesn't seem to close properly; it blows open and shut very slightly with a squeak. Honey circles the house, whining. She stops, throws back her head and howls, then resumes her running – back and forth, round and round. Distracted and slightly mad.

Presumably Honey's been here before with Matthew and remembers. She might smell his presence, or the memory of his presence. Like us, she hopes for resolution.

Gil looks agitated. Takes a deep breath. No one peers at us through the windows, no one comes to greet us. He calls hello. We approach the house and I take his hand. Honey has stopped running and stands very still, sniffing the air.

What have we here? Gil asks softly.

What we have here is a person staying at a cabin in the middle of the woods, who is either not here right now or pretending not to be here right now in the hope that we'll go away.

Look, I say to Gil.

There's a cat. And one thing I know for absolute certain is that big well-fed cats don't live alone in the woods. This cat is a stripy black-and-brown tortoiseshell, which makes her almost invisible in the shadows beside the house. She crouches perfectly still, watching us as if we're prey. Her eyes are yellowish green, and she knows I've seen her. Cats may not be the world's most intellectual creatures but they're excellent observers. This cat turns its attention from us to something in front of it. Maybe that's what she was doing before we arrived, waiting for something to come out of a hole. No sane cat would crouch all day waiting for a translator and his daughter to wander down the path looking for someone who may or may not happen to live here.

I watch the cat, watch it freeze, eyes intent on the ground, watch her swipe with her front paw, then straighten up, paw planted firmly on the ground. She stares down as if mesmerized, then sinks forward, swift as thought, coming up again with the mouse in her mouth. She tosses the mouse a little up in the air and I can actually see the tiny creature scramble, trying to regain its feet, too late. The cat has the advantage. When the mouse reconnects with earth, the cat is already batting at it with its two front paws, like a footballer dribbling a ball. I find it almost impossible to stop watching this game, despite the fact that I am not entirely certain whose side I'm on.

Gil is walking towards the cabin. He opens the screen door and knocks loudly but there is no answer. He calls out. Hello! Anybody here? Then tries the door. It's locked. He looks at me, cups his hands together and presses his face to the window. Curtains block his view.

The cat hates him, I can see it. It resents having its game

ruined by this shouting man. A moment of inattention and suddenly the cat rises up on its hind legs, looks left and right like a cartoon cat seeking a cartoon mouse, then sits and begins to lick one paw, casually, as if it couldn't care less that the best game of the day has been spoilt.

In all our nervous imaginings of the big confrontation, we hadn't really considered that someone might be here but not here. We circle the cabin but there's nothing to see. It is occupied, I know that much. It isn't just the cat. There is nothing empty or abandoned about the place – the flower beds are tidy and look as if someone might recently have been planting flowers. Metal hooks hold back heavy wooden shutters. The house seems to breathe slightly with occupation.

Gil looks in, through the door this time.

Someone's living here, he says. And as he says it I swing round to look at a little outhouse, nearly invisible in a stand of trees. I walk towards it and Gil follows. It's very basic. Beside the outhouse there's a compost pit for rubbish – a square wooden door weighed down with a large stone. I lift it and there's our evidence: egg cartons, newspapers and kitchen waste. Peelings, banana skins, bones. All recent, including the newspapers.

I concentrate and let the feelings of the little cabin seep into my head. It is a woman here, I feel that strongly. But someone else too. Could it be Matthew?

A woman lives here, I say.

How do you know? asks Gil, and I look at him because he and I have had the how-do-I-know conversation too many times in our lives.

I know because I know. Sometimes I can say, Aha! An

91

empty bottle of nail varnish. That's how I know. Meat in a can – no woman eats meat in a can. A dozen empty beer cans, the cheap sort, there's a hint. But usually it's nothing so obvious. I look at a picture and I see the things that aren't visible at that moment. It's not that I'm some sort of mystic; I just see a constellation of tiny facts too small for other people to notice. I don't specifically register each element of the constellation but the overall impression will be clear. The Bear. The Hunter. The Swan.

Do you know the story of Clever Hans?

Clever Hans was an Arab horse living in Germany around the turn of the last century. His owner billed him as the cleverest horse on earth. He could add, subtract, multiply, calculate square roots and tell time, and would communicate the answers to his astonished audience by tapping out numbers with his hoof. Even with his master's back turned, or different questioners, Clever Hans was uncannily accurate.

In 1907, thirteen external examiners were sent from Berlin to validate Hans's feats. And for some time they were stuck. It seemed the horse really could perform difficult mathematical calculations.

But then they began to experiment. They tried blindfolding Hans and his accuracy dropped. At last, they hit upon the idea of asking questions that the questioner himself couldn't answer. And that was it. Hans faltered, refusing even to make an attempt. What was it? Could he read minds?

It turned out that Clever Hans was picking up almost imperceptible clues from his questioner's posture that told him when to stop tapping. When Hans reached the correct answer, the questioner's heart rate might increase, his shoulders might tense slightly or relax slightly – not enough of a sign for any of the humans in the room to recognize or interpret, not so much that the questioner himself recognized what he was doing. But enough for the horse. In other words, poor Hans wasn't so clever at mathematics after all.

Merely astonishingly gifted at interpreting that which no one else could see.

Mila is a perfectly nice name and I have never been dissatisfied with it, but if my parents had happened to name me after that horse, I would have been greatly honoured.

18

If the person or persons who are living at Matthew's cabin is or are actually Matthew, then our hunt is over. If they are not Matthew, they may know where he is. Something tells me that he's not here. I can't explain the feeling. Something about Honey's howl, the way her excitement waned, a dog following an old trail.

We will have to return.

It is three quarters of an hour back to the Mountain View Motor Inn where we stop and tell them we will be staying another night. Then we head into town. We have some time to kill and Gil needs to buy a new razor.

While he decides between the blue and the silver, I ask him for five dollars to buy a small stuffed moose.

We're so far north here that you might say we're inundated with moose. There's the Mighty Moose Café in town and Moose Martin Antiques, in front of which is a huge wooden carved moose, almost as big as a real one. There are paintings of moose in the office of the Mountain View Motor Inn. The place we have breakfast, though not named after a moose, has a drawing of a moose on the menu.

I'd like to see a real moose. Given that I live in North London, I'm guessing it's now or never.

We've been here less than twenty-four hours and already everything looks familiar. It's a small town; you can walk from one end to the other in about ten minutes. It would be strange to live here for twenty years when in just a few hours it's begun to feel like home.

Though I like being with Gil and having a mission and possibly being able to make a difference by finding Matthew, I'm also fairly homesick and there's something nice about feeling that we belong here in this funny place. I fantasize about staying here forever. Marieka comes to join us and we buy one of the pretty wooden farmhouses on the road out of town, I ride a big farm horse to school every day, Catlin comes to visit in the summer, Gil works by a wood fire all winter and Marieka practises her violin in a cosy studio that used to be the dairy.

Then I turn off the fantasy because, really? I can't see any of us living here at all.

Whenever I remember, I text Cat. **No fun without you**, **Missing your face** or **What's the latest?** But she doesn't answer. It's hard to know with texts whether someone isn't getting your messages or doesn't like you or what. Maybe she's gone back to her cool gang and doesn't want to be my friend any more or maybe she's run out of credit and can't ask her parents for money cos they're getting divorced.

There's a whole rack of cards in the bookshop and I buy some with silk-screened pictures of loons and owls for Marieka then wander next door to Ammo Depot, which sells big padded jackets up to size XXXL in camouflage green print and bright orange, and tartan wool duck-hunting hats straight out of an Elmer Fudd cartoon (complete with flaps you can unsnap to pull down over your ears), and other stuff like leather and rubber boots, hunting knives with bone handles, canteens, tents, groundsheets and duck whistles. I love this shop. Everything in it is so foreign. There's a young guy lounging around among the tents and fishing rods, and he's about to ask if he can help me but I look away quickly, shy in front of a stranger in this shop full of things I'd have no clue what to do with.

Then he goes behind the counter, unlocks a cabinet and starts straightening up boxes of bullets, and it dawns on me that, actually, this shop is all about killing. Suddenly everything I notice is a skinning knife or a laser scope. I get freaked out and leave.

In the doorway I glance back and the boy is looking at me. At first I think he might have noticed that I'm interesting and foreign, but it's far more likely that he thinks I'm a shoplifter. Who else would run out of a shop so fast?

Next door there's a second-hand bookshop that might be full of treasures but isn't, quite. I find a book about Laura Ingalls Wilder's real life, complete with actual photographs of her parents, and I kind of wish I hadn't because I love her books and the photos of Laura Ingalls Wilder's real-life parents make them look like religious fundamentalists. The drawings of Pa with his beard playing the fiddle made him seem cheerful and warm, but the man in the photos looks cold and distant. And weird. Ma, who was beautiful and kind in the books, here just looks sour. Gil says that in the early days of photography it wasn't considered proper to smile at the camera.

A few minutes later I find him at the other side of the shop staring at a book.

Look at this, he says. It's old and a bit damp, with brown spots on the pages, but he's so excited that I'm excited too. He opens the cover to look for a price. The mark in pencil says $3.

What on earth is this doing here? he asks, showing me the title. It's an old translation of the book he's working on now. What a strange coincidence, he says. Not exactly the sort of book you'd find just anywhere.

It's the town, I think, welcoming us with little gifts.

When I was eight I found a violin in a skip that turned out to be worth £9,000. I just caught a glimpse of it out of the corner of my eye as I walked home from school and of course felt sorry for a violin thrown in a skip, no matter how terrible it might be, but when I pulled it out of the rubble I knew at once it was something special. I knew nothing about what makes a violin valuable but I could feel it through my fingers. Something made lovingly and with care feels different from something made by machine. Something old glows in a way that something new doesn't. It's not one characteristic but a thousand – a thousand tiny stars slowly forming themselves into a constellation.

I look at Matthew's message one more time.

I'm nowhere

I haven't answered it. I don't know what the right answer would be, or if there is one.

19

We eat lunch late. I order a chicken club sandwich on white toast and it arrives with toothpicks holding it together. Gil asks for toasted ham, cheese and tomato. We both get little white paper tubs of coleslaw. Like most meals in America, my sandwich is gigantic. I give up less than halfway through and wrap it up in a napkin for Honey. Gil says my eyes are bigger than my stomach and that all these leftovers are making the poor dog ill. Like this has nothing to do with him.

The waitress says she likes my accent and wants to know where we're from.

London, I say, and she says, London, England? You're so lucky to come from a place like that, and I think, she's right, I am lucky.

It's getting late and we should set off soon. As I sip lemonade out of a tall glass, I look outside and nearly choke.

Dad, I say, and point.

Oh my god, Gil mutters. It's April.

The waitress catches this last comment. Nothing at all strange about snow in April, she says. Had a blizzard at Easter once that shut down the whole state for nearly a month. Which is saying something around here. Nobody blinks about snow in April. June, you might get a few surprised looks. You might. Or you might not.

But it's been so warm.

She shrugs.

Holey Moley and Heavens to Betsy, Gil says.

The waitress doesn't notice this departure from regulation BBC English but I throw him a look. Don't turn native on me now, I whisper when she's gone. You're my last link to normality.

No such thing, he whispers back, raising an eyebrow.

You're the best I've got.

Ditto, says he.

We pay for lunch and go out to fetch the car.

Hey, Cat I text. **It's snowing! Get over here fast!**

And she bleeps back almost at once, **Wish I cud**, which I can't help reading as fairly mournful. But at least it's an answer, so maybe she's not not-talking to me after all.

The snow isn't sticking but it's whirling down so thick and soft that it's only a matter of time. We set off at a crawl and for once I don't blame Gil. He doesn't much like driving in any weather much less this weather and his face is nearly pressed to the windscreen in an attempt to see. I get the feeling we'll be up to our eyeballs quite soon but in the meantime I like the way it sweeps sideways and then straight up, not actually *falling*. You can squint at it and pretend you're in a snow globe.

It takes more than an hour to reach the cabin and by the time we arrive the world is covered over white with no sign of it stopping.

There's a little red car parked just where we parked this morning. Gil and I look at each other. We stop next to it,

99

and I get out and brush the snow off the windows. Peering in, I see a pair of shoes in the back seat, hiking boots in a small size, a box with book CDs in it (*Anna Karenina* read by a posh actress) and greatest hits of James Taylor. Plus a bag of dried apple rings. I'd call it 100 per cent female except for a dark-blue baseball cap on the back seat with a Mets logo, which looks distinctly male.

I don't think it's Matthew, I say to Gil, and he nods.

Honey jumps out of the car and lands gingerly in the snow without looking particularly surprised. Once again, I'm wondering how Matthew left Honey behind. He obviously knows how Suzanne feels about his dog, knows she won't be lavishing Honey with affection and care. Which makes his leaving her even stranger. He loves her. He must, given how much she loves him. Has he gone somewhere he couldn't take a dog? On a plane?

Come on, says Gil, pulling his jacket around him and tucking his chin down into the collar. We head down the path once more. A bit more hesitantly this time, in case folks round these parts shoot first and ask questions later. You never know with Americans.

Hello! calls Gil when we get to the clearing, and I hope someone answers soon because my shoes are soaked and my hair has begun to drip. If the snow decides to stick around for any length of time, I'm going to have to kit up.

The door is closed but there are lights on, and I can see grey smoke climbing out of the chimney. A woman comes to the door and looks out at us. Her expression is puzzled and for an instant the same thought flashes through my head and Gil's: we're at the wrong house.

She's wearing a denim apron over a long skirt and a heavy dark-blue Norwegian sweater with white flecks in it. She wipes her hands and stares out at us.

Honey stands close beside me, the snow landing but not melting on her coat. She's leaning a little on my leg. I'm watching and watching and even though it's only seconds in real life, time slows down so it feels like ages.

All of a sudden the woman raises one hand to her mouth, flings open the door and runs out into the snow to embrace Gil, who hugs her back.

What in god's name are you doing here? You're getting wet, she laughs. Don't just stand there, come in, come in!

When she unhugs him at last, she turns to me and I notice that her eyes are slanted up at the outside, like a cat's, so it's Mila-dog meets anonymous-cat and I wonder if we're going to bristle at each other and she's going to hunch up her back and start hissing, but she just grabs Gil's arm and mine, and half-drags us inside out of the cold.

Then she stands and looks at Gil, at me, back to Gil.

Mila, says Gil, this is Lynda. A very old friend of mine and Matthew's. From way before you were born.

Lynda smiles. About a century ago, she says.

We stand there, the three of us, Gil and I dripping on the floor of her tiny house, Lynda looking at Gil as if she can't get enough of him. At last she breaks the spell, hurrying off to a chest of drawers from which she pulls an armful of towels. Dry your hair, she says, handing me a blue one, or you'll catch cold.

It's so warm in the cabin that we start to steam. Gil ruffles my hair with his towel and I ask Lynda if it's OK to use mine to dry Honey, who's snuffling around every nook and cranny like we're playing Find the Rabbit.

She's not dirty or smelly, I say, and Lynda says, Of course she's not.

What a crazy day, she says. Snow! At Easter. And now you turning up out of the blue, Gil, how completely – she stops, searching for a word strong enough to do justice to it all – *astonishing*.

I catch Honey and when I'm done drying her, she gives a big dog-shake in an attempt to unruffle her fur, and I look at Lynda. She's younger than Gil, her hair shoulder length and dark with hardly any grey in it and she's tall. It occurs to me that she could possibly be the girl in the picture from so long ago, the girl they both loved, and I wonder if Matthew is keeping her hidden away up here like Rapunzel in a tower.

Gil just stares at her. Well, he says. You'd better tell me what you're doing here.

I've been living here since we came back from Scotland. Nearly three years ago. What on earth are *you* doing here?

We're searching for Matthew, says Gil. You heard he disappeared?

What? Lynda blinks. What do you mean, disappeared? How would I have heard?

He set off a few days ago, taking nothing special with him, no money, passport, clothes. Just his car. And that was it. He didn't come home. We thought he might have come here.

He didn't, she says. We haven't seen him in months. And she opens her palms in a gesture that suggests we look around under the bed or in the drawers if we don't believe her.

OK, so...*we haven't seen him in months*. Which suggests *we* did see him before that? And by the way, I'm thinking, who's *we*? I suppose it could be another man, currently hiding in the woods, but there's a T-shirt draped on the back of a chair with the name of a band on it, an empty box of M&Ms in the bin and a plate on the floor with the remains of breakfast, all of which suggests some version of kid.

Gil sighs and then seems aware that he's being ungracious. Never mind, he says. As surprises go, I couldn't ask for a nicer one.

You're shameless, Lynda smiles. But it's lovely to see you. And Mila! She drags her attention away from my father. That's the trouble with break-ups, she says. You lose everyone else too. But your father and I always got along. I always suspected I chose the wrong friend.

Break-ups. The wrong friend. So she *is* the girl in the photograph.

Lynda smiles again and gives me a look to show that she's not serious about the wrong-friend thing, though it strikes me with some force that she is.

I check Gil to confirm this impression and yes, there is something. My father is attracted to this woman, this old girlfriend of Matthew's. I narrow my eyes, but neither of them is looking at me.

Matt didn't tell you I was living here?

Gil shakes his head. We're not great at keeping in touch. Even less since Owen died. The occasional email, not much else. Suzanne thought he might have come here. Gil looks anxious. You know he's married?

Of course.

But Suzanne doesn't know about this arrangement?

I never asked, says Lynda. But on the evidence, it would appear not.

Even with my lack of worldly knowledge, this strikes me as a bad idea. Should Matthew be keeping this sort of secret? And why, exactly, is their relationship such a secret if she was his girlfriend a hundred years ago?

Look, Lynda says, please sit down, sit down. Let me get you something warm to drink. You must be freezing.

It's warm in here and we aren't freezing, but we both sit at the wooden gateleg table and watch as she heats coffee and milk on her little gas stove.

I teach English at the local high school, she says. Doesn't pay fabulously but they like me. Matt visits occasionally and sends money though I tell him not to. I keep meaning to move into a more sensible house but he doesn't charge us to live here. Basic as it is, that counts for something.

I glance at Gil, who acts as if there's nothing wrong with this picture. We just happen to be here in Matthew's cabin with his secret ex-girlfriend + one, who Matthew sends money to and doesn't charge rent, and none of this has any bearing on our mystery?

Lynda bends down and puts her hand out to Honey, who is stand-offish and withdraws as much as possible without moving her feet. Most dogs would sniff the hand.

She's Matt's dog, Gil says. Her name is Honey.

Lynda nods. I thought so. We've met, actually.

Gil's eyes widen for an instant. Of course you have, he says. But he looks wrong-footed.

Honey backs away and resumes sniffing every corner of

the room. Every once in a while she stops and tries to inhale a particular object. Matthew may not have been here for some time, but Honey's sense of smell is a lot better than mine. The house remembers him, whispering his name at a frequency only dogs can hear.

And then she stops, having collected all the information available. She's still damp, Lynda says, digging around in the bottom of a drawer and pulling out an old grey blanket. She puts it down by the stove and Honey steps over carefully, sniffing to make sure there's no trick, then turns in a circle and lies down. Maybe the blanket smells of Matthew too.

So. Lynda frowns at Gil. Why exactly have you got Matt's dog?

It's kind of a long story, he says.

He left her behind? That's not like him.

Gil sighs.

Unless he was going somewhere he can't take a dog?

We kind of hoped he'd be here. But you're right.

Could he have gone back to England?

We have no idea, Gil says. Though why would he? When he knew we were coming.

Lynda says nothing, setting coffee on the table for Gil and hot chocolate for me.

Gil and I are both trying to take all this in and Gil looks at me questioningly. I shrug and wonder how much he sees and whether he thinks Matthew has been here recently. I have as many questions as he does. Maybe Matthew is having an affair with Lynda and just visits occasionally? Is she the reason he disappeared? And, if so, where is he now?

I look around. Bowls and saucepans are cordoned off in

the kitchen corner with the tiny old-fashioned gas cooker. On the other side, corduroy cushions are piled next to a collection of duck decoys, two ancient folding chairs, and piles of books. It's just one rectangular room, divided into sections that confirm the idea that more than one person lives here. The partition wall at one end must have a bed behind it, and a large grey sofa takes up most of the middle of the room along with a small desk pushed against the wall and a scarred leather armchair. The floor is almost entirely covered by an old Persian rug, faded and threadbare. Lynda has arranged a bunch of lily of the valley in a glass by the window and the sweet smell of it fills the house. She must have picked them before the weather turned psycho.

Lynda slides half a carrot cake on to a large blue-and-white plate and says she's glad we're there to help her eat it.

Despite it being the wilds of northern New York State, you wouldn't know it by the sound of our little group of three representing Scotland, Lancashire and London.

So he's disappeared, Lynda says thoughtfully, and then looks up at Gil, a bit hesitant. He's done it before, you know.

What?

Gil frowns. No, I didn't know.

After Owen died. He walked out of the hospital and no one heard from him for two days. I guess under the circumstances you might expect a person to do something crazy.

Gil looks suitably shocked. Well, he says, yes. But it wouldn't be everyone's choice. Especially when it meant leaving Suzanne alone.

How horrible, I think. What a cruel thing to do.

At the inquest, he couldn't account for those days, couldn't remember where he'd been or what he'd done. We were still in Scotland, but I read about it online.

I look at Gil. *He's disappeared before and Suzanne didn't mention it?* Gil's expression hasn't changed.

It must have been so terrible for him, Lynda says. I always thought he was the world's kindest man.

Unless you're his wife, left alone for two days with a dead son. I refrain from saying this out loud.

Lynda's tone changes again. When you say disappeared, Gil . . . has he run away *to* somewhere? *With* someone? How do you know he's not having an affair or –?

Dead, she means.

Oh, says Gil, I'm pretty sure he's alive. I'm guessing he just needed to be away for a bit. You know what he's like.

Lynda looks doubtful. Yes, but to walk off like that without a word. Not even a note? She frowns. Making everyone worry. Dragging you over from London and all.

We'd planned the visit some time ago, Gil says.

Lynda stares at him, puts her hand on his arm. But that's even worse. Surely it's not just coincidence?

Gil shrugs. You think he didn't want to see me? After all this time? He sounded pleased when I said we were coming.

It can't be coincidence, Lynda says. But why wouldn't he want to see you?

Lynda's right, I think. It doesn't strike me as the act of a rational man who just needs a bit of space, which is how Gil interprets it. People who need to get away don't drop everything and disappear just when their long-lost friend is coming three thousand miles to visit.

Has he been in touch with Oliver? Gil asks.

I don't think so.

Gil addresses me now. Lynda's brother, Oliver, he says, pleasantly and for my information (as if we were not just four seconds ago discussing his oldest friend's strange-possibly-desperate behaviour) and Matt were at university together. That's how they met. Oliver introduced them.

I was living with another woman, Lynda says, also to me.

How fascinating, Lynda, I think. Possibly not entirely pertinent, however. What is it with this woman? All of a sudden she and Gil are talking as if they're an old married couple and I'm some jolly house guest.

Do you remember her, Gil?

He nods. Of course.

Lynda turns towards me so as not to make me feel left out, but it's Gil she's addressing.

She was one of those old-fashioned, men are the enemy, all-sex-is-rape type of lesbians. Well, what did I know. I was young.

I stare at her, telegraphing that I am entirely uninterested in the details of her sex life, past or present. There is more than enough for me to absorb here without extraneous facts. And by the way, Lynda, do you think you might stop flirting with my dad?

Anyway. Lynda smiles. It took me decades to get it right.

Gil looks at her. But you have now?

I hope so. One of my colleagues at school.

That's good to hear. Some people never get it right.

You did though.

I've been lucky, Gil says.

108

She laughs. You've always been lucky. I am just so glad to lay eyes on you, even for an hour or two. And Mila. I've missed you. Really I have.

She beams at us both but I'm sincerely doubting that she's missed me.

The front door opens.

What now? Matthew? Lynda's lesbian lover? Marley's ghost?

Jake! Is it still snowing? Come say hello to Matthew's old friend – my old friend – this is Gil and his daughter, Mila. She points to me as a tall, dark-haired boy of about fifteen with brown eyes and a big blue puffa jacket shuffles through the door. This is my son, says Lynda. Get something to eat and come sit, Jake.

Hold on a minute. Why would Matthew send money to his ex-girlfriend and her son? Unless. Is it possible that Jake is also Matthew's son? Is that why Matthew sends money? Or is he just helping out an old friend? Do people send money to needy ex-girlfriends? I look at Gil and wonder if he's keeping up with what Lynda's saying or has utterly failed to absorb the information coming our way.

Quick-wittedness can be very lonely.

Lynda keeps talking like there's nothing at all weird about a sometimes lesbian, who may or may not be the mother of Gil's best friend's secret teenage son, flirting with my father. I feel dizzy.

He sent me an announcement when Gabriel was born, she's saying, sweeping her hair up off her neck and holding it in a bunch behind her head. I was happy for them. Matt said Suzanne wanted another child even before Owen.

She means before Owen died, but won't say it. And what about Matt? Did he want another child?

We all fall silent, though I have less falling to do than the others, my contribution consisting mainly of gaping with incomprehension. Honey lies quietly beside me, head on paws, eyes open, watching. I wish she and I could compare notes.

I'm sorry we can't help you, Lynda says. We would if we could.

Don't worry, Gil answers. It was a long shot that we'd find him here.

I look at him. As far as I'm concerned it was our shortest and only shot.

Where will you look next?

I've no idea, says Gil. We were pretty much gambling on this place.

Lynda looks from Gil to me, her face anxious. Jake has made himself a sandwich and flopped down on the sofa to eat it. I turn round to look at him and he meets my eyes as if noticing for the first time that I'm here. Hi, he says.

Hi.

This is Mila, says Lynda. Gil's daughter. Gil is an old friend of Matthew's.

You said that, Jake says.

I'm looking at Jake and wondering what his line is on his maybe-father, whether he dislikes him for being married to someone else and hiding Jake's existence from his new family. Assuming he has. And Jake is.

But hold on a minute. Let's say that Jake is actually Matthew's son and *is* actually around fifteen, then isn't he pretty much the same age Owen would be? I'm twelve and a half, and Owen and I were born three years and three days apart.

So Matthew couldn't possibly be his father. Unless . . . oh god.

Use a plate, Lynda says to Jake, and picks one up from a shelf behind the table. I take it from her and she thanks me, then turns back to Gil. I really do wish I could help. But I don't have any idea where he might be. I don't even know who his friends are.

I walk over to the sofa with the plate and look down at Jake. How old are you? I ask him, and he looks a bit nonplussed. It's a somewhat strange conversation-opener but I have to know.

Fifteen, Lynda says from across the room. Last September.

September? And he's fifteen? Owen was born in October. My theory must be wrong. It would mean Lynda got pregnant about the same time as Suzanne, by the same man. Do people even *do* things like that?

It would certainly explain why Suzanne doesn't know they're staying here. I stare at Jake but he's taken the plate from me, smiled politely, replaced his earphones, half closed his eyes and switched his concentration inward.

Across the room, Gil and Lynda are still talking.

I walk back to my chair and sit down. Gil smiles at me. He is probably experiencing regrets for his friend and Lynda and the relationship between them that didn't work out, and not concentrating on the big story at all. I blink at him in a meaningful way, but he merely looks puzzled.

It's starting to get dark and Lynda gets up to light oil lamps in glass hurricane shades. Jake has somehow managed to disappear in this tiny house, still stretched out on the sofa, eyes closed, plugged in to his iPod. I need to use the toilet and when I ask if it's OK, Lynda hands me Jake's big puffa jacket and a torch. Do you want me to come out with you? The snow is quite heavy.

But I know where to go and I'm desperate to be alone for a few minutes to clear my head. The coat feels nice, light and warm and smelling of boy. Honey follows silently as I pick my way across the new snow. The door creaks a little when I open it and it's cold in here, but I'm cosy in my cocoon and the wooden seat is wide and smooth. Honey squeezes into the tiny room beside me, not wanting to be left out in the snow. She presses up against my legs and I sit down, grateful beyond words to be away from that house full of silent drama.

I do the maths once more to be absolutely certain, but it just adds up the same. Barring premature births, if Jake is Matthew's son, he was conceived the same month as Owen.

Despite the turmoil in my head, sitting in the dark with only the torch is quite a nice feeling. Peaceful. I switch it on and make slow circles on the walls, thinking. I'm completely warm inside the jacket with Honey leaning up against my legs. Something about the warm coat and the cold air and the dark and the quiet and the strangeness and all the revelations of the past half hour make me want to sit here forever. I feel almost drowsy staring at the swirls of light I'm making on the wall, turning my brain away by force from the confusion in it and wondering how Lynda and Jake manage in winter when there's tons of snow. Could you even get to the toilet or would it be buried? I shudder. And who would clear the road? In London when it snows, everything shuts down. Maybe Lynda went back to Scotland in order for Jake to be born as far away from Matthew and Suzanne as possible. Under the circumstances, I can see her point.

I wonder why they came back, and to so primitive a place.

Eventually my feet start to feel cold so I get up and open the door, then jump back with my heart flipping over in my chest because there's a dark shape looming near a tree about ten feet away and I'm about to scream and run when I realize that bears don't wear boots and sweaters, and as bears go, this one looks a lot like Jake.

I'm here to make sure you haven't got lost in the woods and frozen to death, he says.

What about getting scared to death?

Sorry, he says. What on earth were you doing in there all that time, if you don't mind my asking? He rubs his hands together and blows on them, watching me.

Well, this is embarrassing, but at least it's too dark for him to see. I was just thinking, I tell him, and even in the dark I can see him roll his eyes.

Come on, he says, and grabs a handful of my jacket. No one cares if I freeze to death while you sit around in the cold thinking. But his tone isn't annoyed; it's actually quite nice and friendly.

He and Honey and I shuffle back through the snow in single file. White smoke is curling out of the little tin chimney. Back inside, Lynda's built up the fire. The cosiness of the place probably makes up for a lot of inconvenience. It smells of wood smoke. I wonder how the two of them can live here. There's not exactly a lot of privacy.

Found her, says Jake, flopping down on the sofa once more and slipping his earphones back on. Honey surprises me by padding over to him. She lies down on the floor beside him and he reaches down to stroke her.

She's an old girl, isn't she? Lynda says, looking at them. I guess she got left behind too? Honey makes a rumbling noise in her chest and I look at her and Jake.

Once more I wonder: Why would he leave Honey?

I'm afraid we'd better go, Gil says, peering out at the snow.

He's worried about finding his way back with no visibility and all the road signs covered in snow. What he ought to be worried about is the countless surprising revelations Lynda's sprung on us.

Will you come again? At least let me make you lunch tomorrow. Lynda has one hand on my arm, though I suspect it's Gil she'd rather arm-hold.

Even though I know we haven't got all the time in the world and the roads will be completely covered in snow and we have flights back to London and need to find Matthew, I know before Gil says anything that we'll be coming back tomorrow for lunch. Though to be fair, where else can we go?

What about the roads? I ask, feeling obscurely resentful.

I guess we just wait and see what it looks like in the morning, says Gil.

We say goodbye to Lynda, who gives me a hug and tells us to drive carefully. I'll try and contact Matt tonight, she says, though I doubt he'll answer my calls if he hasn't answered yours.

Jake doesn't get up, though his mum grumbles at him for being rude, so he waves at us from the sofa and then shuts his eyes again.

Despite all the strange quasi-revelations, I can't bring myself to dislike Jake and Lynda. They seem half like displaced people waiting for something to happen and half like woodland creatures who've always lived here. I'm guessing that Lynda's lonely for people who've known her a long time, or maybe just someone who doesn't live plugged into an iPod. Perhaps Gil isn't acting in anything more than the friendly manner of a person who was once fond of another person.

Seeing them together, I get a funny feeling that Lynda, Jake and Honey have all been discarded in Matthew's wake. Once again, I wonder what sort of person Matthew must be to walk out on the people who love him.

I take out the phone to reply to his text.

Matthew

I stare at the single word for a long time, wondering what else I can possibly say. It is impossible to put into a text everything I want to know. Where are you? Why did you go? Do Jake and Lynda have anything to do with all this? Why did you leave Honey behind? And perhaps most urgently, What happened to your life?

Instead, I write: **Is Jake your son?**

I leave the message as it is and press send, but I can't help noticing that the people in his orbit are beginning, slowly, to add up. Suzanne, Gabriel, Owen, Jake, Lynda, Honey. All circling some sort of story that only Matthew can see completely.

As for Gil and me? We're searching for Matthew but keep finding other things.

20

My own next of kin has some explaining to do.

But, he protests, think about it. I didn't have the faintest clue we were going to run into Lynda. She didn't seem especially relevant when we set off. I haven't seen or heard from her – haven't thought about her – in years. And Matthew somehow never got around to telling me about Jake, *if* in fact Jake is his son and Matt isn't just sending money to Lynda for any of a hundred other reasons.

A hundred? Name one.

You know what I mean.

I guess you couldn't just ask?

Gil looks uncomfortable. I suppose. But wouldn't she have told us if she wanted us to know?

Maybe she thinks you know already. Being Matthew's best friend and all.

Of course, if it's true, it's quite shocking, Gil says, frowning. I wonder if Suzanne knows. Do you think he'd have told her?

Do *I* think? I'm twelve.

Gil smiles. Yes, of course. I keep forgetting.

Uh huh. I don't say anything but, just on the fly, I'm guessing he didn't tell Suzanne.

This whole story gets messier and messier, says Gil, and he sounds weary all of a sudden. There's Matt's disappearance after the accident as well.

Why would he do that?

Gil shakes his head. I have no idea.

It's very snowy and he is concentrating on not sliding into other cars. There's so much going on in my own head that I don't know where to start. It feels as if the landscape has cracked open to reveal a river of lava flowing beneath.

Gil pulls in at the Mountain View Motor Inn, which is undergoing that strange kind of transformation that happens when a completely alien place begins to feel like home. First you say, I'd like to go *home* now, or, Let's go *home*, and suddenly realize that you don't mean your lifelong home in London, but the Mountain View Motor Inn.

The motel is nice inside with huge comfortable beds. Gil plugs his computer into the converter plug from the airport and reaches down to find the socket. The manuscript of the book he is translating covers most of his bed, and the book he found in the second-hand shop sits on a pillow like Cinderella's glass slipper.

I liked the idea that there was no one but me in Gil's life at the moment, but Lynda and Jake and the ghosts of Matthew and Owen have all crowded in on the party and ruined the illusion. It is very weird to see your father look at another woman as a woman, even if it is completely harmless. It is also fairly strange to discover that your father's best friend may have been cheating on his wife about the same time he got her pregnant.

Gil says a bit peevishly that he's not getting any work done, which is hardly surprising given the circumstances.

Never mind, I say, it's only a few days. Try to enjoy the company.

He kisses my forehead and replies, How could I not?

Lynda seems nice, I say cautiously.

Yes, he says. She is. But her life is messy, as ever.

I think about this. What do you mean?

Oh, well, he says. If it wasn't one thing it was another. Two men. A woman and a man. Always some combination that didn't quite work. I found it intriguing years ago – now it just makes me feel tired.

Do you think Matthew knew she was pregnant?

You're making a huge assumption here, Mila. It's only a theory.

But what if I'm right?

Gil shrugs. Who knows? But he does send them money. If you're right, then it would appear he found out eventually.

I look at him. Tell me, I say, is there some huge adult conspiracy where people lead unimaginably complex lives and pretend it's normal?

No such thing as –

I cut him off. *Don't say it.*

He sighs. But don't you see? It's possible to make one mistake, which leads to more and bigger mistakes until you can't find your way back. And then you drag other people in and the complications escalate. Life can get messy very quickly. And Matt's always been quite an individual sort of a person.

What does that mean?

He was always happiest on his own. On a rock face, away from the world. Not a domestic paragon like me, he says. Now go to bed. He gives me his stern look, kisses me and goes back to work.

I send one last text under the covers.

Please tell me why you left.

No answer comes. I fall asleep and the snow tries to bury us in the night.

The nice waitress at our breakfast place isn't on duty next morning. Of course, Gil says, it's Saturday. The new waitress is a friendly girl with fair hair pulled back in a ponytail. She has a slightly displaced air and I decide she followed some boyfriend up to this place and then got stranded. A wild guess.

I skip the muffins, pancakes and waffles, spinach omelettes, smoothies and smoked salmon bagels in favour of toast and orange juice. Infinite variety is beginning to wear me down.

As soon as we've finished breakfast, we start the slow drive out to Lynda's. The roads are clear, sanded and salted like they actually expect this sort of thing to happen, with massive snow piles big enough to hollow out and live in by the side of the road. I guess they do expect this sort of thing to happen.

It's still snowing, but the snow is delicate now, light and dry. The sun is shining, the sky impossibly blue. The world looks so dazzling I almost can't bear to look at it.

Even Lynda's little narrow road has been ploughed and we pull over at the usual place to park. Her car is completely covered in snow and I draw a smiley face on the windscreen with one finger. She hears our car and calls us in out of the cold.

Inside, the wood burner is throwing out masses of heat and it's cosy and sociable, but I can't help wondering if it might feel lonely and remote when we're not here.

Jake's out shovelling driveways, she tells us. He'll be back for lunch. But within minutes of our arrival he bursts in covered with snow, grinning like Tom after a hearty meal of Jerry.

I'm rich! he says, pulling out a wad of notes and throwing off his Mets cap. I hope it snows till August. He strips off his jacket and gloves and hangs them, dripping, over a chair by the fire. His mother pours him a hot chocolate.

It's hard work, and freezing out there. Gotta get my strength back. Jake slumps down in a chair and once more Honey gets up and pads over to lie next to him. He pats her absently. So, he says, how's the mystery of the missing Matthew going? Course, it's not a particularly fascinating mystery for us. He's been missing from our lives more or less, let's see, forever.

Lynda and Gil are talking quietly about other things, so I look at him, take a deep breath and say in a low voice, Is Matthew your father?

You don't exactly beat around the bush, do you? he says with half a smile. Matthew's not much of a father, but technically speaking? Yes. Didn't you know?

I shake my head. The tone Jake takes is so matter of fact

that it's impossible to figure out whether he cares. That his father is Matthew. That his father is missing. Anything. He'd be a good poker player, Jake would.

After a few minutes, he gets up to check if his things are dry and puts his cap back on. I'm going out again, he says. Do you want to come? You could make a small fortune to take back to England. Genuine American dinero. He rubs his fingers together.

Very tempting, I say.

You'll have to take my coat and boots, Lynda says, but doesn't wait for an answer, just fetches both. And a hat. I wonder if the grown-ups want to be alone.

Before I know it I'm wearing a pair of slightly too big fur-lined boots and a long down coat and a fleece hat and gloves, and Jake and I are trudging through the snow.

I feel like a hobbit, I say. Do I look like one too?

Uncannily, he says.

I have to skip a little to keep up. Don't you get freaked out living so far from everything? I look at him. I mean, what do you do around here if something happens? Don't get me wrong, it's beautiful and all, but what about, like, axe murderers and zombies?

Having lived in a city my whole life, the country feels like a horror film waiting to happen, where some crazy person is always lurking in the bushes ready to pounce.

Jake looks at me sideways. I haven't seen a zombie in weeks, he says. Or an axe murderer. There are actually tons of people around here, they just hide up at the end of little roads so you can't see them. If you chopped a tree down on top of yourself and broke both legs, you could always find someone who'd stuff you into the back of a pick-up and ferry you to the hospital. Of course, afterwards they'd tell everyone in town what an incompetent moron you are.

There doesn't seem to be an obvious answer to this.

I like your accent by the way, he says as we trudge along, and I laugh.

What's funny? He shifts the shovels to his other shoulder.

Nothing, it's just that everyone says that. It doesn't sound like an accent to me. You're the one with the accent.

Me? Jake snorts. I grew up in Scotland but I thought I sounded American now.

You do. Almost.

Almost? He feigns outrage. I've won awards for my American accent.

Really? I stop and look at him. Awards?

Well, no. Not actual awards.

I'd give you an award, I say. I like the way you sound.

Thank you, he says. Very kind.

We trudge along for another few minutes. So what do we do, just go up to perfect strangers' doors and ask for a job?

That's it, he says. Only we use careful scientific methods to figure out if they're likely to hire us.

Like if the drive is covered in snow?

Yup.

And that's what we do. The only hitch is getting to the end of all the little roads before we find out if they might need us. We do lots of backtracking but finally we ring the bell of a house with snow on the driveway and Jake makes me talk because of my cool accent, and the woman who answers the door offers us less than the going rate, but Jake says she's kind of old so we'll be doing a good deed. She gives us the money and we take her little dog out for a walk as well, and she seems really grateful. But it's hard work and my arms are killing me after just one job.

Anyone who's not dug out by now, Jake says, is going to be either old or away or a husband-free zone. Which turns out to be true, because all the people who answer the door are either over seventy or women you can't quite imagine wearing snow boots and doing manual labour. We're out for three hours and get two more jobs.

There's not much talk while we're working because it takes all my energy just to throw the snow around.

It's not particularly heavy, Jake says, which is great because they don't pay you any more for wet snow and we'd both be dead of exhaustion by now. Or at least you would be.

I'm kind of getting into the rhythm of shovelling, though my shoulders are killing me. Dig, toss. Dig, toss. When I get tired of tossing I try to kick the back of the shovel to move the snow over, but Jake says there's no point, it just gets packed up hard and more difficult to move when the time comes to clear it. He sends me over to the front path, but it's started snowing once more, so by the time I clear the whole thing it's turning white again.

Everyone's got sand and salt, so we salt first and sand afterwards, collect our money and go on to the next.

You're a good worker, Jake says. I knew you would be.

What, do I look like a lady weightlifter or something? I flex my arm, but the effect is muffled by three inches of padded coat.

He grins. Nah. You don't look that strong. But you're not the complaining type.

Totally untrue, I say. Complaining's one of my best things. Right now I'm starving and cold and really sick of the sight of snow.

Yeah, he says, me too. Let's go home.

Jake divides the money up as we walk along and hands me half. It looks like a fortune. Yikes, I say. Do you think I could buy a house around here with this?

He nods. At least one.

We walk in silence for a minute. So what do you think of Matthew disappearing? I ask him. The minute I've said it, I wish I hadn't. I've already got a reputation for blunt questions.

But he answers. I've met him a bunch of times since we've been here, he says, but I don't exactly know him well. Before that we'd see him once a year or every other year. I like him enough, but he's always quite formal with me. Do you want my theory? I haven't got one. Maybe he's got twelve sons like me hidden away and he can't stand the guilt. He stops and looks at me. What's your theory?

This is not an easy question to answer. I don't know enough to have a theory, I tell him. I don't know anything about him, really. I pause. And you've made the story even more confusing. Do you think his wife knows about you and your mum?

I doubt it, Jake says. It's weird being someone's dirty secret. That's one thing I don't like about the whole deal. He shrugs. But I'm used to it.

Really? I don't say anything to Jake, but I can see that it would be weird. Horrible, even, and I'm hating Matthew more with every new thing I know about him. Why are we searching for this man? Why is he my father's friend?

It's not really fair, I say.

He looks at me. When I leave home I get to choose. I've already decided I'm moving back to Scotland when I can. I liked it. Except in winter, when it's dark most of the time.

How long did you live there?

My whole life till I was twelve, he says. Mum worked in New York City for a while. That's how she kept in touch with Matthew. When she found out she was pregnant, she decided to move closer to her sister, in Aberdeen. But she and her sister never got along all that well, how funny is that? Anyway, she got her teaching qualification and decided to move back. I think she likes it better here.

What about you?

We lived on a big council estate over there. It was OK. There was a decent skate park. And thousands of kids. I liked it. The social life around here isn't exactly riveting.

You're sounding Scottish all of a sudden.

I'm not.

You *are*.

He looks away but I can tell he's pleased.

So far, nothing earth-shattering has happened between us, but just talking about anything can be big when you're on the same wavelength. I've noticed that the magic of getting on with someone isn't really magic. If you break it down, you can see how it happens. You say something a bit off-centre and see if they react. If they get it, they push it a bit further. Then it's your turn again. And theirs. And so on, until it's banter. Once it's banter, it's friendship.

We open the door to the cabin and across the room talking to Gil is a slim woman in her forties with short red hair and neat features, wearing an expensive-looking suit. She looks almost weirdly fashionable for someone in a snowstorm in the middle of nowhere.

This is my friend, Joy, says Lynda. She offers no other explanation, filling the space where an explanation might have gone by bustling around with our wet things and more hot drinks.

The girlfriend, says Jake in a low voice.

Oh.

Lynda hands us cocoa and she and Joy go back to telling Gil about their school and how teachers have to spend so much time with paperwork, and that's where I tune out.

Given how many people have now squashed into this little place, Jake's sofa has become a kind of refuge. He must think so too cos he pulls up his knees to make room for me and after a minute hands me one of his earphones.

Good song, I say.

He nods. Not famous yet, but someday you'll be able to tell everyone you heard it here first, on the somethingth day of something, two thousand and something, on my sofa right here. It'll be just like the first time your parents ever heard the Beatles.

I find it hard to imagine that Gil remembers where he first heard the Beatles, or maybe even who the Beatles are. His radar for popular culture is, shall we say, imperfect.

Who's the singer? I ask, and he looks hurt.

Oh my god! I say, realizing. That's amazing! You've got a totally amazing voice. (This happens to be true.)

I write songs with my friend Chris.

Oh, I think. Chris boy or Chris girl?

I have to squinch up if we're going to share the same earphones and he makes room for me at his end and before long we're sitting squashed up together like it's the most natural thing in the world.

Jake is friendly but a little reserved. I think Honey likes him for the same reasons I do.

Lynda's nodding in our direction, like, isn't it nice that they get on, but Gil thinks she's pointing at the still-life painting on the shelf above us, which happens to be one of Joy's so the conversation veers off. I stifle a laugh.

What are you going to do now? Lynda asks Gil, and I tune in immediately, aware that I've missed a lot of conversation while we were out. I've only got one earphone, which is useful for eavesdropping.

Gil shrugs. Still no plan B. Back to Suzanne's, I guess. Not much else we can do unless we hear from him. Gil is slicing cucumber for the salad while Lynda lays the table and Joy opens a beer, which she offers to Gil.

You know, Gil says, I've been wondering why Matthew disappeared after the car accident.

For possibly the first time in his long, eventful life, my father has asked the right question. But the question has caused a definite atmospheric shift, and it makes me think they haven't brought up the subject of Matthew today at all. I'm watching Joy now, who hasn't said a word but is clearly about to.

Lynda glances at her uneasily, then back at Gil.

The reason he disappeared, Joy says, with exaggerated

calm, is that he's a total shit who doesn't know the first thing about responsibility or commitment.

Lynda looks away, but Joy is just warming up.

He's a loner, that's his problem. And he doesn't give a damn about anyone but himself.

You know that's not true. Lynda casts an anxious glance in her son's direction, but Jake appears able to blank everything beyond the confines of his personal space.

Gil looks from Joy to Lynda.

I've known Matthew a long time, Gil begins, but Joy interrupts.

Look at his track record, she says, nearly spitting the words. One dead son, one abandoned. He left his girlfriend, cheated on his wife, now he's left her *and* the baby –

That's enough, says Lynda in a quiet voice, and it's clear that this is not the first time Joy's opinion has been aired.

It's not, actually, enough, Joy says in a clipped voice. Of course, *I've* never met the man, never been hypnotized into thinking he's some kind of hero who just *happens* to ruin the lives of everyone he comes in contact with, so what would *I* know?

Gil glances at me but I pretend to be immersed in Jake's music.

She likes this line of discourse, Jake whispers, close to my ear.

I nod. It's pretty uncomfortable on that side of the house, what with Joy all pursed up and cross and Lynda's desire for everyone to play nice. But over on our side it's kind of cosy. What I like about Jake is how much he observes and how little any of it seems to ruffle his feathers. It's like he's taken the entire adult world on board and decided it's mildly amusing and mildly irrelevant.

He taps my knee and I look at him sideways. Anyway, he whispers, back to the original question about why Matthew disappeared after the car crash? He makes an imaginary glass with one hand, tips it into his mouth, then closes his eyes and goes back to the music.

Matthew was *drinking*?

My mind races. He was *drinking*? Did he drink a *lot*? Did Lynda and Matthew's relationship break up because Matthew drank? Or Matthew and Suzanne's? But wait, if he'd been drinking on the day of the accident, then of course he disappeared right after. He needed to disappear till all the signs were gone or he'd go to jail for murdering his son. If he had been drinking that day, the guilt would eat away at him for the rest of his life. What more would a person need to go off the rails? Or run away? Or even kill himself? Or does Jake mean he started drinking after the accident? Went on a bender? I look at Jake, trying to ask my questions via psychic transfer, but his eyes are closed, his expression serene.

Joy is in the process of struggling into her coat.

Don't go, Lynda says, but she doesn't sound very convincing.

Nice meeting you, Joy says to Gil as she opens the door. Hope you find what you're looking for.

She lets herself out and the door bangs shut behind her.

Lynda looks at Gil. Sorry about that, she says. Matt's not her favourite person. She thinks she's protecting me, I guess. Though I wish she wouldn't.

Gil waves a dismissive hand. Yes, of course, of course. But

Joy's outburst has shaken him. Perhaps he never looked at Matthew objectively. Perhaps the Matthew he remembers is out of date.

Lynda sighs. Maybe you should tell the police.

I am taken aback, until I realize that my brain has rushed on to a whole new story. Lynda's talking about finding a missing person and I've jumped to an alcoholic child killer.

The police aren't interested, says Gil. Adults don't get to be missing persons in the eyes of the law unless they leave a suicide note or a trail of blood. Otherwise it's assumed they just wanted to be somewhere else. Which in this case is probably true.

He's walked out on another child, Lynda says quietly, as if the reality has just occurred to her.

That makes two, Gil says.

Three. Her voice is quiet.

It's not a great track record.

No, Lynda says. It's crap, actually. For the first time she doesn't sound gentle and tolerant, and I'm wondering what happened to everyone's best friend, the kindest man in the world.

Looking at Lynda, I can see that old relationships leave a flare behind them, an uneven tail of light that doesn't go away when people split up.

I remove my one earphone to hear better and Jake leans in close.

Stop listening, he whispers. It's. Not. Polite.

I poke him. He pokes me back, and then we're struggling half-on half-off the sofa, and I'm laughing so hard I can hardly breathe. You win, I gasp, and replace the earphone.

Lunch, kids, says Lynda.

Jake and I get to our feet a little sheepishly and shuffle over to the table together, still plugged in.

Off, says Lynda, pointing, and I hand him back his earphone. The lunch Lynda serves is nice: beef stew with white beans and salad.

The last thing I expected was to find a person like Jake here in the middle of nowhere, but aside from him, this whole story is starting to make me angry. All these people flung around on the end of a rope because one man keeps on making problems and running away. Or at least that's what it looks like from where I'm sitting.

While Lynda's clearing up, I wrap myself in Jake's big down jacket and step outside for a bit of privacy, and to write one more text.

What happened on the day Owen died?

I stare at the phone and press send. It is not a question I would ever dare ask in person. But in the absence of anyone else getting to the bottom of this mystery I have started to feel a bit desperate.

The little ping of the message flying off calms me. When I go back inside, Jake gives me a look. My father is shaking out his coat in preparation for our departure. I feel suddenly sad.

Jake takes my UK and US mobile numbers and my email and says he'll have to keep in touch with me because other-wise I won't know anything about cutting-edge bands back in my sad little English hick town.

You should come and visit, Gil says. London's not so bad really.

Yeah, come, I say, and Lynda says, Maybe this summer.

We all hug and kiss, even Jake, and everyone feels happy to have met and sad to be parting so soon.

Lynda and Jake walk out to the car with us and at the last minute Jake grabs my arm and pulls his Mets cap down on to my head. I try to take it off but he won't let me, so I get into the car and wave out the back window until we go round a bend and they disappear.

21

We've put it off as long as possible, but it's clear that Gil has to tell Suzanne that Matthew wasn't where we thought he'd be.

Gil stares at my phone, bracing himself, and finally takes out his laptop and writes her an email.

He looks up at me, a little guilty. Do you think I'm a coward?

Only a little, I say, thinking, I wouldn't want to tell Suzanne in person either. I'm guessing that Gil doesn't mention Lynda or Jake in his email; Suzanne is not the sort of woman who would think it was fine to have Matthew's old girlfriend and the son he's never told her about living in his bachelor pad.

I keep wondering how Matthew is going to keep Jake a secret forever. Surely Suzanne will find out someday. If Matthew and Suzanne stay together, how on earth will he explain? There are so many unexploded bombs in Matthew's life. Every day must bring the possibility of discovery. It seems to me like a living hell. Maybe he's used to it. Maybe it's why he left home.

For the first time I'm conscious that Jake is Gabriel's half-brother. Will they meet? Will they grow up to be like their father? Who will I grow up to be like?

I wonder at what point a child becomes a person. Does it happen all at once, or slowly, in stages? Is there an age, a week, a moment, at which all the secrets of the universe are revealed and adulthood descends on a cloud from heaven, altering the brain forever? Will the child-me slink off one day, never to return?

I can't imagine living a real life, or how I'll ever be an adult. It seems like such an unlikely transformation. Someday I may be someone's partner or someone's mother or someone's forensic pathologist. Someday I may drink too much or have a child I never tell anyone about. Someday I might run away from everything, for reasons of my own.

That me is impossible for present-me to imagine.

I cannot picture me grown up. I cannot picture me any different from the me I am now. I cannot picture me old or married or dead.

Crouching down on the floor with Honey, I press my cheek against her face. She smells warm and woodsy, like dog. Her thoughts are in the moment, not the future or the past. She longs for something she can't define, for a state of equilibrium. If Matthew were to walk through the door now, she would feel complete; her terrible yearning would go. It is impossible to tell her that we may see him soon, or next week, or never. She has only two ways of understanding her situation: *yearning* and *yearning gone*. On–off.

Simple.

I wonder if we should tell Suzanne that we're just filling up time to make ourselves look useful. But that would be like saying *We're really grasping at straws here trying to find some vague connection to the husband who ran out on you and*

Gabriel, leaving no trail at all, because I suppose he doesn't really want to be found. Found by you, anyway. Which feels so close to the truth, barring unexpected murder/suicide/kidnapping, that I really can't bring myself even to think it in the same room as Gil emailing Suzanne, in case she overhears.

I hear the whoosh of the email flying off across New York State and for a moment we both sit perfectly still.

Well? So . . . what next?

Excellent question, Gil says. I guess we return to Suzanne's if we can't think of anything else.

I can't imagine what else we might think of, but I don't say that.

We are failing. Not only that, but we have come all the way from England to fail. When I turn to Gil, he has just closed his laptop and is staring at it, looking as lost as I feel.

Well, Perguntadora, he says. We're not terribly good detectives.

But the first rule of being a detective, I tell him, is Do No Harm, and we're not doing any harm, are we?

That's doctors, Mila, not detectives. The first rule of detection is Find Your Man. And we're not doing that either.

A long silence sits in the air and in it we feel separate dejections. Way in the back of my head something nags and nags but I still can't grasp it.

How much do you like Lynda?

Gil frowns. Why on earth do you ask that?

I look at him.

Just the normal amount. It was a long time ago that we were close, he says. What are you thinking? He peers at me closely.

I don't answer.

Then he says, You don't think I'm in love with her? He removes his glasses, rubs his eyes with one hand and replaces them. I'm not. Of course I'm not. He sighs. Perguntadora, he says softly. The past is littered with people we've loved, or might have loved. You'll find out in time.

I say nothing for a while. And then, Let's go.

Yes, OK, Gil says, a bit wearily.

I'll bring my charts and maybe we can read something between the lines.

Or allow ideas to connect where they may.

Willy-nilly. At random. I give him a look.

One must have faith.

One does, I say, and take his hand, thinking of all the people he might have loved.

We pack up. I finish before Gil and press my nose to the window. The snow is still falling.

Where does it all come from?

Too many questions, Gil says. Something to do with ice crystals attaching to each other in groups of six. It's pretty odd, when you think about it.

And no two alike.

That's right. Almost makes you believe in God.

Does it make you believe in God?

He shakes his head. No, I said almost. What about you?

No. But no two alike is strange. I wonder how they can be sure.

And who *they* are. Gil is smiling now. The snowflake scientists. Legions of them, catching and examining billions of snowflakes every year, just on the off-chance . . .

And what if they see one they think they recognize but the twin has already melted?

They'd take pictures, wouldn't they? Give them some credit, Mila. They're scientists. They'd be wonderfully scientific.

Does thinking about snowflakes make your head hurt?

Yes, he says.

It make me feel small.

Ah, Gil says. That all depends. If you're right in the foreground, you're huge. In my head, you're bigger than Big Ben or the Andromeda Galaxy. Much bigger.

The Andromeda Galaxy? Really?

Much bigger. Now let's check out and buy some snow gear. This doesn't look like it's going to end any time soon.

Gil pays at reception and they don't charge extra for not checking out at noon.

Doubt we'll be getting much of an influx tonight, the receptionist says. Not many people driving in this weather.

We head back into town. Gil drops me across from the local minimart and drives further up the road to find waterproof jackets and boots for us both, and mittens and matching hats. My job is to stock up on provisions: bananas, apples, bread, jam, sliced ham, cheese. When I've paid for all of that, plus a large bottle of water, there's enough left over to buy a special offer of chocolate marshmallow Wagon Wheels, Rock Bottom Price, Limited Time Only! They're piled high in boxes by the till and, looking at them, I imagine the limited time to be something like forever.

I lug the groceries in the direction Gil headed, and see the car almost immediately. Gil is waiting for me, looking at a map.

I should phone Lynda to say goodbye, he says, and I hand him my phone.

They chat for a few minutes about Matthew, and Gil promises he'll let her know how it all turns out. Goodbye, Lynda, he says at last. Let's not leave it another twenty years. And then he presses end. He looks at what I've bought. Perfect, he says, now let's get going. Apparently there's a storm coming from the east. If we're lucky we'll miss the worst of it.

He hands me back the phone and a few seconds later it bleeps.

Oh god. What if it's Matthew?

But it's not Matthew. It says: **Ta ta old chap. See you in London.**

And it's signed: **Jake**

I wrap my hand over the screen and place it carefully in my pocket.

On the way out of town we stop one last time and I run into the camping supply place where they're advertising cheap blankets on special offer. They're printed like old-fashioned woollen Navajo blankets but made of recycled plastic bottles. The same guy is working and he recognizes me.

Some storm, eh? he says.

We don't have storms like this in London.

London? Is that where you're from?

Yup. London, England.

What're you doing here? he asks, waiting for the receipt to come out of the till.

We're looking for someone who's lost.

His expression tells me that this is a strange and unexpected answer to a polite and ordinary question.

Lost in the snow? His eyes widen.

No. Lost before the snow started. He might not even be lost, for all I know. I guess he knows exactly where he is.

I am aware that he is staring at me.

I sigh. It's complicated, actually.

Yeah, he says, and hands me the bag with the two blankets and the change. I hope you find him.

Thanks.

That is, if you want to find him.

As I get to the door, I turn round and look at him. Yes, I do want to find him. I want to know why he left.

And then I go out.

Well done, Gil says, appraising the bags. I hope we won't need them, but it's better to be safe.

To tell the truth, I don't mind the thought of needing them, imagining Honey and Gil and me curled up like hibernating bears in our car, eating chocolate-covered Wagon Wheels and waiting for the snow to melt.

We set off. It's getting dark. Kids in town are throwing snowballs at each other while their mothers shout at them to stop. The world has turned a deep and dreamy white and I don't ever want to stop looking at it. I think of Jake with a secret thrill that cancels out the sick feeling I get thinking of Matthew.

My eyes shut and the whirling snow takes me into a dream of the cabin and the fire and the music.

We drive for a while, the windscreen wipers skwooshing snow back and forth, the traffic report muttering out of the radio, Gil hunched up over the wheel of the car with his face nearly up against the windscreen, his usual position now. Our headlights light up more snow.

Whenever I open one eye there's nothing but snowflakes. The traffic is moving slowly, and despite worrying that road conditions might make this my last ever journey on earth, I like the feeling of being here in this strange, warm, murmuring place while nature blows billions of non-identical crystals at us.

I glance over at Gil. He hates driving in London, much less in a blizzard in upper New York State with no known destination.

I send another text to Matthew. **If we die in the snow it's your fault.**

And then I text Jake. **See you in London. Xxx Mila**

It's a little risky adding the 'x's when he didn't put any on his, but it might be the last message I ever send so what the hell. Pressing send gives me the feeling that something between us has been sealed.

Gil finds the highway and it's crowded, everyone moving slowly as the snow whirls harder. Occasionally a gust of wind hits the side of the car like a slap and tries to push us out of our lane. Ahead and to the side I see cars skidding. I suppose I should be nervous but I'm feeling strangely flat. There's nothing I can do except not distract Gil. I climb over into the back seat, put my seat belt on and curl up with my head against Honey's back. It's bonier than it looks but she's warm and her breathing is deep and slow. The snowflakes spin and reel and Gil switches over to a classical music station that comes in full of static; I think about Jake, and a cello lulls me to sleep.

When I wake up it's still snowing but we're moving reasonably well. The traffic station is on again – a young woman's voice – and we pass a big snowplough with flashing lights, growling along in the other direction like a great yellow beast.

I lean forward through the gap in the front seats. How far do we have to go?

We'll come off the highway where we can and stay the night, Perguntadora. We're not far away. With no weather this would be a breeze.

I wonder what no weather would feel like. White sky, invisible temperature. Comfortable, weightless. I'm not all that anxious to get back to Suzanne's.

The red tail lights ahead all flash on at once and Gil steps on the brake. We slide a little and slow. What's this? he murmurs as we crawl along, until about a mile later the traffic comes to a complete stop. Oh Christ, he says, must be an accident.

And sure enough, after ten minutes sat perfectly still in the snow with the wipers still going and the traffic station blathering about wind and snow like we can't see for ourselves, and the heat blowing out of all the vents, a police car flies past in the breakdown lane followed by another, followed by an ambulance.

There, says Gil. Glad it's not us.

We sit for ages and finally Gil turns off the engine. It's nearly eight, he says, time for supper. So I make us ham and cheese sandwiches with apples and Wagon Wheels for dessert. Instead of dog food, I make Honey a sandwich too. Emergency rations, I tell Gil. Honey takes her sandwich politely and doesn't grab, but then scarfs it down in three bites. She seems restless all of a sudden and I venture out into the snow to walk her. Gil says, Be careful, but nothing's moving. The only danger is losing the car; they all look the same in the snow. But there's a big blue van behind us so we won't get lost. Honey's got an upset stomach and I guess it's the food I've been giving her. She's probably a bit old to change to a whole new diet, even if she likes it better.

We're not out very long but the temperature in the car has dropped. We settle down in the back with my blanket. Gil says he's getting cold too, so I unzip the plastic protector bag and hand him the second one. I can see my breath now but feel cosy enough. We find the local news, in which a government official's arrest for misdeeds gets equal billing with the storm. In London, this would be the biggest news for a century.

I text Jake.

We're stuck on the motorway in the snow. Hope we survive. x Mila

The snow collects on the windows and it's impossible to see out. An hour passes, an hour and a half.

At last Jake texts back. **We call it a highway. Don't freeze to death before I get a chance to visit.**

This makes me smile.

We wait. I doze. Gil listens to the radio.

After what seems a very long time, a policeman with a huge orange jacket looms out of the dark, knocking on the window of every car to make sure we're OK, that we're not elderly and freezing to death, or about to give birth. Sorry, folks, he says, we'll have you moving just as soon as we can. In the meantime, stay warm and don't run your battery down. Well done, he says to us when he sees our blankets. And when Gil answers with a question about the accident, the cop just says, Figures it's a bunch of Brits who come prepared.

His radio crackles and he talks into it. Good, he says. Roger. And signs off.

Dad looks at him enquiringly and he says, We're moving. Got two lanes clear. Start your engine, let it warm up. See you folks later, enjoy your stay in the great state of New York.

I hear him banging on the window of the van behind us.

I wish I could have asked what the accident was, but I didn't dare and he probably wouldn't have told me anyway. I hope it wasn't a whole family killed.

The brake lights of the cars ahead light up and clouds of steam rise from cold engines. I feel a little rush of excitement that we'll be on the move again. A flashing blue strobe light appears inside the car. I look out of the back window and see another police car.

Gil starts the wipers. What a predicament, eh? It's non-stop adventure here in the New World.

There's no arguing with that.

We're moving now, slowly, with a bit of slippage at first but picking up speed, and as we approach the accident, we can see a big grey people mover and a smaller car completely scrunched up beside it. There are a few officials standing huddled around, and some cops directing traffic and shouting at everyone to Keep Moving, Keep Moving! The ambulances have gone.

Gil blinks.

What?

Nothing. I was just thinking about Owen. A highway, a winter's night. Gil shakes his head. Icy roads, maybe.

I close my eyes and imagine how it must have been that night. For the child who died on the road. For the father who survived.

Rubbernecking delays, says Gil. He nods at the cars just ahead of us, passing the accident. *Now* I get it.

Get what?

People craning to see what's happened, in case there's some awful scene of carnage. Rubber. Necks.

I feel ashamed of not wanting to miss it either.

How many years since Owen died?

Gil thinks. Three years, he says, and as he says it, something occurs to him. He must have been just the age you are now.

For some reason this information makes my stomach lurch. I remember the phone call late at night, the news that Matthew's son had died. It didn't mean much to me at the time. People I hardly knew.

Meeting Jake makes Owen seem more real. Also, someone exactly my age being dead makes me think about dying more than someone younger or older. The ghost of Owen will always be the same age as Jake. How could Matthew ever stop thinking about that?

I tap Gil on the shoulder. Why did you and Matthew stop seeing each other?

He glances at me in the mirror, even though it means taking his eyes off the road. We didn't exactly stop seeing each other, he says. When he and Suzanne moved upstate, it just wasn't so easy any more. Not like dropping in when I was in New York City. And I got busy too; I didn't travel to New York so much. Gil frowns. I don't know, sweetheart. Time passes, relationships drift.

And Lynda?

I didn't know anything about that part of his life. It's not the sort of thing Matt would have told me in any case.

Because you fancied her too?

He rolls his eyes. A very long time ago, he says. More likely because it's not the sort of mess you want to talk about.

Even to your oldest friend?

Especially to your oldest friend.

Why not?

People don't like talking about the bits of life that don't add up. The bad stuff. The mistakes.

Do you think he felt guilty?

I don't know. Probably.

Have you done things you can't talk about?

I suppose I have, Gil says. But not lately. And no other children that I know about. You can stop worrying about that at least.

I'm not, I say. But maybe I am. How am I supposed to know what adults are capable of?

Gil doesn't like Suzanne much, which is understandable, because in my opinion, she's not very likeable. But the more I hear about Matthew, the more I think it's not so simple. Maybe Suzanne was fine before she hooked up with him.

We've left the police and the truck and the rubbernecking behind, and are moving at a good pace again. It feels really late, though it's only nine thirty. Look for a place to stop, Gil says.

I need the toilet so we stop at the next service area. The lights seem unnaturally bright after all our time in the car. Gil takes Honey for a walk.

You're right about her stomach, he says. Suzanne will have to wean her off highway food.

For the first time I realize that we'll have to leave Honey alone with Suzanne when we go back to London. If Matthew doesn't show up, that is. What a depressing thought. The nagging feeling has returned but my brain is too tired to think.

It's after ten by the time we find a motel. The car park has been ploughed but the man at the desk apologizes for not having shovelled snow off all the walkways. In the short distance between car and room, we get covered with snow. I use the biggest towel from the bathroom to dry Honey while Gil shuffles back to the car for the rest of our stuff. After a long drink, Honey curls up on her bed in the usual waiting position while Gil props himself up on his bed and pours a large whisky.

The room is warm and although the bedspread is a hideous mix of purple, red and blue, the beds are big and comfortable. After all those hours in the car, it feels luxurious to change into pyjamas and stretch out. Tomorrow we'll be back at Suzanne's and after that, home.

I try Catlin again. **What's happening? How are you? What's the news?** But no answer comes. Gil opens his laptop and I hear the ping of mail. I'm almost asleep; too tired to care who Gil's emailing at this hour.

The last thing I hear is his voice, speaking very quietly into my phone. She's asleep, he's saying, though it won't be true for another thirty seconds or so. See you soon, is the last thing I hear.

See *who* soon? Marieka? Suzanne? At this hour?

The question rumbles through my dreams.

22

In the night I dream about Matthew and Gil. They're the age they are now, but they're acting like kids, sitting up in a tree and throwing stones in a pool of water. In my dream, Matthew loses his balance and slips off the branch and Gil doesn't even reach out to him. He watches his friend fall into the pond, watches the bubbles come up from the place he fell. I stare and stare, more and more panicked, but his head doesn't emerge from the pond, and when I grab Gil's arm and scream that we have to save him, Gil merely frowns and says, There's nothing to worry about, he'll be fine.

But he can't swim! I shout, and Gil answers calmly: It doesn't matter. He can breathe underwater.

I wake up terrified with my heart pounding, relieved to be conscious. Gil has just come in with coffee, a bag of bagels and a carton of orange juice. We're not having Wagon Wheels for breakfast, he says, smiling. Come and have a look outside, it's beautiful.

I had the worst dream, I tell him, trying to shake it out of my head.

Poor you, he says, and sits down on the bed beside me, waiting for me to tell him what it was. But as I go over the dream, the picture that's been trying to take shape in my head for a few days now stutters into focus and all of a sudden I wonder why it's taken so long.

The thing is, Gil doesn't seem all that worried about his friend. Not once on this whole trip has he seemed genuinely anxious or depressed. Not once. Thoughtful, yes. Puzzled, yes. But genuinely, seriously worried? No. And I know him. I know he worries about Marieka when she doesn't phone after a concert or her plane takes off in a storm. He worries about me when I'm late home from school even when I told him in the morning I was staying late or going to someone's house. He doesn't sleep when he's worried and he's slept fine this week. He's even done a bit of work.

Is it that he doesn't care that his friend is drowning? Or perhaps Matthew *can* breathe underwater. Perhaps he's not in danger after all.

I sit very still on the edge of the bed, and luckily Gil is leafing through his papers now, waiting for me to calm down, not noticing.

All of a sudden I'm the one who can't breathe. Gil knows where Matthew is. He knows. I am like Clever Hans. For all my powers of perception I have been unable to add up two and two. I've been so busy reading every other situation around us and drawing flow charts that I didn't pay attention to my own father. It took a message in a dream as clear as a typed letter to tell me that something's going on here that isn't right.

I look at Gil and he looks back at me and his expression flickers. He looks away.

We know each other very well.

So, I say.

So?

So. Let me tell you about my dream.

My father is not remotely as tuned in to the world as I am. But even he can tell that the wind has changed.

OK, he says.

In my dream, I start, you and Matthew are sitting on the branch of a tree, over the swimming pond.

Gil stays very very still.

You're grown-ups, but children at the same time. You know how it is in dreams?

He nods.

And suddenly Matthew falls off the branch, or maybe he jumps in. And I'm there now, and screaming at you, I'm all panicky, shouting, Do something! Do Something! Matthew's drowning! And guess what?

What? says Gil. He looks down.

You do nothing. You tell me he can breathe underwater.

There is a pause. Neither of us says a word.

So, I say. How do you interpret that dream?

Gil still says nothing.

You're not actually worried, are you?

I am, in fact, quite worried, he says.

But not about whether he's dead or not. Not about whether he's killed himself or is missing or anything like that. I glare at him.

He sighs. No.

You know where he is.

My statement hangs in the air.

Yes, says Gil. I do.

You've talked to him?

Email, he says. Mostly.

I cannot *believe* it. Fury overtakes me and, for the first time in my life, I'm actually shouting at my father. I can't *believe* it! What kind of *fake trip* has this been? *It's all just a bunch of lies.*

He rubs his forehead with one hand and reaches out to me with the other but I shove his hand away and move across the bed so he can't touch me.

I'm too angry to speak. Two deep breaths. Four. How long have you known?

Mila, he says. I've been in touch with Matthew since he phoned me in London. He told me he'd left home, but he didn't say why. Or where he'd gone. I said I'd come anyway, as planned, and talk to him when he was ready. He said it was important, that he needed time on his own to think. I don't approve of him leaving home, but he didn't ask my opinion. What else could I do? He pauses and looks at me. He's my best friend.

I'm your *daughter.*

You are. And I'm so sorry I involved you in all of this, really I am, my sweetheart. I didn't know what we were getting into. But, Mila, don't you see? I couldn't tell you I was in touch with him because then you'd have had to lie to Suzanne, and that would have been worse. And in any case, marital problems are . . .

I wait, trembling.

Well. They happen. It's not the end of the world. Especially after all they've been through. He falls silent for a moment. I always regret that I didn't fly over when Owen died. I let him down. Of course I offered, but . . . it was such a complicated time. And later, when I heard Suzanne was pregnant, I thought maybe things would be better, that they were putting their lives back to–

Something occurs to me. *And Marieka?*

He sighs. Mum knows.

I think of the texts she sent me about being good detectives when she knew the whole thing was a fraud. I feel like smashing something.

So it's a great big *bloody* conspiracy, then. Including everyone but me. Do you actually know where he is?

I didn't until last night, says Gil, very quietly. He emailed and I phoned him. He wants to see me. At last.

I stare at him, aghast. How can you *ever* expect me to trust you again?

Very gently, he takes hold of my hands and pulls me towards him. He looks at me, his eyes hard and soft at the same time. He takes a deep breath and says, I'm sorry I had to lie to you. I wouldn't have done it if it hadn't been important. But this isn't about you, my darling.

Why not? I grab my hand back. Why can't it just be a *little bit* about me and the rest about Matthew? Why does it *all* have to be about him?

Gil doesn't answer and, for some reason, this makes me angrier.

What was your plan? To tell me eventually? Or just to arrive at Matthew's door one day and say, What a coincidence, why, look who's here!

His expression is miserable. I didn't exactly lie to you. I didn't know where he was. I actually thought he might have been at the cabin; it seemed worth a shot, anyway. And of course I was going to tell you.

But if you were in touch with Matthew . . . he *knew* we were going to the cabin?

Gil nods.

So you knew he wasn't there?

I didn't know for sure, Gil says, looking away.

But he *knew* what we'd find there?

Gil sighs. I suppose he wanted me to know everything.

He could have sent you a bloody postcard. He's a *control freak*. Joy is right about him. He's a *monster*.

Mila . . . Gil reaches out to me again but I slide away from him. I'm much too upset to acknowledge that there was no way for me to know the truth without being complicit in the lie. I leave the room, slamming the door behind me, and then just walk around in the snow for ten minutes. I make a snowball and eat some of it. The snow tastes wet and concentrated, like chewy water. I hurl the rest of it against the window of our room as hard as I can and it hits with a crash. Fake! I shout, throwing another and another and another. Fake fake fake! But he doesn't appear.

It's cold out here and all I can do is cry. My tears come out hot but are slush by the time they hit my chin.

How did it come to this? This furious me hurling snow-balls at a motel window? The me despising my father?

It's freezing cold. I pound on the door and when he opens it, I stand rigid. When he hugs me, I don't hug him back. Tears stream from my eyes.

What is it? I ask, looking up at him at last. Why did he run away? Are he and Suzanne getting divorced?

I don't know, Perguntadora. Honestly, I don't. He kisses the top of my head, strokes my hair.

I pull back.

I keep asking myself, Gil says, and I still don't know. It must be a whole combination of things. Us arriving. Guilt over Owen. And Jake. Being a father again. I don't know how I would survive if anything happened to you, Mila. Maybe he doesn't know how to survive either. I guess he'll tell us when we see him.

But what if it's something else? I'm thinking about the gesture Jake made, with the glass.

Something more? Gil frowns. Don't you think enough has happened to him? There doesn't have to be some huge drama, you know. People sometimes just reach a sort of tipping point and . . .

And run away? They *run away*?

I don't know, Mila. I –

But it could be, couldn't it? It could be something else?

I suppose. It could be. He looks at me carefully. What are you thinking?

Jake says he drinks.

When did he say that? Gil appears shocked. What else did he say?

Nothing. He barely even said that. He just did this. I repeat the gesture, a hand tipping, a glass.

Oh my god, Gil says. My god. Could he have been drunk that night? Is that what Jake meant?

I feel like saying, How should I know? Something happened, that's for sure. Something made Matthew unable to face Gil. Something made him leave his wife and baby. I had trouble leaving Gabriel, and I only knew him for ten seconds.

The words Gil said a minute ago hit my brain at last. Did you say *when* we see him? When are we going to see him?

This morning, says Gil.

Oh.

23

When Catlin and I were eleven, we finally did run away from home.

It was Cat's idea but I was happy to go along with it and, as usual, Cat seemed to have sorted all the technical details. How she knew what to do, I had no idea. It was part of her wisdom about the world, like knowing all about sex before anyone else.

The plan was to pretend to head off to school with our rucksacks so as not to draw attention to ourselves, only we'd dump our sports kit and fill our bags with running-away stuff instead.

According to Cat, the biggest danger in running away was starving to death, so we loaded up all the food we could find – biscuits, bread, jam, Cokes, an entire box of After Eights – and set off for the Eurostar terminal. Bring your passport, Cat said, so I did.

When we got to St Pancras we piled our stuff against the wall outside a shop selling watches and jewellery. There were so many students sitting around waiting for trains that no one took any notice of us despite our age. The plan was to say our parents had just gone to buy lunch if anyone challenged us, but nobody did.

Cat told me to guard our things and went off to take a picture of the departures board. Returning, she carefully copied down the train times from her phone into a notebook. Our plan today, she announced, is to get to Brussels, infiltrate the European Parliament, contact our agent there and pass on the computer codes.

Ambitious plan. I wondered who our agent was in Brussels, but knew better than to ask.

Couldn't we just email them? I said. Or send a text?

Cat looked at me like I was insane. Security, she hissed. Everything we do is surveilled to the nth.

I sighed. I didn't think she'd manage to get two unaccompanied eleven-year-olds on a train to Brussels, but you never knew with her. I was fine skiving off school for a day, but unsupervised international travel made me a little nervous.

She stared at her phone and I stared at her, and eventually she looked up and explained that she was waiting for our contact to make himself known. I thought we might have quite a wait ahead of us.

We passed the time practising encryption, which consisted of texting mildly obscene codes to each other. When things got really slow, Cat would send me out to check for enemy agents, or she'd go out to steal chocolates.

By late morning I'd had enough. Can we go home now? I asked Cat.

Soon, she told me. And we went back to code practice, painstakingly translating texts in a bubble of silence surrounded by the boiling chaos of the huge station.

At lunchtime we haunted the cafés set around the long station corridor and got lucky when a pale young foreign couple ordered a lot of food and left most of it behind. We ate the remains of their posh sandwiches and Cat pocketed the tip they'd left, slinking off to check for spies while I faced the waiter's glare.

When it came down to the actual stowing away to Brussels, we pretty much fell at the first hurdle.

Damn them, Catlin growled, patting her pockets furiously, and when I said, Damn who? she said they'd stolen her passport.

It wouldn't have done us any good anyway as we had no tickets and not nearly enough money to buy any, and besides, I happened to know she didn't own a passport so they didn't have to bother stealing it. I know someone who'll forge me a clean one, she said. For a price. And off she shot once more, disappearing into her fantasy.

I sat and watched the crowd, and browsed the bookshop across the way, and eventually returned to our spot and texted **I'm tired** and a few minutes later Cat wandered back and flopped down beside me. About ten minutes after that (which was how long it took to write the average three-word code due to the unnecessary complexity of our cipher) my phone bleeped again and she looked away, as if distracted.

'I love you', said the text. I translated it twice to make sure I'd read it properly and then just sat, not knowing what it meant or how to answer or what to do next.

We stayed like that, a silent island of two, while the crowds flowed over and around us in a steady torrent.

Let's go, Catlin said at last. And without looking at me,

she fastened the flap of her rucksack, stood up, and trudged off towards the Underground station, towing me behind in her wake like an Arctic sledge.

At her house, Cat shot off up the path and I didn't bother to wave. I arrived home at pretty much the exact time I should have been back from school, and went off to my room, where I sat on the bed and thought.

We never were found out. Cat forged sick notes for both of us, knowing I'd forget to forge one for myself, and our teacher accepted them without a murmur. The lack of suspicion was disappointing; Catlin was ready to withstand torture.

I never had the courage to talk to her about the day we almost went to Brussels or to ask about the text. As time passed, I began to think I'd imagined it.

24

I have learned today that my father can lie to me and that I will put all my instincts on hold and believe him because I want to believe that he wouldn't. I didn't discover that he was a murderer or had a secret son, like Matthew. But none-theless. So much relies on one person assuming the other is telling the truth. If a person can lie to you about one thing, he can lie about something else.

Of course I lied to him too, in a way, but it wasn't the same. Matthew's text was, after all, for me. I was merely protecting Gil from feeling sad. Or was I? Perhaps it was just me thinking I could handle something Gil couldn't.

Another lie.

It makes me think about the nature of truth. I don't lie as a general rule because I've never thought there was much to be gained by it. My parents don't bully me or impose expec-tations in ways that inspire me to make things up.

I blame the quietness of this arrangement for my inno-cence. Though it's not as if I've never experienced dishonesty. It starts early in life with girls at school, saying they're only allowed eight friends at a sleepover and you would be the ninth. Or talking about what they've done with some boy when you're pretty sure they haven't. Some lies barely deserve the effort that goes into telling them.

In theory, I would like to lead a transparent life. I would like my life to be as clear as a new pane of glass, without anything shameful and no dark shadows. I would like that. But if I am completely honest, I have to acknowledge secrets too painful even to tell myself. There are things I consider in the deep dark of night; secret terrors. Why are they secrets? I could easily tell either of my parents how I feel, but what would they say? Don't worry, darling, we will do our best never to die? We will never ever leave you, never contract cancer or walk in front of a bus or collapse of old age? We will not leave you alone, not ever, to navigate the world and all of its complexities without us?

They will leave me. It is the first thing you learn that makes you no longer a child. Someday I will die too, but I'm not nearly as frightened of that as I am of being left alone. This is my darkness. Nothing anyone says can console me.

Is Matthew coming here? I ask.

Gil shakes his head. No, we'll go to him. He's staying nearby.

I would hate to have parents who were always looking over my shoulder, reading my diary, checking my thoughts. I would hate to be exposed. And so, perhaps, when I say I long to be a pane of glass, I am lying. I long for partial obscurity at the same time as I long for someone to know me.

25

Matthew is staying thirteen miles from here. His disappearance, when you come right down to it, was modest in scale. For all the driving we've done up and down the state, his big break for freedom took him less than ninety minutes from home.

I am recalculating all the coordinates I've known so far, but am still lost. I take out my phone and text Jake.

We're seeing Matthew today.

I want to tell him more but don't know how. The phone bleeps back almost immediately.

What???

I text back. **Long story.**

There's a pause. I wonder if he's gone and then the phone bleeps again.

Ok. And then a second later: **Report back.**

I will. Wish us luck.

Luck ☺

*

The landscape we drive through is dazzlingly white, every angle and corner softened by great drifts of snow. Icicles have appeared like magic, giant dripping stalactites anchored to the edges of roofs and gutters. I have never held an icicle before and feel an almost unbearable desire to do so. They look precious as fairy jewels and if I broke one off I could wave it about like a sceptre.

I sit in the back with Honey. Gil glances round at us occasionally but says nothing. He holds a map between his knees. I could be helping, but I don't.

We've left the town and are driving through a hilly landscape that's white as far as the eye can see. Fences and stone walls have become soft slopes, and farmhouses wear high slouchy hats. Everything looks clean and new and I like this world of perfection despite knowing that all sorts of barbed wire and dead things lie beneath. The road is clear and black, which makes a change from England, where they'd just wait for it to turn to ice and then melt eventually, while not going to work and complaining that the services can't cope.

I like the way snow piles itself at the top of telephone poles and even collects on the wires in long thin white lines. There are gaps where birds have landed, spelling out Morse-code messages. Dot dot dot. Dash dash dash. Dot dot dot.

We pull off the road into what looks like a low-rent shopping mall and see the MOTEL sign. We're moving slowly now and I'm glad for Suzanne's big car, which feels solid even when we skid.

Gil leaves Honey and me in the car while he goes in. The path is drifted with snow that no one's bothered to re-shovel in the past hour. Gutters all along the front glitter and sag with ice. He comes slithering back out and moves the car nearer to Matthew's part of the motel.

We'll see what happens, he says. As I get out of the car, I step through ice into a deep pool of freezing water. It fills my boot and feels horrible. Honey neatly avoids the puddle. She seems unnaturally alert, head high.

I blame Gil for my frozen leg and follow him up the path, dragging my foot and limping. He ignores me, which is just as well. I'm behaving badly and don't feel like being cajoled.

The girl at the front desk buzzes us in. We follow the corridor round and knock on Matthew's door. I can hear footsteps. Gil looks down at me suddenly and reaches out his hand. I am not so horrible that I refuse to take it. His face is full of anxiety.

I don't recognize the man who opens the door but Honey does. She bounds at him, launching herself through the air like a missile. Darling Honey, I hear him say, laughing, his voice cracked with emotion. Darling dog. Honey is incandescent with joy, ecstatic, and it's contagious. If I had a tail I'd wag it too.

At last.

Matthew buries his head in her thick white ruff. He holds her face in his hands and his tired features fill with light. At last he stands up and embraces my father. Their faces disappear and the two men seem to merge. They could be twins, so similar are they in height and stature. I can imagine them as children, or on the side of a mountain, the closest either had to a brother.

Honey stands looking up at her master, alert to every expression, every inch of her electric with love. She has lost the melancholic expression of the last few days. Matthew cannot resist kneeling again, and she licks his face and neck till he grasps her head in his two hands and pushes her gently away. Not content to step back, she turns sideways and rubs the length of her body across his chest, first one way, then the other. If she could eat him, she would.

Matthew has strong features and unnaturally intense eyes; his hair is thick and grey. Even I can see that despite his age he is handsome. He doesn't attempt hugging or kissing, just looks at me, his head tilted slightly, watching.

It is hard to get over the habit of dislike that has grown in my head, but Matthew is not what I expected. His expression is complex; he looks athletic, but holds his shoulders stiffly, as if in pain. I wish now that I hadn't sent those texts.

While he speaks to Gil I examine his face. There are purple shadows under his eyes. He smells clean and has recently shaved; he wears a faded green flannel shirt. I expected desperation, but instead he is quiet and reserved. It is impossible to ignore the fact that he looks unspeakably sad.

We sit down, me on the bed, Gil and Matthew in chairs. Matthew asks Gil if he wants a drink, doesn't wait for an answer and pours wine into two glasses. I don't need to check my watch. It is not yet ten in the morning. Gil looks ill at ease. When I tune in to my father, the signals all line up. Is this because I know him so well or because he has nothing left to hide?

I get no clear signal from Matthew. What little comes through is scribbly and erratic. Something scrambled is not the same as a lack of information; it suggests interference. Matthew's signals are blocked, as if he has a glass wall buried a few inches beneath his skin. He is accustomed to hiding.

It is fairly obvious that they would like to talk without me present, but I am not in a mood to cooperate. I sit absolutely still, waiting for resolution. Matthew drinks with steady deliberation and pours another. They make small talk about our trip. Gil tells him about Lynda and Jake. Matthew listens quietly, asking questions that may or may not mask a depth of emotional involvement. The mood in the room becomes increasingly odd. Honey searches Matthew's face. I do too, and am abashed, suddenly, to feel that I may be contributing to his unhappiness.

Just as I'm trying to figure out how to excuse myself, Matthew asks if I would mind sitting in the lobby for a bit while they talk. He asks politely, as to a social and intellectual equal. I appreciate this. It is not commonly the way people speak to children. Gil takes me out to the lobby, which has been designed as a pretend study, with a desk, an ugly red leather sofa, a lamp, a small bookshelf filled with paperback books, two chairs and a television. The room is filled with strange light from all the snow outside. No one sits in the reception area, which connects to a small office. Perhaps whoever is on duty hides back there when not required.

Gil kisses the top of my head and apologizes for . . . well, he says, for everything. Then he goes. I look around for Honey and realize that she has stayed with Matthew.

Horrible music is playing through tinny speakers in the

reception area. I get up from the chair and go exploring. All the public areas are empty.

I miss Honey, and despite the fact that she has been Matthew's dog her entire life, I resent her absence. Gil and I brought her here. She should be grateful. Matthew's the one who left her behind with Suzanne. He left Gabriel behind as well. And Jake. But dogs don't hold grudges. At least this one doesn't.

There's nothing else to do but return to the fake study.

I text Jake again. **We found him.**

What do you think?

Not what I expected.

There's a longish pause and I can almost hear Jake thinking on the other end. I wait and wait but no answer comes. Maybe he doesn't know what to say.

I look up and Gil is there, talking in a low voice to the receptionist. She hands him a key.

I've taken a room, Gil says, just for the night. So I can talk to Matt some more.

Matt is nowhere to be seen. We walk out to the car to fetch our bags. I'm waiting to hear what Gil tells me next.

Perguntadora.

I'm busy collecting my things and only turn to him after a minute. Yes?

Forgive me, he says. I'm trying to do what's best for everyone.

I stare at him, studying his face. You didn't have to lie to me.

I know, he says.

I'm not an idiot.

Far from it. But everyone alive has secrets, he says. It's terrible being a keeper of them. Worse, maybe, than being kept in the dark.

I say nothing.

Mila, I need your help.

Like he needs to point that out. Our eyes meet again and I feel grubby and false. I am withholding help because it is the only power I have, except the power to be kind.

I reach over and take his hand, the one that is not gripping his suitcase, and so the drama between us melts away.

Who knows? Someday I may need him to lie for me.

26

All pretence of happiness has drained out of our journey. We have settled into our motel room and I feel tired and young. Too young to do what Marieka has asked me to do. Too young to look after my father.

Also, I miss Honey. Why is she so loyal to Matthew but not at all loyal to me?

Gil has come back from another conversation with Matthew. He smells of wine.

What did you find out?

I'm not a very good cross-examiner, he says.

You could just ask him what's going on.

I tried. He doesn't seem to know himself. He says he didn't want me to see him this way.

What way?

Oh, I don't know. Gil shrugs. All of it. It's a mess of a corner he's backed himself into. Whichever way you look at it.

I think about this. And then I think about Catlin.

Maybe he can't bear not turning out better than you.

I can see the cogs in Gil's brain turning. This won't be the sort of thing he'd think of. I wouldn't have thought of it either, without Catlin.

Maybe you remind him of when he was young and hopeful. Before everything went wrong.

It didn't have to be such a mess, Gil says. If it had been just –

But he stops himself. He realizes that saying *just Owen* is impossible. Yet I know what he means. It may be possible to lose a child and survive. But to lose one child and possibly be the reason he's dead? And to have another you've kept secret? And then to leave the third? Even with my incomplete understanding of life I can tell that it's too much. You would begin to twist, like a floorboard cut against the grain. And keep twisting, until it was impossible ever again to be straight.

And *now* to have the friend come to visit. The one whose life you saved. The weaker one.

Gil goes out to find dinner and Marieka picks up on the first ring.

Hello, my dear heart. How are you?

We've found Matthew, I say. Gil was in touch with him all along.

My words hang in the air.

I knew, she says.

Yes.

Oh, my love, she says softly. There is silence on the line and it crackles a little.

I'm fine, I say out loud. But really? I don't feel at all fine.

My sweet girl, she says. Mila, please don't cry. She speaks

so softly now that I can barely hear her. Please, sweetheart. Matthew seemed so . . .

Desperate?

She sounds a bit surprised and says, No, adamant. Do you want to come home?

I want to go home, of course I do. I want to go home more than anything I've ever wanted ever. But I also want to stay with Gil and see this thing through. Maybe now that Matthew is found our job will be over and we can go home together. Maybe now that Matthew is found he will go back to Gabriel and Suzanne and they will all live happily ever after. Maybe it could all still work out.

Marieka's voice interrupts my thoughts. Tell me what you saw, she says. Tell me what you noticed about Matthew.

He looks like Dad.

Yes, Marieka says. Yes, I remember that.

He's very intense.

What else?

But I do not know how to explain what I see – the scribbly signals, the intelligent face, the stiff shoulders, the eerie calm, the dark, dark feeling flowing off him. The wine.

He drinks a lot.

Oh, she says. I wish we hadn't let you go. I should have said no.

We're coming home soon, I say. It's nearly over.

Gil bustles in with bags full of Chinese takeaway so I send Marieka kisses and hand him the phone. They talk softly for a few minutes. I hear Gil say, Yes. No, we haven't talked about it. And then, I know, I know. Soon. I've had enough of this. His voice sounds tired and he rubs his head as if trying to rub thoughts away.

When he hangs up the phone, we talk about Marieka. She sounds worried, he says, and I nod.

She may as well join the club.

Yes, says Gil. She may as well. Let's go home, Perguntadora, it's time to go home. We'll leave tomorrow.

But as it happens, we don't.

27

Matthew does not come to breakfast until we are the last people left. He only has coffee and I can see his point. The food is awful, even the toast. Fake jam, fake juice, fake bread. Honey, at least, seems relieved with the outcome of our hunt. She never strays more than a few inches from Matthew's side. When he stands, she stands. When he paces the room, she pads behind him.

Dogs inhabit a world full of different information. Matthew is in the foreground of Honey's life, throwing everything else into shadow, like Big Ben or the Andromeda Galaxy. She fears separation, can smell it hovering around Matthew. If Matthew goes, she will have nothing. Being without him makes her life impossible.

How could he leave her behind?

The receptionist comes in and asks Matthew to move his car to let the snowplough through. I watch from the window as he opens the door for Honey and she jumps in beside him.

Matthew rejoins us, fetching more coffee for himself and Gil. I don't like the look in his eye; it is oddly fixed. He stirs fake milk into the fake coffee but doesn't drink it, instead filling a small glass from a flask he keeps in his pocket. Gil watches, his expression neutral.

The funny thing about Matthew is that he never seems drunk. He seems the same as yesterday. He does not slur his words or fall over or anything.

I take my book and go to another table so they can talk, but it is close enough to hear most of what they say.

Look, Gil says, leaning in towards his friend. It's not too late. You can start again.

Matthew looks up at him. Shakes his head.

You have to want to. Don't you want to?

A loud flat noise makes me jump. Matthew has slammed his hand down on the table. Of course I want to, he says. It's. Too. Late.

There's a long silence and then I hear an awful noise. It's Matthew crying.

There's not another woman? Gil's voice is low.

Matthew actually laughs. No, he says. Not another woman.

Look, says Gil, there's always a way out.

This time Matthew looks up at him, interested, amused. I know, he says.

The two men sit unmoving, each coming to the separate realization that he has misunderstood the other.

The ashes of an old friendship flutter and settle in a delicate heap beneath the breakfast table.

Please, says Gil, and I can hear a rich chattering of emotions in the word. His *please* means *Please* let this all end, *please* let's resolve this so I can go home.

Matthew smiles at him. It'll all be fine, he says.

I want to help.

Oh, I'm well beyond help, Matthew says calmly.

I look over and see Matthew and Gil, their eyes locked across the table, concentrating like chess players.

You're not, Gil says.

No? There is the ghost of a smile on Matthew's face, as if behind the thick dull pain there is a funny side to all of this. I appreciate your faith, he says.

Suddenly I am frightened. My father's faith in Matthew is one of the instruments of his destruction. It reminds him of what he was. How much he has lost.

Matt, come back with us. Come home. Please. Gabriel misses you.

Matthew nods. He looks exhausted.

I'll stay as long as you need me to.

No, says Matthew. Go back to London. There's nothing more you can do.

Are you sure? But I can hear in Gil's voice that he's relieved. No doubt Matthew can hear it too.

Matthew nods. I wonder if he is already drunk, always drunk, in a way that doesn't quite show.

What happened? Ask him what happened that day, Gil, ask him properly, for god's sake. I edge closer, drawn by the dark tug of missing facts.

Gil is still talking, tentatively, saying all the wrong things. I'm sure you can sort things out with Suzanne. For Gabriel's sake.

But Matthew has stopped listening. The very air around him has ceased to move. I look at Gil. Listen! I want to shout. Something happened that day. Something's happening *now*.

I am struggling, trying to read a story written in a language I don't quite speak. Why can't Gil translate?

Perhaps Matt chose a brother who would not see into his soul.

The puzzle pieces in my brain dance just out of reach. I turn to Matthew and focus hard.

Gil speaks of getting back to normal. Matthew stares out of fathomless eyes. He sits perfectly still but the hand that grips his glass trembles.

With an air of resignation, Gil gets up from the table and goes to check out, leaving the two of us together.

I focus harder. Gil has told me that in order to translate you need to be a chameleon, to put on the skin of another person, to creep inside his head. I have seen this transformation take place within him – his features and sometimes his personality seem to alter with each voice he takes on, with each book.

And then the pieces begin to line up. I am back on the day of the accident, the day Owen died.

It is dusk.

My head aches, my skin feels tight. Has Matthew been drinking? I can't tell. Owen is sitting in the back seat.

And then I think of Matthew opening the car door for Honey and, *of course*! *Honey* was in the front. Matthew took her everywhere, Suzanne said. She loved the car. So Owen sat in the back because his father's dog was in the front. If their places had been reversed, the child would have lived and the dog died.

With Honey in the front, Matthew had to turn to look at Owen, to talk to him. At that hour, in winter, with ice on the road and everyone driving too fast, that's all it would have taken. One backwards glance. Or two. A lorry coming up from behind.

The picture comes together. *That's* why Suzanne hates Honey. For surviving when Owen didn't. And it's another reason to hate Matthew. For putting Owen in the back. She knew the dog would have been in the front.

Something else occurs to me.

What if Suzanne knew everything? What if she not only knew everything that happened that night, but *everything*? About Lynda and Jake. Matthew's drinking. Maybe she sent him away after Owen died. She'd lost her son and wasn't prepared to lose her husband to a manslaughter charge on the same day. What if she saved him from arrest on the day she was called to the hospital to identify her dead son?

I feel dizzy with the shifting ground of the story. Matthew is staring at me now.

Recalculating, says my brain. Recalculating.

I judged Suzanne to be angry and trivial, the sort of woman who drives people away. But what if she is the hero of the story, the one who has kept all of Matthew's secrets? That's why she never seems to be telling the truth, because it's *his* lies she's hiding. That's why she looks angry all the time.

But now Suzanne has decided that she can no longer lie for him, or has fallen out of love or out of sympathy. Her impulse to protect him has expired. She has fallen in love with someone else.

I meet Matthew's eyes. The contact seems to last forever. It sucks me down into a furious black fog, a muttering hell. I struggle in the cloying dark. Get me out of here, get me out!

And then suddenly everything clears and I tremble with the force of what I see.

Matthew doesn't want some time away, he wants forever. He wants to die. I feel it so strongly it chokes me. He left Honey behind because he didn't plan to come back.

His eyes are intense and serious. He seems surprised and – could it be? – slightly amused by what has passed between us.

I am floating up to the ceiling, looking down on this scene. I can't speak.

Gil returns with the room key and a printout of our bill. His smile fades when he sees us and he looks from one to the other, puzzled. But Matt is a conjurer of moods and he sets questions for Gil to ease the moment: When will you return to London? How is Marieka? Will you see Suzanne?

I turn to leave and my chair slides back more violently than I intend, tipping backwards with a crash.

Honey leaps to her feet, her whole body poised, a low noise in her chest. I wonder how far she will go to protect him. Would she tear out my throat?

Come on, Gil says to me, let's pack up. I've got some calls to make, he says to Matthew, who nods assent. We'll leave in an hour. You can follow us when you're ready.

I text Jake. **It's awful here.**

And within seconds he texts back. **It'll be over soon.**

Which is true, one way or another.

28

Gil phones Suzanne and talks for a long time. I am glad not to be included. I want to go back to being a child.

There are hundreds of channels on American TV and I flick through without paying much attention to anything on the screen. It is mostly commercials. I come to the high numbers, where a topless woman rubs her breasts and starts to ask if I want to get to know her better before I click past. I pause on a nature show where a quiet-voiced man admires a beautiful stag in a clearing, saying, Isn't he a magnificent creature? and then raises his rifle and shoots him through the heart. The animal staggers and falls to his knees. I want to throw up.

A week ago America felt like the friendliest place in the world but I am starting to see darkness everywhere I look. The worst thing is, I don't think it is America. I think it is me.

Gil phones Marieka next. I don't hear much of what he's saying. It's OK, he says. We'll be there before you know it.

He's too worried to lie to anyone now. He's worried for Matthew, as well he should be – the time I spent in Matthew's head felt like drowning. Maybe he's even worried for me.

I slip under Gil's arm so that he has to hold me close. I wish he could clasp me tight enough to squeeze the images out of my head. They are not real pictures but they are more vivid than any I have ever seen. I do not need to close my eyes to see them.

Gil, I say. Do you think Matthew will be OK? What if he does something desperate? I look intently at my father. Think, I beg him silently. Look at your friend. Figure it out.

Gil tightens his arm round me. Don't worry, Mila. Matthew will sort himself out. He always does.

I want to tell my father that maybe this time he won't sort himself out. But I am twelve years old, should I be the one to know?

Make him promise to come home with us, I beg. *Please.* Gil looks surprised. Make him *promise.*

OK. I'll make him promise.

Just then my phone rings and Gil reaches over to answer it, fumbling the buttons but eventually hitting the right one. He says hello and then, to my surprise, hands it over.

CAT!!

Dad's moved to Leeds, she says, with no preamble, not even hello.

No! I say. *Leeds?*

With his girlfriend.

His *what?* Are you kidding?

Ha ha ha, she says grimly. Yes, I are making the funny joke.

That's awful! Have you met her?

Despite the distance between us, I can see the expression on her face. Yeah, she says. I've met her.

I don't suppose she's nice?

Evil viper troll-bitch from hell.

Oh, Cat. I'm so sorry.

I don't care if I never see him again. Mum hates him too. She says she's damned if she'll pay for me to visit him. Are you still there?

Yes, I'm here. I'm coming home soon. We'll make voodoo dolls.

Perfect, she says. How's my egg?

Oh Christ, her egg. It's big all right, I say. How's mine?

I've been far too busy having my *life wrecked* to think about chocolate, she says, in her most self-righteous voice.

Neither of us says anything.

Are you having fun in America? Her voice is sulky.

Fun? I say. For some reason this strikes me as hilarious. Fun? I say again, and start to laugh. Not really, Cat. Not really very much actual so-called *fun*. What I'm having is what you might call the *opposite* of fun. *Anti-fun*.

Perfect, says Cat, and that's it, I'm off, laughing so hard I can't stop.

What do you mean *perfect*? I can barely choke out the words. What kind of friend are you?

The best kind, she says, trying to sound serious but giving way to snorts of hilarity. It would be *unbearable* if you were having the time of your life while I suffered the torments of hell. At the words *torments of hell* she explodes into guffaws, which sets me off even more.

Tears are running down my face and I'm about to answer that the torments of *her* hell are nothing compared to the torments of *mine*, but there's a click and she's gone.

Gil comes back into the room and looks at me quizzically but I just groan and dry my eyes on my sleeve.

My sides actually ache from laughing so hard and for a minute I can't move.

I love you too, Cat, I want to say, even though the phone line is completely silent and my answer is a year too late.

29

We drive back to Suzanne's in silence. Neither of us is looking forward to this reunion.

I don't know what Gil said to him, but Matthew arrives an hour after we do and Suzanne walks out to the car to greet him. They embrace and she drops her head on to his shoulder. For an instant the flow of emotion between them is powerful, unmistakeable. But she pulls away too soon, her lips pursed tight. His eyes search her face but she turns away.

Gabriel flaps his hands up and down like a penguin when he sees me. He starts to laugh and say me-me-me, which could be his version of Mila. I scoop him up, kiss him noisily on his fat neck to make him laugh even more and bounce him up and down. Gabriel B-B-B-Billington! Silly Billy Billing-ton!

But when Matthew appears, Gabriel's happiness hits a different note. He would fly out of my arms if only it were possible.

Matthew catches him up and the two spin round, gabbling in some private language. Honey watches quietly. When at last they stop, Gabriel reaches over a bit dizzily and grabs my hair with one fist. He holds on to steady the world, then shifts, his face suddenly serious, closes his eyes and lays his head against Matthew's chest. He is a simple mechanism, like a toy aeroplane with a twisted-up rubber band to make him fly. When the rubber band untwists, he falls to earth. I remove his hand from my hair, opening each finger softly, but grateful, somehow, for the gesture. He is nearly asleep.

Suzanne comes out of the kitchen and takes him off Matthew, saying it's time for bed and that she's made sandwiches for us if we're hungry. She disappears with Gabriel and we can hear the bath running.

I look at the sandwiches Suzanne has made – cheese and tomato on brown bread – and am suddenly ravenous. We sit on high stools at what she calls the breakfast bar and eat our supper. Gil opens a beer and holds it out to Matthew, who doesn't take it.

None of us speaks. After a minute or two, Matthew gets up and leaves the room. We hear his tread on the stair. A door closing.

What did we expect to find when we set out? Something nice? Did we imagine Matthew ran away to join the circus? That it was like searching for a lost cat, one you might find up a tree, grateful to be rescued? Frightened cats will claw you to pieces when you try to save them. I glance at Gil. Did he not think any of this through?

A gulf has opened between us and I am angry. I am a child, I want to shout at him. *Protect me.*

My head hurts. Despite a greater than average ability to see clearly, I have been conned. The people I have expected to take care of me – the wise ones, with life experience – have got it wrong.

I return to my room (Owen's room), climb under the covers fully clothed and pull the dark woollen blankets up over my knees and head, like a tent. It's boring being with messed-up people all the time and after all those hours and days in cars and motel rooms I have a desperate urge to be by myself, to escape the tension in the house and the failure of our trip. (Was it a failure? Or an unhappy success?)

The snow is nearly gone but a wild wind whips the trees against my window. Under the pillow is Suzanne's (Matthew's?) book on caravanserais; I slip it out and illuminate the camel's strange head on the cover with my phone torch. Long red and gold tassels decorate his bridle, which is set with discs of hammered silver. A low building with a teardrop-shaped entrance covers the background. I turn the pages past beautiful photographs of tents and woven rugs and men with burning eyes and imagine other journeys, with camels instead of cars and palm dates instead of sandwiches; messengers moving in long slow arcs across empty deserts with news of life and death.

Caravanserai.

I close my eyes and imagine the cool interior of the rest stop, the whitening sun. After the endless bounce and sway of the camels, the ground feels unsteady. They drink, noses deep in stone troughs. Twenty gallons. Forty. Fifty.

If I were on the Silk Trail I could cross Persia, China, Arabia. Just for a while, I would be happy moving through empty spaces, knowing no one, living a different life.

I close my eyes and think about Jake.

30

Matthew and Suzanne speak politely, their faces empty of feeling.

She has moved out of the house, returning with Gabriel so he can see Matthew, who only comes alive when they are together. I am touched by father and son; you don't have to be a genius to recognize that they are full of love for each other. Honey lies beside them, forming a holy trinity. She does not take her eyes off Matthew, and he, in turn, keeps one hand laid gently on her head or back nearly all of the time. Suzanne is staying, she tells us, with a friend. I think it is probably more than a friend but I'm tired of knowing things.

Down the phone line I hear Marieka's sharp intake of breath. What sort of friend is she staying with? Who is it?

But this I can't answer. Age, height, colour of eyes? I am not the KGB.

I have barely spoken to Matthew since we returned.

Our last day is sunny and Matthew and Gil work outdoors to keep busy. They dig up the garden, each working a different end, absorbed in different thoughts. Or the same ones, thought separately. Honey lies nearby with her head on her paws, constantly alert. I cannot bring myself to be inside her head.

Our flight is tomorrow. Easter Sunday.

I sit with Gabriel and draw eggs for him in bright crayons and he slaps them triumphantly with his hands and shouts Ek! I get overconfident and try ducks and bunnies, but they don't look right. He recognizes them though, despite my wobbly pictures, and I wonder how he translates bad drawings of ducks and bunnies into the animals he sees at the zoo or the park. Three dimensions into two, feathers and fur into pink and yellow crayon. An ordinary miracle.

Duck! he says proudly and points. And then, Ek! Has he ever seen a painted egg? Or only the ones his nanny scrambles sometimes for his breakfast? She uses brown ones that look nothing like the ones I've drawn. How can he decode the world so expertly?

We are all together for one last night, Gabriel in his pyjamas with feet, Suzanne making dinner as if this were still her home. But no one is fooled. She is like a horse whose eyes have turned to the next jump.

Matthew pours wine for his wife and his friend but not for himself. The conversation is stilted and he and Suzanne never address each other directly. When I offer to set the table, she looks grateful and then, instead of simply handing me the cutlery, she places it carefully in my outstretched hands and closes her fingers round mine. I look up into her eyes.

I'm sorry, she says in a soft voice meant only for me. I'm sorry we made such a mess of your holiday . . . and everything else. She shrugs and clasps my hands tighter for an instant before releasing them. It's all a mess, she says. A big fucking horrible bloody mess.

Her eyes swim with tears.

It's OK, I tell her. It's not your fault.

No? she says, pushing the hair off her face and almost smiling. I don't know any more. Maybe it is my fault. She turns away.

I set the table and Suzanne calls everyone in to dinner. We make small talk that no one will ever remember and directly after dinner, Suzanne fetches Garbriel and kisses Gil and me goodnight.

As she turns to leave, Matthew stops her and takes Gabriel from her arms. The child is more asleep than awake, but he wraps his arms tightly round his father's neck and Matthew kisses his cheek, pressing his face against Gabriel's, before gently freeing the child's arms and giving him up to an impatient Suzanne.

Gil follows her out to the car, leaving me with Matthew, and I'm desperate to escape, panicked at the thought of another confrontation. But before I can follow Gil, Matthew stops me.

Don't worry, Mila, he says. It'll be OK.

I shake my head. No it won't.

He tilts his head slightly, enquiringly.

What sort of person are you? Anger chokes me. Have you even thought about how Gabriel will feel? Or Honey? It's not just you. It's not just your life.

I know that, he says.

Well, if you know then how can you consider *doing it*? I cannot bring myself to say the words: *killing yourself.*

It's complicated, he says. You'll understand someday.

I understand *now*, I shout at him. I understand that your life is a mess. But I don't understand how you think *that* is going to make it better for anyone but you.

You're not an ordinary child, Matthew says.

What about what you told Gil? I say, ignoring him. About not lying down in the snow? Gil always remembered. You're the one who's forgotten.

I haven't forgotten, Matt says.

Then *don't do it.*

We stand facing each other, squared off. I'm breathing hard. One minute Matthew is there; the next he has turned inward, as if I am no longer in the room.

I follow Gil out to the car.

Suzanne arranges Gabriel in his car seat and clicks the seat belt, which swings over his head in one piece like the roof of a fighter jet. She circles round to the driver's side of the little blue car (whose?) and then she and Gil talk about the airport and the times of our flights. I lean in to kiss Gabriel's fat cheek in the dark, tears dripping from my face on to his. He is fast asleep, his hands grabbed into fists, his eyes screwed up as if battling an unseen foe. He opens his eyes for an instant and blinks and smiles, but he's not properly awake and a second later he's out once more. I kiss his damp fist and hope his sleep is not always full of shadows, then shut the car door as quietly as I can.

Over at the front door of the house, Honey and Matthew stand looking out at us, framed in a halo of light, suspended between this world and the next.

31

The following morning, Matthew and Gil take our bags out to the driveway to wait for Suzanne. The two men embrace. There are no speeches, no final words.

Matthew stands back a little and looks at me carefully.

Take care of Honey, I say to him, and he nods. And Gabriel.

He nods again.

And you, I say.

And you too, Mila, he says.

He disappears into the house before Suzanne arrives, alone. Gabriel is at playgroup, she tells us. We pile our bags into her car and set off. No one speaks. At international departures in New York, it is impossible to stop for more than a minute or two, so our parting is brief. A quick hug and Suzanne is gone.

As we check for passports and arrange ourselves at the terminal, Gil hands me an extra bag to carry, a large one with handles.

I peer inside and there it is – the cowboy Easter egg, vast and unwieldy, the box a bit shopworn. I look up, astonished.

He took some convincing, Gil says. Oh yes. Hi ho, Silver. It took some doing, all right.

I'm gaping at him. What on earth did you say?

Gil shakes his head. Shouldn't tell you, really. I told him I worked for Frommer's. Updating travel guides for the European market.

You didn't.

Gil nods. I did. It was amazing. He practically forced the thing on me. Wouldn't take a penny.

At this moment, I am loving my father almost to distraction. You're a genius, I say, grinning. I'm so proud. Cat will love it.

But secretly it's I who loves it, loves Gil for going back with his extremely clever, extremely dodgy story. His lie, actually.

How on earth will it go on the plane? I ask him. You could fit a family of four in that egg. We'll be arrested for smuggling.

It's your problem now, Gil says. I've done my bit. He picks up the rest of the bags and heads off.

I refuse to check the egg with my luggage, so they attach a tag and a big red sticker reading FRAGILE, and I lug it through departures and on to the plane and manage to wedge it up in the overhead locker. It takes up nearly the whole space.

I should have bought it a seat, Gil says.

We stow our bags and do up our seat belts and the captain says there'll be a half-hour delay before take-off. Gil opens his book and is gone from me. I don't bug him, knowing he will remain silent until he has thought everything through. It might be a few minutes or a few hours or a few days.

I'm leafing through the in-flight magazine when my phone bleeps. I hope it's Jake, but when I open the message, it says:

Goodbye Mila

I'm glad Gil isn't paying attention.

Goodbye Matthew I text back, wishing there were something I could add, something old-fashioned like *fare thee well* or *godspeed*. And then, on impulse, I paste Jake's contact details into the text. And press send.

Outside of my window the planes turn, speed along the runway, rise up and are gone. Gradually, as we wait to take off, I begin to shed some of the sorrows of this journey. Watching planes take off makes me feel like a child again, like Gabriel shouting *Again, again!* We're something like twenty-eighth in line; the repetitive magic soothes me.

At long last our plane turns on to the runway, the engines roar and I'm about to turn off the phone when it bleeps one last time.

See you soon it says. And is signed **Jake xoxo**

I quickly switch it off and snuggle down in the seat. For the moment, all I care about is this.

So much of translating, Gil once told me, takes place in an imaginary space where the writer and the translator come together. It is not necessary to sympathize with the writer, to agree with what he's written. But it is necessary to walk alongside and stay in step. It's harder, he says, when the other person has a bad limp or stops and starts all the time or moves erratically. It is hardest of all when the story comes from a place the translator himself can't go.

We have been in the air for two hours when he turns to me. Very gently, he takes hold of my hands in both of his.

What a thing to have put you through, he says, shaking his head. I'm so sorry. I should never have brought you here. I thought . . . I don't know what I thought. I thought that it was just a blip, that everything would be OK.

Maybe it will be.

He nods. It's up to Matthew.

I look at him. Do you think he was drunk the night Owen died?

Gil shrugs. Does it matter? The child is dead and everything else that follows has followed.

For a while we say nothing.

Well, I say at last. At least he has Honey.

Yes . . . Gil draws out the single syllable and looks at me. But Honey's a dog.

He says this as if it's something I've failed to notice, but I can see what he's thinking: a dog isn't the most important thing.

And I think, OK. So a dog isn't the most important thing. But a dog like Honey loves one person completely, unwaveringly, with perfect faith. That has to be more important than most things.

And Gabriel, I say. He has Gabriel too.

Gil says nothing but I know the answer. The answer is that Gabriel can't save Matthew any more than Gil can, or Honey. Or Jake. But we are all woven together, like a piece of cloth, and we all support each other, for better or worse. Gabriel is just a baby but eventually he will see the world and his father as they are: imperfect, dangerous, peppered with betrayals and also with love.

I cannot think about these things any longer. I droop against Gil and inhale the familiar scent of him, and he puts his arm round my shoulders and tells me to go to sleep now, not to worry about anything.

The world will trundle along, he says, and kisses the top of my head. Despite us thinking it must grind to a halt. The world has seen worse than us, Perguntadora. It is not so easily shocked.

I rest against him, aware of how tightly we are bound together, through thick and thin. For the moment I have stopped thinking of a time when we will no longer have each other. Marieka was right to tell me to take care of Gil. He and I will watch over one another for as long as we are alive, and Marieka will watch over us both, each of us according to our capacity for care. I will not always be happy, but perhaps, if I'm lucky, I will be spared the agony of adding pain to the world.

And then I close my eyes and drift off to the great white noise of the engines, dreaming of a future I know nothing about.

how
I live
now

winner of the
Guardian Fiction Prize

DON'T MISS THE MAJOR FILM

meg rosoff

'Intense and startling . . . heartbreakingly romantic'
– *The Times*

WINNER OF THE CARNEGIE MEDAL

The author of the brilliant *How I Live Now*

meg rosoff

'Intelligent, ironic and darkly funny'
– *Time Out*

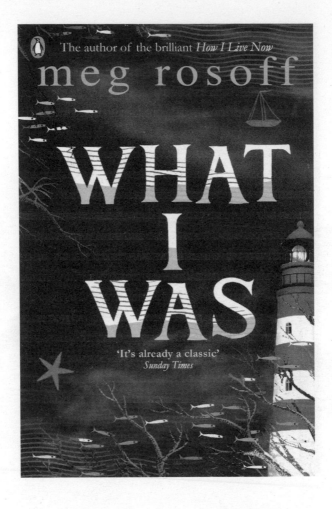

THE author of the brilliant *How I Live Now*

meg rosoff

WHAT I WAS

'It's already a classic'
Sunday Times

'Thrilling and sensitively told'
– *Observer*

'A wonderful, captivating writer. 5 *****'
Daily Telegraph

THE
BRIDE'S
FAREWELL

The author of the brilliant *How I Live Now*

meg rosoff

'Rosoff's writing is luminously beautiful'
– *Financial Times*

'Genius'
ANTHONY HOROWITZ

WHAT IF GOD WERE
A TEENAGE BOY?

THERE
IS NO
DOG

The author of the brilliant *How I Live Now*

meg rosoff

'A wild, wise, cartwheeling explanation of life,
the universe and everything' – Mal Peet

EXTREME PREMATURITY
Practices, Bioethics, and the Law

GEOFFREY MILLER

Yale University School of Medicine

CAMBRIDGE
UNIVERSITY PRESS

CAMBRIDGE UNIVERSITY PRESS
Cambridge, New York, Melbourne, Madrid, Cape Town, Singapore, São Paulo

Cambridge University Press
32 Avenue of the Americas, New York, NY 10013-2473, USA

www.cambridge.org
Information on this title: www.cambridge.org/9780521862219

First published 2007

Printed in the United States of America

A *catalog record for this publication is available from the British Library.*

Library of Congress Cataloging in Publication Data
Miller, Geoffrey, 1947–
Extreme prematurity : practices, bioethics, and the law / Geoffrey Miller.
    p.   cm.
Includes bibliographical references and index.
ISBN-13: 978-0-521-86221-9 (hardback)
ISBN-10: 0-521-86221-3 (hardback)
ISBN-13: 978-0-521-68053-0 (pbk.)
ISBN-10: 0-521-68053-0 (pbk.)
1. Infants (Premature)   2. Infants (Premature) – Moral and ethical aspects.
3. Medical ethics.   I. Title.
[DNLM: 1. Premature Birth – epidemiology.   2. Intensive Care, Neonatal.
3. Neonatology – ethics.   4. Neonatology – legislation & jurisprudence.
WQ 330 M648e   2006]
RJ250.M55   2006
174.2′9892 – dc22   2006016288

ISBN-13   978-0-521-86221-9 hardback
ISBN-10   0-521-86221-3 hardback

ISBN-13   978-0-521-68053-0 paperback
ISBN-10   0-521-68053-0 paperback

FOR TRICIA

CONTENTS

**Part 1: THE EXTREMELY PRETERM INFANT:
EPIDEMIOLOGY, PERCEPTIONS, AND PRACTICES**

1	Introduction	*page* 3
2	Historical Aspects	9
3	Survival	11
4	Influence of Obstetric Management	16
5	Effect of Resuscitation in the Delivery Room	18
6	National Comparisons	20
7	Prediction of Outcome	23
8	Limit of Viability	24
9	Morbidity	25
10	School Age Outcome	29
11	Adolescence	32
12	Perceptions and Practices	34
13	Resource Expenditure	45

Part 2: BIOETHICS

14	Moral Theory	51
15	Autonomy	59
16	Beneficence and Nonmaleficence	62

17 Justice   68
18 Sanctity of Life   70
19 Active and Passive Euthanasia   72
20 Personhood   74
21 Quality of Life and Best Interests   80
22 Futility   86

Part 3: REPORTS, OFFICIAL OPINIONS, AND
GUIDELINES

23 United States   91
24 Canada   106
25 United Kingdom (UK)   110
26 France   116
27 Italy   121
28 Germany   122
29 International   123

Part 4: THE LAW

30 Introduction   135
31 U.S. Law   138
32 The United Kingdom   160
33 Canada   168
34 Australia   173
35 Japan   176
36 Italy, Germany, and Poland   177
37 France   179
38 The Netherlands   181

Part 5: EPILOGUE: TRUTH, TRUST, AND
BOUNDARIES

Epilogue: Truth, Trust, and Boundaries   187

References   197
Index   221

PART 1

THE EXTREMELY PRETERM INFANT

Epidemiology, Perceptions, and Practices

INTRODUCTION

Three-year-old D is a vivacious small child who smiles and giggles freely. Her abdomen is criss-crossed with scars, the result of neonatal surgery for necrotizing enterocolitis for which she had surgical resection of some of her bowel. This was followed by the fashioning of an ileostomy that was closed at two years of age. There is also a scar over her left axilla, which followed a thoracotomy and the closing of a patent ductus arteriosus that had caused heart failure during the early neonatal period. She is the elder of twins, born at an uncertain gestation of 25 weeks weighing 810gs. Both babies were resuscitated at birth, but one twin died on day of life 4. Baby D received prolonged ventilation, required tracheostomy, and was discharged home on a ventilator after many months in the hospital. The daily nursing assistance the family received in their apartment was discontinued following the weaning of ventilation when the baby was aged 15 months. Her early years are remarkable for frequent visits to different specialists in the hospital who have monitored and managed her neurological development, pulmonary status, eyes, and gastrointestinal function. Her family, who have limited economic resources, have undergone the most challenging of economic and emotional strains, and although they have faced the challenges most often with determined stoicism and love, there has often been anguish. However, D has conducted her only known life with the full gamut of emotional sparkle and oppositional irritation that would be expected from any able-bodied child. She has done this without the use of speech – a consequence of her tracheostomy and her profound deafness, the latter perhaps related to either her prematurity or aminoglycosides she received during the neonatal period. She is now a candidate for a cochlear implant, an option that would not have been available only a short time ago. She has started to use consistent sign to communicate, and her nonverbal developmental quotient is within the normal range.

Five-year-old B was born at 24 weeks' gestation, weighing 580gs. At birth she did not breathe spontaneously, had a gelatinous feel to her skin, and could be held in the hand like a pound of butter. She was resuscitated and ventilated without much difficulty, and required about two weeks of intermittent positive pressure ventilation followed by a period of continuous positive airway pressure ventilation. She developed a grade II intraventricular hemorrhage, and following weaning from the ventilator there were many episodes of apnea and bradycardia, which responded to tactile stimulation. After 10 weeks in the hospital, she was bottle-feeding well and was discharged home one week later on an apnea monitor. During her early months, she was often an irritable baby who required frequent feeding, which was followed by episodes of regurgitation. The consequence of this gastroesophageal reflux was failure to thrive and choking episodes. The reflux failed to respond to medical treatment and after an admission to the hospital, because of severe aspiration pneumonia, she underwent a gastric fundoplication. Her irritability improved and she began to thrive. However, her development was relatively slow. She walked independently at 19 months and started to use two-word phrases at about three years of age. Her single-parent mother, who was aged 17 years at the birth of the baby, is now concerned and challenged because B demonstrates a reduced attention span, poor frustration tolerance, impulsivity, and emotional lability. These neurobehavioral difficulties have had an impact on her schooling, where she has difficulty staying in her seat, and with social interaction. Despite this, she is often a loving, affectionate child, with considerable charm. Psychometric evaluation was hampered by variable attention, but a minimum IQ level was measured at 86. There were some findings that suggested she may be at risk of demonstrating a specific learning disability, such as dyslexia, in elementary school. Despite her present difficulties, for which there are successful management strategies, and her extreme prematurity, she is expected to become an independent adult whose life will be governed by similar influences and fates that mould the outcome of any individual who was born normal at term.

J is a four-year-old boy who has recently started to walk using a walker. He is small, with relative undergrowth of the lower half of his body. He has a scaphocephalic head on which are perched thick glasses, and below these is an infectious open-mouthed grin, which is occasionally disfigured by a small amount of drooling. This, when he is reminded, is wiped away by an incoordinated splayed hand. He loves to demonstrate his walking ability and can hurtle down a corridor, albeit in an ungainly fashion, with hips and knees bent and knees knocking and on his toes. This is accompanied by much mirth shared by J and his onlookers. He is adored by his parents and two older sisters, and he adores them. J was born at 24 weeks, weighing 610gs. He required several weeks of artificial ventilation and developed a grade III intraventricular hemorrhage and pronounced periventricular leukomalacia. He required gastrostomy feeding for the first two years of his life, and he has had surgery for retinopathy of prematurity and for a strabismus. His cerebral palsy and poor development was apparent during the first year of life, and repeated cognitive assessments place him in the mild mental retardation range with non–gross motor developmental quotients ranging from 60 to 70. He is expected to achieve adulthood and live a life that, although requiring some assistance and protection by others, will be one in which he is competent in the activities of daily living and able to benefit from some basic education and training.

T is aged five years. He was born at 25 weeks' gestation, weighing 700gs. Resuscitation was achieved easily after birth, and he was ventilated with relative ease for about three weeks. On day of life 5, he had developed a grade IV intraventricular hemorrhage, which was accompanied by severe periventricular leukomalacia. By one month of life, he was breathing independently but was unable to feed and would later require a gastrostomy. It was soon clear that he would develop substantial neurological handicap. Severe spastic quadriparesis, anarthria, pseudobulbar palsy, microcephaly, and what appears to be severe mental retardation now confine him to a wheelchair. He is unable to feed himself and continues to be fed by gastrostomy. He is incontinent and cannot indicate his needs. However, he appears to respond to familiar voices and smile socially and laughs with his siblings. Successful voluntary movements are not possible, and any stimulus or attempt at movement invokes mass, uncoordinated, stereotypic postures. There are contractures in his arms and legs that hamper dressing, toileting, and hygiene.

These cameos are very familiar to anyone involved in neonatal care and follow-up. They represent some of the complications of prematurity, which vary in their severity and cause considerable individual, social, and economic burden. Although it is the severely disabled child that may be most readily remembered, this outcome is not the rule. However, all adverse outcomes become more likely as birth weight and gestation decrease. Survival rates for low birth weight and preterm infants are giving rise, it appears, to an increasing prevalence of childhood neurodevelopmental disability, including severe forms of cerebral palsy. This has raised bioethical and legal questions concerning this population of children. These include topical and debatable concepts such as the limits of viability, end of life decisions for those without capacity, futility, parental and physician autonomy, distributive justice, the role of statutory and case law, and so on.

For the purposes of this book, I define the extremely preterm infant (EPTI) as one who is born at less than 28 weeks' gestation. I also include the extremely low birth weight (ELBW) infant born weighing less than 1,000g. The two are not synonymous as the latter may include infants who are small for gestational age and more mature than the former. However, the literature includes both groups, and for the purposes of argument I do the same.

Extreme prematurity is uncommon, occurring in about 1% of live births(1). However, the moral dilemmas that arise from intensive care for EPTIs is a continuing cause for concern. Although, for some attitudes are fixed, for many the situation is fluid. But the question remains the same. How far should those go, who care for children, to preserve life at the inevitable expense to some babies, families, and society of disability, emotional trauma, and financial cost? Furthermore, attempts to answer this question are clouded by uncertainty arising from the limitations of early prognosis, variable and changing results of management, and differing subjective judgments from health professionals, parents, guardians, and the creators and arbiters of the law. Attempts to resolve the conflict are sought from religion, bioethics and moral philosophy, sociocultural acceptance of certain behaviors, and the law, both civil and criminal. But before these can be considered, it is necessary to briefly provide some history and then document the epidemiology of EPTIs, the perceptions of those involved in their care, and the resources expended.

HISTORICAL ASPECTS

Depending on cultural, religious, and socioeconomic circumstance, infanticide occurred throughout history.(2,3) During the classical period, infants deemed abnormal were left to
die in the open,(4) and infanticide was not unusual up until the
20th century.(5,6) But as medical expertise and technology have
become increasingly sophisticated, active measures are now taken
to keep alive such infants, and the degree of this endeavor has
mirrored changes in societal attitude. This is particularly evident
for the EPTI. However, the requirement that physicians should
not provide treatment that they believe will be of no benefit can
also be dated back to the classical era, and there may well be a positive obligation not to do so. Hippocrates wrote that: "[W]henever
therefore a man suffers from an ill which is too strong for the means
at the disposal of medicine he surely must not expect that it be
overcome by medicine," and, he continued, for the physician to
provide treatment in such a situation was "allied to madness."(7)

And Plato, in *The Republic*, advised that the physician
should:

For those whose bodies were always in a state of inner sickness he did not attempt to prescribe a regime . . . to make their life a prolonged misery . . . medicine was not intended for them and they should not be treated even if they were richer than Midas.(8)

Out of this history has arisen a requirement to care for the EPTI, but not to oblige a physician to provide treatment that is perceived as not beneficial. However, because of differing beliefs, perceptions, and interpretations, there may be a conflict between the requirement and the obligation.

3

SURVIVAL

From 1980 to 2000, the infant mortality rate in the United States has been reduced from 12.6 to 6.9 per 1,000 live births.(9,10) This has occurred with an approximately 17% increase in preterm birth rates,(9,11) and reductions in mortality have been highest for those with the lowest birth weights.(9) This has been mainly attributable to gains in technology as well as improvements in medical practice.(12–15) ELBW infants account for nearly half of total perinatal mortality, despite being only a very small percentage of total live births.(16) Much of the improvement in mortality has occurred in the very and extremely preterm groups.(17,18) There can be considerable variation in the results of studies reporting mortality for the EPTI. To some extent this is governed by the conduct of the studies,(19,20) for example, whether the figures reported include total births, live births, or neonatal intensive care unit (NICU) admissions; whether the numbers were small or based on geographic populations; and whether there were consistent approaches to management. Clearly this variability may introduce uncertainty and incomprehensibility into the counseling of parents. Furthermore, one can speculate whether it might encourage a paternalistic use of figures by physicians, when counseling, allowing for a reflection of their biases. One physician might aggressively resuscitate, whereas another might not.(21,22) But most well-conducted studies quote similar figures, or if there is variability, explanations can be found. More recent improvements in survival are particularly notable for those born at less than 26 weeks' gestation. Reasons for this include the use of surfactant and steroids and an increase in the provision of artificial ventilation, as well as a change in attitudes.

In the United States, during the 1990s, survival for infants born at 24 weeks' gestation was reported as 33–57% and at 25 weeks was 60–75%.(21–29) In the NICHD Neonatal Network Study, the findings were that babies born during 1994 to 1995 weighing 501–800g have a mortality rate of 43%, and 15% of these were not artificially ventilated.(30) The reported survival for those born at 23 weeks is 20–25%, with reports in some centers of 41–48%.(31) El-Metwally, Vohr, and Tucker determined the survival rates of infants born at 22 to 25 weeks' gestation during the 1990s in Rhode Island.(21) The rate of fetal death (stillborn) was 24%. Of those born alive, 46% survived to discharge. Survival rates, including fetal death, at 22, 23, 24, and 25 weeks were 1.8%, 34%, 49%, and 76% respectively; and excluding fetal death, they were 4.6%, 46%, 59%, and 82% respectively. In addition to gestational age, variables associated with increased chances of survival were birth weight, female gender, and the use of surfactant. These authors concluded that it was important, when considering survival rates at the limits of viability, that interpretation took account of whether all births or just live births were analyzed. This was a retrospective study and there were circumstances where treatment decisions could affect outcome. For example, if the infant had no heart rate at birth, resuscitation often was not started, although, as the authors wrote: "[O]ccasionally chest compressions were started and resuscitative medicines given if the neonatologist thought the infant appeared more mature than the estimated gestational age, or if requested by parents." Thus it appears that survival at 22 weeks' gestation is extremely unusual, although it does occur,(21,32) but it dramatically increases for each week of gestation.

In a Canadian report of infants born weighing less than 500g, between 1983 and 1994, 25% were not given intensive care and all died.(33) In 2001, Chan et al. reported survival rates for EPTIs from 17 Canadian NICUs(34) born at less than 26 weeks' gestation from 1996 through 1997. These EPTIs were 4% of NICU admissions, but accounted for 22% of deaths. Of the 949 EPTIs delivered, 42% died in the delivery room. The percentage of those admitted to the NICU increased from 20% at 22 weeks to 91% at 25 weeks. Survival rate after admission was 14% at 22 weeks (range 0–33%), 40% at 23 weeks (range 0–100%), 57% at 24 weeks (range 0–87%), and 76% at 25 weeks (range 57–100%). The overall survival rate for all infants was 1% at 22 weeks, 17% at 23 weeks, 44% at 24 weeks, and 68% at 25 weeks. Of interest was the finding that surviving lower gestational age infants had fewer low Apgar scores, which, to the authors, suggested that resuscitation bias may have existed. In another Canadian study, Effer and colleagues published the survival rates of 860 live births born at 24 and 25 weeks' gestation from 13 tertiary centers.(35) At 24 weeks, survival was 56%, and it was 68% at 25 weeks.

Figures from Japan show impressive improvement over time. Japanese neonatal mortality rates have fallen from 27.4 to 2.3 per 1,000 live births between 1950 and 1993, and in 1991 the survival of infants born less than 1,000g reached about 72%.(36,37) For 1,655 infants born with birth weights less than 600g between 1984 and 1993, studied by Oishi, Nishida, and Sasaki,(38), about 28% survived to hospital discharge. Of those born less than 24 weeks,

17% survived, and of those over 24 weeks about 36% survived. The survival rate for those less than 600g increased, when surfactant therapy became widely available, from 22% in 1988 to 33% in 1989. The majority of deaths (68%) were within the first week of life, and only 10% died after the neonatal period. Improved survival for the smallest and most immature EPTI was likely also affected by the Japanese Eugenic Protection Act, which defines the fetal viability limit as "minimal duration of gestation which renders fetuses capable of extrauterine life."(39) This was amended to 22 completed weeks in 1991.

In Australia, survival rates for the EPTI are similar to those found in recent reports from other developed countries.(31) In a study from Melbourne,(40) Gultom and colleagues reported changes over time in attitudes to treatment and survival for infants born at 23 to 27 weeks' gestation. The authors noted increases in survival rates over time and more frequent active management of labor for gestations, they stated, that were previously considered as nonviable. Overall, 85% were treated intensively, but the pro-portion rose from 74% in 1983–1985 to 91% in 1992–1994. In 1983–1990, 51% of live born infants born 23 to 27 weeks' gesta-tion died, and this decreased to 28% for those born from 1992 to 1996.(41) The authors' conclusions were that improving survival rates were not only because of treatment factors such as antenatal steroids and exogenous surfactant, but also because of a willingness to treat the EPTI intensively.

In the large United Kingdom (UK) and Ireland population-based study, reported in 2000 by Wood and colleagues,(42) data was derived from 4,004 births born between 20 and 25 weeks' gestation. There were only 1,185 live births, of which about one-third died in the delivery room, and a further 43% died in the hospital. That is, the survival rate overall was only 27% for live births and 39% for those admitted to intensive care. For this latter group, intensive care was withdrawn from 55% who died in the unit. Consistent criteria for this were not documented. In a 2002 report from Paris, France,(43) on infants born between 24 and 28 weeks' gestation, about one-third died before discharge. All received resuscitation at birth. Survival was most affected by birth weight, with 42% surviving below 700g and 83% above 900g.

INFLUENCE OF OBSTETRIC MANAGEMENT

How physicians, in particular obstetricians, view and assess viability can affect perinatal survival figures. In an American study(44) that examined the relationship between obstetric care during labor and delivery and the survival of EPTIs, the authors compared the outcomes of those who were considered viable antenatally and those who were not. The factors evaluated in the judgment of viability were estimated age (> 26 weeks) and estimated weight (> 650g), lethal anomalies, and parental requests. In the total population studied, some were misclassified (usually weight estimation), or parents had requested aggressive management or the opposite. This "allowed" the authors to study the survival of infants who, by their standards, would have been considered nonviable but who received antenatal and perinatal care as if they were viable. Although in some groups the numbers were small, the chances of survival were strongly associated with the antenatal assessment of viability. The odds of survival for all fetuses treated as viable were 17 times the odds for those considered nonviable. Birth weight alone did not explain wholly the relationship between antepartum viability assessment and outcome. Thus, in this study, survival of the EPTI was related to judgments of viability that determined their care. Silver et al. also published similar findings.(45) These studies, which had relatively small numbers, do not suggest that there is no limit to fetal viability, but they do caution the reader to take into account obstetric management strategies when examining figures concerning the outcome of the EPTI. Obstetricians evaluate antenatal data to make decisions concerning the management of an anticipated extremely preterm delivery. Bottoms et al.(46,47) evaluated whether antenatal information could accurately predict the survival of ELBW infants with and without major morbidity, using data collected in 1992–1993. The reported findings were that the willingness of an obstetrician to perform a cesarean section at 24 weeks' gestation was associated with an improvement in survival from 33% to 57%, but the risk of serious morbidity doubled from 20% to 40%. Survivals, and survival without disability, were significantly better when birth resulted from active medical management, compared to a passive approach, with or without cesarean section. The use of prepartum ultrasonographic data could not reliably distinguish who would survive without serious morbidity, although there was a threshold below which no survivors were found.

5

EFFECT OF RESUSCITATION IN THE
DELIVERY ROOM

In 1996, Rennie wrote that outcome after full cardiopulmonary resuscitation (CPR) following delivery of a very preterm infant was "appalling."(48) Her justifications for this conclusion were reports published in the early 1990s. In one, from Manchester, England, three of five babies born less than 28 weeks' gestation, who received full CPR, including adrenaline, died and the survivors were handicapped.(49) In a report from Oklahoma, there were no survivors of very low birth weight (VLBW) infants who required more than one resuscitative attempt.(50) In similar circumstances there were only two normal survivors, during the years 1989–1993, reported in a study from Cambridge, England, and all six infants given full CPR in Ottawa, Canada, with birth weights less than 750g, during 1989–1992, died.(51) In sharp contrast to these reports are later ones that suggest that condition at birth of an EPTI may not be a good indicator of viability or later outcome.(52) Jankov, Asztalos, and Skidmore evaluated whether vigorous resuscitation of ELBW infants at birth improved survival or increased the chances of major neurodevelopmental disability. They reported the outcome of a group of infants born weighing

750g or less who received CPR (positive pressure ventilation, cardiac compression, +/− adrenaline) in the delivery room. About 57% survived, and 88% were free of major neurodevelopmental disability at follow-up.(53) Similar findings have been published by several other authors(54–56) and it does appear that CPR in the delivery room for the EPTI does not necessarily lead to a large decrease in survival or an increase in major neurologic sequelae compared to those who survived following only intubation and positive pressure ventilation.

6

NATIONAL COMPARISONS

Outcomes for the EPTI may differ from country to country; the reasons include economic resources and access to sophisticated technological care in developing countries and varying attitudes and perceptions in the more developed countries. The latter will be discussed later in this chapter, but here I briefly document findings concerning the Netherlands and survival in some developing countries. Lorenz et al.(22) reported on the outcome of EPTIs born less than 26 weeks in two population-based cohorts, New Jersey (NJ), United States and the Netherlands, who received systematically different approaches to their care during the mid-1980s. In the NJ cohort, almost all babies received intensive care, whereas the policy was more selective in the Netherlands. Assisted ventilation was more commonly used in NJ, 95% versus 64%, and almost all the difference resulted from the use of assisted ventilation in infants who subsequently died. Mortality at 28 days was about 46% in NJ and 73% in the Netherlands. No infant less than 25 weeks' gestation survived to 28 days in the Netherlands. Survival to 2 years in NJ was twice that in the

Netherlands. The prevalence of disabling cerebral palsy was 17.2% among survivors in NJ and 3.4% in the Netherlands. In the NJ cohort, 1,820 ventilator days were expended per 100 live births compared to 448 days in the Netherlands, but the difference in nonventilator days was not statistically different. In summary, the management approach in NJ resulted in 24 additional survivors per 100 live births, 7 additional cases of disabling cerebral palsy per 100 live births, and at a cost of 1,372 additional ventilator days per 100 live births.(22) That there is a significant difference in approach to the management of the EPTI in the Netherlands compared to NJ that is of great consequence is clear. How this is accomplished can be found in an article by Van der Heide and associates published in 1997.(57) They reported on end of life decisions for neonates in the Netherlands, and although only some of the babies were EPTIs, it does reflect attitude and practice. In the report, they stated that 57% of all infant and neonatal deaths had been preceded by a decision to forego life-sustaining treatment, and was accompanied by the administration of potentially life-shortening drugs to relieve pain or other symptoms in 23% and by the administration of drugs with the explicit aim of hastening death in 8%. Parents were involved in 79% of decisions. The most common reason for not involving parents was stated as "it was so obviously the only correct decision."(57)

The rates for neonatal mortality differ between developing and developed countries, as does the practice of neonatal care. Most worldwide neonatal deaths occur in the developing world, and at least one-third of these are in preterm infants.(58,59) In a study published in 2003,(58) the mortality rate for infants born at 28–29 weeks was 478 per 1,000 live births in a geographically diverse group of developing countries (Brazil, Colombia, Thailand, India, and the Philippines) compared to 83 in two developed countries

(United States, Ireland). In the developing countries, interventions such as surfactant, ventilators, blood gases, and oximetry were variable, and several physicians considered pregnancies less than 28 weeks nonviable. How physicians judge viability affects perinatal interventions and mortality not only in developed countries but also in developing ones.

PREDICTION OF OUTCOME

There can be substantial error rate when physicians estimate outcome for the EPTI.(60–63) Tyson and associates(30) reported error rates of 52% and 21% in the prediction of death and survival for infants weighing 501–800g at birth. Despite the requirement that physicians practice according to the best available evidence, this may not always be the case, and in such circumstances they may incorrectly estimate the chances of death and disability,(64) which affects their decisions as well as the counseling of parents.(44,60)

In 2001, it was reported that at the University Medical Center in Leiden, a leading center for the the treatment of preterm infants in the Netherlands, a decision, in principle, was taken to stop active intensive treatment of babies born less than 25 weeks' gestation.(65) However, the head of neonatology at the center stated that, "infants born before 25 weeks would still be given 'vigorous support' if the parents wished and the medical team considered the infant viable at birth."(65) The decision was made because, in their study of premature births from 1996 through 1997, 66% of those born at 23 and 24 weeks died, and half the survivors had severe physical or mental handicaps.(65)

8

LIMIT OF VIABILITY

Although there is no sharp demarcation point, over time the limit of viability has become progressively lower, from a birth weight of 1,500g before 1940, to 1,000g and 28 weeks' gestation by the 1970s.(20) Survival is now common for infants of less than 750g and for those of 25 weeks' gestation. The lower limit of viability appears, at present, to be approximately 22–23 completed weeks of gestation, with survival and morbidity improving markedly with each later week of gestation. It is now governed by technological capacity, medical intervention, and the attitudes of the medical profession.(63,66)

MORBIDITY

Extremely preterm birth is associated with several morbidities ranging from the very severe to the relatively mild, and the risk increases as gestational age decreases.(67) The morbidities include cerebral palsy, mental retardation, learning and language disability, disorders of attention and behavior, visual and hearing impairment, chronic lung disease, gastrointestinal dysfunction, and poor growth.(68–74) Furthermore, survivors may require prolonged hospital stays, in-home nursing and technological services, and societal and state support, all of which add to emotional and financial family burdens.(75,76) Although there is some relationship between disorders of higher brain function and psychosocial, socioeconomic, and environmental factors,(77,78) there is now substantial evidence that neurodevelopmental disability arises from poor brain development apart from frank parenchymal brain injury. Former EPTIs have been reported to show decreased regional brain volumes, compared to term controls, including reduced volumes of cortical gray matter, the hippocampi, and corpus callosum, in addition to an increase in the size of the lateral ventricles,(79–87) all of which have adverse neurodevelopmental correlates.

Many articles have documented the short- and long-term outcome of EPTIs. However, as with reports on survival, there can be variability in the results both within and between countries. The causes include variable perinatal and neonatal practices; case ascertainment and attrition rates; gestational age limits and birth weight restrictions; age at follow-up; diagnoses sought; criteria for disability with differing definitions and inclusions; and the use of different methodologies when assessing outcome, including a failure to use concurrent norms.(20,31,88–93) But despite a plethora of outcome studies, there is a relative dearth of reports on the functional outcome of disabilities and their effect on quality of life.(31,94) The characteristics of different national populations studied, and the conduct of their health delivery systems, may also appear to affect the statistics reported, even when these populations are geographically close. Field and colleagues(95) compared the neonatal intensive care services of two European countries, the UK and Denmark, during the period 1994–1995; these countries have different approaches to neonatal intensive care. The populations compared were live born infants 22–27 weeks' gestation or less than 1,000g. The British services were more centralized and specialist based, but they had higher rates of prematurity and sicker babies with worse outcomes, despite the delivery of more intensive care. The authors rejected the notion that this was the result of systematically worse care and suggested it was "a reflection of innate reproductive health in the two countries" and social circumstances, as the teenage pregnancy rate was about four times higher in the UK,(96) as well as the lower social spending per head of population.(97)

El-Metwally et al.(21) determined neonatal morbidity rates for infants born in Rhode Island, United States, during the 1990s, at 22 to 25 weeks' gestation. The rate of severe intraventricular hemorrhage or periventricular leukomalacia was 27% but was higher at lower gestational ages. Chan and associates(34) reported the neonatal morbidity for babies born less than 26 weeks, in 17 Canadian centers, during 1996 and 1997. Major neonatal morbidity, defined by the authors as grades III or IV intraventricular hemorrhage, stage 3 or worse retinopathy of prematurity (ROP), chronic lung disease, and necrotizing enterocolitis, was found in some form in 77%. The percentage was 89% at 22 weeks and 71% at 25 weeks. As with survival, there was wide intercenter variation with survival without major early morbidity ranging from 0% to 26%. Vohr and associates, in a U.S. multicenter cohort study,(98) reported the outcome of 1,151 ELBW infants at a corrected age of 18 to 22 months. This number represented only 78% of the total survivors, which could represent an underestimate of the disability rate.(91) Abnormal neurologic examinations were found in 25% and an abnormal Bayley Mental and Psychomotor Developmental Index of less than 70 in 37% and 29% respectively. Vision impairment occurred in 9%, hearing impairment in 11%, and cerebral palsy in 17%. The probability of abnormal neurological findings increased as birth weight decreased – 25% for birth weights 901–1,000g and 43% for those weighing 401–500g. The risk of cerebral palsy also increased with decreasing birth weight – 15% for 901–1,000g and 29% for 401–501g. In a prospective population-based study from the UK and Ireland, Wood et al.(42) published the outcome of infants born less than 26 weeks' gestation during a 10-month period, beginning in March 1995, who were admitted to a NICU. The survivors were assessed at a median age of 30 months after the expected date of delivery. The mean Bayley Mental Developmental Index was 84 +/− 12, and the mean Psychomotor Developmental Index was 87 +/− 13. Nineteen percent of the children had scores more than 3 standard deviations below the mean and were classified as severely disabled. There were 11% who scored between 2 and 3 standard deviations below the mean ("other disability"). Interestingly, the scores did not vary substantially with gestational age, but boys had significantly lower psychomotor scores than girls. Cerebral palsy was diagnosed in 18%, and in about one-half of these it was characterized as severe. Again there were no differences related to gestation. About 2% were blind, and 3% had uncorrectable hearing loss. Overall, 23% were reported to have severe disability in the developmental, neuromotor, sensory, or communication domains. In a multicenter study involving NICUs in Canada, the United States, Australia, and Hong Kong,(99) on infants born weighing 500–999g between 1996 and 1998, 18% developed cerebral palsy, 26% had cognitive impairment, 2% had hearing loss requiring amplification, and 2% had bilateral blindness. In San Francisco, Piecuch et al.(100) reported on 24- to 26-week gestation survivors. About 25% had a developmental quotient of less than 70, and 14% had cerebral palsy. When the same group reported on a larger number of infants of ELBW born between 1979 and 1991, and reported on in 1997,(101) about 14% were reported to have cerebral palsy, 1% were blind, 0.2% were deaf, and 14% had cognitive dysfunction. Other reports have placed the risk of cerebral palsy at early follow-up as between 7% and 18%.(102–106)

10

SCHOOL AGE OUTCOME

There have been several reports of follow-up to school age, as well as into adolescence, which show some variability in their results for the reasons previously stated. Although major disability does not occur in the majority of survivors, when they reach school age, a high percentage appear to experience functional impairments, including disorders of higher mental function, that affect education and behavior.(78,90,107–109) Psychosocial and socioeconomic factors may also play a role in these outcomes.(78) The Victorian Infant collaborative study from Australia(90) reported that the IQ of their extremely preterm study group (gestation less than 28 weeks, birth weight less than 1,000g) was within the normal range but averaged about 9 points less than abnormal birth weight control group. In the preterm group, poorer scores were found in verbal comprehension, perceptual organization, freedom from distractibility, and processing speed. The infants were born in 1991 and 1992, and although they have lower mean test scores than normal birth weight controls in reading, spelling, and arithmetic, these scores were much improved when compared to earlier previous reports. Saigal and colleagues, from Canada,(110) reported on the outcomes of ELBW infants at 5.5 years. Their findings were that 9.5% had cerebral palsy, 4.8% were blind, and 20% had mental retardation. Using the Vineland Adaptive Behaviour Scales they found that approximately 8% were significantly functionally disabled (composite score more than 2 standard deviations below the mean). Areas of limitation included motor skills, activities of daily living, communication, and socialization. In a similar population at a similar age, Msall et al., from the United States,(111) found that 5% had cerebral palsy, 10% had mental retardation, 1% were blind, and 5% had multiple impairments. Basic functional limitations were uncommon, and most functional disability was mild to moderate.(112) However, when actual school performance is examined many authors have found that nearly half of EPTIs require resource or special educational support at some time.(68,98,110,113,114) In 2003, Saigal et al.(89) compared the outcomes of infants born weighing 500–1,000g in four international population-based cohorts and reported their cognitive abilities and school achievement. The four cohorts were from central New Jersey, central-west Ontario, Bavaria, and Holland. Adjustments were made for comparison of all measures based on reference norms within each country. The live births in the United States and Canadian populations were more immature and smaller than those in the European groups, although the survival rates were similar between the international groups, ranging from 44 to 45%. There were also differences between the populations when neonatal management was compared, and some of these differences were striking. The proportion of survivors ventilated in Holland was 53%, and in Bavaria, New Jersey, and Ontario, it was 95%, 93%, and 82% respectively. The median number of days of ventilation was 6 days in the Dutch group, compared with 16 days in New Jersey, 32 days for Ontario, and 38 days for Bavaria. There were also differences in the length of hospitalization. As the authors stated: neonatal intensive care was most aggressive in Bavaria, and then Ontario and New Jersey, and more selective in Holland. The prevalences of cerebral palsy, deafness, blindness, and mental retardation more than 3 standard deviations below the mean were recorded as 22%, 27%, and 25% respectively. The prevalence in the Dutch population was 11%. The cerebral palsy rates were 19% for New Jersey, 13% for Ontario, 16% for Bavaria, and 8% for Holland. Although a significant number of children, who were ELBW, have serious neurodevelopmental disabilities, the majority do not, and the rate is least in the Dutch population. However, when cognition and achievement, in those without serious neurodevelopmental disability, is evaluated, high numbers fall below the normal range. Overall, the percentages of children who performed within the normal range on IQ testing ranged from 44% to 66%; for reading the range fell between 46% and 81%, arithmetic 31% and 76%, and spelling 39% and 65%. Those from New Jersey had the highest cognitive and achievement results, and those from Bavaria the lowest, relative to their peers and the other populations. It should be noted that for New Jersey the ascertainment rate for psychometric testing was only 60% compared to 87% and 90% for the Bavarian and Ontario research subjects. It has been reported that similar nonparticipants in other studies are more likely to have intellectual and behavioral difficulties.(115) Furthermore, the Canadian and German researchers used concurrent norms whereas the U.S. researchers used older standardized test norms, which may have produced overestimations. What is clear is that ELBW and EPTIs may perform poorly on tests of school performance in all of the four populations. Whereas these figures might provoke a fear of socioeconomic burden within the populations examined, it should be noted that the total numbers of survivors are relatively small, ranging from 397 in Ontario to 263 in Bavaria.

11

ADOLESCENCE

There have been a number of studies documenting adolescent outcomes. Most of these adolescents do not have major motor, sensory, or intellectual handicap, but as a group, they do not fare as well in school as their normal birth weight peers. However, they do not view their quality of life as different.(116) A 14-year follow-up study of ELBW infants born during 1970–1980 was reported from Melbourne (117) and compared to a normal birth weight control group. Survival rate was 25%, and of the survivors 10% have cerebral palsy, 6% are blind, 5% are deaf and required hearing aids, and 46% have an IQ score more than 1 standard deviation below the mean compared to controls. Overall, 14% are severely disabled. In a Canadian population of ELBW infants followed into adolescence,(118) 28% had neurosensory impairments compared to 1% of term controls. Reading scores were significantly low in 38% of those born less than 750gs and 18% of those born weighing 750 to 1,000g compared to 2.5% of terms controls. Special educational services were required at some time in 50% of the study group and 10% of the controls. The ELBW cohort tended to be smaller and use health and educational resources far more than controls.(119) Similar findings have been reported from Britain(120) and the United States.(121,122) However, although adolescents who were born extremely preterm are more likely to have to cope with more health and educational challenges, studies on quality of life seem to demonstrate that most of this group do not feel that their quality of life is very different from others.(123,124)

Despite some variability in the reported rates of impairment and disability, a reasonable figure for the rate of major disability among survivors of extremely preterm birth is 20–25%(125) and for cerebral palsy 10–18%.(126) Even more common are disorders of higher mental function such as attention deficit and specific learning disabilities, which can occur in more than 50%.(127–129) However, local results should be taken into account when counseling parents, and it is thus incumbent on those who run NICUs to collect these data and make them available.

12

PERCEPTIONS AND PRACTICES

It has been stated that the decisions to forego life-sustaining treatment for an EPTI should be a joint one combining the knowledge of the physician with the wishes of the parents.(130) But the purported decision makers are not homogeneous groups, the knowledge of the physicians is not necessarily reliable or certain in all cases, and the wishes of all parents are also not necessarily realistic or reasonable. There are different times at which a decision to forego life-sustaining treatment could be made. The first is at the time of birth, although obstetric decisions prior to this might affect the perinatal outcome. But at birth, there is often a competent team of doctors and nurses who initiate resuscitation, often perhaps without all the information required for prognosis. Birth weight may be only estimated and gestational age uncertain. Even so, care is not rendered only when absolute success is assured. As Lorenz and Paneth wrote,(131) treatment of the EPTI often falls into one of the three categories. The first is where most would treat. The second is where most would not treat, and a third group exists where there is variability and disagreement. They also noted that the personal characteristics and views of the physicians strongly influence their decision making, and that they may impose their own values on the family. But the situation is one in which there is often uncertainty. Because of this, many neonatologists, Rhoden wrote,(132) follow a "least-worst" strategy, that is, intensive care treatment followed by repeated prognostic evaluation and a decision on whether to treat or withdraw care. But there are still problems with this approach as it assumes the ability to very accurately predict prognosis, which is often not the case, and the question of deciding between a quality of life decision and the worth of life still exists.

In a study from the United States in 1997, Wall and Partridge(133) reported the frequency of selective nontreatment of extremely preterm, critically ill, or malformed infants in the NICU at the University of California San Francisco between 1989 and 1992. There were 108 infant deaths, the majority of whom were ELBW, following the withdrawal of life support, and 13 deaths followed the withholding of treatment. These deaths represented 73% of the total deaths, the others occurring while the infants continued to receive maximal life support. For 74% of the deaths attributable to foregoing of life-sustaining treatment, the reasons given were that death was imminent and treatment was futile. Quality of life concerns were also given as reasons in about one-half of these. Quality of life was the only reason given for limiting treatment in 23% of the deaths ascribed to foregoing of life-sustaining treatment.

Despite an aversion toward allowing the courts to interfere in the practice of medicine in the United States, some physicians may still act in accordance with a fear of litigation. In a study reported in 2002,(134) Ballard and colleagues surveyed a large representative population of U.S. neonatologists on whether they would be willing to resuscitate a hypothetical 23-week gestation baby weighing 480g. With no information about the parents, 47%

thought that resuscitation was "the most appropriate treatment." If requested by the parents to "do everything possible," 91% would resuscitate; however, if the parents requested them "to provide comfort care only," only 11% would resuscitate. From these figures, it appears that there is a clear desire to respect parent requests. On further questioning and analysis, the authors showed that a perceived risk of litigation (litigious parents) influenced the possible action of several physicians whose initial judgment was not to resuscitate and who had predicted a very poor prognosis. These physicians were more likely to follow parental wishes if there was a perceived risk of litigation. This did not apply to those whose initial uninfluenced judgment was to resuscitate. They indicated that they would defer to parental requests regardless of how they might perceive prognosis or the risk of litigation. Thus in some circumstances, some physicians in the United States, as stated by the authors, "may resuscitate infants against their better judgment," if they believed the parents were litigious. The converse also applied. If the physicians were informed that the parents were unlikely to be litigious, and were "easy to deal with," they were more likely to favor nontreatment. Although this study has methodological flaws, and in particular it reports responses to a hypothetical situation, it does demonstrate not only the influence of parental wishes, but also how the response to these wishes may be altered in some by a fear of litigation. Perhaps at the limit of viability, because there is uncertainty not only concerning prognosis but also concerning what the right action is, the introduction of some reasonable factor, be it a parental wish or a fear of litigation, can bear weight on a decision and alter it.

In a Canadian study, Saigal et al.(135) collected and compared preferences for selected health states from the perspectives of neonatologists, nurses, parents of ELBW or normal birth weight infants, and adolescents who were either ELBW or normal birth weight infants. The different health states the participants were asked to rate were ones in which there were varying degrees of disability, from mild to severe. Physicians and nurses, for the five health states defined, had similar preferences, and similar proportions viewed some health states as worse than death (59% of neonatologists, 68% of nurses). There was a significant difference between how physicians and nurses rated health states and how parents of ELBW and term infants rated them. One or more of the health states was rated as worse than death by 64% of the health professionals and 45% of the parents. The difference was statistically significant. Differences in scores between health professionals, parents, and adolescents were greatest for the two health states in which there was the most severe disability. Health professionals rated these two health states significantly lower than parents ($p < 0.001$). A significantly fewer number of adolescents rated at least one of the health states worse than death. Health professionals and parents rated mild to moderate disability similarly, but parents were far more likely to accept disability. Adolescents who were ELBW or term infants, as a group, rated the same health states lower than their parents, but there was more consistent agreement between adolescents and parents than there was between these two and health professionals when severe disability was considered.(136) In a similar vein, other studies have suggested that patients appear to perceive their own disability states, or life-threatening situations, in a better light than do health professionals.(137,138)

The same Canadian group examined the attitudes of parents and health professionals toward the treatment of ELBW infants.(139) The health professional group was composed of neonatal physicians and nurses, and the parents' groups were two matched groups, one of which had experienced the birth of a preterm infant less than 1,000g and the other a full-term infant.

About 64% of parents agreed, or strongly agreed, that an attempt should be made to save all infants regardless of birth weight or condition at birth compared with only 6% of health professionals. There was no difference between the two-parent groups, or between the physicians and nurses. Although the majority of both groups, parents and health professionals, believed that there should not be a standard policy on whether to save such infants, a greater proportion of parents than health professionals believed this. Among those who did not believe that all infants should be saved, 65% of physicians and 75% of nurses gave the economic costs of intensive and lifelong care as a reason, compared with 7% of parents of ELBW infants and 26% of parents of full-term infants. In this study, having a child with a disability did not greatly affect the responses of the parents of an ELBW infant. As for who should make the final decision regarding whether to forego life-sustaining treatment, the majority, in all groups, believed parents should "have the final say." However, there was a difference between the groups. Health professionals believed that they should have "the last word" significantly more than parents believed they should. The role of hospital ethics committees was accorded less influence, although nurses were more supportive of their role than parents, who were more supportive than physicians. As for other potential sources of authority, health professionals were more in favor of standards issued by medical bodies than parents, and only a minority in all groups supported a role for the courts. This occurred in 20% of nurses, 13% of parents, and only 2% of physicians. The conclusion from this study that, in general, parents support the aggressive treatment of EPTIs also has been reported in other studies.(54,140,141) Furthermore, the literature seems to support the notion that physicians are more likely than parents to forego treatment based on a perception of a later poor quality of life.(133,142–144)

In Scotland, McHaffie, Laing, Parker, and McMillan(145) examined the practices of 176 neonatologists and nurses, in addition to the perceptions of 108 parents of 62 babies for whom there was discussion about withholding invasive treatment. All the infants had a prognosis of either early death or a serious disabling impairment. All of them died, and the parents were interviewed at 3 and 13 months after the death. The conclusions were that the actual decisions to forego life-sustaining treatment were made by the physicians with or without the parents. Although the majority believed that parents should be involved, only 3% of physicians and 6% of nurses thought parents should "take the ultimate decision," even though 58% of physicians and 73% of nurses were in favor of a joint approach. In contrast, when the parents were interviewed 56% perceived that the ultimate decision had been theirs, of which 46% believed they were alone in accepting the responsibility and 14% felt it had been a joint decision along with the physicians, following advice or a recommendation. The authors noted that even though professional opinion may consider that it is "too great a burden" for parents to decide to withdraw treatment, the majority of parents saw this as "part of parental responsibility." At the second interview, 13 months after the event, 98% felt the decision had been right, although there was some concern over the validity of the prognosis and the distressing dying process. The authors determined that the role of the physicians is strongly influential as they "are not only the purveyors of fact but also of arguments," which in themselves may be self-fulfilling prophecies that bolster future argument.

In a study from Denmark it was reported that most Danish physicians would treat a 24-week infant at birth but would withdraw treatment if severe complications occurred. However, they would continue life-sustaining treatment if the parents wished this.(146) An Australian survey published in 2001,(147) examined when and how a neonatologist would counsel parents expecting the delivery of an EPTI. Counseling included the survival prognosis and almost always morbidity. The most important factor was the gestational age of the infant. At 22 weeks' gestation only 24% always or often counseled, and this rose to 77% at 25 weeks. Otherwise it was the obstetrician who did the counseling. Of the neonatologists who did counsel, 86% would recommend nonresuscitation at 22 weeks, and 14% at 24 weeks. The majority of neonatologists believed that legal action to limit parental decisions "had no useful place . . . regardless of the gestation." Where there was disagreement, 58% believed the parents should decide, and 35% believed it should be the neonatologist. Only 6% believed a court or an ethics committee should decide. When questioned concerning the withdrawal of life support, only 2% supported that "all interventions should be taken to preserve life, however severe the prognosis," and a similar low percentage agreed that "even with severe physical disability, life is better than death." Only 8% supported the notion that "even with severe mental disability, life is better than death."

The experience of foregoing life-sustaining treatment in the Muslim country of Oman was reported by DaCosta, Ghazal, and AlKhusaiby.(148) They believed that for religious and sociocultural reasons "when the question of withdrawal of life support measures is raised . . . we meet with near universal refusal." They stated that parents and extended family do not want to be seen as having acquiesced in their child's demise. However, when the child is not ventilated, but a decision not to resuscitate or to limit vital support is made, none have objections to limiting therapy. The authors wrote that they always say, "in our opinion, and if this was my child, I would not put the child on the ventilator," and the parental response to this is to acquiesce silently, or say, "[Y]ou do what is best for my child." The authors interpreted this as parents not wanting to make a life or death decision themselves, "but are willing to accept transferring the responsibility onto a person in authority."

It is apparent that there are conflicting views between parents and physicians, as well as varying opinions within and between countries.(44,149–153) De Leeuw et al.(154) compared the treatment choices of physicians and nurses in 11 European countries for a hypothetical case of an EPTI born weighing 560g at 24 weeks' gestation and an Apgar score of 1 at 1 minute. The responses, collected in 1996 through 1997, came from 143 NICUs in Italy, Spain, France, Germany, the Netherlands, Luxembourg, Britain, Sweden, Hungary, Estonia, and Lithuania. In summary, most physicians in every country, except the Netherlands, would resuscitate the baby. However, should the baby's condition deteriorate following seizures and a severe, although unilateral, intraventricular hemorrhage with parenchymal involvement, most physicians in France, the Netherlands, and Luxembourg, and most, but fewer, in Sweden, Britain, Spain, and Lithuania would favor limiting or withdrawing intensive care. Physicians in Estonia, Hungary, Germany, and Italy were less likely to support this approach. Of interest was that most in Estonia, France, and Italy, and a significant number in Hungary, Sweden, Spain, and Lithuania, would carry out their decision, whatever it was, without involving the parents. In Estonia, Hungary, Italy, Germany, and Spain, most physicians would only withhold treatment in circumstances such as a cardiac arrest, if the parents requested a withdrawing of intensive care, in the circumstance described. However, in Britain, the Netherlands, and Sweden, they would withdraw mechanical ventilation, and a substantial number of physicians in France and the Netherlands would administer drugs with the purpose of ending the baby's life. There were other factors, apart from parental wishes, that influenced the decisions of physicians. For example, those who claimed that they personally found religion "fairly" or "extremely" important were less willing to make nontreatment choices. Male physicians who held junior professional positions, and those with experience of neonatal follow-up, were more willing to involve parents in decision making. But overall, the main significant predictor of attitude was country. This finding was similar for neonatal nurses. In a similar U.S. 1992 study,(142) about 95% would resuscitate and 60% would start "full intensive care." If there was marked deterioration, about 45% would encourage withdrawal. These studies demonstrate that the attitudes of physicians vary within, and between, countries. Although the individual characteristics of the physicians affect their attitudes, it is the nation in which they practice that appears to influence their responses the most.

In 2000 Rebagliato and associates(155) reported the neonatal end of life decision-making practices in 10 European countries, as part of a study for EURONIC (European Project on Parents' Information and Ethical Decision Making in Neonatal Intensive Care Units: Staff Attitudes and Opinions). The group had previously reported(156) that the frequency of withdrawing mechanical ventilation was highest in Northern European countries and lowest in south Mediterranean ones. In the 2000 study they examined physicians' attitudes toward the value of life and life with a disability; the appropriate use of medical technology; the relevance of family burden, economic costs, and legal constraints; the influence of country of origin; personal and professional characteristics; and the relationship between attitudes of self-reported practices. The countries included were France, Germany, Italy, the Netherlands, Spain, Sweden, Britain, Estonia, Hungary, and Lithuania. About one-fourth to one-third of physicians in Italy, Lithuania, and Hungary agreed with a sanctity of life principle, and "that everything possible should be done to ensure a neonate's survival, however severe the prognosis." In contrast, most physicians in every country equated severe mental disability as "an outcome equal to or worse than death." There was less agreement when severe physical handicap was considered. In all countries the majority of physicians believed that family burden was an important concept when making end of life decisions. However, more than half of those in Baltic countries thought their ability to limit treatment was legally constrained. This was in stark contrast to those who believed this in Sweden (3%) and France (5%). As for the argument invoking economic justice, most did not believe that this should affect their decisions, although about 25% in France, Britain, and the Baltic countries did believe that there should be a consideration of cost. Considerable variation was found when the mode of foregoing life-sustaining treatment was evaluated. Most physicians in every country but Lithuania appeared to make an ethical distinction between withholding intensive care from the very beginning and withdrawing it afterward. Interestingly, and perhaps disturbingly, about one-third of the physicians form France, the Netherlands, and Estonia "found no ethical difference between treatment withdrawal and the administration of drugs with the purpose of ending a patient's life," and in France and the Baltic countries more than half agreed that "withholding intensive care without simultaneously taking active measures to end life" may increase the chances of future severe disability. Using multiple linear regression analysis the authors attempted to identify variables that might help to explain the variation in findings. The characteristics that were more likely to be associated with a quality of life stance versus a sanctity of life one were being female, having no children, being Protestant or having no religious background, considering religion not important, an intermediate length of professional experience (6–15 years), and working in units with a higher number of ELBW admissions.

Among physicians who found religion important, those from Italy, Hungary, and the Baltic countries were significantly more in favor of sanctity of life approach. For those physicians who did not report religion as important, Italian physicians did not differ from those in Spain, France, and Germany, whereas those in Hungary and Estonia continued to follow a pro-life stance. However, country remained the strongest single factor explaining differences in practice, even though there was variability of beliefs within countries.

RESOURCE EXPENDITURE

S ome might argue that intensive care for the smallest of EPTIs raises the level of societal economic burden in an unjustified manner. But the cost of such care should be examined in relationship to how much and the manner in which society spends on other aspects of health care and the proportion of this that is generated by the population in question. Neonatal intensive care cost per life year gained is likely to be considerably less than that for many adults given intensive care.(30) When the figures for resource use by NICUs on caring for the EPTI are examined in isolation, they appear daunting. For example, in a study of 17 Canadian NICUs(34) it was found that although EPTIs comprised only 4% of admissions, they accounted for 22% of deaths, 31% of severe intraventricular hemorrhage, 22% of chronic lung disease, 59% of severe retinopathy of prematurity, and 20% of necrotizing enterocolitis. They consumed 11% of NICU days, 20% of mechanical ventilator use, 35% of transfusions, 21% of surgically inserted central venous catheters, and 8% of major surgical procedures. Lorenz et al.(22) reported on the resource expenditure in the perinatal period generated by EPTIs born less than 26 weeks in two population-based cohorts, New Jersey (NJ) and the Netherlands, who received systematically different approaches to their care during the midmed-1980s. In the NJ cohort, almost all the babies received intensive care, whereas the policy was more selective in the Netherlands. Assisted ventilation was more commonly used in NJ, 95% versus 64%, and almost all the difference resulted from the use of assisted ventilation in infants who subsequently died. Mortality at 28 days was about 46% in NJ and 73% in the Netherlands. No infant less than 25 weeks' gestation survived in the Netherlands cohort. Survival to 2 years in NJ was twice that in the Netherlands. In the NJ cohort 1,820 ventilator days were expended per 100 live births compared to 448 days in the Netherlands, but the difference in nonventilator days was not statistically different. In summary, the management approach in NJ resulted in 24 additional survivors per 100 live births, 7 additional cases of disabling cerebral palsy per 100 live births, and at a cost of 1,372 additional ventilator days per 100 live births.

It is important, when considering cost, to realize that most EPTI deaths occur in the first 3 days, and it is the least mature who die the earliest.(157) Those who survive day 4 are very likely to survive to discharge. Meadow and Lantos(157) make the argument that as the smallest babies, for example, those who weigh 600g, are more likely to die, and to die in the first few days after birth, they consume fewer resources than the larger babies, for example, those weighing 900g.(157) About 85% of bed days are allocated to infants who will be discharged home, independent of the initial mortality risk. Furthermore, as Meadow and Lantos wrote, "the vast majority of NICU resources are directed to infants who ultimately survive to go home to their families," that is, the longer the EPTI stays in the NICU the more likely that infant will survive, which is not necessarily the case in the adult ICU. In Japan, Nishida(39,158) calculated the economic cost of providing for ELBW infants, including lifelong costs, and concluded that there was a net financial benefit, which was generated by "normal" survivors. Also, when considering cost, it should be remembered that the number of survivors is relatively very small compared to the numbers in the rest of the population who consume health care and social services. In the Saigal et al. paper(89) comparing outcome in four national regional cohorts (NJ, Ontario, Bavaria, and Holland), the total number of survivors ranged from 397 in Ontario to 263 in Bavaria. Thus, the financial cost of intensive care for EPTIs, at least in countries with advanced health care systems, should be evaluated in relationship to how they compare to other expensive health resource allocation. It might also be argued that a relatively favorable outcome for an EPTI generates potentially more lifelong beneficence than that gained from resource allocation to the elderly.

PART 2

BIOETHICS

14

MORAL THEORY

Beauchamp defines the term *morality* as traditions of belief about right and wrong human conduct.(159) In particular this book is concerned with the morality of special groups, that is, health care professionals, those who care for children, and the state. Right and wrong conduct is conduct that affects the interests of others.(159) The theories that are used to argue what constitutes morality are ethics (although the term is also used as a synonym for morality), and the ethics that apply to a special group, such as health care professionals, are bioethics. The application of bioethics can be used when there are different choices concerning health care that affect the interests of individuals. Fundamental to what might be deemed the right choice is correct knowledge, which is the explanation for the first section that includes the epidemiology and prognosis of extreme prematurity, even though these topics may not always be "cut and dried." However, central to the use of bioethics, or any argument, is that there are clear shared definitions. In addition, for a conclusion to be reached, and a course of action agreed on, boundaries should be delineated and common moral theories, codes, and principles adopted.(160) This does not mean that there always should be a universally adopted answer to any moral question or dilemma, but that any conclusion reached should have consistency and generalizable coherence.

Although we might view bioethics as a subject that encompasses codes and concepts on how physicians should behave, it is much broader than that, for within the discipline are philosophies and principles enshrined within the culture in which the physician practises. As such, although themes may remain constant, or some new ones appear, the moral interpretation of what may be the correct approach to these themes has not always been constant throughout recorded time. Jonsen wrote that Hippocrates in *Epidemics I* declares that the physician "help and not harm."(161) A modern interpretation of this is that a physician should weigh carefully the risks and benefits of treatment. However, according to Jonsen, the context is one of prognostication and that the "good physician" should distinguish between fatal and nonfatal disease so that "the patient can benefit from medical ministrations."(162) The interpretation is "that the experienced physician should never be blamed for refusing to take on desperate cases."(162) Harm, in this context, occurs when medicine is practiced with no hope of effect. In medieval times, Western medicine was primarily governed by the work of the church. This cemented a tie between Christian ethics and a duty to the sick. As Jonsen noted,(163) there was a version of the Hippocratic Oath in which the Greek gods are replaced by "God the Father of our Lord Jesus Christ," and the prohibition against abortion is strengthened and the requirement against "cutting for the stone" is removed.(164) From the 13th century the practice of medicine began to return to the lay sector, although the behavior of physicians continued to be advised strongly by ecclesiastical doctrine, which commanded that there was a duty to the sick and the poor.(165) Medical ethics were also influenced by Islamic and Jewish teachings, particularly in Spain and the near East, with the common themes of sanctity of life, duty toward all patients, and the absolute power of a higher being.(166) As Western medical practice entered into the renaissance, medical ethics were characterized by decorum, duties and obligations, and politic ethics. The latter, which had risen in importance, is defined by Jonsen(167) as "the duties of those whose work is intimately related to the welfare of a political unit, a community." The physician is now viewed as one who not only has an obligation to provide services for any individual who seeks help, rich or poor, but also has to act in a manner that benefits the community as a whole.(168) This notion of politic ethics and a duty to society can also be found in the influential 19th-century text by Thomas Percival,(169) and it is during that century that it is now written that the duties of physicians should be balanced by their rights,(170) which included an expectation that their prescriptions be followed and their duty to sustain life be respected. However, by the end of the 19th century, although deontological forces were still in play in medical ethics, the science of statistical probabilities was available and allowed for utilitarian choices whereby the aim was to provide the greater good.(171) In addition, as expounded by Cabot from the Massachusetts General Hospital, incompetent practice was unethical, to the dismay of some practitioners who believed that the public exposure of medical mistakes was not an act of decorum.(172,173) As the 20th century passed, medical ethics brought into play concepts such as autonomy, patients' rights, justice, and the regulation of research. But it was not until the 1960s and early 1970s, and the ability to care better for very premature and disabled infants, that moral questions began to be asked about the extent and consequences of their care.

There are various ethical theories and schools of thought that can be invoked when considering the care of the extremely preterm infant, and in particular foregoing life-sustaining treatment, the topic with which this book is mainly concerned. Although virtue ethics will not be discussed, an integral part of moral behavior derives from this. This is the consistent performance of that behavior and the desire to do good. These are classical virtues and can, and should, be integrated into other theories.(174) One of these theories is deontology. This involves acting in accordance with duties and obligations. These can be based on religious teachings or on the "categorical imperative" proposed by Kant(174) in which an action should only be taken if it is right for anyone to take the action. That is, there is a universal law concerning what is right and that some actions are intrinsically immoral. He stated that one should: "act so that you treat humanity, both in your own person and in that of another, always as an end and never merely as a means."(174) This is the respect principle.

This obligation may be special to a group. A special obligation is created by a specific relationship, and the obligation is limited to people in this relationship. Parents have special obligations to their children, and physicians to their patients, such as sick preterm infants. Kantian moral theory applies to an act that is under the control of the individual and not the outcome. An act is judged by how it accords to negative or positive duties. A negative duty is "do not kill." A positive duty might be "to let a patient die when death is inevitable." Negative duties are universally binding and have priority over positive ones. As Freeman and McDonnell wrote:(175) the physician has a positive duty to provide medical care that is effective and available and to respect the wishes of an informed individual. If the patient is a baby it is usually the parents who are surrogate decision makers. But their autonomy is restricted, as they have a special negative duty not to harm their child. The strengths of deontology are that it is consistent and takes account of special obligations and individual justice.

Its weaknesses are that there are no real rational justifications for the rules; there may be conflicting duties and obligations; it is not situational; and it is not necessarily benevolent as it is indifferent to the consequences of an action.(176)

Another ethical theory that is used to address various questions of morality is act utilitarianism. This follows from the work of Jeremy Bentham (1748–1832) and John Stuart Mill (1806–1873). Utilitarianism teaches that a course of action is morally right if it leads to overall benefit. How an individual acts is judged on the net utility of that action. Akin to utilitarianism is consequentialism that argues that actions are good or bad based on their consequences(177) and that it is good to take actions that lead to happiness. The actor should treat the parties who are affected as if the consequences to them are equal. Inevitably, in this approach, net happiness is pitted against varying individual states and interests. Furthermore, it requires that the future can be predicted, even though the consequentialist might argue that we need only to act in a way that reasonably predicts the outcome. In act utilitarianism it would be desirable to forego life-sustaining treatment for the disabled infant if the death of the child would relieve the family and society of a burden and inconvenience and would lead to the greatest good for the greatest number. A utilitarian approach might be accepting that actions that either promote the death of the extremely preterm infant or enable the child to survive but with certain disability, the nature of which is not entirely predictable, are two moral evils. Then the lesser of the two evils is the one that promotes the greatest happiness. However, from the perspective of the infant, one has to accept that death is a state that can be measured against an arguably undesirable life. The moral calculation would be an abstraction versus an uncertainty and thus would negate any conclusion on the basis of noncommensurability. A calculation might still be made from the perspective of the parents or society. Examining the case of the former, the happiness of the parents and family should have as least as much moral weight as that of the infant. But the happiness of the infant is incalculable. Furthermore, parents as surrogate decision makers for their child would still have to decide between incommensurable states. That is the net happiness derived from the death of the baby versus life with a disabled child. From the family's perspective alone, life with a disabled baby might be less happy than life without. In this calculation, the interests of the baby are not taken into account. As for society, its well-being will depend on local and general resources. In a local situation where resources are limited, for example, ventilators, the moral calculation might favor other infants who require ventilation and would survive without disability. Similarly, in poor countries where the need for food, sanitation, and security is acute, an attempt to set up sophisticated neonatal intensive care units would have a lower moral priority and result in less well-being in that society where resources may be better spent. But in relatively rich societies it has been argued that neonatal intensive care, for the extremely preterm infant, does not substantially take away resources that would lead to more happiness in society,(38,158) and it could be said that living in a society that provides for the very vulnerable, in itself, raises the overall sense of well-being in that society. Thus, as Ridley wrote,(176) the utilitarian method surveys all possible courses of action and predicts what consequences, in terms of happiness and suffering, each of these courses will have. A calculation is made that produces the best balance of good results over bad results. No one individual's happiness or suffering is intrinsically more important than anyone else's. The goal is to maximize happiness and satisfaction on the basis of a calculation and on a case-by-case basis. The strengths of act utilitarianism are that it is rational, situational, and benevolent.(176) Its weaknesses are that it has too much faith in predictability; it does not account for incommensurable values or special obligations; and it is inconsistent and has no concern for justice.(176) A modification, which addresses some of these weaknesses, is rule utilitarianism.(176) This theory states that one should act in accordance with rules that if you and everyone else always acted on would produce the greatest amount of happiness for the greatest number.(176) There is still the deontological problem of finding a rational procedure to decide which rules to adopt. However, the strengths of rule utilitarianism are that it is consistent, benevolent, takes account of special obligations, and has a concern for justice.(176) Weaknesses are still present as there may still be incommensurable values, conflicting rules, and too much faith in predictability.(176)

Another approach is rights theory. This can be used with any ethical theory that includes mention of obligations and can be used in tandem with wider ethical perspectives.(176) In this theory, rights are balanced by duties, and there are rights that everyone has, regardless. Any duty one might have corresponds to someone's right. Thus a patient has a right to the best medical care that a physician can provide, and a physician has a duty to provide it. But physicians also have rights, and patients have duties, and these can clash. Furthermore, rights, in general, are often loudly expounded, but duties less so. The right to "Life, liberty, and the pursuit of happiness" is appreciated better than any correlative duties.(175) Individual rights may oppose each other, or be said to apply to one group but not another. Also, as with moral imperatives, there is a problem with the origin of rights.(175) For rights theory to stand on its own and carry moral weight it requires a metaphysical or religious origin. A moral right should compete with, and be part of, rules, obligations, and consequences. That is, without invoking an overriding abstract source, rights theory should be subject to, or made part of, other major moral theories.

The ethical theories described have their strengths and weaknesses. To better address bioethical questions and dilemmas, we can apply principilism. This is based on the notion that a common morality contains a set of moral norms that includes principles,(178) and these principles can be applied in moral discourse concerning the extremely preterm infant. These principles guide moral argument and provide a structure on which the direction of an argument can be made. The commonly used principles are respect for autonomy, beneficence, nonmaleficence, and justice. But is there a common morality? This is defined by Veatch as a "pretheoretical awareness of certain moral norms."(179) Whether this is the case across different cultures and during different epochs is not proven empirically.(180) But there could be an element of calming reassurance if there were some moral norms we all hold in common.(181) Even if there was some consensus on common moral norms, it is unlikely that this would easily resolve moral dilemmas but rather provide a common language across cultures with which to address the dilemmas. As Macklin wrote, there may not be ethical absolutes, but there are ethical norms.(182) Support for the concept of the universality of some principles, across cultures, can be found in the teachings of the 13th-century Muslim scholar Mawlana.(183)

15

AUTONOMY

An important principle in bioethics is respect for autonomy. Clearly, extremely preterm infants do not have autonomy, and surrogates, usually parents, are granted the right to make decisions for them, on the basis of a special relationship. This is not without limits, and where consent to treatment is concerned they have a duty to act in the best interests of the child, from the perspective of the child. Determining this may be difficult. Correct respect for autonomy demands that parents are given ample opportunity to express their views and that these are heard and addressed in a considerate manner. Physicians have a duty to recognize and protect the future of the child, who is both vulnerable and without autonomy.(184) Babies, of any gestation, require the protection of parents, health professionals, and society and have a moral and legal right to receive this protection. Other physicians' duties, which relate directly to the health-related interests of the baby, include the correct exercise of knowledge and expertise; the acknowledgment of any lack of knowledge; and a requirement to seek knowledge and guidance, not to provide ineffectual treatment, to respect the law, and to provide alternative care when required. The duty of physicians, and their perceptions of these, when they are centered on the infant, may conflict with parental wishes and lead to severe emotional and economic family burden and threaten its very integrity. Conflict may arise that leads to intervention by ethics committees, and sometimes the courts, which in itself may further division.(185,186) Based on the reasonable expectation of extreme family burden, in the presence of a clear severe outcome for the infant, there are those who argue that there is an obligation to respect parental requests to forego life-sustaining treatment.(185) But how well parents make such choices, and how much they are influenced by others, health professionals or otherwise, is variable and complex. Although parents or guardians are granted a limited surrogate autonomy, as Meyers wrote:

> genuine autonomy entails more than the mere making of decisions. It requires both the capacity to make free and informed decisions and the active development of character by which persons understand and are able to act upon self-defining choices . . . autonomy undercutting power asymmetries prevail and decision making in routine care relies much more on assent than on consent . . . health-care in general, and critical care in particular, represent profoundly difficult contexts for genuinely autonomous choices.(187)

The decisions of surrogates are not only influenced by their own prejudices, pressures to avoid perceived taboos, incriminating statements, and other emotional, social, and economic pressures, they are also shaped by the fear of an alien environment and the, perhaps unintentional, posture of physicians whose requirements are, in an intensive care situation, that they control the variables. There is an undoubted pressure on physicians to make decisions and move on. This provides an impetus that not only impedes shared knowledgeable decision making but also fashions how physicians may be perceived and how they see themselves.

16

BENEFICENCE AND NONMALEFICENCE

From classical times health care professionals have been obliged to avoid harming their patients and to promote their welfare. But in the medical and surgical management of preterm infants harm is often inflicted that is considered justified because of the presumed benefits. The harm may be relatively minor, such as taking blood samples or placing intravenous lines, or it may have the potential to cause long-term damage, such as with prolonged high pressure artificial ventilation or the surgical removal of bowel damaged by necrotizing enterocolitis. At what point does treatment no longer offer a benefit? Some may argue that a supposed long-term benefit, for example, survival, may not further the welfare of the infant, the family, or society. This argument might arise when it is proposed to place a ventriculo-peritoneal shunt into a severely brain-damaged preterm infant with progressive posthemorrhagic hydrocephalus. In all aspects of health care there is a balance between beneficence and nonmaleficence. The principle of nonmaleficence would support foregoing treatment if it was of no benefit and the treatment would inflict harm and suffering. But the use of the principle correctly requires that lack of benefit, harm, and suffering can be recognized and predicted. The principle of beneficence would support an action, or lack thereof, if it was in the best interests of the infant. Correct use of the principle requires that it is understood what interests the infant has, or perhaps will have, from the perspective of the infant. The principle of beneficence is the primary principle when dealing with medical decisions that concern the welfare of children. It can be a subjective notion that generates different interpretation depending on circumstance, situation, prognostic knowledge, and the moral notions of those involved in the care of an infant. Those who invoke the best interests standard state they are acting to maximize benefits and minimize harms.(188) Its use as a general guideline is clearly important when deciding between different options for the treatment of a child. It allows for standards to be set and boundaries to be drawn. However, it should be recognized that there may be situations in which its use is not applicable, and where its use, as Kopelman wrote, is "unknowable, vague, dangerous, and open to abuse."(188)

She argued that it should be understood "not as absolute duty, but as a *prima facie* duty, or an ideal that should guide choices."(189) As may occur, ideals may not be possible always. It would be ideal for an extremely preterm infant, once resuscitated and supported, not to have to live a life challenged by serious disability. But if this ideal cannot be met, and the infant survives, then as Holmes stated, we must consider what our prima facie duties toward the child are and how we justify these.(190) For this to occur, we have to state that the infant has moral rights, which it is not able, nor obliged, to reciprocate.

Does providing life-sustaining treatment to the extremely preterm infant cause more harm than benefit and violate the nonmaleficence principle?(191) Jonsen and Garland wrote that the principle is not violated if there is "inability to survive infancy, inability to live without severe pain, and inability to participate, at least minimally, in human experience."(192)

This assumes prognostic accuracy, which may be uncertain. However, there are circumstances where application of the principle might apply in the newborn nursery, for example, with anencephaly and an extremely preterm infant may suffer such complications that the conditions laid down by Jonsen and Garland would clearly apply.

How much brain injury should constitute such harm that continuing treatment would be immoral? Later mental retardation is not relevant when determining treatment. What interests the infant has should take priority over those of the family and society when weighing the options. It is true that a patient may have an interest in the welfare of his or her family, but if the incompetent patient has never been competent, it is wrong to impute altruism, or any other motive, to that patient, against his or her interests.(178)

Freeman and O'Donnell noted that physicians do not have the luxury of retrospective analysis of a situation(175) in the way that some philosophers, lawyers, and judges have but must make prospective judgments based on knowledge, which may be uncertain, and experience, which is not stereotypic. But it is important not only to know the facts, but also to recognize the ambiguity and power of words. For example, a ventilator-dependent preterm infant with a grade IV intraventricular hemorrhage (enlarged ventricles and hemorrhage into the ventricle in addition to the substance of the brain) may be described as neurologically devastated by some. Clearly the infant is at high risk for varying degrees of neurologic disability. But it is not always clear how to distinguish which infant will survive with a moderate degree of cerebral palsy and sufficient cognition to be a sentient, but dependent, human being from one who is truly unable to interact in any meaningful way. It is important not to make value judgments and to act in the best interests of the infant, from the perspective of the infant. This is not easy, nor wholly possible, for we do not know the future perspective of the infant. The best interests concept is a fuzzy notion. However, making the infant central to the process narrows the argument. But can existence itself be an injury? When one states that an infant would be "better off dead," is it possible to compare the dead state with the state that would have occurred should the infant have lived? The two states are not commensurable, as one is nonexistence. This is not to say that continued existence will be good for the infant. But it is to say that when deciding whether to forego life-sustaining treatment for an extremely preterm infant, a utilitarian calculation comparing lack of existence to a life with disability should not apply. Feinberg argued that a surrogate

> exercises his judgment that whatever interests the impaired party might have, or come to have, they would already be doomed to defeat by his present incurable condition. Thus, it would be irrational – contrary to what reason decrees – for a representative and protector of those interests to prefer the continuance of that condition to non-existence.(193)

The problem with this is predicting when potential interests will be "doomed to defeat." It is not only uncertainty that clouds the decision-making process, but also the perceptions, and perhaps even the knowledge of those who discuss these situations. Paris, when giving his opinions on a legal case in which a baby was disconnected from a ventilator by a parent, stated that the parents of this 25-week gestation infant were given a 20–40% risk of severe intracranial hemorrhage should the baby survive. Paris viewed this as "more than sufficient evidence of the disproportion-ate burden that awaited this child to justify a decision to withhold resuscitation."(194)

This conclusion was made even though should the infant have survived, the statistical risk of a major disability was considerably less than not having a major disability. Furthermore, should the major neurological complications of extreme prematurity occur, prediction of the degree of disability may be difficult, particularly during the early stages after birth. Paris also proposed a "popular fallacy" argument by stating that treatment is based on objective criteria such as birth weight throughout Europe. Even if this was totally true, which it is not as there is much variability (see Section I), it is not a moral justification. He also wrote that because the baby was described as "lifeless, hypotonic, hypoxic, purple-blue, with no grasp or grimace, at birth," that this should have precluded resuscitation, even though the baby had a heart rate of 90. Many extremely preterm infants have this appearance at birth. The reasoning that the baby's appearance should have precluded resuscitation begs the question, are infants such as these, who are resuscitated at birth, more likely to have severe neurologic dis-ability if they survive? Or, if they die, are they more likely to have a long lingering dying process? The scientific literature appears to support an answer of no to both these questions.(49–53,157)

Whereas considering the interests of the infant is paramount, this is not to discount the interests of others. Parents who are left to raise a disabled extremely preterm infant suffer significant stress. They may enter a morass of frustration, guilt, denial, anger, and disbelief that may be rekindled during their years of caring. It should be argued that if the state has a strong duty to protect the vulnerable and the susceptible, then it also has an obligation to provide social, educational, psychological, and economic support for those who care for disabled children.

So it can be seen that principles may compete, and the interpretation of their uses vary. Phrases such as *best interests* are difficult to define for an infant, and it is arguable whether the use of such a phrase can apply to nonexistence. Parents may find themselves enveloped in myth and uncertainty. It is in such circumstances that physicians, who may have little time or expertise in moral argument, shape the discussions with parents and in effect determine the decision. This is not to say that physicians should not impart their knowledge and wisdom to inform and guide parents. Rather it is recognition of the prejudices and moral fallibility of all involved and the slippery nature of moral standards and boundaries. Some might argue that physicians should stay within the sphere of their technical and scientific knowledge. But the practice of medicine has never had this as its sole aim. The origin of the word *doctor* is learned teacher, a *sensei* who is expected to act like a priest and think like a scientist. Most physicians recognize this professional burden and may feel compelled, or duty bound, to shape life and death decisions according to their moral judgment.

17

JUSTICE

In general, the principle of justice concerns fairness and rights and dictates that the extremely preterm infant should be treated in the same way as other infants with the same treatable condition, for example, the extremely preterm infant and the full-term infant with progressive hydrocephalus. This ethical principle protects certain moral rights even though, it can be argued, it may conflict with the principle of beneficence.(195) As Foot wrote: "an act which is 'more humane' than its alternative may be morally objectionable because it infringes rights."(196)

Invoking justice as a principle can become arguable if it cannot be agreed that the recipients of an action are equal in some agreed on respect. Another form of justice is distributive justice. This refers to a fair and equitable distribution of resources. It might be argued that the costs of neonatal intensive care for the extremely preterm infant, and the costs and burdens to society of providing for disabled children, are not justified as they threaten the overall welfare of society. If a justification is to be made for limiting such neonatal intensive care on these grounds, then the proponent must provide some measure of the social burden and compare it with other burdens that society agrees to take. The proponent would be required to show that other accepted commitments such as military defense, education, and other aspects of healthcare would be substantially lessened. Costs are relatively small when compared with some treatments in adults(2) and represent only a small proportion of total health costs for children.(197) If resources are limited, it could also be argued that they are more effectively spent on the very young than on the very old.(198)

18

SANCTITY OF LIFE

In the Judeo-Christian tradition, the sanctity of life principle might be stated as follows:

> human life is of infinite value. This in turn means that a piece of infinity is also infinite and a person who has but a few moments of life is no less of value than a person who has sixty years to live . . . a handicapped individual is a perfect specimen when viewed as an ethical concept. The value is an absolute value. It is not relative to life expectancy, to state of health, or to usefulness to society.(199)

The sanctity of life principle is sometimes employed in such a way that would suggest that the use of the words themselves should put an end to moral argument,(200) what could be seen as an exchange of reasoning for dogma rather than seeking an understanding of what life is, when it has moral worth, and what the relative role of other principles is. Even in a strictly religious context, in the Western tradition, the need to sustain human life, purely because it is that, is not overriding.(201–203) Glover defined the sanctity of life principle as one in which taking life is intrinsically wrong.(204) He argued that the doctrine "is not acceptable, but there is embedded in it a moral view we should retain." He does not argue that it is not wrong to take away life, but that "conventional moral views about killing are often intellectually unsatisfactory."

In the sanctity of life doctrine, the act of killing can never have a justification, or there can never be a circumstance where it is morally correct. It cannot be justified to save the life of another or oneself. However, many would support the concept of deadly self-defense, or the prosecution of a "just war," but might not agree with allowing nonterminal, severely handicapped infants to die.

19

ACTIVE AND PASSIVE EUTHANASIA

Kuhse wrote that killing is not always morally worse than letting die and sometimes may be better.(205) She argued that active euthanasia is morally no worse than passive euthanasia and sometimes morally better. This, she stated, is based on the motivation of the agent, as the two acts have the same outcome. The actors, parents and physicians believe they are doing good, which, in itself, is based on the notion that the outcome, death, is good, or much better, than the alternative, a life with severe disability. Although the moral notion, in some circumstances, may be seen by some as acceptable, it is based on an abstraction akin to the legal term *non actus reus nisi mens sit rea* (knowledge of the wrongfulness of an act at the time of its commission) and in the case of foregoing life-sustaining treatment for an extremely preterm infant, is not a verifiable proposition. Whereas the actors may believe they are doing good, this is based on their perceptions and judgments, which have been molded by anecdote, bias, prejudice, custom, and taboo. For example, it was not that long ago that children with Down syndrome were left to die from conditions that were correctable. Recent history is replete with acts performed by professionals that at the time were not believed by them to be bad but would be judged as such now.(206,207) Thus if a coherent argument for foregoing life-sustaining treatment for an extremely preterm infant cannot be made on the basis of the beneficence of the actors, nor on a verifiable outcome, if the life-sustaining treatment is continued, can the action be considered allowable? Apparently the action can only be good based on the motivation of the actors, which is predicated on their belief in the outcome. It would appear that an impasse has been reached. But this is not necessarily the case for, while not disregarding the arguments, it can be said that for ethical rules that determine behavior to work there needs to be a degree of trust, both in the actions of agents and in a reasonably foreseeable future. The former are required morally to be virtuous, and the outcome is not required to be absolutely verifiable. The physicians can agree on what is required to be the actor, and what the outcome will be on a probabilistic basis, and society, through its representatives are required to take into account the fallibility of the actors, and the uncertainty of the outcome. As Kuhse stated, "answers to public-policy questions are rarely derived from first ethical principles, but are, quite properly, based on common intuitions."(205)

20

PERSONHOOD

According to Englehardt,(208) it is morally acceptable to allow a severely disabled infant to die when it is unlikely that the infant can attain a developed personal life, that is, become a person, and when it seems clear that providing continued care would constitute a severe burden for the family. He argued that there is "an injury of continued existence"(208) and that a child has a right not to have his or her life prolonged in those cases where life would be "painful and futile."(208) He does not define futile. He proposed that allowing a severely disabled infant to die is not only morally acceptable but also morally demanded. Although Englehardt used the principles of nonmaleficence – beneficence and justice and preventing a continuing injury – removing a burden from the family and the right not to have a painful futile life, as well as suggested that there might be a universal law that demands that a severely disabled infant be allowed to die, he also stated that the attainment of personhood is important to the argument. Singer defined a person as an individual who has rationality and selfawareness.(209) He asked if the life of a being that is conscious, but not self-conscious, has moral value, and if so, how the value of such a life compares with the life of a person. Singer believed infants are beings that are neither rational nor self-conscious.(209) They have not reached a neuropsychological standard required to attain personhood, but will do so some time after birth. Tooley also argued that to have a moral right to life a human should possess those characteristics that identify that human as a person.(210) He suggested that a person, in the moral sense, must be able to envisage the future for itself and have desires about its own future states. The personhood argument is that only personal life has a unique moral claim to existence.(211) If this characteristic, the possession of higher brain functions such as self-awareness, rationality, and a sense of the future is accepted as the basis for a moral claim to life, it does carry with it the weight of logical consideration. However, in our society, this approach might be considered counterintuitive and viewed as unreasonable by many.(211)

If one is to argue that the potential to become a person is the criterion for claiming a moral right to life, and that this claim is diminished in proportion to degrees of disability, then not only does this presuppose prognostic accuracy, particularly in terms of higher mental functions, it also suggests that there is a potential personhood continuum that can be viewed in a categorical rather than a continuous fashion. That is, there is some specific time in development, normal or abnormal, when a person appears, rather than viewing the continuum as a threaded chain that, if broken at any point, destroys that chain. There is, of course, a point at which the continuum starts. This point starts when an organism will develop into a person given a normal course of events. The potentiality argument is refuted by those who state that if it is followed it leads to accepting that a sperm or an ovum are potential people.(212) But a tree is not a table in the normal course of events. There comes a time when the constituent parts of a human come together to form an organism that unarguably has the developmental potential to become a human person. The constituent parts, and their origins, do not, in themselves, have this potential. I do not argue when this occurs, but it is certainly present after birth.

If the reasoning of those who champion a neuropsychological standard for personhood, which they argue will appear in infants at some ill-defined time during their development, is followed, then unless there is absolute certainty that this will never occur, and there is often uncertainty concerning this, then a certain time period will need to be determined before life-sustaining support is removed from a disabled infant. It might be argued that the concept of personhood, or potential personhood, should not be used as the sole determinant for foregoing life-sustaining treatment from a disabled infant in the absence of more rigorous ways of defining and recognizing its presence. In addition, this notion of self that grants a person rights and duties does not necessarily remove moral consideration from a nonperson. Many cannot justify cruelty to animals but have no qualms about considering exterminating cockroaches with noxious substances. Perhaps we allow moral consideration based on a tier of situational acceptability that is built according to moral consensus. Qualms are moral intuitions. That is, they are doubts and uncertainties concerning what is right or wrong, in a particular situation, without reasoning.(213) These intuitions may vary between people and will depend on knowledge, preconceived notions, and cultural education. In addition, an intuition will depend on the language used to deliver a proposition. So there may be qualms when the statement is we need to kill this baby because it is a burden to itself and others, but it may be more acceptable to state that it is in the best interests of the baby, and secondarily for others, to let this baby die. The response to these statements is still intuitive, as the words *burden* and *best interests* are not defined, reasoned, or argued. An intuition is sought rather than a moral truth based on theory or principle. In such a situation, agreeing with one of the propositions may be counterintuitive. The first requirement for testing moral intuitions, whatever language is used, is acceptable fact, and only then can moral theory and principle be applied. If the conclusion is still counterintuitive, then there should be a reexamination of whether facts are incorrect or whether reasoning or principles are inconsistent. An example could be that moral status is granted by an arbitrary definition of personhood. This definition then determines that an infant does not have moral status and a right to life.

The definition of a person comes from Locke in the 19th century, who wrote that a person is "a thinking intelligent being that has reason and reflection and can consider itself as itself, the same thinking thing, in different times and places."(214)

This person, human or otherwise, has moral status with rights, duties, and obligations. Those without this rationality and self-consciousness are not entitled to this moral status. This neurological standard, if followed logically, would lead to an unacceptable conclusion, for example, that it is morally acceptable to experiment on human newborn infants – nonpersons – to study disease in adult gorillas – persons. This does not necessarily mean that the converse is morally acceptable – experiments on primates to benefit babies. Clearly, however, we do practice speciesism, even though it may not be morally justifiable. So do those who propose a personhood argument to justify foregoing life-sustaining treatment for an extremely preterm infant propose something that is counterintuitive and morally absurd? Is it because they equate a right to life with moral status and moral status with personhood? It seems that the argument centers on moral status. It could be argued that we should grant moral status to those with both continuing consciousness and developmental potential, and not necessarily just rationality. It may be arguable just how much, or the degree of, consciousness an extremely preterm infant has, but in biological terms the infant is not just a brain stem preparation. If we grant the infant moral status then we grant a right to life, and there are duties that we owe the infant. In fact there are special duties that physicians owe the baby, not only because of the degree of vulnerability and susceptibility of the baby, but also because the baby is a patient. The baby deserves the dignity and respect that comes with moral status. It is intuitively the virtuous thing to do, and it would be morally wrong not to do so. Although the concept of personhood may be a long-standing topic among philosophers, who argue what it is to be a person and gain moral status, the concept has little if any practical application in the practice of managing the extremely preterm infant. It would be highly unlikely that anyone in this practice would consider that a living 24-week gestation infant was any less a person than a 24-year-old, however philosophically incorrect. That is, those decisions, including the foregoing of life-sustaining treatment, ought not be made on the basis of the moral worth of the infant. As Higginson wrote: "it is not obvious that doctors have any special expertise that allows them to presume to judge the ultimate value or significance of another human life."(215)

Thus the application of any personhood argument would have no clear application given the real nature of clinical decision making and would be out of social context. That is not to say that the concept of personhood is unworthy of examination. That is up to the philosophers. But it is to say that, in all likelihood, the concept would be rejected by others actually involved in the clinical situation. Other reasons and arguments would be used, and the personhood argument would be rejected on cultural grounds, which afford the most vulnerable, human dignity.(216)

It is a powerful general view that the life of an infant is a very highly placed value, and the death of a baby is a sad and undesirable occurrence. Is there something in us, nonmetaphysical, that places this high value on life and particularly on the life of an infant? Neuroscientists have demonstrated that there are strong neurochemical rewards, expressed as pleasure, but seen as activation of neurochemical pathways, that are triggered by interaction with infants, and in particular our own.(217,218) This visualized response is the passion aspect that is pitted against a reasoning personhood argument. This is probably why the latter is counterintuitive. The passion is not necessarily directed in favor of life-sustaining treatment, but might be strongly felt when a parent, or a physician, strongly believes that he or she may be severely harming a disabled infant by allowing life-sustaining treatment.

As Wocial wrote: "ethics involves not only understanding principles and respecting rights, but reasoning through deep emotions."(219)

With this may come moral distress that occurs when an individual perceives that what he or she believes is the right thing to do is obstructed in some way.(219)

However personhood is defined and described, it is not the only basis for moral standing(220) and use of the term, in arguments concerning foregoing life-sustaining treatment for extremely preterm infants, does not appear to be operational.

21

QUALITY OF LIFE AND BEST INTERESTS

Is it true that the life of an individual with a severe disability may be so difficult for that individual that should the opportunity arise, during early infancy, to extinguish the possibility of that life, taking that opportunity is a morally good act and not a morally harmful one? In the best interests argument it is held that treatment for a severely disabled infant should be such that it is based on a reasonable assessment that its benefits outweigh its burdens. In this approach there is an acknowledgment that there is a balance to be struck between the value of an infant's life, and "a life that, on balance, does not warrant aggressive treatment."(211) The proposal is that treatment of certain infants harms their interests. How can we judge this for infants who are unable to express their interests? It is clear that some severely disabled infants endure painful surgical interventions, and medical complications, that are performed and managed to improve, as well as sustain, their lives. In terms of the interests of such infants, is the endeavor worth the outcome? It is not the act that is morally indefensible, as we allow medical and surgical interventions to be performed on others, and attempt to alleviate their pain and maximize their outcome. Is it, then, the outcome that is nonbeneficial? That is life as a severely disabled individual. The argument cannot be sustained for the majority of disabled infants who will live lives of sentience and individual significance. But what of the infant who is destined to be profoundly retarded and multiply handicapped?

Robertson wrote that:

> the essence of the quality of life argument is a proxy's judgment that no reasonable person can prefer pain, suffering, and the loneliness of, for example, life in a crib with an IQ level of 20, to an immediate painless death . . . a standard based on healthy ordinary development may be entirely inappropriate to this situation. One who has never known the pleasure of mental operation, ambulation, and social interaction surely does not suffer from their loss as much as one who has . . . life and life alone, whatever its limitations, might be of sufficient worth . . . one should also be hesitant to accept proxy assessments of quality of life because the margin of error in such predictions may be very great . . . even if the judgment occasionally may be defensible, the potential danger of quality of life assessments may be a compelling reason for rejecting this rationale for withholding treatment.(221)

The argument is that we cannot truly objectively judge what a profoundly handicapped individual might prefer. This was not the way authors of a Hastings Center Report saw it.(222) They supported the use of a quality of life standard that, they stated, should be made in reference to the well-being of the infant. They concluded that it was in the best interests of an infant not to receive treatment when continued life would be worse for the infant than an early death. Foregoing treatment, they believed, would not be unjust discrimination when the infant's handicap was so severe that there could not be a meaningful comparison with an otherwise normal child. They did make it clear that any decision should be made from the child's perspective, but did not state how this was to be determined, other than that there were certain states marked by pain and suffering that could be viewed as worse than death. They did allow themselves another option, but without dismissing the best interests approach. They stated that they were proposing not only a best interests standard, but also an alternative relational potential standard, where it could be said that if an infant lacked any present or future potential for human relationships, because of severe neurological impairment, they could be said to have no interests, except to be free from pain and discomfort. If the child is judged not to have interests, apart from being free from pain and discomfort, foregoing treatment is allowable, but not obligatory, as although continued treatment would not benefit the infant, neither would it cause harm. According to the Hastings Center Report participants, the relational standard differs from the best interests standard in that it allows the interests of others, such as family and society, to decide whether to treat.

There is thus a dilemma that revolves around the indefinable nature of best interests, a lack of interests, and the notion that there is not an absolute requirement to attempt to prolong life in all situations. Singer, in arguing for nonvoluntary euthanasia of severely disabled infants, wrote:

[His] arguments presuppose that life is better without a disability than with one, and is this not itself a form of prejudice held by people without disabilities . . . the error in this argument is not difficult to detect. It is one thing to argue that people with disabilities who want to live their lives to the full should be given every possible assistance in doing so. It is another, and quite different thing, to argue that if we are in a position to choose, for our next child, whether that child shall begin life with or without a disability, it is mere prejudice or bias that leads us to choose to have a child without disability. If disabled people who must use a wheelchair to get around were suddenly offered a miracle drug that would, with no side effects, give them full use of their legs, how many of them would refuse to take it on the grounds that life without a disability is in no way inferior to life with a disability? In seeking medical assistance to overcome and eliminate disability, when it is available, disabled people themselves show that the preference for a life without disability is no mere prejudice.(223)

To use this as an argument to support nonvoluntary euthanasia of disabled infants does not appear to be coherent. First, even if we could predict, a supposed good life for a disabled infant is not necessarily commensurable with a possible good life for a nondisabled infant. If you ask a nondisabled adult, Which would you prefer, to live as you are now or in a wheelchair with poor sphincter control?, a reasonable response would be that, with the choices available, remaining ambulant and continent is not a bad or biased choice. However, if the choice is one between wheelchair existence or death in early infancy, then the response might be different. The argument is not which is a preferable life, if one could choose, but it is whether adult persons can make that decision for a disabled infant, based on the argument that it is so much more preferable to live a life as a nondisabled person. Of course we would prefer to have bright able-bodied children. There are many things we would all prefer, but the vulnerable have a right to protection, morally, socially, and in law, whether it is a preference to live a disabled life. This right to protection is bound by the duty of those with special interests in the child, such as parents or physicians, to protect the child. Preference utilitarianism is not only incorrect and unjust, it could justify a eugenics theory that many would find unacceptable.

Understanding, and agreeing on, what is meant by quality of life for another individual is subjective, a value judgment. Despite this, most of us can agree on disorders that would detract from the quality of living, chronic pain, frequent unpredictable poorly controlled seizures, chronic emotional distress and anguish, and so on. We also acknowledge that it is the duty of a physician to attempt to relieve these disorders, without further adding or substituting another unacceptable disorder. In general, physicians attempt this, and competent patients readily consent. There is no ethical discord here. But there is when the patient is not capable of consent and intervention will sustain life that is deemed by some to be of poor quality. The degree of this poor quality may not be entirely predictable. This is the situation that exists for an extremely preterm infant with brain damage. Prediction of this infant's present and future quality of life may be based on ignorance and prejudice. There may be ignorance of the type of lives lived by severely multiply handicapped individuals and prejudice toward the deformed and intellectually impaired. Quality of life judgments, in this situation, as with best interests, should be from the perspective of the disabled infant. As this is not knowable, in the present, and perhaps in the future, it could be argued that quality of life judgments should not be used to justify foregoing life-sustaining treatment for the extremely preterm infant. But there are those who believe there are situations where, in all likelihood, the future quality of life of a damaged infant "can confidently be judged to be undesirable for, and undesired by, any human being."(224)

They would then argue that it is ethically justifiable, in this situation, to forego life-sustaining treatment. Good people might disagree. Not based on a sanctity of life argument, but rather on the inability of the observer to know the mind of the infant with severe disability, however undesirable that future life might appear.

When making a decision to forego life-sustaining treatment for an extremely preterm infant is there a boundary beyond which most would agree stopping treatment is not unethical? There probably is, in our society, but there are difficulties recognizing this boundary in advance. There might be a high degree of consensus between all involved if there was certainty that the outcome would be a chronic vegetative state. The consensus would lessen if the outcome was a final mental age of 3 years. If we could predict this in the neonatal unit, would this be an acceptable boundary? To some it might, as the capacity for self-determination would be limited; to others it would not, for all the reasons previously stated. Specific prognostic uncertainty clouds the ability to make these decisions. Even when there is clear evidence, from clinical and radiological information, that a cerebral palsy syndrome will develop, the degree of severity may be difficult to predict. When outcome statistics are given for extremely preterm infants, they tell us little about the severity of handicap and the quality of life from the perspective of the disabled individual.

22

FUTILITY

Although often stated in medicine, the term *futility* has little agreed-on meaning without definition or qualification. The term should only be used with respect to a stated outcome. Physiologic futility is an ability to produce a desired physiologic response by any intervention.(225) Quantitative futility is the probable failure of any intervention to provide a benefit to a patient derived from previous knowledge and experience.(225) Qualitative futility refers to an intervention whose outcome is deemed not worthwhile.(225) The use of the term, defined and qualified, does not necessarily prescribe procedure and lead to a readily agreed on conclusion. Its use, defined and qualified, does provide an understandable topic for discussion that can be used in conjunction with moral theory and concepts. For example, when considering foregoing life-sustaining treatment for an extremely preterm infant, providing further intervention may be futile in terms of short-term survival or in terms of leading to a worthwhile life. These are qualifications of the term *futility*. The use of the term in this way helps to set the stage for discussion of scientifically derived facts and moral arguments that might apply to the act and consequences of life-sustaining treatment for an extremely preterm infant.

However, the term *futile* can trigger an emotional response that is counterproductive. For example, if parents disagree with physicians concerning the withdrawal of life-sustaining treatment from their infant, and they are told that the treatment is futile (qualified or otherwise), what they may hear is that they are being told that the treatment is not worthwhile, it is a waste of time, which may quickly become it is a bothersome waste of time. When the physician uses the term, what is meant is that the treatment in question cannot achieve a certain goal, and the use of the term strongly reflects his or her feelings concerning the continuation of treatment. Because the term has been used, it might only serve to entrench differences of opinion, however valid either opinion is. The word is best avoided in these situations. It might also best be avoided in discussions between health and allied professionals and reduce the risk of euphemistic misunderstanding. Professionals may still argue that they are not obliged to provide treatments they consider useless or harmful. One of the difficulties generated by the use of the term *futility*, and its pejorative nature, is that it threatens to change the focus of the argument from when it is right to forego life-sustaining treatment to one concerning power and influence, the right of parents to control what is happening to their child against a perceived professional authority of physicians. Tactful language is as much a part of the practice of medicine as it is of political diplomacy. That physicians, in practice, have the determining role in recognizing when it may be appropriate to forego life-sustaining treatment does not constitute the final step in the process. The next step is one of counseling, which is a complex subtle exercise that may turn on the use of a word. Skill in this counseling process is part of the art of medicine and can be the exercise of an ideal virtue. The virtue is that proper conduct leads to a lessening of harm, that is, conflict and misunderstanding, and the promotion of good, that is, the resolution of a question based on sound moral principles.

PART 3

REPORTS, OFFICIAL OPINIONS, AND GUIDELINES

23

UNITED STATES

The first important U.S. report that related to the extremely preterm infant came from a president's commission published in 1983.(226) In the section on seriously ill newborns, the commission reported that between 1970 and 1980 the neonatal mortality rate almost halved and that this was the greatest proportional decrease in any decade since national birth statistics were first recorded in 1915. The decrease was "especially dramatic" in the very low birth weight (<1,500g) and the extremely low birth weight (<1,000g) infants, with 50% of the latter surviving (at that time) compared to less than 20% twenty years previously. However, they noted that there was a downside to this, as the survivors could be impaired. This, they stated, tested "the limits of medical certainty in diagnosis" and "raises profound ethical issues." The commission attempted to provide ethical and legal guidelines in order to provide a framework for those in health care and the law. To aid them in this, testimony was provided by various experts. One such testimony came from Carole Kennon, a neonatal intensive care social worker, who stated that anguished parents "watching the suffering of an infant the size of an adult's hand – connected to awesome machinery and offered only distant prospects of a somewhat normal survival – inevitably takes an emotional toll"; and for those families who leave the unit with a handicapped child: "they must often travel a financially and emotionally perilous path." The commission also noted that withdrawing life support from a seriously impaired infant was a relatively frequent occurrence in U.S. neonatal intensive care units and this was usually following parent and physician agreement. But questioning of this system was reflected by the statement of parents Paul and Marlys Bridge that "we regard any decision making by concerned physician and parents behind closed doors of the pediatric unit as a haphazard approach."(227) This sentiment was supported by the commission who wrote that:

> appropriate information may not be communicated to all those involved in the decision;
> professionals as well as parents do not at times understand the bases of a decision to treat or not to treat; and
> actions can be taken without the informed approval of parents or other surrogates.

Further emphasis was made concerning the problems of adequate communication between physicians and parents, with a particular note on the "preconceptions held by physicians and parents about the quality of life of handicapped individuals." Physicians and parents may differ on who, in reality, has the final responsibility for continuing life-sustaining management. As Diane Crane wrote: "[V]ery few doctors seem to have given such matters enough consideration to have worked out a philosophical position toward them,"(228) and one parent told the commission: "I am very uncomfortable with the doctor assuming that if there are two equal choices, he will decide and take the responsibility."

In coming to their conclusions, the commission relied on the following concepts. The first was parental autonomy, and they stated that: "Public policy should resist state intrusion into family decision making unless serious issues are at stake and the intrusion is likely to achieve better outcomes without undue liabilities." Parental autonomy was to be balanced by the best interests of the child. If these interests did not appear to be followed, "the stage is set for public intervention." Quoting a U.S. Supreme Court decision (*Prince v. Massachusetts*, 321 US 158, 166, (1944)) they stated that "parents are not entitled to make martyrs of their children." They emphasized that parents or guardians must be given up-to-date relevant information from caring and empathic health care professionals. The commission acknowledged that best interests might be difficult to assess and recommended that conclusions be based on whether:

1. a treatment is available that would clearly benefit the infant.
2. all treatment is expected to be futile, or
3. the probable benefits to an infant from different choices are quite uncertain.

Beneficial therapies were those where there was "medical consensus that they would provide a net benefit to a child." Parents could choose between reasonable alternatives but should not "reject treatment that is reliably expected to benefit a seriously ill newborn substantially, as is usually true if life can be saved." Where the expectation of handicap entered into the consideration, the commission applied what they termed a very restrictive standard. That was that "permanent handicaps justify a decision not to provide life-sustaining treatment only when they are so severe that continued existence would not be a benefit to the

infant." Although they agreed that this was imprecise and subjective, their view was that applying this concept would exclude
idiosyncratic views, particularly if benefits and burdens were evaluated from the perspective of the infant.

The commission were clearer in their description of futile
therapies, which were those that offer no benefit and "no reasonable probability of saving life for a substantial period." Comfort,
pain relief, and respect for the dying patient and grieving family
were paramount. Where a course of action or where the interests of an infant are uncertain, the commission wrote that professional associations and health care institutions should "ensure
that the best information is available and is used when decisions about life-sustaining treatment are made." Specialist consultation should be available and sought. Although the commission acknowledged that the courts might adjudicate, in situations
where there was a dispute, they did not find this was a very satisfactory course. They observed that judicial proceedings take time.
This was stated ably by Kennon when she said in her testimony
that:

> I think we have . . . a real contrast in time-frame analysis
> between the medical and the legal profession. . . . When
> we talk about quick court decisions we are talking about
> 12 days. When I talk about quick, it means running down
> the stairs rather than taking an elevator . . . you have to
> understand when physicians want an answer they want
> it in 10 minutes. When lawyers produce an answer, they
> congratulate themselves for producing it in 10 days.

The commission were also critical of the adversarial nature
of the courts in these situations. They were particularly scathing
when considering the government regulations that followed the

Infant Doe case (*Infant Doe,* 52 US LW 3369 (1983)), of which more will be discussed later in this book. The commission wrote:

> Instead of adding further uncertainty to an already complex situation, the Federal government would do better to encourage hospitals to improve their procedures for overseeing life and death decisions, especially regarding seriously ill newborns. Using financial sanctions against institutions to punish an 'incorrect' decision in particular cases is likely to be ineffective and to lead to excessively detailed regulations that would involve government reimbursement officials in bedside decision making.

The commission concluded that "hospitals that care for seriously ill newborns should have explicit policies on decision making procedures in cases involving life sustaining treatment for these infants." This might require specialist consultation about a condition, or if the benefits of therapy are in dispute, or unclear, an ethics committee might be designated to review the decisions. Finally, they stressed that society should make provisions for handicapped children as there is "an obligation . . . to provide life continuing care that makes a reasonable range of life choices possible."

Thus the commission set the stage on which other opinion makers could perform, and on which bioethicists could pontificate, governments could regulate, and lawyers dissect.

In 1994, the American Academy of Pediatrics issued their guidelines on foregoing life-sustaining treatment.(229) They noted early in their statement that: "sometimes limiting or stopping life support seems most appropriate, especially if treatment only preserved biological existence or if the overall goal of therapy has shifted to the maintenance of comfort." They acknowledged that, philosophically speaking, there was little distinction between not starting treatment and discontinuing it. However, because uncertainty was often present, they recommended initiating an intervention that, if later proved to be unhelpful, could be stopped. Not only could it be stopped, it should be stopped, according to the Academy, as "continuing non-beneficial treatment harms many patients and may constitute a legal, as well as moral, wrong." This approach, they stated, was supported by the moral notion that the reasons to start or stop treatments are "based primarily on the relative benefits and burdens for the patient." Thus the introductory remarks in the Academy's guidelines favor a best interests approach and suggest consideration of quality of life when deciding on life-sustaining treatment for children. As with the recommendations in the earlier president's commission,(226) it was advised that informed parents should be the decision makers, when advised by the responsible physician. If there are disagreements that cannot be resolved, despite appropriate consultation, the courts can become involved. Physicians are responsible for providing adequate information and alternatives, but, the guidelines state, "they should recommend what they believe is the best option for the patient under the circumstances and give any reasons, based on medical, experiential, or moral factors, for such judgments. However, physicians should remind families that they may accept or reject the physician's recommendations." Although there is no clear answer to this, that is, who guards the guardians, the reader may want to consider the presumption that physicians may be the best moral arbiters when considering life and death decisions for children based on a best interests approach.

Over the next 2 years, the American Academy of Pediatrics published three more pertinent reports. Two were in 1995 through the Committee on Fetus and Newborn and one of these was in association with the American College of Obstetricians and Gynecologists.(230,231) The first report published concerned foregoing life-sustaining treatment for high-risk newborns, which included extremely preterm infants.(230) As with previous reports, this one stated that treatment should be based on what is in the best interests of the infant but qualified this by stating that what constituted "best interests" was not always clear. They stated that "intensive treatment . . . sometimes results in prolongation of dying or occasionally iatrogenic illness; nonintensive treatment results in increased mortality and unnecessary morbidity." The report's recommendations were as follows:

1. Ongoing evaluation of the condition and prognosis of the infant is essential, and the physician as the spokesperson for the healthcare team must convey this information accurately and openly to the parents of the infant.
2. Parents should be active participants in the decision-making process concerning the treatment of severely ill infants.
3. Humane care must be provided to all infants, including those from whom specific treatment is being withheld. Parents should be encouraged to participate in the care of their infant as much as they wish.
4. If the viability of the infant is unknown, or if the curative value of the treatment is uncertain, the decision to initiate or continue treatment should be based only on the benefit to the infant that might be derived from such action. It is inappropriate for life-prolonging treatment to be continued when the condition is incompatible with life or when the treatment is judged to be futile.(230)

The first three statements are no more than should be expected from good medical practice. The fourth statement only partially addresses the dilemma. Most would agree that life-prolonging treatment, such as artificial ventilation, is inappropriate for conditions that in the near future are inevitably terminal, whatever the management. However, in the last part of the sentence the committee stated that treatment is inappropriate when it is judged to be futile. Futility is not defined or qualified, but as conditions incompatible with life have been stated as reason for foregoing life-sustaining treatment, one can only presume that it is a life with unacceptable quality that is the criterion. No mention is made of how well the perceived criterion can be predicted nor what types or levels of disability are acceptable and why. The only guideline is the infant's best interest.

The second report is on perinatal care at the threshold of viability.(231) The committees acknowledge the relatively high mortality rates of preterm infants born at 25 weeks or less and the high proportion of disability, of varying severity, in the survivors. They noted that mortality and morbidity changes with each additional week of gestation and caution that practitioners "should allow for some error in the best estimate of gestational age and fetal weight." As they stated, even in ideal circumstances, the 95% confidence limits for a formula-based estimate of fetal weight are $\pm15\%$ to 20%,(232) and small discrepancies in the estimation of gestational age have major implications for survival and morbidity. They therefore recommended that when counseling, a range of possible outcomes should be given. They also noted that multiple gestation complicates the prognosis, as it relates to weight and gestation. The report then goes on to discuss modes of delivery and the need for frequent evaluations of the infant, including at birth, to determine management, as well as compassionate, dignified, treatment of the infant and family should there be a foregoing of life-sustaining medical treatment. However, no guidelines are given to help in how to determine when this should occur.

The third policy statement from the American Academy of Pediatrics came from the committee on Bioethics(233) and concerned the ethics and care of critically ill infants. The committee again followed a best interests approach, which they believed should be individualized for all children, regardless of age. They did make it clear that decisions regarding resource allocation, and distributive justice, should be addressed at the public policy level and not at the bedside. They allowed that "good medical practice may favor initiation of life sustaining medical treatment until clarification of the clinical situation and relevant ethical values can occur." However, they stated that "many think that laws, regulations, and government policies have unduly constrained parents and physicians from exercising reasonable judgments about whether to forgo life sustaining medical treatment." There was no clear guidance on what constituted a reasonable judgment for an extremely preterm infant, except that it should be made, by parents on the advice of physicians, on a case-by-case basis, and the judgments that are made should be equivalent to those made for critically ill older children. The inference here is that the recognition of benefits and burdens of life-sustaining treatment for the extremely preterm infant may be similar to, for example, that for an older child with end stage cancer. But the uncertainty of outcome may be very different. That the justice principle should apply to children, no matter what their age, is clear. But the principle is applied properly only if they have similar conditions. The committee summarized their recommendations as follows:

1. Decisions about critical care for newborns, and children should be made similarly and with informed parental permission.

2. Physicians should recommend the provision or for-going of critical care services based on the projected benefits and burdens of treatment, recognizing that parents may perceive and value these benefits and burdens differently from medical professionals.
3. Decisions to forgo critical care services on the grounds of resource allocation, generally speaking, are not clinical decisions, and physicians should avoid such "bedside rationing."(233)

This third policy statement provides little clarification on what constitutes moral legitimacy for forgoing life-sustaining treatment for the extremely preterm infant, except the use of the ill-defined terms *benefits* and *burdens*, which appear to have become a mantra. The statement, however, is useful, in part, because it invokes the principle of individual justice, which can be argued for the individual and for allocation of resources, but in different ways, in different venues.

In 2002, the American College of Gynecology and Obstetrics (ACOG) issued a practice bulletin on perinatal care at the threshold of viability,(234) which they defined as 25 or fewer completed weeks of gestation. They noted the very low prevalence of these births but their high contribution to perinatal mortality. They also recognized a past difficulty with interpretating the results of outcome studies because of variable methodologies, incomplete data, and small populations but believed the results from large multicenter studies provide sufficient detailed data to assist in the management of the extremely preterm infant (see Part 1). They emphasized the need to counsel parents on the basis of specific gestational age, estimated weight, and gender, as each affects outcome, and they quoted the National Institute of Child Health and Human Development (NICHD) Neonatal Research Network trial, which was a large prospective study of 4,633 infants weighing between 400g and 1,500g at birth, conducted at 14 tertiary centers across the United States between 1995 and 1996.(236) Based on this, and similar studies, three types of counseling recommendations were given. The first recommendations were based on good and consistent scientific evidence as follow:

> In general, parents of anticipated extremely preterm fetuses can be counseled that the neonatal survival rate for newborns increases from 0% at 21 weeks of gestation to 75% at 25 weeks of gestation, and from 11% at 401–500g birth weight to 75% at 701–800g birth weight. In addition, females generally have a better prognosis than males.

> In general, parents of anticipated extremely preterm fetuses can be counseled that infants delivered before 24 weeks gestation are less likely to survive, and those who do are not likely to survive intact. Disabilities in mental and psychomotor development, neuromotor function, or sensory and communication function are present in approximately one half of extremely preterm fetuses.(236)

These appear to be reasonable recommendations. But if the morbidity outcomes were stated as written to parents, they could be misleading. Using the study quoted by the college,(42) about 25% of the survivors would have severe disability. The remainder of the impaired survivors would have varying lesser degrees of disability, which include relatively mild learning and attentional difficulties. If the morbidity outcomes, for survivors, derived from birth weight reported by the NICHD study(98) are used, as they are in the text of the ACOG report, at age 18 months 57% of the tiniest babies with birth weights of 401–500g and 71% of those

REPORTS, OFFICIAL OPINIONS, AND GUIDELINES

weighing 501–600g had normal examinations. Although some of these survivors may have had intrauterine growth retardation, and therefore a potentially better prognosis, the point is that language can be manipulated, purposefully or otherwise, which affects communication with parents and thus their perceptions. The next type of counseling recommendations were stated to be based on limited or inconsistent scientific evidence and were as follows:

> Based on data from retrospective studies, maternal transport to a tertiary care center before delivery should be considered when possible.
>
> The effects of aggressive resuscitation at birth on the outcome of the extremely preterm fetus also are unclear. Therefore, management decisions regarding the extremely preterm fetus must be individualized.
>
> Prospectively collected outcome data for extremely preterm fetuses are available. Whenever possible data specific to the age, weight, and sex of the individual extremely preterm fetus should be used to aid management decisions made by obstetricians and parents of fetuses at risk for preterm delivery before 26 completed weeks of gestation. This information may be developed by each institution and should indicate the population used in determining estimates of survivability.(236)

The second recommendation in this set reflects the difficult conjectural nature of decision making when considering foregoing life-sustaining treatment for the extremely preterm infant. Stating that management decisions should be individualized begs the question and does little to clarify the dilemma. That is, in matters concerning life and death decisions, can a best interests approach be used, or a more substantive, but not certain, approach, such as survivability? The text of the report does not mention two papers published in 2000 by Jankov, Asztalos, and Skidmore(53) and Costeloe et al.,(56) that suggested that aggressive resuscitation at birth on an extremely preterm infant improved survival and did not appear to increase morbidity. The committee does state in the text that the ethics of this situation are complex and "the decision to withhold or withdraw support should not be made entirely on the basis of gestational age or birth weight, but should be individualized based on the newborn's condition at birth, survival and morbidity data, and the parents' preferences." But if the efficacy of aggressive resuscitation at birth is unclear, that just leaves parents' preferences. As the boundaries of parental preference remain arguable, the ethical dilemma remains but does allow for the resolution of a situation in a functional manner. How U.S. law responds to this will be seen later.

The final set of recommendations are based primarily on consensus and expert opinion and are:

> When extremely preterm birth is anticipated, the estimated gestational age and weight should be carefully assessed, the prognosis for the fetus should be determined, and each member of the health care team should make every effort to maintain a consistent theme in their discussion with family members regarding the assessment, prognosis, and recommendations for care.
>
> Because it is difficult to predict how an extremely preterm newborn will develop, proactive programs to assess and support the infant through early school years are desirable. When the extremely preterm newborn does not survive, support should be provided to the family by physicians, nurses, and other staff after the infant's death.(236)

In the same year as the ACOG report, the Committee on Fetus and Newborn of the American Academy of Pediatrics issued a further report on perinatal care at the threshold of viability.(236) This is similar to the ACOG report and covers the recorded mortality and morbidity rates of extremely preterm infants, the potential flaws in estimated birth weight and gestational age, the uncertainty of early prognosis, and the need for repeated reevaluations and repeated knowledge-based counseling of parents providing a range of possible outcomes. There were some important specific recommendations that, in full, were as follows:

> . . . non initiation of resuscitation for newborns of less than 23 weeks gestational age and/or 400g in birth weight is appropriate. Parents should be counseled that decisions about viability and neonatal management made before delivery may need to be altered in the delivery room and beyond depending on the condition of the neonate at birth, the postnatal gestational age assessment, and the infant's response to resuscitative and stabilization measures. Decisions regarding the extent of continuing support require frequent re-evaluations of the infant's condition and prognosis and reconsideration with the parents.
>
> When a decision is made to withhold resuscitation, discontinue resuscitation, or forgo other life-supporting treatments, the family should be treated with compassion, focusing on their needs. Humane and compassionate care must be provided to the nonviable or dying infant and the family. This includes careful handling, maintaining warmth, avoidance of invasive procedures, and unobtrusive monitoring – sometimes called comfort care.
>
> When medical support is discontinued or death is inevitable, time and opportunity should be provided for

the parents and other family members to hold, touch, and interact with the infant before and after the infant dies. Simple personalizing acts, such as naming the infant, obtaining a photograph, footprint sheet, crib card, name band, or even a lock of hair; and recording birth weight and other measurements may be important to the parents and should be provided. Clergy and supportive family and friends should be encouraged to have access to the infant in a setting that maintains dignity.

Support should be provided to the family by physicians, nurses, and other staff beyond the time of the infant's death. This may include referral to perinatal loss support groups, repeated telephone contact, other simple acts of condolence, and a conference with the family to review the medical events surrounding the infant's death and to evaluate the grieving response of the parents.

These are clearly virtuous statements and reemphasize the importance of decorum and empathy in the practice of pediatrics.

24

CANADA

In 1994 the Fetus and Newborn Committee of the Canadian Paediatric Society and the Maternal-Fetal Medicine Committee of the Society of Obstetricians and Gynaecologists of Canada published guidelines for the management of the woman with a threatened birth of an infant of extremely low gestational age.(237) Their recommendations were:

> According to current Canadian outcome data, fetuses with a gestational age of less than 22 completed weeks are not viable, and those with an age of 22 weeks rarely viable. Their mothers are not, therefore, candidates for cesarian section, and the newborns should be provided with compassionate care, rather than active treatment. The outcomes for infants with a gestational age of 23 to 24 completed weeks vary greatly. Careful consideration should be given to the limited benefits for the infant and potential harms of cesarian section, as well as to the expected results of resuscitation at birth. Cesarian section,

when indicated, and any required neonatal treatment are recommended for infants with gestational ages of 25 and 26 completed weeks; most infants of this age will survive and most survivors will not be severely disabled. Treatment of all infants with a gestational age of 22 to 26 weeks should be tailored to the infant and family and should have fully informed parents.

In the text of the report, the committees acknowledged the ethical complexities surrounding the extremely preterm infant and noted that the birth of a child with a gestational age of 22 to 26 weeks "is fraught with uncertainty concerning the chance of survival and the risk of impairment and disability." They noted the extreme difficulty of making a prognosis before birth and during the first few days after birth. The guidelines did not deal with later management in the neonatal intensive care unit. This was addressed in a position statement by the Bioethics Committee of the Canadian Paediatric Society.(238) They also invoked the best interests concept, but their interpretation allowed only a limited consideration of quality of life. They stated that the primary concern of physicians caring for children must be the best interests of the individual child, and all infants have intrinsic value and deserve respect and protection. Their view on mental or physical handicap as a determining factor was that "all children, regardless of handicap either actual or potential, have a justified claim to life and therefore to such medical treatment as is necessary to either improve or prolong life." They emphasized that the interests of the child were paramount over other interests and that "usually, the best interests of the child will favour the provision of life-sustaining treatment. This is self-evident where the result of the treatment will be survival of a child with no or little handicap, but should be equally true even when a chronic physical or mental handicap will continue to be present." Their exceptions to the general duty of providing life-sustaining treatment were:

1. irreversible progression to imminent death;
2. treatment that is clearly ineffective or harmful;
3. instances where life will be severely shortened regardless of treatment and where non-treatment will allow a greater degree of caring and comfort than treatment;
4. lives filled with intolerable and intractable pain and suffering.

Further guidelines were given concerning the responsibility for decision making and its implementation. Parents were morally and legally responsible for their children and for providing consent to their treatment. Exceptions to this were:

1. they are incompetent to make decisions for themselves,
2. there are unresolvable differences between the parents, or
3. they have clearly relinquished responsibility for the child. In that case, the identification of a legal guardian should precede any decisions regarding withholding treatment.

Other points included the intervention of the court should there be irreconcilable disagreement between physicians and parents. Where there was agreement, and life-sustaining treatment was foregone, it was recommended that there be a post hoc ethical review. The Canadian Paediatric Society issued a further position statement (B2004–01) in 2004, concerning treatment decisions for children.(239) It contained new information concerning consent and assent for treatment of children and adolescents but contained no new information or recommendation pertaining to the extremely preterm infant.

25

UNITED KINGDOM (UK)

In the UK, in 1997, the Royal College of Paediatrics and Child Health issued guidelines on foregoing life-sustaining treatment for children.(240) These were based on a best interests approach. Five situations were given where the foregoing of life-sustaining treatment might be considered:

1. Brain death
2. Permanent vegetative state
3. The "no chance" situation. The child has such severe disease that life-sustaining treatment simply delays death without significant alleviation of suffering. Medical treatment in this situation may thus be deemed inappropriate.
4. The "no purpose" situation. Although the patient may be able to survive with treatment, the degree of physical or mental impairment will be so great that it is unreasonable to expect them to bear it. The child in this situation will never be capable of taking part in decisions regarding treatment or its withdrawal.

5. The "unbearable" situation. The child and/or family feel that in the face of progressive and irreversible illness further treatment is more than can be borne. They wish to have a particular treatment withdrawn or to refuse further treatment irrespective of the medical opinion on its potential benefit.

Some might find the language used in these guidelines unsuitable (no purpose, no chance). Be that as it may, situation 4 demands specific accurate prognosis, is vague, and requires value judgments.

In 2000, the British Association of Perinatal Medicine (BAPM) issued a memorandum concerning fetuses and newborns at the threshold of viability.(241) They defined threshold viability as a gestation of 22 to less than 28 weeks (about 500–1,000g) but acknowledged that in developed countries the term was more often used in reference to infants of less than 26 weeks. The authors stated that because of the risk of disability or early death, serious ethical dilemmas were raised. The specifics of how these dilemmas should be addressed are not discussed. They do advise the use of a best interests approach but leave this to be interpreted by the reader. Some of their recommendations for management are as follows:

Decisions on management should be based on what is perceived by parents and their medical advisors to be in the child's best interest, uninfluenced by the child's gender or by religious, eugenic, demographic or financial factors.

Medical staff have a responsibility to keep parents informed as to the likely clinical outcome resulting from the decisions in which the parents need to participate.

Counseling must be honest and accurate. Parents may have unrealistic expectations not only as to what is medically possible but also as to future prospects for their infant . . . .

Perinatal mortality, morbidity and future outcome relate closely to gestational age at birth. There needs to be an agreed policy for the antenatal estimation of the expected date of delivery. This is usually based on early ultrasound measurements and the menstrual history. Physical examination of the infant after birth may lead to a revision of the original estimate. This needs to be explained in advance to parents who otherwise may be confused or feel that an error has been made . . . .

The perinatal team needs to be aware of up-to-date national statistics on infant mortality and morbidity outcome according to gestational age, as well as results of local audit. This should include the incidence and severity of disability amongst survivors at the age of 2 years or more. Following delivery, more accurate on-going advice concerning the individual child's prognosis will become available with the passage of time as the result of clinical observation and investigation.

Following counseling on the likely prognosis, some parents may wish to give advance authorisation for the non-resuscitation and non-provision of intensive car for infants at the extreme margin of viability. While appreciating their wishes, such authorization cannot be considered binding on the health care team . . . .

. . . It may be appropriate to institute intensive care to threshold-viability infants at birth until the clinical progress of the infant and further consultation with the parents has clarified whether it is better to continue or withdraw this form of medical care . . . .

. . . The doctor counseling parents on the withholding or withdrawal of life support should be senior and experienced. When appropriate the doctor may wish to consult colleagues or, in exceptional circumstances, an ethics committee or the courts . . . .

. . . The doctor counseling parents should be careful not to impose his or her own cultural and religious convictions on those whose beliefs may be different, bearing in mind the requirements of the law. When a doctor's beliefs prevent the disclosure of all possible management options open to the parents, the doctor has a duty to refer them to a colleague who is able to do so.

. . . When the parents do not agree with each other, or when they do not accept their doctor's advice on whether or not to withhold or withdraw care, treatment should be pursued until a change in the baby's status or further counseling and discussion clarifies the situation. Only as a last resort and in exceptional circumstances after all other options have been exhausted, should the problem be referred to the Courts.(241)

These examples of the guidelines issued by the British association are sensitive to a difficult situation. It is clear that they come from experienced clinicians who acknowledge uncertainty and the principle role of parents in the decision making but recognize limits to their autonomy. However, there is still no clear resolution of how much a perceived quality of life for a disabled child should play in the decision to forego life-sustaining treatment. There is not a clear answer to this, when the guidelines ask that a best interests standard be applied in a compassionate paternalistic manner. In the final analysis, this may be the best functional approach, but it places on the physicians an assumption that they have a uniformity of excellence in ethical and prognostic analysis that may not be the case.

In 2001, the British Medical Association published guidelines for foregoing life-sustaining treatment.(242) Although they continued to support the use of the term *best interests*, they were more specific in their interpretation and provided more detail than other definitions. The report stated that:

Legally and ethically decisions to treat or not to treat are justifiable only where this is in the child's best interests. But reasons for differences in perception may be significant and require further analysis. Willingness to continue with treatment may reflect the fact that a decision to stop striving to maintain life is emotionally more difficult to make for children than adults or that outcomes may be less predictable for children due to a small evidence base from which to judge the likely outcome. The developmental potential of children is also important and paediatricians will consider the quality of this potential for progression from incompetence as a factor in decision making . . . the ethical underpinnings of paediatric, adult, and geriatric medicine are the same . . . where there is reasonable uncertainty about the benefit of life-prolonging treatment, there should be a presumption in favour of initiating it, although there are circumstances in which active intervention (other than basic care) would not be appropriate since best interests is not synonymous with prolongation of life. Criteria for deciding best interests are the same as those for adults, including whether the child has the potential to develop awareness, the ability to interact and the capacity for self-directed action and whether the child will suffer severe unavoidable pain and distress. If the child's condition is incompatible with survival or where there is broad consensus that the condition is so severe that treatment would not provide a benefit in terms of being able to restore or maintain the patient's health, intervention may be unjustified. Similarly, where treatments would involve suffering or distress to the child, these and other burdens must be weighed against the anticipated benefit, even if life cannot be prolonged without treatment.(242)

The guidelines, as they relate to the extremely preterm infant, are now narrower. What constitutes a life not in the best interests of the child is one in which there is no awareness, no ability to interact, no capacity for self-directed action, as well as unavoidable severe pain and distress. This may be difficult to predict and only applies to a relatively small proportion of survivors. It would not apply to those destined to be moderately disabled.

26

FRANCE

In 2000, the French National Consultative Ethics Committee reported on ethical considerations regarding neonatal resuscitation.(243) They noted that in France extreme prematurity causes 50% of neonatal mortality and is associated with a high risk of serious sequelae. They reported that the survival rate for live births less than 24 weeks was 0%, and for those at 24 and 25 weeks, survival rates were 31% and 50% respectively. This is substantially less than U.S. figures. The committee noted the history and ethical dilemmas associated with extreme prematurity and stated that they did not aim to "set up rules or recommendations" but to help those involved find solutions by "highlighting the issues which need to be taken into account." The first issue they emphasized was prevention, which they strongly believed was a priority for health policy. They had previously noted a recent increase in prematurity that they had, in part, related to late pregnancies, multiple pregnancies and faulty or poorly monitored medical prescription of ovulation induction drugs, and the transfer of several embryos during in vitro fertilization. They urged control and research in this area, as well as accountable improvements in prenatal services

and further research into the causes and consequences of prematurity.

The next issue they wished to highlight was the practice of
nonmaleficence. This was expressed as respect for four "categorical
prescriptions": do no harm, prevent a harmful effect, eliminate a
harmful effect, and provide a beneficial effect. They realized that
for this to work it was necessary to consider what was desirable
and what we wish to avoid. They noted that what was desirable
was only defined "in the light of a person's rights, but what we
wish to avoid was the onset of major disability which would not
be beneficent." However, they stated that "independently of age,
state of health, and particularly handicaps human dignity and
value must be recognized as worthy of respect" and "a child is
obviously to be considered in the same way as any other human
being. Ethical principles applying to a person can and must apply
to a child." The committee recognized that because of an infant's
dependence, he or she deserved special consideration, but

> . . . to question or worry about the quality of life of a
> particular newly born infant or the child's future capacity
> for autonomy, and the kind of relationship which he or
> she may or may not establish with loved ones and the sur-
> rounding world is perfectly legitimate. However, that is no
> justification for a process of dehumanization which denies
> an endangered human child the right to dignity.(243)

The difficulty was putting into practice this respect for dignity.
They believed there was a further major difficulty, and that was that
severe disabilities are "sometimes . . . the adverse result of deliberate human action, the fruits of increasingly sophisticated medical
practice." Because of this, they pronounced that the nonmaleficence principle was "eminently applicable" and defined aggressive

and futile therapy as "irrational obstinacy," a failure of recognition that a newborn may be dying and cannot be cured. Following these strong words, they acknowledged prognostic uncertainty but tempered this with the statement that "there is also the issue of responsibility for irreversible damage which may be attributed to the treatment delivered . . . the actual process of neonatal resuscitation." The committee, having swayed the reader one way and then the other, stirred the stormy sea further by discussing the decision-making process. They stated that "the appraisement" of parents, even if they did not originate the medical decision, was the "sole criterion for evaluating the ethical demands of consent." Decisions concerning foregoing life-sustaining treatment must involve both health professionals and parents, but health professionals must avoid placing a burden of guilt on the parents, and they have an obligation to take full responsibility for professional decisions. I believe this infers incorrectly that one can differentiate between the ethical and the professional, in this situation. But the committee appreciates that there are intertwining ethical dilemmas. There is "conflict between several moral standards, all of which have a restricted degree of legitimacy." But having appreciated this, the committee returned to their previous strong reproachful tone:

> . . . [T]he lure of performance for performance's sake and ensuring survival of even younger infants, at the risk of severe future consequences for the child, is obviously (sic) non-ethical because it denies the notion of another's identity to satisfy either a narcissistic pursuit of personal satisfaction or a view of medical progress which has become completely disconnected from its true object, that is the well being of patients . . . these possibilities, including

extreme action, must be considered when discussing initiation of resuscitation, in spite of (or perhaps because of) uncertainty regarding consequences . . . it therefore does seem that all ethical considerations and responsibilities originate from the moment when the initial decision to resuscitate is taken.(243)

The committee opened their report by stating that they were not providing rules or guidelines and that decisions should not be based totally on the possible later chance of disability. However, their tone appears to contradict this: "when at the time of delivery, the possibility of disability-free survival is nil or negligible, initiating systematic or standby resuscitation raises the issue of futile therapy." This suggests that therapy that prevents death but ends in disability may be futile. The committee might argue that they are only referring to the severest of disabilities, perhaps bordering on a minimally conscious state. But this is not made clear, nor is it recognized that this latter outcome is a small proportion and not easily predicted early in the course of management. The committee goes further when they discuss the purposeful ending of life, not just foregoing life-sustaining treatment:

. . . [T]he issue of a medical ending of life sometimes arises. It is clear that this would be an obvious transgression of the law. . . . However when faced with tragedies for which no satisfactory solution can be found, there could perhaps be a measure of understanding for such transgression. Whatever outcome is chosen, whether or not it constitutes a transgression of texts of law as they are now applicable, there must be a guarantee that the decision is taken as a result of conscience-bound, humane, open and progressive processes, with due regard for the wishes of parents who alone are able to measure the burden of the life ahead of them.(243)

Some might find these frightening words that attempt to justify nonvoluntary euthanasia of an infant. However, the committee end their report by stressing the need to avoid difficult decisions relating to foregoing life-sustaining treatment for the disabled infant by early definitive measures, but then state that "these necessary efforts should not blind us to the lack of social investment in the management of disabled children." Whether there is general consensus among French neonatologists concerning the general approach given by the committee is arguable. In 2001, neonatologists from Marseille recommended that in the majority of situations intensive care should be given at birth *a priori*, (244) and decisions to withdraw treatment, on an individual basis, should be made later. They believed that gestational age– or birth weight–based restriction of access to intensive care may not be acceptable in most countries.

ITALY

The Italian Code of Profession Medical Ethics warns against treatment that will not bring a benefit or an improvement in quality of life (Codice di Deontologia Medica 1998 art 14). However, as will be described later, Italian law is very restrictive concerning quality of life decisions for neonates.

28

GERMANY

The German Society for Medical Law has strict recommendations concerning foregoing life-sustaining treatment for neonates. They are specific about stating that an infant's life should be protected, whether severely damaged or not. Any deliberate shortening of life is an act of killing.(247)

INTERNATIONAL

In 1988, 33 delegates from 10 countries met to produce a set of guidelines for discussion concerning decisions to forego medical treatment. A study edition of the guideline was distributed to 152 discussion groups that met in 15 countries for study and comment. Their responses were summarized for 24 delegates who met in Appleton, Wisconsin, and produced the document *The Appleton International Conference: Developing Guidelines for Decisions to Forego Life-Prolonging Medical Treatment.*(245) Part III dealt with decisions involving neonates. The guidelines were as follows:

1. Regard for the value of life does not imply a duty always to employ life-prolonging treatment for patients in this category. In setting reasonable limits for such treatment 'third person' judgments about quality of life are inevitable. Responsible third-person quality-of-life judgments consider, in so far as possible, how the options must appear from the perspective

of one in the patient's condition and determine what
would most reasonably be thought to count as quality
for most such patients.

The delegates warned that the quality of life judgment should
not be based on concepts of minimal social worth, which was
not morally justifiable. Some argued that to consider how options
appear to an infant, who has never been competent, is misguided.
They considered that this was an "inappropriate projection of others' interests onto the infant." Even so, it was felt that if a quality
of life judgment was to be made it was the responsibility of those
making the judgment to ascertain ". . . as far as possible, what most
such patients would count as quality."

2. Assessing quality of life of these patients for purposes
    of medical decisions involves weighing the ratio of
    benefits and burdens.(245)

Although it was agreed that there were differences between
people when weighting benefits and burdens, sometimes irreconcilable, the delegates, nonetheless, believed the terms useful "to
help focus on clinically significant variables and to avoid employ-
ing judgments of social worth." Perhaps, but it still begs the question what constitutes a benefit or a burden and to what degree do
they need to be present to justify foregoing life support?

3. In most decisions involving patients in this category,
    at least four sets of interest may be discerned:
    (a) the patient's
    (b) the surrogate's or family's
    (c) the doctor's and those of other caregivers
    (d) society's

Normally, the patient's interests should be regarded as paramount. However, difficult moral dilemmas arise when the patient's interests are unclear or clearly conflict with a number of other interests . . . it is important to remember . . . in the cases most commonly encountered, the various interests are not necessarily in conflict. Often the patient's own interest is integrally interwoven with the interest of the family and the community. Part of the doctor's clinical wisdom consists of responsibly weighing interests and creatively resolving apparently irreconcilable conflicts.(245)

This approach has been discussed in the previous section. But in summary, it is felt to be a mistake to impute altruism from an extremely preterm infant. Furthermore, there is no universal generic ethical wisdom that comes with a degree in medicine, though it may be easier to argue that there may be paternalistic hubris. The next two recommendations concern honest, effective communication and adequate documentation and are not dealt with here, in any more detail. The last two recommendations concern weighing benefits and burdens.

6.   When a patient lacks a surrogate, little difficulty arises when the benefit-burden ratio clearly favours administration and continuation of life-prolonging treatment. When the benefit-burden ratio is less certain or reversed, a wide variety of mechanisms have been proposed to aid or to review the doctor's decision-making.(245)

The reader is referred to a 1987 Hastings Center report,(222) which, as discussed in the previous section, uses a fairly restrictive, but subjective, quality of life standard to justify foregoing treatment. That is a condition that lacks potential for future relations or the probability of a life full of pain and suffering, which is worse than death. The problem with this is accurate prognosis. If uncertainty is acknowledged in the majority of situations, then those cases where the above criteria are undoubtedly fulfilled will be relatively few.

7. The doctor may appropriately withdraw or withhold life-prolonging treatment when, in the view of the informed surrogate and doctor, continued treatment would lead to unacceptable burdens without sufficient compensating benefits to the patient. What counts as a benefit or a burden and the relative ratio between them depends on specific situational factors and, therefore, good decisions in this category of patients demand individual discretion. While these patients possess vulnerability which makes them frequently subject to social discrimination and stigmatism, their interests are not protected by the elimination of decisional discretion. On the contrary, a trustworthy doctor and the processes of appropriate review are better means of protecting the interests of vulnerable patients.(245)

There seems to be little basis for this reasoning. The questions are not so much whether the infants' interests are not protected by the elimination of decisional discretion but whether the infant is particularly at risk if decisional discretion is too broad. Of course there needs to be trust between physicians and parents, and it is hoped that vulnerability and susceptibility to bias and ignorance will be appreciated by a physician. However, in matters concerning life and death the question must be asked, how much can we allow when the statement is "trust me, I'm a physician"?

In 1997 the International Federation of Gynecology and Obstetrics published a report on ethical aspects in the management of newborn infants at the threshold of viability.(246) The recommendations in this report are similar to those stated in the more recent guidelines in the United States and the UK concerning a threshold of viability (vide supra). A best interests approach is advocated, and this is determined by patients on the advice of experienced knowledgeable physicians.

In 2000, international guidelines for neonatal resuscitation were published by an international consensus group.(248) In these it was recommended that noninitiation of resuscitation in the delivery room was appropriate for infants with a confirmed gestation of less than 23 weeks or a birth weight of less than 400g. When there is an uncertain gestational age, options included a trial of therapy and noninitiation or discontinuation of resuscitation after assessment of the infant. Initiation of resuscitation at delivery did not mandate continued support. Withholding and withdrawing of life support were viewed as ethically equivalent, but the advantages of resuscitation and later withdrawal were that it allowed ongoing evaluation and counseling. Delayed, graded, or partial support were not encouraged.

In 2001, the Confederation of European Specialists in Paediatrics published recommendations concerning ethical dilemmas in neonatology.(249) They listed a number of ethical principles that could be applied to each newborn infant. These "principles" appeared to be tightly prescriptive. However, the confederation then placed their interpretations on these principles, which left the reader with more latitude on which to act, should he or she choose to follow these interpretations. Some of these principles and the confederation's interpretations are as follows:

Every human individual is unique and has the right to live its own life.

Every human individual has its own integrity which must be acknowledged and protected.

Every human individual has the right to optimal treatment and care.

Every human individual has the right to take part in society and what society has to offer.

The optimal purpose of all measures and decisions should focus on the "best interests" of the patients. It is acknowledged that the definition of "best interests" can be more difficult to establish in the newborn infant.

Decisions should not be influenced by personal or social views on the value of life or absence thereof by the caregivers.

Retardation or disability alone is not a sufficient reason to stop treatment.

Withholding or discontinuation of life support measures are ethically equivalent.

The opinion of parents or the responsible representatives should be included in all medical decisions. Doctors treating the sick infant first should come to the conclusion on the basis of comprehensive facts. This should then be discussed with parents in thoughtful dialogue.

Every form of intentional killing should be rejected in paediatrics. However, giving medication to relieve suffering in hopeless situations which may, as a side effect, accelerate death, can be justified.

All decisions have to be based on evidence as solid as possible.(249)

Some of these statements are not strictly principles but contain interpretations and qualifications. Be that as it may, further interpretations followed. In their discussion on whether every human has a right to be treated, the confederation made it clear that treatment need not necessarily be life sustaining: "When there is a right to be treated, then there is also the right to withhold treatment based on the best interests of the patient. Treatment can also consist merely of symptom relief."(249) The committee had already stated that the best interests of a newborn infant has difficulties. They noted the autonomy of an adult in situations of intractable suffering or imminent death and that parents act as surrogates for infants in decision making. The extent of this obligation was uncertain. Similarly, the duty of physicians to sustain life in all situations was uncertain. To address this, some ill-defined, but useful, recommendations were given to the reader when considering the prediction of the expected life of an infant:

Projected suffering and burden. If it can be foreseen that the life of the infant will be full of suffering and pain that cannot easily be relieved, one has to ask whether this is a life to be lived.

Communication with the environment. A unique feature of a human being is its possibility to interact with its environment. If this will never be possible, an important quality of life is lost.(249)

These conditions are difficult to predict in the extremely preterm infant, and if they could be predicted, a future life of intractable pain and suffering, or a life in which there is no possibility of any meaningful interaction, would apply to only a relatively few potential survivors.

> Dependence on medical care. The option for the child to live his or her own life can be severely impaired when they are almost completely dependent on medical care for survival. This can limit the development of the infant to an inaccessible degree.(249)

In itself, this is a reasonable statement. The question is whether this degree of dependency, on its own, is sufficient to justify foregoing life-sustaining treatment. The important part of the statement is, "almost completely dependent on medical care for survival."(249) Presumably this means survival, which is dependent on lifelong artificial ventilation, or dialysis and renal transplant followed by the burdens of immunosuppression. This is a difficult dilemma. But it is certainly an action that is taken for older children and adults, who have the ability to share in the decision. Even so, the situation would apply to very few extremely preterm infants.

> What is the life expectancy of the infant? One has to balance the life expectancy against the burden of treatment. If the burden of treatment is intense and the life expectancy rather short, initiation or continuation can be questionable.(249)

The term *rather short* is rather subjective and needs defining. Even so, foregoing life-sustaining treatment when death is imminent and irreversible is justifiable. Some judgment would have to be made concerning imminence. Further in their discussion, the confederation discuss the role of physicians and parents when death of the infant is imminent. They state that:

(a) the paediatrician should stop further medical treatment and use all possible resources to prevent suffering and pain of the infant and of the parents.

(b) the decision to stop treatment is a medical decision. The decision has to be communicated to the parents. The parents, however, cannot force the paediatrician to institute or continue a treatment when this treatment will only increase the suffering of the patient without any chance of survival.

In the reverse situation, where the parents want to forego life-sustaining treatment but the physicians do not, it is recommended that, after consultation with colleagues, treatment is continued and legal measures be taken.

PART 4

THE LAW

30

INTRODUCTION

Decisions regarding life-sustaining treatment for extremely preterm infants are frequent in neonatal intensive care units. These decisions are determined by prognostic judgment, the perceptions and ethical beliefs of health professionals and parents, and the prevailing law of the land. However, specific prognoses may be difficult and perceptions of later outcome and ethical beliefs are variable. There is disagreement concerning the circumstances in which life-sustaining treatment should be withdrawn or withheld and who should decide this. In different ways, legal practices have developed around the world that attempt to address this problem. Laws have arisen – cases, statutes, and legal code that, to a varying degree, indicate the authority and actions of physicians, parents, and the courts. Legal systems differ between countries and they may be single systems or federations where provinces or states can regulate medicine. Countries such as Britain, Canada, and Australia have common law systems where the law is based on judicial precedent and legislation. Holland, Poland, Germany, France, and Japan have civil and criminal codes, although courts of appeal can make authoritative rulings.(250)

The relationship between ethics and law has been discussed and argued since classical times and will continue to be argued. However, those that frame and adjudicate the law, at a minimum, are required to set clear acceptable operational boundaries. Laws are not determined, necessarily, by ethical rules. For example, in law the clinical conduct of a physician and the standard of care delivered may be considered acceptable if it follows the professional behavior of similar physicians in the community. But this is a legal standard not a moral one. Customary behavior is not perforce a moral justification. The arguments for moral and legal rules may share similar origins, but they are not, by definition, the same. An act that an agent commits in a special relationship may be justifiable morally, but the reasoning that makes it so may be insufficient, or incorrect, for that act to be permissible as a matter of public policy or law. How much the law should proscribe behavior will continue to be debated. To a large extent, in Western civilization there is a belief that the law will not intervene in moral matters except where society, through its representatives and the courts, finds it necessary to create or apply law to protect the public interest.(251) The boundaries of public interest are defined by the political process and are created to proscribe the conduct of people in a community whose moral values and behavior may vary. For it to be acceptable, the law must arise out of reason and thus be reasonable and prudent.

When considering types of treatment for, or the foregoing of life-sustaining treatment from, the extremely preterm infant, questions arise that concern both the law and morality. These involve concepts such as parental autonomy, state or physician paternalism to avoid harm, and the right of a physician not to have to give treatment that is of no benefit. Many approach these bioethical questions in a "legal frame of mind."(252) As Capron wrote, the focus is more often on the right of an individual to do something and who is the proper decision maker than it is on what is the right thing to do,(253) and as Hart stated,(254) there is ". . . the danger that law and its authority may be dissolved in man's conceptions of what law ought to be and the danger that the existing law may supplant morality as a final test of conduct and so escape criticism."

31

U.S. LAW

During the 1970s, it was a matter of public record that large numbers of infants died each year in U.S. hospitals as a result of the withdrawal or withholding of treatment,(255) and surveys demonstrated that a large percentage of physicians were willing to forego life-sustaining treatment for disabled infants.(256) In one study it was revealed that 85% of pediatric surgeons and 65% of pediatricians surveyed were willing to honor parental wishes not to perform necessary surgery on an infant with Down syndrome, but less than 6% would deny similar treatment for a child without the disability.(256) Furthermore, some physicians made decisions not to treat without parental consultation,(257) although on the basis of the law at the time it was generally considered unlawful.(258) In 1975, John Robertson, professor of law, wrote:

> In the case of a defective infant the withholding of essential care would appear to present a possible cause of homicide by omission on the part of parents, physicians, and nurses, with the degree of homicide depending on the extent of premeditation. Following a live birth the law

generally presumes that personhood exists and that there is entitlement to the usual protections, whatever the specific physical or mental characteristics of the infant may be. Every state imposes on parents a legal duty to provide necessary medical assistance to a helpless minor child. If they withhold such care, and the child dies, they may be prosecuted for manslaughter or murder . . . likewise physicians and nurses may face criminal liability . . . even when all parties, including the parents, are in agreement.(259)

In the United States, the treatment of a patient without valid consent constitutes a battery,(260) and it is parents who ordinarily decide what medical treatment is appropriate for their children:

It is cardinal with us that the custody, care, and nurture of the child resides first in the parents. . . . (261)

If there is disagreement between parents and physicians a court can consider prognosis without treatment. In *Newmark v. Williams*, the court refused to order painful and invasive chemotherapy for a child with leukemia where it was judged that the treatment had only a 40% chance of success.(262) However, the state has a compelling interest to preserve human life, which justifies interference with individual rights.[263] These include the right of parents to make medical decisions for their children(264–266) and a constitutional right of privacy in child rearing.(267–268) But this parental authority is limited if it is held that parental actions might threaten the health or safety of a child,(261,269) for example, parents' decisions to withhold consent for necessary blood transfusions for religious reasons.(270–271) The common law doctrine of *parens patriae* permits the state to exercise protection and guardianship over persons disabled by means of minority, insanity, or incompetency,(272) and this doctrine has a long legal history. However, 30 years ago parents and physicians were left to make life and death treatment decisions concerning disabled infants. In 1971, three babies with Down syndrome and intestinal atresia were born at Johns Hopkins hospital. Two were "allowed" to die, at the parents' request, and the parents of the third requested treatment for their infant, who survived.(273–274) This type of approach was made more evident by two Yale pediatricians who published that they had accepted parents' decisions to forego treatment on 43 impaired infants who, they stated, subsequently died early.(275) This article was, to some extent, a response to one published in 1971 by the English physician John Lorber, who suggested that some babies with myelomeningoceles were so severely impaired that it was better for them not to receive treatment.(276) Similar criteria to those selected by Lorber for deciding on nontreatment of an infant with a myelomeningocele were used in some U.S. centers.(273) But there was a reaction to this type of approach at the federal level of government. In Bloomington, Indiana, in 1982, Baby Doe was born with Down syndrome and a tracheo-esophageal fistula.(277) The child's parents and obstetrician wanted no surgical intervention, as the obstetrician believed there was a dismal prognosis. The hospital administrators and members of the pediatric staff disagreed.(273) An unrecorded nighttime hearing was conducted in the hospital by county judge John Baker, without the appointment of a guardian ad litem for the infant, and he ruled that the parents had the right to make the decision about treatment versus nontreatment.(278) The case was appealed up to the U.S. Supreme Court,(279) but was not heard as the baby had died. The U.S. Commission on Civil Rights, when reviewing this case, stated that the prognosis given by the obstetrician was: ". . . strikingly out of touch with the contemporary evidence on the capabilities of people with Down syndrome."[278]

Prior to the commission, there was a reaction from the White House administration. The publicity surrounding the Infant Doe case was the impetus that prompted President Reagan to direct the Departments of Justice and Health and Human Services (HHS) to mandate treatment services in future similar cases.(277) To avoid a conflict between federal and state law, the latter defining crimes such as homicide and gross negligence,(273) new rules were announced pursuant to section 504 of the Rehabilitation Act of 1973, which bars discrimination against the handicapped in programs receiving federal assistance, such as hospitals that accept Medicare and Medicaid patients. The new rules barred hospitals from denying medical care to infants on the basis of handicap, and violation of this would lead to loss of federal funds. Opposition to any such denial was encouraged by the creation of "Baby Doe squads" comprised of lawyers, administrators, and physicians who could be available at short notice to investigate alleged violations of the Act.(277) Accusations that these had occurred could be made anonymously through a toll-free number that was openly advertised and easily seen by anyone visiting or working in neonatal units. But the courts did not support this interpretation of the Rehabilitation Act, and the U.S. District Court for the District of Columbia, in *AAP v. Heckler 280*, ruled that it "could never be applied blindly and without consideration of the burdens and intrusions which might result." The regulations were revised but were again invalidated by the court.[281] Around the same time, two lawsuits were in the courts concerning Baby Jane Doe.(282) This baby was born with a myelomeningocele and hydrocephalus and transferred to the State University of New York campus at Stonybrook. The attending surgeon, Arjen Kenscamp, recommended immediate surgery, but the child neurologist who was involved, George Newman, advised against this, stating later that "the child was not likely ever to achieve any meaningful interaction with her environment, nor ever achieve any interpersonal relationships, the very qualities which we consider human."(282) The parents did not consent to surgery but requested palliative care, which included food, water, and antibiotics. The parental refusal to consent to surgery was challenged in court by an independent attorney, who sought to be appointed guardian ad litem for the child, although he had no legal relationship to the child or the circumstances of the birth. A New York State lower court ruled that surgery should be performed, but the ruling was reversed on appeal, and this was affirmed by the state's highest court, but on the grounds that the attorney had no genuine connection with the circumstances and thus had no standing or right to bring such litigation, which, they stated was the responsibility of the state's child protection services.(283) Furthermore, as there were, in the opinion of the court, two medically reasonable options, the law allowed the parents the choice. The second, and more important, Baby Jane Doe lawsuit was brought by the U.S. Department of Health and Human Services and was based on the Rehabilitation Act revised rules concerning disabled infants. The department wanted to inspect the hospital records to evaluate whether there had been a violation of Baby Jane Doe's civil rights. The hospital refused to make available the records, in part because of parental refusal to consent to the release. Two lower Federal courts held that Congress did not intend to authorize review of individual medical decisions for disabled infants under section 504 of the Act, and the case went to the U.S. Supreme Court,(284) which affirmed this decision, stating:

> In broad outline, state law vests decisional responsibility in the parents, in the first instance, subject to review in exceptional cases by the state acting as *parens patriae* ... the

Federal government was not a participant in the process of making treatment decisions for newborn infants. We presume that this general framework was familiar to Congress when it enacted section 504 . . . the Secretary has acknowledged that a hospital has no statutory treatment obligation in the absence of parental consent and it has become clear that the "Final Rules" are not needed to prevent hospitals from denying treatment to handicapped infants. . . . By itself, section 504 imposes no duty to report instances of medical neglect . . . that undertaking derives from state law reporting obligations or a hospital's own voluntary practice.

The Supreme Court made it clear that parental consent was a matter of state law, and exercise of this consent, as well as other rights, accorded to the traditional family were protected under the Constitution.(285,286) The Court was particularly critical of HHS when they ruled that:(284)

1. HHS has no authority to compel medical treatment absent parental consent.
2. Parental refusal to consent does "not equate with" refusal by a hospital or physician to treat.
3. HHS's "perception that the withholding of treatment in accordance with parental instructions necessitates federal regulation is manifestly incorrect."
4. "[S]tate child protective service agencies are not field offices of HHS bureaucracy and they may not be conscripted against their will as foot soldiers in a federal crusade."
5. HHS's view "that the basic provision of nourishment, fluids, and routine nursing care" was "not an option for medical judgment" was untenable.

The rulings of the Supreme Court should not be viewed as negating the role of the federal government in the protection of life, which is ranked first in the Declaration of Independence. However, it is the states that carry the legislative responsibility for child protection and welfare. In addition, the Supreme Court ruling is an example of the balance of powers that, in this case, curtailed the heavy-handed approach of the White House administration.

The response to *Bowen* came from Congress, rather than directly from the White House administration, and was in the form of amendments to The Child Abuse Prevention and Treatment and Adoption Reform Act (PL 93–247, 88 stat 4 (1974)). These were the Child Abuse Amendments of 1984 (PL 98–457), also known as the Baby Doe rules, and they made conditional the receipt of certain federal funds by a state on that state satisfying certain criteria. These criteria were that a state would respond, under state child abuse laws, to cases of medical neglect (42 USC 5106 (b) (2) (B)). Medical neglect was defined as "withholding of medically indicated treatment" from disabled infants with "life threatening conditions." Medically indicated treatment was then effectively defined as treatment:(287)

> which, in the treating physician's reasonable medical judgment, will be most likely effective in ameliorating or correcting all [of the infant's life threatening] conditions, except that the term does not include the failure to provide treatment . . . to an infant when, in the treating physician's reasonable medical judgment,
>
> (A) the infant is chronically and irreversibly comatose;
> (B) the provision of such treatment would (i) merely prolong dying, (ii) not be effective in ameliorating or correcting all of the infant's life threatening condition,

or (iii) otherwise be futile in terms of the survival of the infant; or

(C) the provision of such treatment would be virtually futile in terms of the survival of the infant and treatment itself under such circumstances would be inhumane.

It is important to note that these amendments were interpretative guidelines and came with commentary.(288) "Virtually futile" was interpreted as:

"highly unlikely to prevent death in the near future" on the basis of reasonable medical judgment (45 CFR pt 1340 app at 306).

A treatment is inhumane if:

the treatment itself involves significant medical contraindications or significant pain and suffering for the infant that clearly outweigh the very slight potential benefit of the treatment for an infant highly unlikely to survive . . . the balance is clearly to be between the very slight chance that treatment will allow the infant to survive and the negative factors relating to the process of the treatment.(288)

A conference committee report added that:

the use of the term inhumane is not intended to suggest that the consideration of the humaneness of a particular treatment is not legitimate in any other context; rather, it is recognized that it is appropriate for a physician, in the exercise of reasonable medical judgment, to consider that factor in selecting among effective treatments (US CCAN 2969, 2970 (1984)).

In the commentary to the amendments, the primary role of parents is made clear, except in specific circumstances, which are defined: ". . . except in highly unusual circumstances, decisions to provide or withhold medically indicated treatment should be made by the parents or legal guardian" (50 Fed. Reg. 14, 878 14, 880 (1985)). Although the commentary also stated that: "the parents role as decision maker must be respected and supported unless they choose a course of action inconsistent with applicable standards established by law" (50 Fed. Reg. 14, 880).

It is state law that applies under such circumstances. The Child Abuse Amendments do not prescribe medical treatment, nor do they determine specific state law, in this respect. Rather they require state child protective services:

> to pursue any legal remedies including the authority to initiate legal proceedings in a court of competent jurisdiction, as may be necessary to prevent the withholding of medically indicated treatment from disabled infants with life threatening conditions (45 CFR s 1340.15 (c) (2) (iii)).

But, as Frader wrote, by the time the Baby Doe rules came into force, practices relating to disabled infants had begun to change in the United States, and the "heavy-handed" federal approach likely had more political significance than production of meaningful changes in the care of most disabled infants.(289)

A further effort by the federal government to regulate physicians' actions can be found in the Born Alive Protection Act of 2001, which became Public Law 107–207 in 2002. The law established that:

infants who are born alive, at any stage in development, are persons entitled to the protections of the law . . . regardless of whether or not the infant's development is believed to be, or is in fact, sufficient to permit long term survival, and regardless of whether the infant survived an abortion.(290)

However, a report from the Committee on the Judiciary stated that the Act: "would not mandate medical treatment where none is currently indicated . . . and would not affect the applicable standard of care, but would only insure that all born alive infants – regardless of their age . . . are treated as persons for purposes of Federal law."(290) It was the opinion of the American Academy of Pediatrics that the debate regarding the efficacy of providing treatment to extremely preterm infants was not relevant in the context of this law.(290)

The situation is that U.S. courts do not judge what they believe is a correct medical option, which might differ from that chosen by parents; rather, it is for state courts to proscribe parental or medical neglect. There is no neglect, in terms of medical care, when parents select from among professionally recommended options for treatment and "have provided an acceptable course of treatment for their child in light of all the surrounding circumstances."(291) The Baby Doe rules do not compel state courts to follow federal regulations. The federal statute stipulates that child protective services, a state body, have the authority, in certain circumstances, to pursue any legal remedies that may be necessary to prevent the foregoing of life-sustaining treatment.(292) This does not guarantee that the federal standard will be applied in state courts as the statute sets criteria for federal funding of state programs and does not set legal standards independent of state law. On this basis, federal law supremacy doctrines probably would not apply.(258)

It is up to the states, through their own law, to judge the matter. As has been shown, there are two doctrines that may clash: respect for parental autonomy when making health care decisions for their children and the state's right to protect children against harm. In general the U.S. courts are unlikely to override a reasonable parental decision not to treat if the condition is not extremely severe or life threatening, particularly if the condition can wait until the child is old enough to participate in the decision(293,294) or if there are risks that outweigh benefits.(266) An infant's lack of capacity allows parents, as natural guardians, to act in the best interests of the child.(288,295–302) The exercise of this legal right is rebuttable if the decisions or actions of the parents are not in the best interests of the child or amount to neglect or abuse.(262,288,295,303–309) But it has not always been certain how state courts will rule in matters concerning disagreements between parents and physicians concerning the foregoing of life-sustaining treatment from an infant. *In re Steinhaus*,(310) shortly after the Baby Doe rules had been issued, it was held that it would not constitute neglect to issue a do not attempt resuscitation order for a baby who was diagnosed as being in a chronic and irreversible comatose state. But *in re KI*, this order was also authorized, despite parental objection, for an infant whose condition, allegedly, did not satisfy the federal criteria for withholding treatment from a disabled infant.(311)

As the states were writing and modifying their statutes dealing with end of life issues, a number of landmark cases were heard that influenced these statutes and the action of health professionals. They have in common the drama of the law courts; intensive care units caring for the most fragile and moribund infants; and the actions and anguish of distraught parents. In Illinois in 1991, the Health Care Surrogate Act was signed into law. It followed a well-publicized case that occurred at the Presbyterian-St. Luke's

Center in Chicago.(312) In August 1988, Sammy Linares, an infant aged 6 months, had become asphyxiated by inhaling a rubber balloon and suffered a cardiac arrest. He was maintained on life support in a persistent vegetative state. In April 1989, following a refusal by the hospital and attending physicians to discontinue life support in the absence of a court order, the father, Rudy Linares, performed this act while keeping hospital workers at bay with a hand gun. This followed an incident the previous December when the father had disconnected the baby from the ventilator, but was physically restrained by security guards while the ventilator was reconnected.(312) Despite the manner in which the father acted, there clearly was much sympathy for him. A coroner found that asphyxiation from a balloon was the primary cause of death,(312) and a grand jury declined to issue an indictment for homicide. Mr. Linares did receive a suspended sentence for a misdemeanor arising from a weapons charge. The statutory law that followed made it clear that life-sustaining treatment could be withdrawn, without judicial involvement, from a patient without decisional capacity. The conditions that would allow this were that a surrogate could request withdrawal if two physicians certified one of the following:

(a) imminent death; that is, when death is inevitable within a short time, "even if life sustaining treatment would be initiated or continued";
(b) permanent unconsciousness, for which initiating or continuing life support, in light of the patient's medical condition, provides only minimal medical benefit;
(c) incurable or irreversible condition that imposes severe pain or an inhumane burden that will ultimately cause the patient's death and for which initiating or continuing life-sustaining treatment provides only minimal medical benefit.

The Act protects the parties involved provided they follow the legislation "with due care."

Perhaps a less clear-cut case for the exercise of the quality of mercy is that involving baby Messenger who was born in Michigan. In this instance, the mother went into premature labor at 25 weeks' gestation. The parents were informed that there was a 50–75% chance of mortality and a 20–40% chance of severe cerebral hemorrhage and neurological damage.(313) I would certainly argue that these estimates are too high, but nevertheless these are the figures that were given to the parents. They instructed the neonatologist not to take "extraordinary" measures. However, it was a physician assistant who attended the baby at birth and she resuscitated the baby despite a previous instruction that this should only occur if the baby was vigorous and active at birth. This was not how the baby appeared at birth,(194) which is not particularly unusual for a 25 week, 750g extremely preterm infant. It was after the neonatologist told the parents that she wanted to continue intensive care, at least in the short term, that the father, in the presence of his wife but no others, disconnected the baby from the ventilator, and the baby died shortly thereafter. Not surprisingly, the father was arrested and charged, but the jury found him not guilty. This was despite the fact that at the time the artificial ventilation was removed the baby was in no imminent danger of dying and there was no evidence of severe neurological damage. The Messengers, in their testimony, denied that their actions were because of fear that their child may survive handicapped, but that he might suffer when the likely outcome, they believed, was death.(314)

Parents have the right to be informed to give consent, in the same manner as a competent adult patient, which includes being given alternatives, provided the alternative is legally acceptable.(315) If there is a genuine emergency situation consent may be waived, but it is doubtful that information can be withheld from parents on the basis of therapeutic privilege.(288) In November 1991, in Georgia, Mary Elizabeth Bethune was delivered by her father at the side of the road. She was 24 weeks gestation and weighed 500g. She was taken to the hospital profoundly hypothermic, where she was resuscitated and placed on a ventilator. However, she was considered to be in the process of dying and that her condition was terminal. Thus life support measures were removed, without consent according to the parents, and they sued for wrongful death (*Velez v. Bethune*(316)). The court stated that: "The doctor had no right to decide, unilaterally, to discontinue medical treatment even if the child was terminally ill and in the process of dying. That decision must be made with the consent of the parents (see *In re Jane Doe*(317))."

In contrast, in Milwaukee, Wisconsin, the parents of a baby born at 24 weeks' gestation sued physicians, alleging that they were not sufficiently informed of the risk of disability to their son and that they should have been allowed to decide on whether to treat.(318) However, the appeals court found that the conditions that allowed the foregoing of life-sustaining treatment had not been met and that there was not an absolute right for parents to decide whether to resuscitate a newborn or withhold life-sustaining treatment following informed consent. The court stated that:

> if the parents' claim is allowed to proceed, courts will be required to decide which potential imperfections or disabilities are . . . "worse than death." They will have to determine which disability entitles a child to live and which disability allows a third party surrogate to withhold or withdraw life sustaining treatment with the intent to allow a disabled person to die . . . such a process, not unreasonably, has kaleidoscopic, unending implications.(319)

Parents were also overruled in *MacDonald v. Milleville* with a judgment that went against the later one given in *Velez v. Bethune*.(316,320) Baby MacDonald was born in Milwaukee at 23–24 weeks' gestation, after a difficult breech extraction. The baby was pale, apneic, and bradycardic. After 10 minutes' resuscitation using an Ambu bag, but not intubation, chest compressions, or medications, the baby remained bradycardic with a heart rate of less than 60/minute. The baby was wrapped in a blanket and handed to the parents, who were told the baby was dying despite the best efforts of the staff. About an hour later, a faint cry was heard, and the baby was found to have a heart rate of 130/minute. At this stage the baby was intubated and placed on a ventilator and went on to show severe brain injury, characterized by incapacitating cerebral palsy and profound mental retardation. The parents sued the doctor and hospital, claiming that failing to fully resuscitate constituted negligence and that stopping the partial resuscitation violated the doctrine of informed consent. The ethical and legal question in this case is whether, at the time of the delivery, a firm judgment could be confidently made that aggressive resuscitation would "offer no immediate or long term benefit."(321) Certainly, in 1989 when the baby was born, this was a widely held belief among neonatologists,(320) and physicians do not have a legal duty to provide ineffectual treatment.(322) The court found that the doctor was not obliged to seek authorization to cease resuscitation in the situation in which he found himself, and his actions were not negligent.

How the law has developed in Texas and been applied in the higher courts may reflect what would happen in the future in other parts of the United States. Between 1977 and 1995, the Texas legislature enacted three advance directive laws for end of life treatment decisions. In 1977, Texas recognized "living wills," which were called "directives to physicians." This statutory law was part of the Natural Death Act,(323) which was followed by the Durable Power of Attorney for Health Care in 1989.(324) In these statutes were included situations in which parents, or legal guardians, in conjunction with physicians, could forego life-sustaining treatment for infants. In 1997, in an attempt to address various inconsistencies in the law, a single comprehensive advance directive law was passed by both houses(325) but was vetoed by then Governor George W. Bush because of, as alleged by some,(326–327) pressure from a Right to Life group. Eventually the Act was passed and resulted in a new chapter 166 of the Health and Safety Code, entitled the Advanced Directives Act.(328) The new act does not specifically provide requirements for infants, disabled or otherwise, but refers inter alia to patients less than 18 years of age. A licensed physician may be directed by parents or a legal guardian (166.035) to forego life-sustaining treatment from these patients if they have a terminal or irreversible condition that has been diagnosed and certified in writing by the attending physician. A terminal condition means "an incurable condition caused by injury, disease, or illness that according to reasonable medical judgment will produce death within six months, even with available life sustaining treatment provided in accordance with the prevailing standard of medical care" (166.002). An irreversible condition means a condition, injury, or illness:

(A) that may be treated but is never cured or eliminated;
(B) that leaves a person unable to care for or make decisions for the person's own self; and
(C) that, without life sustaining treatment provided in accordance with the prevailing standard of medical care is fatal (166.002).

Life-sustaining treatment means treatment that:

> Based on reasonable medical judgment, sustains the life of a patient and without which the patient will die. The term includes both life sustaining medications and artificial life support, such as mechanical breathing machines, kidney dialysis treatment, and artificial nutrition and hydration. The term does not include the administration of pain management medication or the performance of a medical procedure considered to be necessary to provide comfort care, or any other medical care provided to alleviate pain. (166.002)

The Act also specifically states that: "this subchapter does not condone, authorize, or approve mercy killing or permit an affirmative or deliberate act or omission to end life except to permit the natural process of dying as provided by this subchapter" (166.050).

An important aspect of the Act was the inclusion of a process for resolving disagreements between treating physicians and legal guardians (166.046). This process created an unprecedented legal role for ethics committees.(327) The Act also provided legal protection for health care personnel and institutions provided the statutory process was followed (166.045): "a physician, a health professional acting under the direction of a physician, or a health care facility is not civilly or criminally liable or subject to review or disciplinary action by the appropriate licensing board if the person has complied with the procedures outlined. . . ." The new Act now mandated that should there be a dispute between parties concerning the foregoing of life-sustaining treatment, there should be an ethics committee consultation, a reasonable attempt to transfer the patient to another provider, and the continuation of life-sustaining procedures for a minimum of 10 days after the ethics committee has provided a written explanation of its review process to the treating physicians and legal guardians. If the dispute continues after this 10-day period, and a new treating physician or health care establishment has not been found, there is no longer an obligation under the statute to continue the life-sustaining treatment (166.046). The aim of this 10-day rule is to provide time during which transfer of the patient might be arranged, and it also enables discussions to continue between the relevant participants. Furthermore, it provides a more orderly approach for families if they should seek judicial review after all reasonable attempts at agreement have failed (166.046).

Two important cases occurred in the Texas courts, the outcomes of which probably reflect the direction other state courts may take. In *Stolle v. Baylor College of Medicine*,(329) the legal arguments mainly concerned whether section 672.016(b) of the Natural Death Act allowed immunity to physicians who did not comply with a written instruction from parents to withhold life-sustaining treatment from their infant. The parents sought damages for negligent disregard of their instructions not to use "heroic efforts"(329) or artificial means to prolong the life of their child. The circumstances were that in 1991 the mother gave premature birth to twins. One of the twins died soon after mechanical ventilation was withdrawn; the other twin survived and suffered a grade IV intraventricular hemorrhage. She was transferred to a large children's hospital where a neurological consultation concluded that she had irreversible brain damage and would have a neurological deficit.(329) The following day the parents executed a written Directive to Physicians on behalf of their infant in which they stated that her life should not be artificially prolonged under the circumstances provided in the directive. The wording was that life-sustaining treatment could be withheld if the infant was certified by two physicians (the new Advanced Directives Act requires only one physician) as having a terminal condition. About 1 month later, the baby had an apneic episode with brady-cardia following aspiration of some of her feed. A nurse administered chest compressions for about 1 minute and the episode ended.

When the case went to court, a summary judgment was given against the parents and this was affirmed on appeal. Smith J, giving the majority opinion, stated that "... the parents do not cite us any authority that would have allowed the the withdrawal or withhold-ing of life sustaining procedures in a lawful manner." The limits of parental influence were also demonstrated in *Hospital Corporation of America v. Miller.*(330) In 1990, the mother of Sidney Ainsley Miller went into premature labor and was admitted to a Houston hospital. The baby was estimated to be 23 weeks gestation with an approximate weight of 629g.(330) Both the obstetrician and the neonatologist told the parents that should the baby survive she would be impaired, and the parents requested "no heroic mea-sures," which was recorded in the hospital chart. The parents were also informed that if the baby was born alive and weighed over 500g, the medical staff would be obliged by law and hospital policy to perform life-sustaining procedures.(330) The parents expressed again that they did not want the baby resuscitated. Later that night the mother gave birth, and the baby was resuscitated. She survived and subsequently developed severe neurological impairment. The parents sued the Hospital Corporation of America asserting: 1) vicarious liability for the actions of the hospital in: a) treating Sidney without consent; and b) having a policy that mandated the resuscitation of newborn infants weighing over 500g even in the absence of parental consent; and 2) direct liability for failing to have policies to prevent such treatment without consent. Based on the jury's finding of liability, the trial court entered judgment in favor of the parents in the amount of $29,400,000 in past and future medical expenses, $13,500,000 in punitive damages, and $17,503,066 in prejudgment interest. This verdict was appealed to the Court of Appeals and was reversed. The defendant's arguments were that they did not owe the parents the tort duties they claimed had been breached. They could not be liable for battery or negligence in treating Sidney without parental consent and against their instructions as there was a legal obligation to do so and because the parents had no right to withhold life-sustaining treatment from Sidney. Justice Edelman rendered the majority opinion and stated that there were three fundamental but competing legal and policy interests:

> On the one hand Texas law expressly gives parents a right to consent to their children's medical care.(331) Thus, unless a child's need for life sustaining medical treatment is too urgent for consent to be obtained from a parent or other person with legal authority . . . a doctor's treatment of the child without such consent is actionable even if the condition requiring treatment would eventually be life threatening and the treatment is otherwise provided without negligence(332) . . . the logical corollary of a right of consent is a right not to consent . . . in Texas the Advance Directives Act, formerly the Natural Death Act (collectively, the "Act") allows parents to withhold or withdraw life sustaining medical treatment from their child where the child's condition has been certified in writing by a physician to be terminal i.e. incurable or

irreversible, and such that even providing life sustaining treatment will only temporarily postpone death.(333)

Edelman J continued by stating that ". . . parents have a legal duty to provide needed medical care to their children(331) . . . the failure of a parent to provide such care is a criminal offense when it causes injury or impairment to the child."(334–337)

The third competing legal and policy interest was that of the state:

> acting as *parens patriae* . . . even where doing so requires limiting freedom and authority of parents over their children(261) . . . in Texas, the rights and duties of a parent are subject to a court order affecting those rights and duties(331) including an order granting a governmental entity temporary conservatorship of a child with authority to consent to medical treatment refused by the child's parents(297,307,338–341)

Edelman J emphasized that:

> . . . in Texas, the legislature has expressly given parents a right to withhold medical treatment, urgently needed or not, for a child whose medical condition is certifiably terminal, but it has not extended that right to the parents of children with non terminal impairments, deformities, or disabilities, regardless of their severity. In addition, although the Act expressly states that it does not impair or supercede any legal right a person may have to withhold or withdraw life sustaining treatment in a lawful manner, the parties have not cited and we have found no other statutory or common law authority allowing urgently needed

life sustaining medical treatment to be withheld from a non terminally ill child by a parent . . . the state's interest in preserving life is greatest when life *can* be preserved and then weakens as the prognosis dims . . . to withhold urgently needed life sustaining treatment from non terminally ill children would impose imponderable legal and policy issues . . . if parents *had* such a right, would it apply to otherwise healthy, normal children or only those with some degree of abnormality? If the latter, which circumstances would qualify . . . how could any such distinctions be justified legally? . . . we perceive no legal basis or other rationale for concluding that Texas law gives parents a common law right to withhold urgently needed life sustaining medical treatment from children in circumstances in which the Act does not apply.

The appellate court thus made it clear that in these circumstances a best interest approach was not valid. The case went to the Supreme Court, which did not issue an opinion until 2003.(342) They affirmed the appellate court decision and agreed with their reasoning, adding that any decisions concerning treatment for the baby would not be fully informed decisions until birth and that once the infant was born the physician was faced with an emergency situation. The baby might survive with treatment but was likely to die if treatment was not provided before either parental consent or a court order overriding the withholding of such consent could be obtained. The court held that circumstances like these provide an exception to the general rule imposing liability on a physician for treating a child without consent.

32

THE UNITED KINGDOM

Although not dealing with prematurity, it is instructive to examine the *R v. Arthur* case,(207) as it reflects the attitudes and behaviors of many physicians and judges toward disabled children in the early 1980s and thus how they might respond to the disabled preterm infant who could be potentially mentally retarded. In the *Arthur* case, a Down syndrome baby was born without any clinically apparent life-threatening complication. Neither the parents nor the doctor wanted the child kept alive, and the baby was prescribed dihydrocodeine and nursing care only and in addition restricted to oral water. The baby died within about 2 days, which suggests that, in the absence of any other clinical factors, there was inordinate sedation and inadequate hydration. Although the original charge was murder, this was changed to attempted murder, as an eminent pathologist had found (not surprisingly) other congenital defects and could not discount that the baby had died of "natural causes." Dr. Arthur was found not guilty, and one cannot discount the influence of the judge's statements, which included "any child who is a Mongol is faced with the most appalling handicap." Although he made it clear that no doctor has the right to kill a disabled child, the situation in this case was different, he believed, as there was a "setting of conditions within which death may occur more expediently than would otherwise have been the case." Not much more needs to be said about this case except that it reflects the misperceptions and ignorance of those involved, both medical and legal. The decision is not binding on civil cases, and as Mason and McCall Smith wrote, it is unlikely that Dr. Arthur's regime would be acceptable today and the case has lost any credibility as precedent.(343) However, examination of the case reminds us that under UK law physicians have a duty to care for patients they have accepted responsibility for, and if a breach of that duty leads to death then that physician, depending on mens rea, is liable for prosecution for manslaughter or murder.(344–347) But that duty of care does not extend to mandatory treatment to prolong life regardless of the circumstances,(348) and furthermore it has been ruled that the provision of appropriate palliative care in a situation where a patient is known to be dying, and the aim is to relieve suffering, may not be judged criminal.(349)

The UK common law pertinent to the extremely preterm infant is best considered by examining those cases that involve disabled infants and the rights and duties of parents and physicians. As will be seen, it is the best interests test, despite its ambiguity, which drives British common law as it relates to treatment, life sustaining or otherwise, for the disabled infant. As Montgomery wrote, three areas should be examined when considering the law relating to foregoing life-sustaining treatment for these infants.(350) The first is, what limits does the law place on the actions of physicians and parents? The second is, which of these two has the greater legal right to make end of life decisions for the infant? Finally, what is the role of the courts in resolving conflicts that might surround end of life decisions for disabled infants?

Parents have a legal duty to seek medical attention for their children and failure to do so risks prosecution for child neglect under the Children and Young Persons Act 1933 S1(2), but it has to be clear that it is needed,(351) or that a "reasonable parent" would have been aware of this.(352) When there is a conflict between doctors and parents concerning life-sustaining treatment, it may be necessary for the courts to make a judgment. In general, treatment cannot be given to an infant without parental consent, unless it is immediately life saving and comes under the doctrine of necessity.(350) In the situation where life-sustaining treatment is demanded by parents, but believed to be inappropriate by physicians, the courts have ruled that physicians cannot be forced to act, provided their decision is not unreasonable.(353,354) Reasonableness is determined by the best interests of the child, as judged by the courts. Thus parents cannot guarantee treatment for their child without the compliance of physicians, nor can they guarantee nontreatment if the physicians view a situation as an imminent life-threatening one.

The authority of parents was tested *in re B*,(355) which was initially heard around the same time as *Arthur*. Both cases involved a baby born with Down syndrome, but the judgments *in re B* were very different. The baby had Down syndrome and duodenal atresia, which required surgery so that the child might survive. The parents refused to consent to the operation and the local authority made the baby a ward of the court. When the surgeon decided the wishes of the parents should be respected, an order was sought authorizing the operation to be performed by another named surgeon. Eventually the case went to the court of appeal where it was judged that where the welfare of a child was at stake the courts were the final arbiter of how a child should be treated based on the best interests of the child. Templeman LJ stated that:

... It is a decision which of course must be taken in the light of the evidence and views expressed by the parents and the doctors, but at the end of the day it devolves on this court in this particular instance to decide whether the life of this child is demonstrably going to be so awful that in effect the child must be condemned to die, or whether the life of this child is still so imponderable that it would be wrong for her to be condemned to die. There may be cases, I know not, of severe proved damage where the life of the child is bound to be full of pain and suffering that the court might be driven to a different conclusion, but in the present case . . . I have no doubt that it is the duty of this court to decide that the child will live. . . .(355)

There are two conclusions that can be drawn from *re B*. One is that parental rights are subordinate to the welfare of the child, and the other suggests that a quality of life determination might justify legally allowing a disabled infant to die.

The court also went against the wishes of the parents in *re J*.(353) But in contrast to the previous case, it was the parent who demanded treatment for her multiply handicapped child and the physicians who wanted to forego this. Initially the High Court agreed with the mother, but the Court of Appeal overruled this, and it was Lord Donaldson who judged that: "the effect of setting aside the order leaves the health authority and it's medical staff free . . . to treat J in accordance with their best clinical judgment. This does not mean that we thought, and still less required, that in no circumstances should J be subjected to mechanical ventilation."(353) The court made it clear that the determining factors were the best interests of the child. This ruling by Lord Donaldson was consistent with one he made *in re J (a minor)*,(348) in which he judged that:

there is without doubt a very strong presumption in favour of a course of action which will prolong life, but . . . it is not irrebuttable . . . account has to be taken of the pain and suffering and quality of life which the child will experience if life is prolonged. Account also has to be taken of the pain and suffering involved in the proposed treatment itself . . . in the end there will be cases in which the answer must be that it is not in the interests of the child to subject it to treatment which will cause increased suffering and produce no commensurate benefit, giving the fullest possible weight to the child's and mankind's desire to survive.

Where the line is drawn is not very apparent, although Lord Justice Taylor *in re J (a minor)* (348) made it clear that best interests should be viewed from the infant's perspective, and the presence of severe handicap, per se, is not enough to justify the foregoing of life-sustaining treatment:

I consider that the correct approach is for the court to judge the quality of life the child would have to endure if given the treatment and decide whether in all circumstances such a life would be so afflicted as to be intolerable to the child. I say to that child because the test should not be whether the life would be tolerable to the decider. The test must be whether the child in question, if capable of exercising sound judgment, would consider the life tolerable . . . where the child is terminally ill the court will not require treatment to prolong life; but where . . . the child is severely handicapped, although not intolerably so, and treatment for a discrete condition can enable life to continue for an appreciable period, albeit subject to the severe handicap, the treatment should be given.

Despite these rulings, the use of the best interests test for deciding on whether to forego life-sustaining treatment for a potentially disabled infant is interpreted differently depending on the perceptions of the decision maker. That is, the best interests approach risks an inexact clinical judgment being converted into a judicial value judgment. A best interests argument was also followed in *NHS v. D.*(356) In this case, health professionals recommended palliative care for a disabled child rather than any resuscitation through artificial ventilation, and the parents opposed this. The child was said to have irreversible and worsening lung disease, heart failure, hepatic and renal dysfunction, and developmental delay, and life expectancy was considered to be 1 year at the most.(357) My reading of the clinical situation is that if the child's condition was truly terminal and irreversible, and the remaining time he had left alive was clearly intolerable from the perspective of the child, then foregoing life-sustaining treatment could be justified morally and legally without using a best interests test, and counseling parents on this basis might be more acceptable. Having written this, however, I readily acknowledge the possible inappropriateness of judging from a distance after the event. But the more important legal aspect of this case was whether withholding life-sustaining treatment, in the situation described, contravened the Human Rights Act 1998, which incorporated into UK law the European Convention on Human Rights (ECHR).(358) It was held that there was no conflict with Article 2 of the ECHR, which upholds the right to life, as the best interests of the child was followed,(357) and there was no infringement of Article 3 because in *D v. UK* (359) it was held that the right to dignity is encompassed in the requirement that a person should not be subjected to inhuman or degrading treatment. The principle of best interests of the child also overrules the rights of parents under ECHR Article 8, which grants the right to respect for private and family life (see *re A*).(360) A similar case to *NHS v. D* occurred in Portsmouth and was well publicized. Doctors in a Portsmouth hospital issued a "do not attempt resuscitation" order for baby Charlotte Wyatt on the basis that further "aggressive treatment" was not in the best interests of the child. The parents opposed this. The 11-month-old baby was born at 26 weeks and was said to only experience pain. She had extensive lung and brain damage, was tube fed, and was dependent on supplemental oxygen. The High Court supported the doctors and, in essence, ruled that her quality of life was so poor that she was "better off dead."(361) Some might argue that a correct decision had been reached, but for the wrong reasons.

The last instance involves a British case that was tried in the European Court of Human Rights. This case involved life-sustaining treatment for a severely disabled child and the administration of diamorphine without consent. The events involved physical assault between the medical staff, the family, and the police, in addition to inflexible demands from all involved. The full details of this are not described, but for those interested the situation, as it arose, was an object lesson on how not to proceed when there is a dispute concerning the foregoing of life-sustaining treatment for a severely disabled child.(362) The applicants to the court, the mother and the child, stated that there had been a failure to ensure effective respect for the child's right to physical and moral integrity within the meaning of "private life" as guaranteed by Article 8 of the ECHR. The court considered that the decision to impose treatment (the administration of diamorphine) on the child in defiance of the mother's objection interfered with the child's right to respect for his private life and in particular his right to physical integrity. Surprisingly, the court did not consider it necessary to examine separately the complaint that a "do not attempt resuscitation" notice had been placed in the chart without the consent or knowledge of the mother. The basis for this was that guilt had already been ascertained for a breech of Article 8. The court did observe that: "the notice was only directed against the application of vigorous cardiac massage and intensive respiratory support, and did not exclude the use of other techniques, such as the provision to keep the child alive." This statement fails to address whether there should be legal requirements, including consent, for a "do not resuscitate" order for a patient without capacity. Judge Casadevall entered a separate opinion expressing his judgment that there should have been a ruling on this:

> In the circumstances of this case that notice amounts . . . to an important and aggravating factor regarding the issue in question which helps to understand better the qualms and distress experienced by the mother . . . and her manner of dealing with the situation during the disturbing and unbelievable fight that broke out between certain members of the family and the hospital doctors . . . I can fully understand that the patient's condition was such that it was medically necessary to administer him diamorphine urgently in order to alleviate his suffering . . . however I find it difficult to accept that the doctors unilaterally took the serious decision of putting a Do Not Resuscitate order in the case notes without the mother's consent and knowledge. I find the comment ". . . was only directed against the application of vigorous cardiac massage and intensive respiratory support . . ." inappropriate . . . in my view the complaint deserved an additional examination. (362)

33

CANADA

Although exactly how Canadian courts would rule in cases concerning the foregoing of life-sustaining treatment for extremely preterm infants is uncertain, there are some recent cases that indicate the extent of parental autonomy when they consent or otherwise to medical treatment for their children. As in other jurisdictions, the courts have a *parens patriae* obligation that will be exercised in the best interests of the child. The interpretation of best interests lies finally with the courts, but the law allows, as it should, broad leeway for parents to raise children as they think fit, provided it does not threaten the health and safety of those children. The law also imposes a duty of care on physicians but recognizes that there are circumstances where physicians are not obliged to treat where they believe there would be no overall benefit. In the *Case of Child and Family Services of Central Manitoba v. RL,* (363) a young infant suffered severe nonaccidental brain injury that eventually led to a diagnosis of a permanent vegetative state. The question before the court was whether the infant's physician could issue a "do not attempt resuscitation" order without the consent of the parents, who objected to the order. In ruling against the parents, Twaddle JA stated that:

> there is no legal obligation on a medical doctor to take heroic measures to maintain the life of a patient in an irreversible vegetative state . . . neither consent nor a court order in lieu is required for a medical doctor to issue a non-resuscitation direction where in his or her judgment the patient is in an irreversible vegetative state. Whether or not such a decision should be issued is a judgment call for the doctor to make having regard to the patient's history and condition and the doctor's evaluation of the hopelessness of the case. The wishes of the patient's family or guardian should be taken into account, but neither their consent nor the approval of a court is required.

I assume that the judge is referring to a permanent vegetative state when he refers to the hopelessness of the case. As Sneiderman wrote,(364) the ruling should not necessarily refer to a patient with a different condition. That is, it should not necessarily apply to an infant who is severely neurologically damaged, but not in a permanent vegetative state. However, Twaddle JA appeared not to treat the foregoing of life-sustaining treatment from an infant any differently from any other form of treatment, or rather lack thereof, when he ruled that consent is required in nonemergency situations:(363)

> only when the provision of treatment without it would constitute assault . . . there is no need for consent from anyone for a doctor to refrain from intervening . . . the only fear a doctor need have in denying heroic measures is the

fear of of liability for negligence in circumstances where qualified practitioners would have thought intervention warranted.

Thus if the court does not see a need to intervene in what it views as a medical decision, it could leave the disabled infant vulnerable and without access to the *parens patriae* protection of the court. Furthermore, if active intervention has taken place such as artificial ventilation and hydration, the decision not to intervene further, let us say, with possible life-sustaining treatment such as antibiotics or a vasopressor, is a treatment decision. Legally defining it as nontreatment and nontouching is specious and denies its consequences, despite the risk of a charge of negligence, after the event. I am not arguing here for treatment at all costs but rather that the withholding of life-sustaining treatment should not be viewed legally as nontreatment and not require consent from legitimate surrogates. There are other ways of determining when it is legally permissible to withhold life-sustaining treatment from an infant, as can be found in the statutory and common law of other international jurisdictions, although there is not unanimous agreement on these ways.

The Canadian courts also ruled against parental autonomy in *B (R) v. Children's Aid Society of Metropolitan Toronto*.(365) But the legal approach was different to the *Case of Child and Family Services* cited earlier and more in keeping with the common law reasoning found in other Commonwealth countries as the best interests test was invoked. The case involved the provision of treatment, against parental wishes, rather than the withholding of treatment, and in addition there was an appeal to statutory law. A young infant was given a blood transfusion, despite a specific instruction by the parents, who were Jehovah's Witnesses, not to give this. This was made possible by the granting of wardship by the Provincial Court (Family Division). The case was eventually appealed to the Supreme Court of Ontario, who were required to determine whether section 19 (1) (b) (ix) of the Ontario *Child Welfare Act*, which defines a "child in need of protection," together with the powers in sections 30 and 41 and the procedures in other sections, deny parents a right to choose medical treatment for their infants, contrary to section 7 of the *Canadian Charter of Rights and Freedoms*.(366) The court ruled that:

> an exercise of parental liberty which seriously endangers the survival of the child should be viewed as falling outside section 7 of the *Charter*. While the right to liberty embedded in section 7 may encompass the right of parents . . . to choose among equally effective types of medical treatment for their children, it does not include a parents' right to deny a child medical treatment that has been adjudged necessary by a medical professional and for which there is no legitimate alternative. The child's right to life must not be so completely subsumed to the parental liberty to make decisions regarding that child. Although an individual may refuse any medical procedures upon their own person, it is quite another matter to speak for another especially when that individual cannot speak for herself. Parental duties are to be discharged according to the best interests of the child. The exercise of parental beliefs that grossly invades those best interests is not activity protected by the right to liberty in section 7. There is simply no room within section 7 for parents to override the child's right to life and security of the person. To hold otherwise would be to risk undermining the ability of the state to exercise

its legitimate *parens patriae* jurisdiction and jeopardize the *Charter's* goal of protecting the most vulnerable members of society.

The final Canadian case I mention is *R v. Latimer*.(367) Although this involved a severely disabled 12-year-old girl, her condition was one that might be the outcome of extreme prematurity, although not often. It is also interesting to speculate why the treatment of the father in this case was different than the treatment meted out to the father in a U.S. court, not far from the Canadian border, in the *Baby Messenger* case.(314) In the Canadian case, the father of a severely disabled 12-year-old girl asphyxiated her with carbon monoxide. His reasoning for doing this was that he could not let her suffer further pain from proposed and strongly recommended palliative surgery. The father was convicted of second-degree murder and the case was eventually appealed to the Supreme Court of Canada. Essentially the appeal concerned sentencing, as the verdict was not in doubt. The Supreme Court upheld the sentence, which was a mandatory minimum of life with no chance of parole for at least 10 years. Would, or should, the court have shown more clemency if the sentence had not been mandatory? Many Canadians thought so.(368) Dr. Gregory Messenger was not convicted after he disconnected the life support from his extremely preterm infant.(314) The judgment from the Supreme Court of Canada was: "killing a person, in order to relieve the suffering produced by a medically manageable physical or mental condition, is not a proportionate response to the harm represented by the non life threatening suffering resulting from that condition."

34

AUSTRALIA

As in Canada, there is very limited common law specifically relating to extremely preterm infants. How the courts might act if presented with questions concerning life-sustaining treatment for such infants may be derived by considering the legal history of the extent of parental and physician autonomy over treatment decisions for children, and how the courts might exercise the best interests test for disabled children. Australian law recognizes that once a baby is born alive, that baby becomes a legal person,(369–370) with the full protection of the law. However, in 1988 the National Health and Medical Research Council(371) reported that:

> "contrary to popular belief and common practice, parents do not have the legal right to determine that their infant be refused medical treatment without which the infant would die" and that "in cases of extremely low birth weight babies . . . it is likely both doctors and parents make decisions which are not acceptable under present Australian laws."

In 1986, in *F v. F* (unreported, 2 July) Vincent J, in the Supreme Court of Victoria, judged that physicians have a legal obligation to sustain the life of a child without concern for quality of life: "The law does not permit decisions to be made concerning the quality of life nor any assessment of the value of any human life."(372) But this statement was made in an urgent hearing, and the judge made it clear that he was only dealing with the urgent specific question at hand, which was feeding for the infant, who had spina bifida.(373) However, it is consistent with a later judgment from the High Court of Australia in a wrongful birth suit (which was rejected) when it was stated that:

> . . . in the eyes of the law, the life of a troublesome child is as valuable as that of any other; and a sick child is of no less worth than one who is healthy and strong. The value of human life, which is universal and beyond measurement, is not to be confused with the joys of parenthood, which are distributed unevenly.(374)

The *parens patriae* jurisdiction of the court also applies in Australia and its aim is to protect those who cannot protect themselves. This is a value that Brennan J said in *Marion's Case*(375):

> underlies and informs the law: each person has a unique dignity which the law respects and which it will protect. Human dignity is a value common to our municipal law and to international instruments related to human rights. The law will protect equally the dignity of the hail and hearty and the dignity of the weak and lame; of the frail baby and of the frail aged: of the intellectually able and

the intellectually disabled . . . our law admits of no discrimination against the weak and disadvantaged in their human dignity.

This *parens patriae* jurisdiction *has* to be exercised in the best interests and welfare of the child,[376] and it extends to authorizing medical treatment for an infant, even against the wishes of parents.(377) Thus it would appear that Australian common law is similar to that in the UK. Parents do not have an absolute right to decide treatment for an infant, if there is no reasonable option and without treatment the child is at risk of death or further injury. It also appears that quality of life decisions are discouraged, although to what extent this would be applied if a physician wanted to forego life-sustaining treatment for an extremely preterm infant, and the parents did not, has not been tested in the Australian Courts (at this time of writing). As in the United States there is statutory law that would support the physician if the infant was terminal or in a persistent vegetative state. For example, in South Australia the Consent to Medical Treatment and Palliative Care Act states that a physician who is responsible for the management of a terminally ill patient is:

under no duty to use, or to continue to use, life sustaining measures in treating the patient if the effect of doing so would be merely to prolong life in a moribund state without any real prospect of recovery or in a persistent vegetative state.(378)

35

JAPAN

In Japan, the extremely preterm infant is protected by the Japanese Eugenic Protection Act, which defines the fetal viability limit as "the minimal duration of gestation which renders fetuses capable of extra uterine life(39) and was amended to 22 completed weeks in 1991. Therefore the expectation would be that such an extremely preterm infant would be given resuscitation after birth. How Japanese courts would respond to a request to allow withdrawal of life-sustaining treatment from an extremely preterm infant is uncertain, although this would be unlikely to occur for quality of life reasons alone. In general, Japanese physicians expect their directions to be followed,(379,380) although the courts do recognize the right of competent adults to have their medical decisions respected.(381) If physicians decide that further treatment is not indicated, Article 35 of the Criminal Code offers a defense of justification for acts done "in the course of legitimate business."(379,382)

ITALY, GERMANY, AND POLAND

In Italy, a doctor has a duty to treat conditional on consent (Italian Constitution art 32), and a competent adult can refuse consent (Penal Code art 50). Nontreatment of children with disabling conditions is viewed as a violation of Article 3 of the Constitution, which relates to equality of all human beings.(383,384)

German law takes a strong "pro-life" position, although for the competent adult patient autonomous decision making, as it relates to medical treatment, includes refusing life-sustaining treatment.(379) Withdrawal of treatment from neonates, where death is inevitable, has become acceptable, but the Einbecker Recommendations of the German Society of Medical Law state that the life of a severely damaged neonate should be safeguarded, and any deliberate shortening of that life constitutes killing.(383,385)

In Poland, the Medical Profession Act of 2002 appears to impose "a duty to rescue"(379) as Article 30 states that a physician has a (legal) duty to always save human life when a delay would result in death and or physical or mental injury, and Article 162.1 of the Penal Code provides a punishment of imprisonment for failure to do this.(379) But Article 32 of the Polish Code of Medical Ethics, which does not carry statutory power, states that: (1) in terminal states the physician does not have the duty to undertake and continue resuscitation or persistent treatment, nor to resort to extraordinary measures, and (2) the decision to discontinue resuscitation rests with the physician and should be based on the assessment of the likely therapeutic success.(379) The Medical Profession Act of 2002 does state that a physician may decide to discontinue or not institute a treatment . . . unless prompt medical intervention is necessary. The latter presumably refers to a duty to rescue and save a life.(379) It is unclear whether an intervention would be deemed necessary if it was believed that it would be ineffective in preventing imminent death, but it is clear that Article 150 of the Polish Penal Code 1997 prohibits "mercy killing."(379)

FRANCE

In France, if a child is born alive and able to sustain life it has a legal existence. Ability to sustain life at birth is defined as at least 22 weeks' gestation and a minimum weight of 500g.(243) Reported legal cases involving foregoing of life-sustaining treatment for an extremely preterm infant have not occurred, as far as I could ascertain. The Code of Medical Deontology, which is legally binding, warns physicians to "avoid any unreasonable obstinacy in pursuing investigations and treatments." This presumably refers to treatments that might be viewed as medically ineffective,(386) but Article 37 specifically states that "a dying person must be attended until the last, and given appropriate care and suitable support to preserve the quality of life which is ending. A patient's dignity should be protected, and his or her entourage comforted."(379)

Article 223–6(2) of the criminal code imposes a duty to rescue and proscribes deliberately exposing a person to the danger of death or injury (223–1). In 1996, a physician who extubated and withheld resuscitation from a patient with no chance of survival was convicted of involuntary homicide by the Court of Appeal of Rouen. The doctor was described as acting "against all logic,

medical ethics, and accepted rules of good practice."(379,387)
This decision is in accord with Article 38 of the Code of Medical Deontology, which states that a physician "has no right to
bring about death."(379) This judgment is presumably a statement against euthanasia by the court. However, where extremely
preterm infants are concerned the literature outlined in previous chapters suggests that neonatal euthanasia is practiced and
accepted in French neonatal intensive care units.

THE NETHERLANDS

In the Netherlands, physicians are not required to give treatment they view as "medically futile," and they decide what constitutes this.(383) Euthanasia has been made legal in certain circumstances and there is a provision for children older than age 12 years.(388) Active euthanasia of neonates remains illegal although it has been reported.(389) Although there have not been any reported legal cases involving the foregoing of life-sustaining treatment for an extremely preterm infant, there were two cases in the 1990s that appeared in the Courts of Appeal, which addressed the deliberate termination of life of two severely disabled newborns.(390–392) In one, the *Prins* case, the baby had severe spina bifida, and in the other, the *Kadijk* case, the disorder was trisomy 18. In both these cases, the physicians, after discussion with the parents and colleagues, administered lethal doses of medication. The cases were brought by the Minister of Justice and the physicians were acquitted of the charge of murder on the basis that they had acted in accordance with the legal requirement for careful practice(392) (criteria relating to this are used to justify adult euthanasia). The reasoning was that several major surgical interventions would be necessary that would not offer a later reasonable quality of life and would be accompanied by pain and suffering. The courts accepted, on the testimony of expert medical opinion, that such intervention would be an example of medical futility.(392) The reasoning for the next step was more tenuous. It was believed by the treating physicians that both babies were in great pain that could not be adequately relieved, an opinion that was supported after "expert" consultation with colleagues in anesthesiology. Thus, they reasoned, that as the babies would inevitably die, it was their moral duty to provide a short pain-free death. It should be emphasized that there was no claim that this was an example of the doctrine of double effect. The primary intention was to terminate life.

In 1991 the case of *Baby Jeremy* was heard in Utrecht.(393) The baby was born in August 1989 with brain abnormalities that caused severe handicap. In 1990, he was readmitted into hospital with hydrocephalus. His pediatrician recommended that should the possible situation arise, he should not be resuscitated. The parents disagreed and went to court alleging that the conduct of the doctor was unlawful. In addition, they accused the physician of contravening the European Convention for the Protection of Human Rights and Fundamental Freedoms. They cited Article 2, which protects the right to life, and Article 8, which protects the right to family life.(394) The court ruled that a physician has no obligation to provide treatment that is judged to be ineffective and inappropriate. What constitutes this type of treatment is made on the basis of medical judgment, which is required to follow prevailing professional standards. The court may then, if necessary, judge whether the decision was reasonable, based on these standards. As the physician had consulted a number of experts, who agreed that intubation and ventilation would not alter the course of the disorder, the court found that the pediatrician had acted appropriately with care and beneficence. In addition, it was ruled that Articles 2 and 8 do not allow a right to medical treatment that is deemed of no useful purpose.(394) In 1997, the Dutch government produced a report on physicians' behavior and the shortening of a disabled neonate's life (Toetsing als spiegel van de medische praktijk(395)). This report recommended that all cases of deliberate termination of newborn life should be reported, and that these reports be reviewed by an appointed expert multidisciplinary clinic. The committee would report on whether careful practice had occurred to the Board of Attorneys General, who would decide whether to instigate criminal proceedings. Careful practice includes the adequate recognition of an incurable illness, intractable suffering, and appropriate consultation. In legal terms the deliberate termination of a disabled infant's life still qualifies as homicide in the Netherlands. However, the *Prins* and the *Kadijk* cases would suggest that, provided an acceptable case can be made, a successful prosecution would be unlikely. It remains debatable whether this practice of active euthanasia for the severely disabled infant is a practical ethical recognition of reality or whether it is a cautionary tale.

PART 5

EPILOGUE

Truth, Trust, and Boundaries

EPILOGUE: TRUTH, TRUST, AND BOUNDARIES

The 1989 United Nations Convention on the Rights of the Child, Article 3(1), states: "In all actions concerning children whether undertaken by public or private social welfare institutions, courts of law, administrative authorities or legislative bodies, the best interests of the child shall be a primary consideration."

This principle of best interests also appears in many other parts of the convention (Articles 9, 18, 20, 37, and 40). Clearly, children have interests from the onset of live birth. The question is who should interpret these interests and how can they be protected? Most jurisdictions allow parents to determine the best interests of their child, up to a point. The courts then recognize their duty to intercede, in certain situations. Physicians also have a duty to act in the best interests of their pediatric patients. Although they are required to respond to the wishes of parents or their surrogates, this response is not necessarily the same as it would be for a competent adult.(396) To fulfill their duty toward the child, physicians may attempt to override the instructions of the principal decision makers, should this lead to the good possibility of significant benefit for the child and the avoidance of a serious risk of harm.

For the extremely preterm infant there remains considerable disagreement concerning where this harm threshold is. That is, does a parental decision increase the likelihood of serious harm as compared to other options?(397) Answering this question, if consent for life-sustaining treatment for an extremely preterm infant is refused, requires a comparison between the harms of death versus that of disability, the degree of which may be uncertain. Can such a utilitarian calculation be made, or are the two harms incommensurable? Even though there is evidence that active intervention for the extremely preterm infant improves mortality and morbidity, these remain relatively high,(399) and the incidence of severe disability is not uncommon, although specific degrees of severe disability remain difficult to predict. Improved survival may lead to an increased prevalence of disability but would also lead to an increase in the number of normal survivors or in those only mildly affected.(400) We have seen in the previous chapters that the approach to this situation varies both legally and operationally from country to country, as well as within countries.

In the United States. the *Miller v. HCA* verdict might suggest that there is a clear boundary that defines when parents and physicians may forego life-sustaining treatment and that treatment must take place despite any likelihood of severe disability.(401) Actual practice may be different and occurs when parents and physicians agree to forego life-sustaining treatment for an unqualified infant, and any legal challenge from the state child protection services is unlikely. This is reflected in an article by Wall and Partridge(133), who reported that in a San Francisco neonatal unit treatment was withdrawn or withheld in 23% of those who died based on quality of life decisions alone. Furthermore, the attitudes of physicians may still be governed by parental preferences, as shown by Ballard et al.(134) In this article, neonatologists were asked whether they would resuscitate a 23-week, 480g infant. If the parents requested "do everything possible," 91% would resuscitate, and if parents requested "comfort care only," only 11% would resuscitate. Thus, it is suggested that although the law may require that an infant was in an irreversible coma, was in a permanent vegetative state, or had a condition that was irreversibly terminal, in the near future, before life-sustaining treatment could be foregone, in actual practice this may not occur consistently. This inconsistent practice does not necessarily bolster any argument concerning what the right thing to do is. There remains an ethical dilemma, a lack of moral consensus, and legal differences between and within countries where sophisticated neonatal intensive care exists. Some might argue against a too-strict approach as it imposes an unjustifiable burden on caregivers, particularly if the child does not develop any relational capacity.(401) But reliable, accurate prediction of this may not be possible, especially shortly after birth. There are clinical and investigative methods that can predict later that disability will occur, even severe disability. But predicting the degree of severity eludes us. The difficult question for many is should life-sustaining treatment continue for an extremely preterm infant whose neurological condition is such that should survival eventually occur there is a strong possibility that a life of extremely poor quality would result, with all the attending burdens to the child, family, and the state? Is there even a justification for neonatal euthanasia? In the Netherlands there is a protocol, the Groningen protocol, the following of which determines whether to actively end the life of a newborn infant.(402) How rigorously this is followed in the rest of the Netherlands is unclear, and all cases are not reported to the legal authorities. Infants for whom such an end of life decision might be made are divided into three categories. The first group includes those infants who are said to have no chance of survival. Such infants are, among others, those with renal agenesis, severe pulmonary hypoplasia, or anencephaly. The approach

toward the first two conditions might be different if transplanta-
tion for these were readily available and effective. Furthermore,
can dying from renal failure be described as unbearable suffering?
Similarly, the discomfort of respiratory failure can be managed.
Are there discomforts suffered by the infant that would justify
actively and intentionally ending that infant's life? The next two
categories could apply to some extremely preterm infants. Their
description is couched in wooly terms without specificity. Infants
in the second category are described as having a very poor prognosis and are dependent on intensive care. Although they may
survive, it is said that "expectations regarding their future conditions are very grim. They are infants with severe brain abnormalities or extensive organ damage."(402) They are viewed as having
an extremely poor prognosis and a poor quality of life. The third
category infants are those believed to have "a hopeless prognosis who experience what parents and medical experts deem to be
unbearable suffering."(402) The example given is the child with
the most serious form (undefined) of spina bifida or the infant
who has survived intensive care but whose quality of life will be
"very poor" with no hope of improvement. These are the categories that might allow "deliberate life ending procedures." When
considering an approach such as the Groningen protocol, it is easy
to become embroiled in definition and recognition of what constitutes severe disability. However, it is important to emphasize what
is preferable and what is permissible. We do not prefer to have
severely handicapped children, or welcome the distress it evokes,
but we also have to decide which actions we do not permit parents
and physicians to make.

Society has to trust parents and physicians to provide care for
children, up to a point. Where to draw the boundary is open to
discussion, but not that there should be a boundary. Unfortunately
drawing boundaries can also be problematic, for example, using

gestational ages or weights as sole determinants for care. In the busy confines of hospital practice, and in particular intensive care, there is a pressure to reduce the complexity of decisions and act on rules that offer resolution of a problem at hand. Thus an a priori limit for intervention might be attractive in that setting. No resuscitation, say, for less than 25 weeks, or 24 weeks' gestation, or less than a certain birth weight. Ethically this is hard to justify if the status of a preterm infant is viewed as the same as an adult with respect to the receipt of medical treatment. This becomes more so when early specific individual prognosis may be uncertain. As Simeoni and colleagues wrote(403):

> There is . . . a difference between saying (1) that a limit in terms of gestational age should be set for intensive inter-vention in extremely preterm infants, and (2) that every infant deserves a unique approach concerning the applica-tion of intensive care, backed by the information available on collective outcomes at the various gestational ages and perinatal conditions. The difference lies in intention. Its denial would challenge by extension the ethical bases of decision making in other medical situations.

Thus treatment decisions for extremely preterm infants should be made based on a combination of factors, which are recognized and interpreted by physicians and decided on by parents. How much actual power parents may have will vary depending on the clinical situation, the legal jurisdiction, and the attitudes of the physicians. Orfali and Gordon posed the questions: "does a system that emphasizes parents' autonomy enable them to cope better as some studies and the bioethical theoretical literature strongly suggest? How do parents without decision making power deal with such situations?"(404) They examined decision making in

American and French neonatal intensive care units. The study was based on the assumption that in the United States parents are viewed as the appropriate surrogate decision makers for their infants and may or may not give informed consent following the receipt of appropriate information and options from physicians. In France, as Orfali and Gordon wrote, "physicians tend to use only the child's best interest as the guiding criterion for decision making. Parental consent is taken as implicit . . . since it is presumed that doctors and parents want the same 'good' for the baby." Although it is arguable whether this contrast is completely true, it is reasonable to allow the premise that French physicians act in a more paternalistic manner than their American counterparts and then examine the consequences of this, recognizing that there is not a sharp divide between autonomy and paternalism between the two countries. The authors' conclusions were that a sensitive empathic, but paternalistic, model was viewed by mothers as providing more satisfaction and reassurance when compared to an autonomy model, despite their support for the ethical principle of autonomy. However, other factors may play a role in providing less satisfaction in the American system and include a lack of continuity in physician availability and perhaps a more detached formal contractual relationship between the parents, physicians, and the health care system. Orfali and Gordon's findings do not refute the doctrine of informed consent or the respect for autonomy principle. The French parents in their study strongly believed they were making a "shared decision" with physicians, when end of life issues were decided for their infants, but the burden of considering and arriving at the decision was carried by the physician. In effect, French physicians decide what is "best" for a neurologically damaged neonate, and by acting to "shape" the decision of parents their intention is to avoid further harm. I would suggest that this approach is followed by many pediatric physicians in modern health care systems. The theoretical discord is that giving the beneficence principle primacy requires faith and trust, risks a loss of respect for autonomy, increases the inherent dangers of quality of life decisions, and perhaps encourages a lack of scrutiny. But in practice it may well lead to more comfort and satisfaction. The creation of faith and trust always has been, and remains, an important component of the art of medicine.

There is a special relationship between patients and parents and physicians that demands special obligations. Society allows physicians powers and privileges that potentially could threaten the welfare of their patients. Although the principle of autonomy ostensibly permits parents to agree to treatments for their children, it is the physician who necessarily frames and defines the circumstances. Thus parents seek care for their children from someone they can trust. But they do not always have the time or the opportunity to choose. Systems in which this occurs can erode the trust between health care professionals and parents and requires considerable skill and virtue from the professionals to gain and maintain trust. This is particularly so in an intensive care unit, where interventions may be poorly understood by parents and the situation may be overwhelming. Apparently good physicians gauge how much autonomy parents want to express and by doing so demonstrate the good aspects of paternalism that should not be lost. Present bioethical theoreticians might question this approach and perhaps risk undermining a delicate trust.(405) As Sherlock stated: "the language of rights and the language of trust move in opposite directions from one another."(406)

But there is not only the delicate trust that needs to exist between parents and physicians. Society, through its laws and actions, is also required to trust. That is, there is a public trust.(407) But the question is to what extent and in what circumstances? In situations that are beyond our direct control we expect society, through its laws and the actions of our representatives, to define the limits and boundaries that protect both the integrity of the society and the vulnerable individual. It is not enough to rely completely on the assumed benevolent motives of the health care professional.(405) In fact, the knowledge that there are proscriptions against the behavior of physicians, through both the law and professional codes, should bolster trust. A counterargument is that intrusive overregulation might impair trust and confidence by disturbing the behavior of physicians and their interaction with parents. Despite this, there is still a requirement for methods of monitoring clinicians and their practices, and in particular defining boundaries in end and beginning of life issues.

There remains considerable variability around the world in the approach to extreme prematurity with differing professional and personal perceptions and disparate codes, case laws, and statutes. Perhaps the main conclusions we draw are that the extremely premature state is not a preferable choice, and in addition to addressing its clinical, ethical, and legal impact, we should be spending more resources to reduce the incidence of preterm birth. The growth of neonatal intensive care and its successful lowering of the limits of viability have come at a price. This price is not only financial, which compares favorably with intensive care for adults, but also medical and emotional. The dramatic psychosocial strains that stress families following the birth of an extremely preterm infant can never be welcome, even though those who work in neonatal intensive care do so with laudable care and professionalism and have at their disposal increasing technological expertise. In January 2005, a group from Britain and Ireland reported that the outcome for those studied following birth before 26 weeks, during 1995, was disabling cerebral palsy in 12% and moderate or severe disability in 46%.(408) Furthermore, premature birth rates are increasing and adding to the dilemma.(409,410) Survival rates for the extremely preterm infant increased over the last decade of the 20th century,(411) and most deaths occurred in the first few days after birth.(198) If the determining factor is survival, early intensive care appears to be justified as most will survive after the first week or so of life.(411) The question remains whether there can be an acceptable level of disability and whether this be predicted. Such decisions are further complicated by the fact that outcomes change sharply with each week of added gestational age, which can be over- or underestimated.(412) Furthermore, not all preterm infants are at the same developmental level after delivery because of differing genetic and environmental influences.(413)

It would appear clear that the most effective approach to the difficult questions raised by extreme prematurity is prevention. Considerable clinical resources, research money, and effort are expended on neonatal intensive care, and although the causes of preterm birth are multiple and complex, changes in education, health, and social policy might have a greater impact.(414,415) This includes well-funded, accessible, comprehensive prenatal care, and social and financial support during pregnancy.(416,417) Prematurity affects 12% of births in the United State and 17% of births among African Americans. Hospital care of preterm infants costs over $13 billion each year, apart from the medical and social costs incurred following initial discharge from hospital.(418) The causes of preterm birth are multiple and complex. Infection and the inflammatory response appear to contribute to these causes,(419) but this may be complicated by a gene-environment interaction.(420,421) Further research on infection, host response, and genetic susceptibility offers an avenue into treatment and prevention. However, there may be a greater improvement if more research, action, and resources were directed at poor social circumstances,(422) the effects of demanding work,(423) the reduction of multiple pregnancies, and the role of assisted reproduction technology.(424) In the United States, during the decade prior to 2002, there was a 13% increase in the number of preterm births, and in some states the increase was more than 30%.(425–427) Two major contributions to this were advanced maternal age and multiple pregnancy(428) to some extent as a result of the increasing use of assisted reproductive technologies.(429) In this group of women those with lower socioeconomic status were at higher risk for a poor perinatal outcome.(430) There is a strong association between preterm birth and social disadvantage, linked with maternal stress, infection, and lack of prenatal care,(431–433) and the preterm delivery rate in the United States is nearly twice that in Canada and Western Europe.(434)

REFERENCES

1. Births: final data for 1997. *National Vital Statistics Report* 1999; 47:99–120.
2. Van Reempts PJ, Van Acker KJ. Ethical aspects of cardiopulmonary resuscitation in premature infants: where do we stand? *Resuscitation* 2001; 51:225–232.
3. Bloch H. Abandonment, infanticide, and feticide. An overview of inhumanity to children. *Am J Dis Child* 1988; 142:1058–1060.
4. Boswell J. *The Kindness of Strangers: The Abandonment of Children in Western Europe from Late Antiquity to the Renaissance.* New York: Pantheon; 1989.
5. Lecky W. *History of European Morals from Augustus to Charlemagne.* Vol. 2. New York: Brazillier; 1955:25–26.
6. Langer WL. Europe's initial population explosion. *Am Hist Rev* 1963; 69: 1–17.
7. Selection from the Hippocratic Corpus. The Art (circa 5th–4th century BC). In: Reiser SJ, Dyck AJ, Curran WJ, eds. *Ethics in Medicine: Historical Perspectives and Contemporary Concerns.* Cambridge, MA: MIT Press; 1977:6–7.
8. Plato. *The Republic.* Translated by Grube GMA. Indianapolis: Hacket Publishing; 1974:42.
9. Alexander GR, Slay M. Prematurity at birth: trends, racial disparities, and epidemiology. *MRDD Research Reviews* 2002; 215–220.
10. Centers for Disease Control and Prevention. Infant mortality low birth weight among black and white infants – United States, 1980–2000. *MMWR* 2002; 51:589–592.

REFERENCES

11. Guyer B, Hoyert DL, Martin J et al. Annual summary of vital statistics – 1998. *Pediatrics* 1999; 104:1229–1246.

12. Eichenwald EC, Stark AR. High frequency ventilation: current status. *Pediatr Rev* 1999; 20:e127–e133.

13. Ballard PL. Scientific rationale for the use of antenatal glucocorticoids to promote fetal development. *Pediatr Rev* 2000; 1:e83–e90.

14. Curley AE, Halliday HL. The present status of exogenous surfactant for the newborn. *Early Hum Dev* 2001; 61:67–85.

15. Thorp JM, Hartmann KE, Berkman JD et al. Antibiotic therapy for the treatment of preterm labor. A review of the evidence. *Am J Obstet Gynecol* 2002; 186:587–592.

16. Iams JD, Mercer BM. What we have learned about antenatal prediction of neonatal morbidity and mortality. *Semin Perinatol* 2003; 27:247–252.

17. Murphy SL. Deaths: final data for 1998. *National Vital Statistics Reports* 2000: 48:87.

18. Branum AM, Schoendorf KC. Changing patterns of low birth weight and preterm birth in the United States, 1981–1998. *Paediatr Perinat Epidemiol* 2002: 16:8–15.

19. Evans DJ, Levene MI. Evidence of selection bias in preterm survival studies: a systematic review. *Arch Dis Child Fetal Neonatal Ed* 2001; 84:F79–F84.

20. Allen MC. Preterm outcomes research: a critical component of neonatal intensive care. *MRDD Research Reviews* 2002; 8:221–233.

21. El-Metwally D, Vohr B, Tucker R. Survival and neonatal morbidity at the limits of viability in the mid 1990's. *J Pediatr* 2000: 137:612–622.

22. Lorenz JM, Paneth N, Jetton JR, Den Ouden L, Tyson JE. Comparison of management strategies for extreme prematurity in New Jersey and the Netherlands: outcomes and resource expenditure. *Pediatrics* 2001; 108:1269–1274.

23. Ferrara TB, Hoekstra RE, Couser RJ et al. Survival and follow up of infants born at 23 to 26 weeks of gestational age: effects of surfactant therapy. *J Pediatr* 1994; 124:119–124.

24. Hack M, Friedman H, Fanaroff A. Outcomes of extremely low birth weight infants. *Pediatrics* 1996; 98:931–937.

25. The Victorian Infant Collaborative Study Group. Improved outcome into the 1990s for infants weighing 500–999g at birth. *Arch Dis Child Fetal Neonatal Ed* 1997: 77:F91–F94.

26. Hack M, Fanaroff A. Outcomes of children of extremely low birth weight and gestational age in the 1990s. *Early Hum Dev* 1999: 53:193–218.

27. Gray PH, Jones P, O'Callaghan MJ. Maternal antecedents for cerebral palsy in extremely preterm babies: a case controlled study. *Dev Med Child Neurol* 2001; 43:580–585.

28. Horbar JD, Badger GJ, Carpenter JH et al. Trends in mortality and morbidity for very low birth weight infants, 1991–1999. *Pediatrics* 2002: 110:143–151.

29. Lorenz JM. Survival of the extremely preterm infant in North America in the 1990s. *Clin Perinatol* 2000: 27:255–262.

30. Tyson JE, Younes N, Verter J, Wright LL. Viability, morbidity, and resource use among newborns of 501–800g birth weight. National Institute of Child Health and Human Development Neonatal Research Network. *JAMA* 1996; 276:1645–1651.

31. Lorenz JM. Management decisions in extremely premature infants. *Semin Neonatol* 2003; 8:475–482.

32. Hack M, Wright LL, Shanbaran S et al. Very low birth weight outcomes of the National Institute of Child Health and Human Development Neonatal Network, November 1989 to October 1990. *Am J Obstet Gynecol* 1996: 172:457–464.

33. Sauve RS, Robertson C, Etches P, Byrne PJ, Dayer-Zamora V. Before viability: a geographically based outcome study of infants 500grams or less at birth. *Pediatrics* 1998; 101:438–448.

34. Chan K, Ohlsson A, Synnes A, Lee DSC, Chien L, Lee SK. Survival, morbidity, and resource use of infants of 25 weeks gestational age or less. *Am J Obstet Gynecol* 2001; 185:220–226.

35. Effer SB, Moutquin J-M, Farine D, Saigal S, Nimrod C, Kelly E, Nigorsenga J. Neonatal survival rates in 860 singleton live births at 24 and 25 weeks gestational age. A Canadian multicenter study. *Br J Obstet Gynaecol* 2002; 109:740–745.

36. Committee of Newborn Infant, Japan Society of Pediatrics. Neonatal white paper in Japan. *J Jpn Pediatr Soc* 1986; 90:2827–2855.

37. Committee of Newborn Infant, Japan Society of Pediatrics. Report on the current status of NICU and neonatal mortality in Japan. *J Jpn Pediatr Soc* 1991; 95:2454–2461.

38. Oishi M, Nishida H, Sasaki T. Japanese experience with micropremies weighing less than 600 grams born between 1984 to 1993. *Pediatrics* 1997: 99:1–5.

39. Nishida H. Perinatal care in Japan. *J Perinatol* 1997; 17:70–74.

40. Gultom E, Doyle LW, Davis P, Dharmaluigam A, Bowman E. Changes over time in attitudes to treatment and survival rates for extremely preterm infants 23–27 weeks' gestational age. *Aust NZ J Obstet Gynecol* 1997; 37: 56–58.

41. Doyle LW, Gultom E, Chuang SL, James M, Davis P, Bowman E. Changing mortality and causes of death in infants 23–27 weeks' gestational age. *J Paediatr Child Hlth* 1999; 35:255–259.

42. Wood NS, Marlow N, Costeloe K, Gibson AT, Wilkinson AR, for the EPI Cure Study Group. Neurologic and developmental disability after extremely preterm birth. *N Engl J Med* 2000; 343:378–384.

43. Ayoubi JM, Audibere F, Boithas C, Zupan V, Taylor S, Bosson JL, Frydman R. Perinatal factors affecting survival without disability of extremely premature infants at two years of age. *Eur J Obstet Gynaecol Reprod Biol* 2002; 105:125–131.

44. Reuss ML, Gordon HR. Obstetrical judgments of viability and perinatal survival of extremely low birth weight infants. *Am J Publ Hlth* 1995; 85:362–366.

45. Silver RK, MacGregor SN, Farrell EE, Ragin A, Davis C, Sokol ML. Perinatal factors influencing survival at 24 weeks gestation. *Am J Obstet Gynecol* 1993; 168:1724–1731.

46. Bottoms SF, Paul RH, Iams JD et al. Obstetric determinants of neonatal survival: influence of willingness to perform cesarean section on survival of extremely low birth weight infants. National Institute of Child Health and Human Development Network of Maternal Fetal Medicine Units. *Am J Obstet Gynecol* 1997; 176:960–966.

47. Bottoms SF, Paul RH, Mercer BM et al. Antenatal predictors of neonatal survival and morbidity in extremely low birth weight infants. *Am J Obstet Gynecol* 1999; 180:665–669.

48. Rennie JM. Perinatal management at the margin of viability. *Arch Dis Child Fetal Neonatal Ed* 1996; 74:F214–F218.

49. Sims DG, Heal CA, Bartle Sm. Use of adrenaline and atropine in neonatal resuscitation. *Arch Dis Child Fetal Neonatal Ed* 1994; 70:F3–F9.

50. Sond S, Glacois P. Cardiopulmonary resuscitation in very low birth weight infants. *Am J Perinatol* 1992; 9:130–133.

51. Davis DJ. How aggressive should delivery room CPR be for ELBW neonates? *Pediatrics* 1993; 92:447–450.

52. Macfarlane PI, Wood S, Bennett J. Non-viable delivery at 20–23 weeks gestation: observations and signs of life after birth. *Arch Dis Child Fetal Neonatal Ed* 2003; 83:F199–F202.

53. Jankov RP, Asztalos EV, Skidmore MB. Favourable neurological outcomes following delivery room cardiopulmonary resuscitation of infants < 750gs at birth. *J Paediatr Child Hlth* 2000; 36:19–22.

54. Doron MW, Veness-Meehan KA, Margolis LH et al. Delivery room resuscitation decisions for extremely premature infants. *Pediatrics* 1998; 102:574–582.

55. Finer NN, Tarin T, Vaucher YE, Barrington K, Bejar R. Intact survival in extremely low birth weight infants after delivery room resuscitation. *Pediatrics* 1999; 104:e40–e44.

56. Costeloe K, Hennessy E, Gibson AT et al for the EPICure Study Group. The EPICure Study: outcomes to discharge from hospital for infants born at the threshold viability. *Pediatrics* 2000; 106:659–671.

57. Van der Heide A, Van der Maas PJ, Van der Wal G et al. Medical end-of-life decisions made for neonates and infants in the Netherlands. *Lancet* 1997; 350:251–255.

58. Straughn HK, Goldenberg RL, Tolosa JE et al. Birthweight-specific neonatal mortality in developing countries and obstetric practices. *Int J Gynecol Obstet* 2003; 80:71–78.

59. Malhotra D, Gopalan S, Narang A. Preterm breech delivery in a developing country. *J Gynaecol Obstet* 1994; 45:27–34.

60. Morse SB, Haywood JL, Goldenberg RL, Bornstein J, Nelson KG, Carlo WA. Estimation of neonatal outcome and perinatal therapy use. *Pediatrics* 2000; 105:1046–1056.

61. Cook LA, Watchko JF. Decision making for the critically ill neonate near the end of life. *J Perinatol* 1996; 16:133–136.

62. Ginsberg HG, Goldsmith JP. Controversies in neonatal resuscitation. *Clin Perinatol* 1998; 25:1–15.

63. Campbell DE, Fleischman AR. Limits of viability: dilemmas, decisions, and decision makers. *Am J Perinatol* 2001; 18:117–128.

64. Heywood JL, Goldenberg RL, Bronstein J, Nelson KG, Carlo WA. Comparison of perceived and actual rates of survival and freedom from handicap in premature infants. *Am J Obstet Gynecol* 1994; 171:432–439.

65. Sheldon T. Dutch doctors change policy on treating preterm babies. *Brit Med J* 2001; 322:1383.

66. Breborowicz GH. Limits of fetal viability and its enhancement. *Early Pregnancy* 2001; 5:49–50.

67. Doyle LW. Outcome at 5 years of age for children 23 to 27 weeks' gestation: refining the prognosis. *Pediatrics* 2001; 108:134–141.

68. Saigal S, Szatzmari P, Rosenbaum P, Campbell D, King S. Cognitive abilities and school performance of extremely low birth weight children and matched term control children at age 8 years: a regional study. *J Pediatr* 1991; 118:751–760.

69. Escobar GJ, Littenberg B, Pettiti DB. Outcome among surviving very low birth weight infants: a meta-analysis. *Arch Dis Child* 1991; 66:204–211.

70. Szatmari P, Saigal S, Rosenbaum P, Campbell D. Psychopathology and adaptive functioning among extremely low birth weight children at eight years of age. *Dev Psychopathol* 1993; 5:345–357.

71. Hille ETM, Den Ouden AL, Bauer L, Van den Oudenrijn C, Brand R, Verloore-Vanhorick SP. School performance at nine years of age in very

premature and low birth weight infants: perinatal risk factors and predictors at 5 years of age. *J Pediatr* 1994; 125:426–434.

72. Hack M, Taylor HG, Klein N, Eiben R, Schatschneider C, Mercuri-Minich N. School-age outcomes in children with birthweights under 750g. *N Engl J Med* 1994; 331:753–759.

73. Hille ETM, Den Ouden AL, Saigal S et al. Behavioural problems in children who weigh 1000g or less at birth in four countries. *Lancet* 2001: 357:1641–1643.

74. Saigal S, Pinelli J, Hoult, Kim M, Boyle M. Psychopathology and social competencies of adolescents who were extremely low birth weights. *Pediatrics* 2003; 111:969–975.

75. Saigal S, Burrows E, Stoskopf BL, Rosenbaum PL, Streiner DL. Impact of extreme prematurity on families of adolescent children. *J Pediatr* 2000; 137:701–706.

76. Singer L, Salvator A, Guo S, Collin M, Lillien M, Bailey J. Maternal psychological distress and parenting stress after the birth of a very low birth weight infant. *JAMA* 1999; 281:799–805.

77. Levy-Shiff R, Einat G, Mogilner MB, Lerman M, Krikler R. Biological and environmental correlates of developmental outcome of prematurely born infants in early adolescence. *J Pediatr Psychol* 1994; 19:63–78.

78. Gross SJ, Mettelbaum BB, Dye TD, Siagle TA. Impact of family structure and stability on academic outcome in preterm children at 10 years of age. *J Pediatr* 2001; 138:169–175.

79. Inder T, Huppi P, Warfield S et al. Periventricular white matter injury in the premature infant is followed by reduced cerebral cortical gray matter volume at term. *Ann Neurol* 1999: 46:755–760.

80. Maalouf E, Duggan P, Rutherford M et al. Magnetic resonance imaging of the brain in a cohort of extremely preterm infants. *J Pediatr* 1999; 135:351–357.

81. Peterson BS, Vohr B, Staib LH et al. Regional brain volume abnormalities and long-term cognitive outcome in preterm infants. *JAMA* 2000; 284:1939–1947.

82. Ajayi-Obe M, Saeed N, Cowan FM, Rutherford MA, Edwards AD. Reduced development of cerebral cortex in extremely preterm infants. *Lancet* 2000; 356:1162–1163.

83. Skranes J, Nilson G, Smevik O, Vik T, Brubakk A. Cerebral MRI of very low birth weight children at 6 years of age compared with the findings at 1 year. *Pediatr Radiol* 1998; 28:471–475.

84. Stewart AL, Rifkin L, Amess PN et al. Brain structure and neurocognitive and behavioural function in adolescents who were born very preterm. *Lancet* 1999; 353:1653–1657.

85. Isaacs EB, Lucas A, Chong WK et al. Hippocompal volume and everyday memory in children of very low birth weight. *Pediatr Res* 2000; 47:713–720.

86. Nosarti C., Al-Asady MHS, Frangou S, Stewart AL, Rifkin L, Murray RM. Adolescents who were born very preterm have decreased brain volumes. *Brain* 2002; 125:1616–1623.

87. Peterson BS, Anderson AW, Ehrenkranz R et al. Regional brain volumes and their later neurodevelopmental correlates in term and preterm infants. *Pediatrics* 2003; 111:939–948.

88. Hack M, Klein N, Taylor HG. Long term developmental outcomes of low birth weight infants. *Future Child* 1995; 5:176–196.

89. Saigal S, Den Ouden L, Wolke O et al. School-age outcomes in children who were extremely low birth weight from four international population-based cohorts. *Pediatrics* 2003; 112:943–950.

90. Anderson P, Doyle LW, Victorian Infant Collaborative Study Group. Neurobehavioral outcomes of school-age children born extremely low birth weight or very preterm in the 1990s. *JAMA* 2003; 289:3264–3272.

91. Wolke D, Ratschinski G, Ohrt B et al. The cognitive outcome of very preterm infants may be poorer than often reported: an empirical investigation of how methodological issues make a big difference. *Eur J Pediatr* 1994; 153:906–915.

92. Morley R, Farewell V. Methodological issues in randomized controlled trials. *Semin Neonatol* 2000; 5:141–148.

93. Ericson A, Kallen B. Very low birth weight boys at the age of 19. *Arch Dis Child Fetal Neonatal Ed* 1998; 78:F171–F174.

94. Msall ME, Tremont MR. Functional outcomes in self-care, mobility, communication, and learning in extremely low birth weight infants. *Clin Perinatol* 2000; 27:281–419.

95. Field D, Peterson S, Clarke M, Draper ES. Extreme prematurity in the UK and Denmark: population differences in viability. *Arch Dis Child Fetal Neonatal Ed* 2002; 87:172–175.

96. Highlights on Health in Denmark. Epidemiology, Statistics, and Health Information Unit, WHO Regional Office for Europe. Available at: http://www.who.dk/country/dan01.pdf (accessed 2005).

97. National statistics. The official UK statistics site. Available at: www.statistics.gov.uk (accessed 2005).

98. Vohr B, Wright LL, Dusick AM et al. Neurodevelopmental and functional outcomes of extremely low birth weight infants in the National Institute of Child Health and Human Development Neonatal Research Network 1993–1994. *Pediatrics* 2000: 105:1216–1222.

99. Schmidt B, Asztalos EV, Roberts RS, Robertson CMT, Sauve RS, Whitfield MF. Impact of bronchopulmonary dysplasia, brain injury, and severe

retinopathy on the outcome of extremely low birth weight infants at 18 months: Results from the trial of indomethacin prophylaxis in preterms. *JAMA* 2003; 289:1124–1129.

100. Piecuch RE, Leonard CH, Cooper BA et al. Outcome of infants born at 24–26 weeks gestation. II. Neurodevelopmental outcome. *Obstet Gynecol* 1997; 90:809–814.

101. Piecuch RE, Leonard CH, Cooper BA et al. Outcome of extremely low birth weight infants (500 to 999 grams) over a 12-year period. *Pediatrics* 1997; 100:633–639.

102. Tudehope D, Burns YR, Gray PH et al. Changing patterns of survival and outcome at 4 years of children who weighed 500–999g at birth. *J Paediatr Child Hlth* 1995; 31:451–456.

103. Victorian Infant Collaborative Study. Neurosensory outcome at 5 years and extremely low birth weight. *Arch Dis Child Fetal Neonatal Ed* 1995; 73:43–46.

104. Casiro O, Bingham W, MacMurray B et al. The Canadian Exosurf neonatal study group and the Canadian Exosurf neonatal study group: one-year follow up of 89 infants with birth weights 500–749 grams and respiratory distress syndrome randomized to 2 rescue doses of surfactant or air placebo. *J Pediatr* 1995; 126:553–560.

105. Ment LR, Vohr B, Oh W et al. Neurodevelopmental outcome at 36 months corrected age of preterm infants in the multicenter indomethacin intraventricular hemorrhage prevention trial. *Pediatrics* 1996; 98:714–718.

106. Hagberg B, Hagberg G, Olow I et al. The changing panorama of cerebral palsy in Sweden VII: prevalence and origin in the birth year 1987–1990. *Acta Paediatr* 1996; 85:954–960.

107. Horwood LJ, Mogridge N, Darlow BA. Cognitive, educational, and behavioural outcomes at 7 to 8 years in a national very low birth weight cohort. *Arch Dis Child Fetal Neonatal Ed* 1998; 79:F12–F20.

108. Buck GM, Msall ME, Schusterman EF et al. Extreme prematurity and school outcomes. Social and biomedical risks. *Pediatr Perinatal Epidemiol* 2000; 14:324–331.

109. Whitfield MF, Grunau RV, Holsti L. Extremely premature (< 800g) school children: multiple areas of disability. *Arch Dis Child Fetal Neonatal Ed* 1997; 77:F85–F90.

110. Saigal S, Szatmari P, Rosenbaum P et al. Intellectual and functional status at school entry of children who weighed 1000 grams or less at birth: a regional perspective of births in the 1980s. *J Pediatr* 1990; 116:409–416.

111. Msall ME, Rogers BT, Buck GM et al. Functional status of extremely preterm infants at kindergarten entry. *Dev Med Child Neurol* 1993; 35:312–320.

112. Msall ME, Tremont MR. Measuring functional outcomes after prematurity: developmental impact of very low birth weight and extremely low birth

weight status on childhood disability. *MRDD Research Reviews* 2002; 8:258–272.

113. Halsey CL, Collin MF, Anderson CL. Extremely low birth weight children and their peers: a comparison of school-age outcomes. *Arch Pediatr Adolesc Med* 1996; 150:790–794.

114. Saigal S, Szatmari M, Rosenbaum P. Can learning disabilities in children who were extremely low birth weight be identified at school entry? *J Dev Behav Pediatr* 1992; 13:356–362.

115. Wolke D, Söhne B, Ohrt B, Riegel K. Follow-up of preterm children: important to document dropouts. *Lancet* 1995; 345–447.

116. Johnson A, Bowler U, Yudkin P et al. Health and school performance of teenagers born before 29 weeks gestation. *Arch Dis Child Fetal Neonatal Ed* 2003; 88: F190–F198.

117. Doyle LW, Casalaz D, for the Victorian Infant Collaborative Study Group. *Arch Dis Child Fetal Neonatal Ed* 2001; F159–F164.

118. Saigal S, Hoult LA, Streiner DL et al. School difficulties at adolescence in a regional cohort of children who were extremely low birth weight. *Pediatrics* 2000; 105:325–331.

119. Saigal S, Stoskopf BL, Streiner DL et al. Physical growth and current health status of infants who were of extremely low birth weight and controls at adolescence. *Pediatrics* 2001; 108:407–415.

120. Roth S, Wyatt J, Boudin J et al. Neurodevelopmental status at 1 year predicts neuropsychiatric outcome at 14–15 years of age in very preterm infants. *Early Hum Dev* 2001; 65:81–89.

121. Hack M, Taylor HG, Klein N et al. Functional limitations and special health care needs of 10–14 year old children weighing less than 750 grams at birth. *Pediatrics* 2000; 106:554–560.

122. D'Angio CT, Sinkin RA, Stevens TP et al. Longitudinal 15-year follow up of children born at less than 29 weeks gestation after introduction of surfactant therapy into a region: neurologic, cognitive, and educational outcomes. *Pediatrics* 2002; 110:1094–1102.

123. Dineson SJ, Greisen G. Quality of life in young adults with very low birth weight. *Arch Dis Child Fetal Neonatal Ed* 2001; F165–F169.

124. Donohue PK. Health related quality of life of preterm children and their caregivers. *MRDD Research Reviews* 2002; 8:293–297.

125. Bennett FC, Scott DT. Long-term perspective on premature infant outcome and contemporary intervention issues. *Semin Perinatol* 1997; 21:190–201.

126. Bracewell M, Marlow N. Patterns of motor disability in very preterm children. *MRDD Research Reviews* 2002; 8:241–248.

127. Taylor HG, Klein N, Hack M. School-age consequences of birth weight less than 750g: a review and update. *Dev Neuropsychol* 2000; 17:289–321.

128. Taylor HG, Klein N, Minich NM. Middle-school-age outcomes in children with very low birth weight. *Child Dev* 2000; 71:1495–1511.

129. Aylward GP. Cognitive and neuropsychological outcomes: more than IQ scores. *MRDD Research Reviews* 2002; 8:234–240.

130. Finer NN, Barrington KJ. Decision-making delivery room resuscitation: a team sport. *Pediatrics* 1998; 102:644–645.

131. Lorenz JM, Paneth N. Treatment decisions for the extremely premature infant. *J Pediatr* 2000; 137:593–595.

132. Rhoden NR. Treating Baby Doe: the ethics of uncertainty. *Hastings Cent Rep* 1986; 16:34–42.

133. Wall SN, Partridge JC. Death in the intensive care nursery: physician practice of withdrawing and withholding life support. *Pediatrics* 1997; 99:64–70.

134. Ballard DW, Li W, Evans J, Ballard RA, Ubel PA. Fear of litigation may increase resuscitation of infants born near the limits of viability. *J Pediatr* 2002; 140:713–718.

135. Saigal S, Stoskopf B, Feeny D et al. Differences in preferences for neonatal outcomes among health care professionals, parents, and adolescents. *JAMA* 1999; 281:1991–1997.

136. Saigal S, Rosenbaum P, Hoult L et al. Conceptual and methodological issues in assessing health-related quality of life in children and adolescents: illustration from studies of extremely low birth weight survivors. In: Drotar D, ed. *Measuring Health-Related Quality of Life in Children and Adolescents: Implications for Research and Practice.* Mahwah, NJ: Lawrence Erlbaum Associates; 1998:151–169.

137. Churchill DN, Torrance GW, Taylor DW et al. Measurement of quality of life in end-stage renal disease: the time trade-off approach. *Clin Invest Med* 1987; 10:14–20.

138. Slevin MI, Stubbs L, Plant HJ et al. Attitudes to chemotherapy: comparing views of patients with cancer with those of doctors, nurses, and general public. *Brit Med J* 1990; 300:1458–1460.

139. Streiner DL, Saigal S, Burrows E, Stoskopf B, Rosenbaum P. Attitudes of parents and health care professionals toward active treatment of extremely premature infants. *Pediatrics* 2002; 108:152–157.

140. Lee SK, Penner PL, Cox M. Impact of very low birth weight infants on the family and its relationship to parental attitudes. *Pediatrics* 1991; 88:105–109.

141. Wainer S, Khuzwayo H. Attitudes of mothers, doctors, and nurses toward neonatal intensive care in a developing society. *Pediatrics* 1993; 91:1171–1175.

142. Sanders MR, Donohue PK, Oberdorf MA, Rosenkrantz TS, Allen MC. Perceptions of the limit of viability: neonatologists' attitudes toward extremely preterm infants. *J Perinatol* 1995; 15:494–502.

143. Norup M. Treatment of extremely premature newborns: a survey of attitudes among Danish physicians. *Acta Paediatr* 1998; 87:896–902.

144. DeLeeuw R, DeBeaufort AJ, DeKleine MJK, VanHarrewijn K, Kiuée LAA. Foregoing intensive care treatment in newborn infants with extremely poor prognoses. *J Pediatr* 1996; 129:661–666.

145. McHaffie HE, Laing IA, Parker M, McMillan J. Deciding for imperiled newborns: medical authority or parental autonomy. *J Med Ethics* 2001; 27: 104–109.

146. Norup M. Limits of neonatal treatment: a survey of attitudes in the Danish population. *J Med Ethics* 1998; 24:200–206.

147. Munro M, Yu V, Partridge JC, Martinez AM. Antenatal counseling, resuscitation practices and attitudes among Australian neonatologists towards life support in extreme prematurity. *Aust NZ J Obstet Gynaecol* 2001; 41:275–280.

148. Da Costa DE, Ghazal H, AlKhusaiby S. Do not resuscitate orders and ethical decisions in a neonatal intensive care unit in a Muslim community. *Arch Dis Child Fetal Neonatal Ed* 2002; 86:F115–F119.

149. Fenton AC, Fields DV, Mason E, Clarke M. Attitudes to viability of preterm infants and their effect on figures for perinatal mortality. *Brit Med J* 1990; 300:434–436.

150. Van der Heide A, Van der Maas PJ, Van der Wal G, Killèe LAA, De Leeuw R, Hou RA. The role of parents in end-of-life decisions in neonatology: physicians' views and practices. *Pediatrics* 1998; 101:413–418.

151. Wolder Levin B. International perspectives on treatment choice in neonatal intensive care units. *Soc Sci Med* 1990; 30:901–912.

152. Silverman WA. Over treatment of neonates? A personal retrospective. *Pediatrics* 1992; 90:971–975.

153. Pinkerton JV, Finnerty JJ, Lombardo PA, Rorty MV, Chapple H, Boyle RJ. Parental rights at the birth of a near-viable infant: conflicting perspectives. *Am J Obstet Gynecol* 1997; 177:283–290.

154. De Leeuw R, Cuttini M, Nadai M et al. Treatment choices for extremely preterm infants: an international perspective. *J Pediatr* 2000; 137:593–595.

155. Rebagliato M, Cuttini M, Broggin L et al. Neonatal end-of-life decision making: physicians' attitudes and relationship with self-reported practices in 10 European countries. *JAMA* 2000; 281:2451–2459.

156. Cuttini M, Nadai M, Kaminski M et al. End-of-life decisions in neonatal intensive care. *Lancet* 2000; 355:2112–2118.

157. Meadow WL, Lantos J. Epidemiology and ethics in the neonatal intensive care unit. *Qual Manage Health Care* 1999; 7:21–31.

158. Nishida H, Oishi M. Survival and disability in extremely tiny babies less than 600g birth weight. *Semin Neonatol* 1996; 1:251–256.

159. Beauchamp T. Introduction to ethics. In: Beauchamp TL, Walters L, eds. *Contemporary Issues in Bioethics*. 5th ed. Boston: Wadsworth Publishing Company; 1999:1.

160. Ibid., p5.

161. Jonsen AR. *A Short History of Medical Ethics*. Oxford: Oxford University Press; 2000:2.

162. Ibid., p3.

163. Ibid., p17.

164. Calvao-Sabrinho C. Hippocratic ideals, medical ethics, and the practice of medicine in the early middle ages: legacy of the Hippocratic Oath. *J History Med Allied Sciences* 1996; 50:438–456.

165. Jonsen, p17–18.

166. Ibid., p21–22.

167. Ibid., p45.

168. Ibid., p45–46.

169. Leake C. Ed. *Percival's Medical Ethics*. Baltimore: Williams & Wilkins; 1927.

170. Jonsen, p70.

171. Ibid., p83.

172. Ibid., p86.

173. Burns C. Richard Cabot and reformation in American medial ethics. *Bull History Med* 1977; 51:353–368.

174. Kant I. *The Moral Law: Groundwork of the Metaphysics of Morals*. New York: Routledge; 1991.

175. Freeman JM, McDonnell K. *Tough Decisions. A Casebook in Medical Ethics*. New York: Oxford University Press; 1987:156.

176. Ridley A. *Beginning Bioethics*. New York: St. Martin's Press; 1998.

177. Kagan S. *The Limits of Morality*. New York: Oxford University Press; 1989.

178. Beauchamp TL, Childress JF. *Principles of Biomedical Ethics*. New York: Oxford University Press; 2001.

179. Veatch RM. Is there a common morality? *Kennedy Inst Ethics J* 2003; 13:189–192.

180. Turner L. Zones of consensus and zones of conflict: questioning the "common morality" presumption in bioethics. *Kennedy Inst Ethics J* 2003; 13:193–201.

181. Beauchamp T. A defense of the common morality. *Kennedy Inst Ethics J* 2003; 13:259–274.

182. Macklin R. *Against Relativism. Cultural Diversity and the Search for Ethical Universals in Medicine*. New York: Oxford University Press; 1999.

183. Aksoy S, Tenik A. The four principles of bioethics as found in 13th century Muslim scholar Mawlana's teachings. *BMC Medical Ethics* 2002; 3:4–10.

184. Fleischman AR, Chervanek FA, McCullough LB. The physician's moral obligations to the pregnant woman, the fetus, and the child. *Semin Perinatol* 1998; 22:184–188.

185. Campbell DE, Fleischman AR. Limits of viability: dilemmas, decisions and decision makers. *Am J Perinatol* 2001; 18:117–128.

186. Yen BM, Schneiderman LJ. Impact of pediatric ethics consultations on patients, families, social workers, and physicians. *J Perinatol* 1999; 19:373–378.

187. Meyers C. Cruel choices: autonomy and critical care decision making. *Bioethics* 2004; 18:104–119.

188. Kopelman LM. Children and bioethics: uses and abuses of the best interests standard. *J Med Philos* 1997; 22:213–217.

189. Kopelman LM. The best interests standard as threshold, ideal, and standard of reasonableness. *J Med Philos* 1997; 22:271–289.

190. Holmes RL. Consent and decisional authority in children's health care decision making: a reply to Dan Brock. In: Kopelman LM, Moskop JC, eds. *Children and Health Care: Moral and Social Issues*. Dordrecht: Kluwer Academic Publishers; 1989:218–220.

191. Chervanak F, McCullough LB. Nonagressive obstetric management. *JAMA* 1989; 261:3439–3440.

192. Jonsen AR, Garland MJ. A moral policy for life/death decisions in the intensive car nursery. In: Jonsen AR, Garland MJ, eds. *Ethics of Newborn Intensive Care*. Berkeley: University of California, Institute of Governmental Studies; 1976:148.

193. Feinberg J. Wrongful life and the counterfactual element in harming. *Soc Philos Policy* 1987; 4:3–36.

194. Paris JJ. Parental right to determine whether to use aggressive treatment for an early gestational age infant: the Messenger case. *Med Law* 1997; 16:679–685.

195. Sklansky M. Neonatal euthanasia: moral considerations and criminal liability. *J Med Ethics* 2001; 27:5–11.

196. Foot P. Euthanasia. In: Ladd J, ed. *Ethical Issues Relating to Life and Death*. New York: Oxford University Press; 1979:30.

197. Lewitt EM Baker LS, Corman H, Shiono PH. The direct cost of low birth weight. *The Future of Children* 1995; 5:40–58.

198. Lantos JD, Mokalla M, Meadow W. Resource allocation in neonatal and medical ICUs. Epidemiology and rationing at the extremes of life. *Am J Respir Crit Care Med* 1997; 156:185–189.

199. Brody H. *Ethical Discussions in Medicine*. Boston: Little Brown; 1976:66.

200. Koop CE. The handicapped child and his family. *Linacre Quarterly* 1981; 48:22–32.

201. Papal encyclical. Evangelium vitae, para 65, 1994.

202. *President's Commission for the Study of Ethical Problems in Medicine and Biomedical and Behavioural Research: Deciding to Forgo Life-Sustaining Treatment.* Washington, DC: Government Printing Office; 1983:85. Publication No 20402.

203. McCormick R. To save or let die. The dilemma of modern medicine. *JAMA* 1974; 229:172–176.

204. Glover J. *Causing Death and Saving Lives.* London: Penguin; 1990:42.

205. Kuhse H. Why killing is not always – and sometimes better than letting die. *Cambridge Q Hlthcare Ethics* 1998; 7:371–374.

206. Lorber J. Results of treatment of myelomeningocele: an analysis of 524 unselected cases with special reference to possible selection for treatment. *Dev Med Child Neurol* 1971; 13:279–303.

207. *R v Arthur,* 13 BMLR 1 (1981).

208. Englehardt HT. Ethical issues in aiding the death of young children. In: Mappes TA, DeGrazia D, eds. *Biomedical Ethics.* 4th ed. New York: McGraw-Hill Inc.; 1996:408–415.

209. Singer P. *Writings on an Ethical Life.* New York: Harper Collins Publishers Inc.; 2000:128.

210. Tooley M. Decisions to terminate life and the concept of a person. In: Ladd J, ed. *Ethical Issues Relating to Life and Death.* New York: Oxford University Press; 1979:64–65.

211. Walter JW. Approaches to ethical decision-making in the neonatal care unit. *AJDC* 1988; 142:825–830.

212. Harris J. The concept of a person and the value of life. *Kennedy Inst Ethics J* 1999; 9:293–308.

213. Shaw AB. Intuitions, principles, and consequences. *J Med Ethics* 2001; 27:16–19.

214. Singer P. *Practical Ethics.* 2nd ed. Cambridge: Cambridge University Press; 1993:87.

215. Higginson R. Life and death and the handicapped newborn: a review of the ethical issues. *Ethics Med* 1987; 3:45–48.

216. Kilmer JF, Miller B, Pellegrino ED. *Dignity and Dying.* Grand Rapids: William B Eerdmans; 1996:98–99.

217. Nitschke JB, Nelson EE, Rusch BD et al. Orbitofrontal cortex tracks positive mood in mothers viewing pictures of their newborn infants. *Neuroimage* 2004; 21:583–592.

218. Bartels A, Zeki S. The neural correlates of maternal and romantic love. *Neuroimage* 2004; 21:1155–1166.

219. Wocial L. Moral distress – the role of ethics consultation in the NICU. *Bioethics Forum* 2002; 18:15–23.

220. Beauchamp TL. The failure of theories of personhood. *Kennedy Inst Ethics J* 1999; 9:309–324.

221. Robertson JA. Involuntary euthanasia of defective newborns. A legal analysis. *Stanford Law Review* 1975; 27:246–261.
222. The Hastings Center research project on the care of imperiled newborns. *Hastings Cent Rep* 1987; 17:13–16.
223. Singer P. *Practical Ethics*. 2nd ed. Cambridge: Cambridge University Press; 1993:395.
224. Jonsen AR, Siegler M, Winslade WJ. *Clinical Ethics. A Practical Approach to Ethical Decisions in Clinical Medicine*. 5th ed. New York: McGraw-Hill; 2002:116.
225. Ibid., p25.
226. President's Commission for the Study of Ethical Problems in Medicine.
227. Bridge P, Bridge M. The brief life and death of Christopher Bridge. *Hastings Cent Rep* 1981; 11:19.
228. Crane D. *The Sanctity of Social Life: Physicians' Treatment of Critically Ill Patients*. New York: Russell Sage Foundation; 1975:78.
229. Committee on Bioethics. American Academy of Pediatrics. Guidelines on foregoing life-sustaining medical treatment. *Pediatrics* 1994; 93:532–536.
230. Committee on Fetus and Newborn, American Academy of Pediatrics. The initiation or withdrawal of treatment for high-risk newborns. *Pediatrics* 1995; 96:362–63.
231. Committee on Fetus and Newborn, American Academy of Pediatrics. Committee on Obstetric Practice, American College of Obstetricians and Gynecologists. Perinatal care at the threshold of viability. *Pediatrics* 1995; 96:974–976.
232. Hadlock FP, Harrist RB, Sharmon RS et al. Estimation of fetal weight with the use of head, body, and femur measurements – a prospective study. *Am J Obst Gynecol* 1985; 151:333–337.
233. Committee on Bioethics, American Academy of Pediatrics. Ethics and the care of critically ill infants and children. *Pediatrics* 1996; 98:149–152.
234. ACOG Practice Bulletin. Perinatal care at the threshold of viability. *Int J Gynecol Obstet* 2002; 79:181–188.
235. Lemons JA, Bauer CR, Oh W et al. Very low birth weight outcomes of the National Institute of Child Health and Human Development Neonatal Research Network, January 1995 through December 1996. NICHD Neonatal Research Network. *Pediatrics* 2001: 107:E1.
236. MacDonald H, and the Committee on Fetus and Newborn. American Academy of Pediatrics. Perinatal care at the threshold of viability. *Pediatrics* 2002; 110: 1024–1027.
237. Fetus and Newborn Committee, Canadian Paediatric Society; Maternal-Fetal Medicine Committee, Society of Obstetricians and Gynecologists of Canada. Management of the woman with threatened birth of an infant of extremely low gestational age. *Can Med Assoc J* 1994; 151:547–553.

238. Bioethics Committee. Canadian Paediatric Society. Treatment decisions for infants, children, and adolescents. Reference No. B86–01. Available at: http://www.cps,ca/english/statements/B/b86–01.htm (accessed 2005).

239. Bioethics Committee, Canadian Paediatric Society. Treatment decisions regarding infants, children, and adolescents. *Paediatr Child Health* 2004; 9:99–103.

240. Royal College of Paediatrics and Child Health (RCPCH). *Withholding or Withdrawing Lifesaving Treatment in Children. A Framework for Practice.* London: RCPCH; 1997.

241. Gee H, Dunn P. *Fetuses and Newborn Infants at the Threshold of Viability.* London: British Association of Perinatal Medicine; 2000.

242. British Medical Association. *Withholding and Withdrawing Life Prolonging Medical Treatment. Guidance for Decision Making.* London: BMJ Publishing Group; 2001.

243. Ethical considerations regarding neonatal resuscitation. Recommendation No. 65 of the National Consultative Ethics Committee for Health and Life Sciences, September 14, 2000.

244. Simeoni U, Lacroze V, Leclaire M, Millet V. Extreme prematurity: the limits of neonatal resuscitation. *J Gynecol Obstet Biol Reprod* (Paris) 2001; 6:S 58–63.

245. The Appleton International Conference: developing guidelines for decisions to forgo life – prolonging medical treatment. *J Med Ethics* 1992; 18:Supplement 1–24.

246. Report of the Committee for the Study of Ethical Aspects in the management of newborn infants at the threshold of viability. *Int J Gynecol Obstet* 1997; 59: 165–168.

247. German Society for Medical Law. *The Einbecker Recommendations.* Munich: German Society for Medical Law; 1992:206.

248. International Guidelines for Neonatal Resuscitation: An excerpt from the guidelines 2000 for cardiopulmonary resuscitation and emergency cardiovascular care: International Consensus on Science. *Pediatrics* 2000: 106:e 29–45.

249. Sauer PJJ and the members of the working group. Ethical dilemmas in neonatology: recommendations of the Ethics Working Group of the CESP (Confederation of the European Specialists in Paediatrics). *Eur J Pediatr* 2001; 160:364–368.

250. Mendelson D, Jost TS. A comparative study of the law of palliative care and end-of-life treatment. *J Law Medicine Ethics* 2003; 31:1–23.

251. McTeer MA. A role for law in matters of morality. *McGill Law J* 1995; 40:893–903.

252. DeVille K, Hassler G. Health care ethics committees and the law: uneasy but inevitable bedfellows. *HEC Forum* 2001; 13:13–31.

253. Capron AM. What contributions have social sciences and the law made to the development of policy on bioethics? *Daedalus* 1999; 128:295–325.

254. Hart HLA. Positivism and the separation of law and morals. *Harvard Law Rev* 1958; 71:593–629.

255. *Medical Ethics: The Right to Survival 1974*: Hearings before the Subcommittee on Health of the Senate Committee on Labor and Welfare 93d Cong 2d Sess 26 (1974).

256. Saw A, Randolph JG, Manard B. Ethical issues in pediatric surgery: a national survey of pediatricians and pediatric surgeons. *Pediatrics* 1977; 60:588–599.

257. Waldman AM. Medical ethics and the hopelessly ill child. *J Pediatr* 1976; 88:890–892.

258. Smith SR. Disabled newborns and the federal child abuse amendments: tenuous protection. *Hastings Law J* 1986; 37:765–827.

259. Robertson J. Involuntary euthanasia of defective newborns: a legal analysis. *Stanford Law Rev* 1975; 27:213–270.

260. *Union Pacific Railway Co v Bostford*, 141 US 250, 251 (1891).

261. *Prince v Massachusetts*, 321 US 158, 166 (1944).

262. *Newmark v Williams*, 588 A2d 1108, 1117–1118 (DeL 1991).

263. *Branzburg v Hayes*, 408 US 665, 700–701 (1972).

264. *Zoski v Gaines*, 271 Mich 1, 9, 260 NW, 101–102 (1935).

265. *Roger v Sells*, 178 Okla. 103, 105, 61 P2d 1018, 1019–1020 (1936).

266. *Re Hudson*, 13 Wash 2d 673, 693–694, 126 P 2d 765, 775–776 (1942).

267. *Paris Adult Theatre I v Slaton*, 413 US 49, 65 (1973).

268. *Carey v Population Servs Int'l*, 431 US 678, 684–685 (1977).

269. *Wisconsin v Yoder*, 406 US 205, 233–234 (1972).

270. *Jehovah's Witnesses v King County Hospital*, 278 F Supp 488, 504–505 (WD Wash 1967) *Aff'd per curiam*, 390 US 598 (1968).

271. *In Re Ivey*, 319 So 2d 53, 58–59 (Fla Dist Ct App 1975).

272. *State v Perricone*, 37 NJ 463, 475, 181 A 2d 751, 758.

273. Pence GE. *Classic Cases in Medical Ethics*. New York: McGraw-Hill Inc.; 1995.

274. Gustafson J. Mongolism, parental desires, and the right to life. *Perspect Biol Med* 1973; 16: 529–534.

275. Duff R, Campbell A. Moral and ethical dilemmas in the special-care nursery. *N Engl J Med* 1973: 289:890–894.

276. Lorber J. Results of treatment of myelomeningocele: an analysis of 524 unselected cases, with special reference to possible selection for treatment. *Dev Med Child Neurol* 1971; 13:279–303.

277. Perrachio A. Government in the nursery: new era for Baby Doe cases. *Newsday* 1983: November 13.

278. United States Commission on Civil Rights. *Medical Discrimination against Children with Disabilities.* Washington, DC: US Government Printing Office; 1989:321.

279. *Infant Doe*, Re GU 8204–004A (1982); on appeal 52 US LW 3369 (1983).

280. *American Academy of Pediatrics v Heckler*, 561 F Supp 395 (DDC 1983).

281. *American Hospital Association v Heckler*, 105 SCt 3475 (1985).

282. Kerr K. An issue of law and ethics. Newsday 1983: October 26.

283. *Weber v Stonybrook Hospital*, 60 NY 2d 208 (1983).

284. *Bowen v American Hospital Association*, 476 US 610, 106 SCt 3101, 90 L Ed 584 (1986).

285. *Parham v JR*, 442 US 584 (1979).

286. *Youngberg v Romeo*, 457 US 307 (1982).

287. Hall MA, Ellman IM, Strouse DS. *Health Care Law and Ethics in a Nutshell.* St. Paul, Mn: West Group; 1999.

288. Meisel A, Cerminara KL. *The Right to Die. The Law of End-of-Life Decision Making.* 3rd ed. New York: Aspen Publishers; 2004.

289. Frader JE. Baby Doe blinders. JAMA 2000; 284:1143.

290. Boyle D, Carlo WA, Goldsmith J et al. Born-Alive Infants Protection Act of 2001, Public Law No. 107–207. *Pediatrics* 2003: 111:680–681.

291. *Matter of Hofbauer*, 47 NY 2d 648, 652 (1979).

292. 42 USCA 5103 (b) (2) (k) (iii) (West Supp 1985).

293. *Re Seiforth*, 309 NY 80, 127 NE 2d 820 (1955).

294. *Re Green*, 220 Pa Super Ct 191, 286 A 2d 681 (1971).

295. *In re Christopher I*, 131 Cal Rptr 2d 122, 138 (Ct App 2003).

296. *In re Phillip B*, 156 Cal Rptr 48 (Ct App) *cert denied* 445 US 949 (1980).

297. *Custody of a Minor*, 379 NE 2d 1053, 1065 (Mass 1978).

298. *In re Rosebush*, 491 NW 2d 633, 637 (Mich Ct App 1992).

299. *Morrison v State*, 252 SW 2d 97 (Mo Ct App 1952).

300. *State v Perricone*, 181 A 2d 751 (NJ 1962).

301. *In re Brooklyn Hosp*, 258 NYS 2d 621 (Sup Ct 1965).

302. *In re Clark*, 185 NE 2d 128 (CP Ohio 1968).

303. *In re KI*, 735 A 2dn448, 454 (DC Ct App 1999).

304. *In re Doe*, 418 SE 2d 3 (GA 1992).

305. *In re Nikolas E*, 720 A 2d 562 (Me 1998).

306. *In re AMB*, 640 NW 2d 262, 295–96 (Mich Ct App 2001).

307. *In re McCauley*, 565 NE 2d 411 (Mass 1991).

308. *Commonwealth v Nixon*, 761 A 2d 1151 (PA 2000).

309. *In re Hamilton*, 657 SW 2d 425 (Tenn Ct App 1983).

310. *In re Steinhaus, a minor*, Juv Ct Div Redwood Minn County Ct 1986.

311. *Re KI*, 98 FS 1767 (District of Columbia 1999).

312. Lantos JD, Miles SH, Cassel CK. The Linares affair. *Law Med Hlth Care* 1989; 17:308–315.

313. Gross M. Avoiding anomalous newborns: preemptive abortion, treatment thresholds. And the case of baby Messenger. *J Med Ethics* 2000; 26:242–248.

314. *People of the State of Michigan v Gregory Messenger.* Ingham County Circuit Court, Lansing, MI 94–67694 FH Feb 2 1995.

315. *Johnson v Thompson,* 971 F 2d 1487, 1499 (10th Cir 1992).

316. *In Velez v Bethune,* 219 Ga APP 679, 466 SE 2d 627 (1995).

317. *In re Jane Doe,* 262 Ga 389, 391(2), 393(2) (c), 418 SE 2d 3 (1992).

318. Parent's "wrongful life" lawsuit against doctors fails. Available at newsmax.com. Thursday, May 30, 2002 (Accessed 2005).

319. *Montalvo v Borkovec,* 647 NW 2d 413, 421 (Ct App Wis 2002).

320. Paris JJ, Goldsmith JP, Cimperman M. Resuscitation of a micropremie: the case of MacDonald v Milleville. *J Perinatol* 1998; 18:302–305.

321. Lantos JD, Miles SH, Silverstein MD, Stocking CB. Survival after cardiopulmonary resuscitation in babies of very low birth weight. *N Engl J Med* 1988; 318:91–96.

322. *Barber v Superior Court,* 147 Cal App 3rd 1006, 95 Cal Rptr 484 (1983).

323. Texas Health and Safety Code 672.004 (1992), repealed by Acts 1999, 76 Leg, Ch 450, 1.05.

324. Texas Civ Prac and Rem Code 135.001 (1997), repealed by Acts 1999, 76 Leg, Ch450. 1.05.

325. Texas SB 414, 76th Leg (1997).

326. Letter from Joseph M Graham, President, Texas Right to Life Committee, to Texas Senator Mike Moncrieff, March 10 1997. Texas Right to Life Committee, Inc. Newsletter; Spring 1997.

327. Heitman E, Gremillion V. Ethics committees under Texas law: effects of the Texas Advanced Directives Act. *HEC Forum* 2001; 13:82–104.

328. Texas Health and Safety Code 166.001 (West Supp 2000).

329. *Stolle v Baylor College of Medicine,* 981 SW 2d 709 (West 2001).

330. *Hospital Corporation of America v Sidney Ainsley Miller,* 36 SW 3d 187 (West 2001).

331. Fam Code Ann 151.003(a)(6)(Vernon 1996).

332. *Moss v Rishworth,* 222SW 225, 226–227 (Tex Comm'n App 1920, holding approved).

333. Texas Health and Safety Code Ann 166.002(13), 166.031, 166.035 (Vernon Supp 2000).

334. Texas Pen Code Ann 22.04(a)(b)(1)(Vernon 1996).

335. *Ahearn v State,* 588 SW 2d 327, 336–337 (Tex Crim App 1979).

336. *Ronk v State,* 544 SW 2d 123, 124–125 (Tex Crim App 1976).

337. *Fuentes v State,* 880 2d 857, 860–861 (Tex App-Amarillo 1994).

338. Texas Fam Code Ann 102.003(a)(5), 105.001(a)(1), 262.201 (c)(Vernon 1996 & Supp 2000).

339. OG v Baum, 790 SW 2d 839, 840–842 (Tex App-Houston [1st Dist] 1990).

340. Mitchell v Davis, 205 SW 2d 812, 813–15 (Tex Civ App-Dallas 1947).

341. In re Cabrera, 381 Pa Super 100, 552 A 2d 1114, 1120 (1989).

342. Miller v HCA, Supreme Court of Texas No 01–0079 (2003).

343. Mason JK, McCall Smith RA. Law and Medical Ethics. 5th ed. London: Butterworths; 1999:370.

344. R v Gibbons, 13 Cr App R 134 (1918).

345. R v Stone, QB 354 (1977).

346. In Re F (Mental patient: sterilization), 2 AC 1, 55–56 (1990).

347. Airedale NHS Trust v Bland, AC 789 (1993).

348. In re J (a minor) (wardship: medical treatment), Fam 33 (1991).

349. R v Adams, Crim LR 365 (1957).

350. Montgomery J. Health Care Law. Oxford: Oxford University Press; 1997:410.

351. R v Sheppard, AC 394 (1981).

352. R v Senior, 1 QB 823 (1899).

353. Re J, 4 ALL ER 614 (1992).

354. R v Cambridge DHA ex p B, 2 AU ER 129 (1995).

355. Re B (a minor) (wardship: medical treatment), 1 WLR 1424 (1981).

356. National Health Service Trust v D, FLR 677 (2000).

357. National Health Service Trust v D. Med Law Rev 2000; 8:339–335.

358. ECHR Act 1998 Sch 1 Part 1 Art 2 and 3.

359. D v UK, 24 EHRR 423 (1997).

360. Re A (permission to remove child: Human Rights), FLR 225 (CA) (2000).

361. BBC News. 'Ill baby should not revived'. Available at: http://news.bbc.co.uk/go/pr/fr/-/l/hi/health/3723656.stm (accessed 2005).

362. Case of Glass v United Kingdom. European Court of Human Rights 9 March 2004.

363. Case of Child and Family Services of Central Manitoba v RL and SLH, 123 Man R (2d) 135 (1997).

364. Sneiderman B. A do not resuscitate order for an infant against parental wishes: a comment on the Case of Child and Family Services of Central Manitoba v RL and SLH. Health Law J 1999; 7:205–231.

365. B (R) v Children's Aid Society of Metropolitan Toronto, 1 SCR 315 (1995).

366. Canadian Charter of Rights and Freedoms. Constitution Act 1982 (79).

367. R v Latimer, 1 SCR 3 (2001).

368. CBC News. Petition demands clemency for jailed Robert Latimer. Available at: http://www.canoe.ca/CNEWSLaw0112/13_latimer-cp.html (accessed 2005).

369. R v Hutty, ALR 689 (1953).

370. R v Castles, QWN 36 (1969).

371. Ethics in Clinical Practice Advisory Panel. *The ethics of limiting life-sustaining treatment*. National Health and Medical Research Council (NHMRC) (Australia). Canberra; 1988.

372. *F v F* The Age. Melbourne, 3 July 1986, p1.

373. Skene L. *Law and Medical Practice*. 2nd ed. Sydney, Lexis Nexis, 2004.

374. *Cattenach v Melchior*, HCA 38 (2003).

375. *Secretary Department of Health and Human Services v JWG and SMB*, 175 CLR 218 – *Marion's Case* (1991–1992).

376. *Dalton v Scuthorpe*. Unreported decision of Supreme Court of New South Wales, 17 November 1992, 5094 377.

377. *Director General of the Department of Community Services v "BB,"* NSWSC 1169 (1999).

378. Consent to Medical Treatment and Palliative Care Act (1995)(SA) section 17(2).

379. Mendelson D, Jost TS. A comparative study of the law of palliative care and end-of life treatment. *J Law Med Ethics* 2003; 31:1–23.

380. LeFlar RB. Informed consent and patients' rights in Japan. *Houston Law Rev* 1996; 33:1–112.

381. *Takeda v State*, 5 (2) Minshu 582, 1710 Hanrei Jiho 97, 1031 Hanrei Taimazu 158 (Sup Ct, Feb 29 2000).

382. Kimura R. Death, dying, and advance Directives in Japan: sociocultural and legal points of view. In: Sass H-M, Veatch RM, Kimura R, eds. *Advance Directives and Surrogate Decision Making in Health Care*. Baltimore: Johns Hopkins University Press; 1998.

383. McHaffie HE, Cuttini M, Brolz-Voit G et al. Withholding/withdrawing treatment from neonates: legislation and official guidelines across Europe. *J Med Ethics* 1999; 25:440–446.

384. Pretura di Genova 13.11.1991, Gallicia, in Fi 1992, 11.586, Italy.

385. German Society for Medical Law.

386. Duguet AM. Euthanasia and assistance to end life legislation in France. *Eur J Hlth* 2001; 8:109–123.

387. Nys H. Physician involvement in a patient's death: a continental European perspective. *Med Law Review* 1999; 7:208–246.

388. Emmanuel EE. Euthanasia: where the Netherlands leads will the world follow? *Brit Med J* 2001; 322:1376–377.

389. Cuttini M, Casotto V, Kaminski M et al. Should euthanasia be legal? An international survey of neonatal intensive care units staff. *Arch Dis Child Fetal N Neonatal Ed* 2004; 89:F19–F24.

390. Sheldon T. Dutch may relent over euthanasia prosecution. *Brit Med J* 1996; 312:76–77.

391. Chao DVK, Chan NY, Chan WY. Euthanasia revisited. *Family Practice* 2002; 19:128–134.

392. Dorscheidt JH. Assessment procedures regarding end of life decisions in neonatology in the Netherlands. Proceedings of the World Congress on Medical Law; 2004. Sydney, Australia.

393. *T v GR*, Regional Court of Utrecht, 11 January 1991.

394. Heinen AL. End of life: some of the legal dilemmas. Proceedings of the World Congress on Medical Law; 2004. Sydney, Australia.

395. Report of the consultancy group on the assessment of careful medical practice regarding the end of life of neonates. Assessment as a mirror of medical practice. Publication of the Minister of Health Care, Welfare and Sport, Rijswijk, September 1997.

396. Rhodes R, Holzman IR. The *not unreasonable standard* for assessment of surrogates and surrogate decisions. *Theor Med* 2004; 25:367–385.

397. Diekma DS. Parental refusals of medical *treatment: the harm principle as threshold for state intervention. Theor Med* 2004; 25:243–264.

398. Griesen G. Meaningful care for babies born after 22, 23, or 24 weeks. *Acta Paediatr* 2004; 93:153–156.

399. Serenius F, Ewald U, Farooqui A, Holmgren P-A, Haakansson S, Sedin G. Short-term outcome after active perinatal management at 23–25 weeks of gestation. A study from 2 Swedish perinatal centres. Part 3: neonatal morbidity. *Acta Paediatr* 2004; 93:1090–1097.

400. Lorenz JM. Proactive management of extremely premature infants. *Pediatrics* 2004; 114:264.

401. Robertson JA. Extreme prematurity and parental rights after Baby Doe. *Hastings Cent Rep* 2004; 34:32–39.

402. Verhagen E, Sauer PJJ. The Groningen protocol – euthanasia in severely ill newborns. *N Engl J Med* 2005; 352: 959–962.

403. Simeoni U, Vendemmia M, Rizzotti A, Gamerre M. Ethical dilemmas in extreme prematurity: recent answers; more questions. *Eur J Obstet Gynecol* 2004; 117:S33–S36.

404. Orfali K, Gordon EJ. Autonomy gone awry: a cross cultural study of parents' experiences in neonatal intensive care units. *Theor Med* 2004; 25: 329–365.

405. Hall MA. The importance of trust for ethics, law, and public policy. *Cambe Q Healthc Ethics* 2005; 14:156–167.

406. Sherlock R. Reasonable men and sick human beings. *Am J Med* 1986; 80: 2–4.

407. Clark CC. Trust in Medicine. *J Med Philos* 2002; 27: 11–29

408. Marlow N, Wolke D, Bracewell MA, Samara M, for the EPIcure Study Group. Neurologic and developmental disability at six years after extremely preterm birth. *N Engl J Med* 2005; 352:9–19.

409. Vohr B, Allen M. Extreme prematurity – the continuing dilemma. *N Engl J Med* 2005; 352:71–72.

410. Arias E, MacDorman MF, Strobino DM, Guyer B. Annual summary of vital statistics – 2002. *Pediatrics* 2003; 112:1215–1230.

411. Meadow W, Lee G, Lin K, Lantos J. Changes in mortality for extremely low birth weight infants in the 1990's: implications for treatment decisions and resource use. *Pediatrics* 2004; 113:1223–1229.

412. Mongelli M, Wilcox M, Gardosi J. Estimating the date of confinement: ultrasonographic biometry versus certain menstrual dates. *Am J Obstet Gynecol* 1996; 174:278–281.

413. Leviton A, Blair E, Damman O, Allred E. The wealth of information conveyed by gestational age. *J Pediatr* 2005; 146:123–127.

414. Hollier LM. Preventing preterm birth: what works, what doesn't. *Obstet Gynecol Survey* 2005; 60:124–131.

415. St John EB, Nelson KG, Cliver SP et al. Cost of neonatal care according to gestational age at birth and survival status. *Am J Obstet Gynecol* 2000; 182:170–175.

416. Gold R, Connell FA, Heagerty P, Bezruchka S, Davis R, Cawthon ML. Income inequality and pregnancy spacing. *Soc Sci Med* 2004; 59:1117–1126.

417. Papiernik E, Goffinet F. Prevention of preterm births, the French experience. *Clin Obstet Gynecol* 2004; 47:755–767.

418. Lackritz E. *Meeting the Challenges of Prematurity: CDC Prevention Efforts.* Hearings before the Subcommittee on Children and Families, Committee on Health Education, Labor and Pensions, US Senate, May 12, 2004. Available at: http://www.hhs.gov/asl/testify/t040512b.html (accessed 2005).

419. Hitti J, Tarczy-Hornoch P, Murphy J, Hillier SL, Aura J, Eschenbach DA. Amniotic fluid infection, cytokines, and adverse outcome among infants born at 34 weeks' gestation or less. *Am J Obstet Gynecol* 2001; 98:1080–1088.

420. Macones G, Parry S, Elkousy M, ClothierB, Ural SH, Strauss JF. A polymorphism in the promoter region of TNF and bacterial vaginosis: preliminary evidence of gene-environment interaction in the etiology of spontaneous preterm birth. *Am J Obstet Gynecol* 2004; 190:1504–1508.

421. Romero R, Chaivorapopngsa T, Kuivaniemi H, Tromp G. Bacterial vaginosis, the inflammatory response and the risk of preterm birth: a role for genetic epidemiology in prevention of preterm birth. *Am J Obstet Gynecol* 2004; 190:1509–1519.

422. Dole N, Savitz DA, Hertz-Picciato I et al. Maternal stress and preterm birth. *Am J Epidemiol* 2003; 157:14–24.

423. Mozurkewich EL, Luke B, Avni M, Wolf FM. Working conditions and adverse pregnancy outcome: a meta-analysis. *Obstet Gynecol* 2000; 95:623–635.

424. Blondel B, Kaminski M. Trends in the occurrence, determinants, and consequences of multiple births. *Semin Perinatol* 2002; 26:239–249.

425. March of Dimes. Premature birth rate in US reaches historic high. Available at: http://www.marchofdimes.com/aboutus/1061_10763.asp (accessed 2005).

426. March of Dimes. Premature Birth Rates. Available at: http://www.marchofdimes.com/files/ptbrates_bystate_final2.pdf (accessed 2005).

427. Cockey CD. Prematurity hits record high. *AWHONN Lifelines* 2004; 8:104–111.

428. Russell RB, Petrini JR, Damus K, Mattison DR, Schwarz RH. The changing epidemiology of multiple births in the United States. *Obstet Gynecol* 2003; 101:129–135.

429. Centers for Disease Control and Prevention. Use of assisted reproductive technology – United States 1996 and 1998. *MMWR Weekly* 2002; 51:97–101.

430. Zhang J, Meikle S, Grainger DA, Trumble A. Multifetal pregnancy in older women and perinatal outcomes. *Fertil Steril* 2002; 78:562–568.

431. Wadhara PD, Culhane JF, Rauh V et al. Stress, infection, and preterm birth: a biobehavioral perspective. *Paediatr Perinat Epidemiol* 2001; 15 (Suppl 2):17–29.

432. Kramer MS, Goulet L, Lydon J et al. Socioeconomic disparities in preterm birth: causal pathways and mechanisms. *Paediatr Perinat Epidemiol* 2001; 15 (Suppl 2):104–123.

433. Vintzileos AM, Ananth CV, Smulian JC, Scorza WE. The impact of prenatal care on preterm births among twin gestations in the United States, 1989–2000. *Am J Obstet Gynecol* 2003; 189:818–823.

434. Joseph KS. Marcoux S, Liu S et al. Changes in stillbirth and infant mortality associated with increase in preterm birth among twins. Fetal and Infant Health Study Group of the Canadian Perinatal Surveillance System. *Pediatrics* 2001; 108:1055–1061.

AAP v. Heckler court case, 141
act utilitarianism, 55
  methodology of, 56
  strengths/weaknesses of, 56–57
active euthanasia, 72–73
adolescence, outcomes of, 32–33
adolescents
  health/educational challenges
    of, 33
  health state comparative study
    of, 36–37
  higher mental function disorders
    of, 33
  self-view of, 32
adulthood, independence in, 5
Advanced Directives Act (Health and
    Safety Code), 153
  disagreement resolution provided by,
    154–155
  ethics committee consultation
    recommendations, 155
  protections provided by, 154
African Americans, premature birth
    statistics for, 195
Alkhusaiby, S., 40
American Academy of Pediatrics
  best interests approach favored
    by, 96
  life-support guidelines by, 95

parental decision-making outlined in
    guidelines of, 96
  physician responsibilities outlined in,
    96
  on treatment choices, 147
American College of Obstetricians and
    Gynecologists, 96–97
  counseling recommendations of,
    101–103
  perinatal care bulletin of, 100–101
antenatal data, obstetrician evaluation of,
    17
antepartum viability, 16
Appleton International Conference,
    123–125
artificial ventilation, 12, 62
assisted reproduction technology, 196
assisted ventilation, 20, 46
Asztalos, EV, 18
attention/behavior disorders, 25
Australia
  baby's legal status in, 173
  Consent to Medical Treatment and
    Palliative Care Act, 175
  F v. F court case, 174
  law issues of, 173–175
  Marion's Case court case, 174
  National Health and Medical
    Research Council of, 173

Australia (*cont.*)
    neonatal mortality reports from,
        14
    neonatologist's parental counseling
        study of, 39–40
    parens patriae in, 174, 175
    Victorian Infant collaborative study
        of, 29
autonomy
    bioethic's respect for, 59–61
    EPTI's lack of, 59
    Meyers on, 60
    parental, 59

B (R) v. Children's Aid Society of
    Metropolitan Toronto court case,
    170–172
Baby Doe cases, 140–143
    Health and Human Services
        Department and, 142–143
    Supreme Court (US) and, 142
Baby Doe rules. *See* Child Abuse
    Amendments of 1984
Baby Doe squads, 141
Baby Jeremy court case, 182
Baby Messenger case (Michigan), 150,
    172
Ballard, PL, 35, 188
Bavaria, cerebral palsy rates in, 31
Bayley Mental and Psychomotor
    Developmental Index, 27
Beauchamps, T., morality defined by, 51
beneficence, non-maleficence and, 62–67
Bentham, Jeremy, 55
Bethune, Mary Elizabeth. *See Velez v.*
    Bethune court case
bioethics
    applications of, 51
    moral theory, 51–58, 59–72
    questions of, 136
    respect for autonomy, 59–61
    shared definition of, 52
Bioethics Committee (Canadian
    Paediatric Society)
    best interest concept of, 107
    life-sustaining treatment
        recommendations/exceptions of,
        107–108
blindness, 30, 32
Born Alive Protection Act of 2001, 146

Bottoms, SF, 17
Bowen v. American Hospital Association
    court case, 144
Bowman, E., 14
brain function(s)
    disorders of, 25–26
    life claim based on, 75
Brennan, J, 174
British Association of Perinatal
    Medicine, 111–113
British Medical Association, 114–115
Buck, GM, 30
Bush, George W., 153

Cabot, Richard, 53
Canada
    B (R) v. Children's Aid Society of
        Metropolitan Toronto court case,
        170–172
    Case of Child and Family Services of
        Manitoba v. RL court case,
        168–169
    cerebral palsy rates in, 31
    Child Welfare Act of, 171
    ELBW study of, 32–33
    Fetus and Newborn Committee of,
        106
    law issues of, 168–172
    Maternal-Fetal Medicine Committee
        of the Society of Obstetricians
        and Gynaecologists of, 106
    neonatal mortality reports from, 13,
        27, 29–30
    NICUs of, 13, 45
    R v. Latimer court case, 172
    reports of, 106–109
    Supreme Court of, 172
    survival rate study in, 27
Canadian Charter of Rights and
    Freedoms, 171
Canadian Paediatric Society, 106
    position statement of, 109
Capron, AM, 136
cardiopulmonary resuscitation (CPR)
    infants receiving, 18–19
Casadevall, Judge, 167
Case of Child and Family Services of
    Manitoba v. RL court case,
    168–169
categorical imperative (Kant), 54

cerebral palsy, 25, 28, 30
country variance of, 31
cesarean sections, 17,200
Chan, K., survival rate study of, 27
Chien, L., 27
Child Abuse Amendments of 1984, 144
child protective services required by, 146
non-prescriptive nature of, 146
parent's role defined by, 146
Child Abuse Prevention and Treatment and Adoption Reform Act, 144
child protective services, Child Abuse Amendments requirements of, 146
child rearing, constitutional rights in, 139
Child Welfare Act (Canada), 171
children, disabled
acceptability of death for, 74
determining life's value for, 80–85
examples of, 3–6
neurodevelopment disabilities, 7
personhood of, 74–79
questions regarding caring for, 7
societal attitudes towards, 9
Children and Young Persons Act (UK), 162
Christianity
duty to sick of, 52
sanctity of life principle of, 70–71
Civil Rights Commission (US), 140
Clarke, M., 26
Code of Medical Deontology (France), 179
Code of Profession Medical Ethics (Italy), 121
cognition, evaluation of, 30, 31
Committee on Fetus and Newborn
perinatal care report of, 104–105
recommendations of, 96–97
common morality, 58
Confederation of European Specialists in Paediatrics recommendations, 127–131
consent
Do Not Resuscitate order and, 167
non emergency requirement of, 169
Supreme Court and parental, 143

Consent to Medical Treatment and Palliative Care Act (South Australia), 175
consequentialism, 55
Cooper, BA, 28
Costeloe, K., 14
court decisions
AAP v. Heckler, , 141
B (R) v. Children's Aid Society of Metropolitan Toronto court case, 170–172
Baby Jeremy, , 182
Baby Messenger case, 150, 172
Bowen v. American Hospital Association, , 144
Case of Child and Family Services of Manitoba v. RL, , 168–169
D v. UK, , 165
end of life issues involving, 148–159
F v. F, , 174
Hospital Corporation of America v. Miller, , 156–159
Kadijk court case, 181, 183
Linnares, Sammy, case, 149
MacDonald v. Milleville, , 152
Marion's Case, , 174
Miller v. HCA, , 188
Milwaukee, Wisconsin, 151
Newmark v. Williams, , 139
NHS v. D, , 165
Prins court case, 181, 183
R v. Arthur, , 160–161
R v. Latimer, , 172
re: B (a minor)(wardship: medical treatment), , 162–163
re: J (a minor)(wardship: medical treatment), , 163–165
Stolle v. Baylor College of Medicine, , 155–156
Velez v. Bethune, , 151, 152
Court of Appeal of Rouen (France), 179
courts
intervention decisions of, 170
on medical neglect, 147
parens patriae obligation of, 139, 168, 170
parent's not overridden by, 148
Crane, Diane, 92
Criminal Code of Japan, 176
Cuttini, M., 41, 42

D v. UK court case, 165
DaCosta, DE, 40
Davis, P., 14
De Leeuw, R., 41
death(s)
    acceptability of, 74
    hastening of, 21
    life-support withdrawal cause of, 35
    1970s US infant, 138
decisions
    National Consultative Ethics
        Committee recommendations,
        119
    parental involvement in, 21, 34–35,
        93, 139
    of surrogates, 60
    worth of life, 35
Declaration of Independence, life
        protected by, 144
delivery room, resuscitation in, 18–20
Denmark
    neonatal intensive care approach of,
        26
    physician treatment withdrawal issues
        in, 39
deontological forces, medical ethics
        influenced by, 53
deontology theory, 54–55
Dharmalugam, A., 14
dignity, right to, 165, 174
disabilities
    attention/behavior, 25
    functional, 26
    health professional rating of, 36–37
    learning/language, 25
    neurodevelopmental, 7
    visual/hearing impairment, 25
Do Not Resuscitate order, consent for,
        167
doctrine of necessity, 162
Donaldson, Lord, 163
Doyle, LW, 14
Draper, ES, 26
Durable Power of Attorney for Health
        Care statute, 153
Dusick, AM, 27
dying, killing v., 72

ECHR. *See* European Convention on
        Human Rights

Edelman, J., 157–159
Effer, SB, 13
El-Metwally, D., survival rate study of, 12,
        26–27
ELBW. *See* extremely low birth weight
        infant
end of life issues, cases involving,
        148–159
Englehardt, HT, 74
Epidemics I (Hippocrates), 52
EPTI. *See* extremely preterm infant
ethics, medical
    committees, 154
    deontological forces influence on, 53
    Islamic/Jewish teaching's influence
        on, 52–53
    law's relationship to, 136
    renaissance influence on, 53
ethics, politic, 53
eugenics theory, 84
EURONIC. *See* European Project on
        Parents' Information and Ethical
        Decision Making in Neonatal
        Intensive Care Units
European Convention for the Protection
        of Human Rights and
        Fundamental Freedoms, 182
European Convention on Human Rights
        (ECHR), 165, 166
European Court of Human Rights,
        166–167
European Project on Parents' Information
        and Ethical Decision Making in
        Neonatal Intensive Care Units
        (EURONIC): Staff Attitudes and
        Opinions study, 42–44
euthanasia
    active v. passive, 72–73
    French National Consultative Ethics
        Committee thoughts on, 120
    French NICU practice of, 180
    Netherlands practice of, 181
extremely low birth weight infant
        (ELBW)
    Canadian study of, 32–33
    defined, 7
    determining value of life for, 80–85
    health state comparative study of,
        36–37
    Japan and economics of, 46–47

Melbourne (Australia) follow-up
    study of, 32
parent's/health professional attitude
    study, 37–38
perinatal mortality of, 11
predicting survival of, 17
resource expenditures for, 45–47
extremely preterm infant (EPTI)
    antepartum viability judgments for, 16
    assisted ventilation for, 20
    Australia (Melbourne) study of, 14
    birth condition indicators, 18
    Canada's reports on, 13
    common law limitations regarding,
        173
    CPR for, 18–19
    decreased brain volumes of, 25
    defined, 7
    determining moral worth of, 78
    early prognosis limitations for, 7
    ethical complexities surrounding, 107
    ethical theories/schools of thought
        on, 53–54
    gestation variance survival rates of,
        24, 26
    hastening death of, 21
    historical obligations to care for, 10
    increases in, 11
    increasing survival rates for, 194–195
    justice for, 68–69
    Lorenz/Panetti on treatment of, 34–35
    morbidities, 25–28
    mortality rates of, 11
    mortality variations for, 11
    national comparisons of, 20–22, 26
    Netherlands and, 20
    New Jersey and, 20
    nonautonomy of, 59
    outcomes, short/long-term, of, 26
    predicting outcomes for, 23
    psychosocial strain on families of, 194
    surrogate's relationship with, 59
    survival possibility for, 46
    UK common law regarding, 161
    uncommonness of, 7

F v. F court case, 174
families
    emotional/financial burden of, 25
    happiness of, 56

psychosocial strain on EPTI, 194
Farine, D., 13
Feinberg, J., 65
fetal viability limit, defined, 14
Fetus and Newborn Committee
        (Canada), 106
    women's guidelines from, 106–107
Field, D., 26
Foot, P., 68
Frader, JE, 146
France
    children's legal existence status in,
        179
    Code of Medical Deontology of, 179
    Court of Appeal of Rouen of, 179
    decision making in NICUs of,
        191–192
    law issues of, 179–180
    National Consultative Ethics
        Committee of, 116–117
    neonatal euthanasia and, 180
    reports of, 116–120
Freeman, JM, 54, 64
futile therapy, 94, 119
futility
    emotional response connected to, 87
    medical, 182
    physiologic, 86
    qualitative, 86
    quantitative, 86
    virtually futile treatment choices, 145

Garland, MJ, 63
gastrointestinal dysfunction, 25
Gemerre, M., 191
Germany
    law issues of, 177–178
    reports of, 122
    Society of Medical Law of, 177
Ghazal, H., 40
Gibson, AT, 14
Glover, J., 71
Gordon, EJ, 191
Groningen protocol (Netherlands),
        189–190
growth, lack of, 25
Gultom, E., 14

harm, justifiability of, 62
Hart, HLA, 137

Hastings Center report, 125–127
Health and Human Services Department (US), 141
    Baby Jane Doe lawsuit and, 142–143
    Supreme Court criticism of, 143
Health and Safety Code, Advanced Directives Act of, 153
Health Care Surrogate Act, 148
hearing disabilities, 25
Higginson, R., 78
Hippocrates, writing of, 9, 52
Hippocratic Oath, 52
Holmes, RL, 63
Hospital Corporation of America v. Miller court case, 156–159
Human Rights Act (1998), 165

Iams, JD, 17
immunity, for physicians, 154
Infant Doe case [52 US LW 3369 (1983)], 95
infanticide
    historical aspects of, 9–11
infants
    happiness of, 56
    highly placed value of, 79
    Singer's definition of, 75
inhumane treatment, definition of, 145
International Federation of Gynecology and Obstetrics report, 127
IQ levels, 5, 29, 31
irreversible condition, definition of, 153
Islam
    medical ethics influenced by, 52–53
Italy
    Code of Profession Medical Ethics of, 121
    law issues of, 177–178
    reports of, 121

Jankov, RP, 18
Japan
    Criminal Code of, 176
    ELBW infant's cost in, 46–47
    law issues of, 176
    neonatal mortality reports from, 14
    physician's expected behavior in, 176
Japanese Eugenic Protection Act, 14, 176

Jehovah's Witnesses, withholding permission by, 170
Jonsen, AR, 52, 53, 63
Judaism
    medical ethics influenced by, 52–53
    sanctity of life principle of, 70–71
justice, for EPTI, 68–69
Justice Department (US), 141

Kadijk court case, 181, 183
Kant, Immanuel, categorical imperative of, 54
Kelly, E., 13
Kennon, Carole, 91, 94
Kenscamp, Arjen, 141
killing, dying v., 72
Kopelman, LM, 63

Laing, IA, 39
Lantos, J., 46
law
    Australia's issues of, 173–175
    Canada's issues of, 168–172
    French issues of, 179–180
    Germany's issues of, 177–178
    Italy's issues of, 177–178
    Japan's issues of, 176
    medical ethics relationship to, 136
    Netherlands' issues of, 181–183
    parens patriae common law doctrine, 139
    Poland's issues of, 177–178
    societal applications of, 136
    UK issues of, 160–167
    US issues of, 138–159
Lee, DSC, 27
Lee, SK, 27
legal systems, international variance in, 135
Leonard, CH, 28
life. *See also* end of life issues
    best interests and quality of, 80–85, 86
    brain functions help define, 75
    concerns regarding quality of, 35
    Declaration of Independence and protection of, 144
    determining value of, 80–85
    non-prolonging of, 74
    sanctity of, 70–71

life-support
American Academy of Pediatrics
guidelines, 95
federal government (US)
involvement deciding, 140
Jehovah's Witnesses and, 170
parental decisions regarding, 34–35
personhood's influence on, 76
physician decisions regarding, 34–36
President's Commission (US) report
on, 92
religious/socio-cultural issues with, 40
withdrawal of, 35
life sustaining treatment, definition of,
154
Linares, Rudy, 149
Linares, Sammy, 149
litigation, physician fears regarding, 36
living wills, 152
Locke, John, 77
Lorber, John, 140
Lorenz, JM, 34–35, 45
lung disease, 25, 27

MacDonald v. Milleville court case,
152
Macklin, R., 58
management strategies, 5
passive v. active, 17
Marion's Case court case, 174
Marlow, N., 14
Maternal-Fetal Medicine Committee of
the Society of Obstetricians and
Gynaecologists (Canada), 106
women's guidelines from, 106–107
Mawlana, 58
McDonnell, K., 54
McHaffie, HE, 39
McMillan, J., 39
Meadow, WL, 46
medical futility, 182
medical neglect
courts on, 147
definition of, 144
Medical Profession Act (Poland),
177
medically indicated treatment, definition
of, 144
mental retardation, 6, 25, 30
Mercer, BM, 17

Messenger, Gregory, 172
Meyers, C., 60
Mill, John Stuart, 55
Miller, Sidney Ainsley. See Hospital
Corporation of America v. Miller
Miller v. HCA court case, 188
Montgomery, J., 161
moral rights, of infants, 63
moral theory, 51–58, 59–72
morality
Beauchamp's definition of, 51
common, 58
and deontology theory, 54–55
Engelhardt on, 74
morbidity, of EPTIs, 25–28
mortality rates
ELBW, 11
EPTI, 11
halving of neonatal, 91
Moutquin, J-M, 13
Msall, ME, 30
Muslims. See Oman

Nadai, M., 41, 42
National Consultative Ethics Committee
(France)
decision-making recommendations
of, 119
on euthanasia, 120
on futile therapy, 119
neonatal resuscitation ethical
considerations of, 116–117
non-maleficence issue highlighted by,
117–119
purposeful ending of life discussion
by, 119
National Health and Medical Research
Council (Australia), 173
National Institute of Child Health and
Human Development (NICHD)
Neonatal Research Network trial of,
100–101
National Institute of Child Heath and
Human Development (NICHD),
12
Natural Death Act, 153
physician immunity in, 154
necessity. See doctrine of necessity
necrotizing enterocolitis, 3, 27, 45,
62

neglect. *See* medical neglect
neonatal euthanasia, 180
neonatal intensive care unit (NICU)
    admissions to, 11
    of Canada, 13, 45
    countries with aggressive use of, 31
    EPTI's economic impact on, 45–47
    French/US decision-making in,
        191–192
    international multicenter study, 28
neonatal management, comparison of, 30
neonatal mortality
    developing v. developed countries
        and, 21–22
    US report on, 91
neonatal mortality reports
    of Canada, 13, 29–30
    of Japan, 14
    of UK, 14–16
Neonatal Network Study (NICHD), 12
Neonatal Research Network trial
    (NICHD), 100–101
neonatal resuscitation, international
    guidelines for, 127
neonatologists
    counseling parents by, 39–40
    disabilities rated by, 36–37
    examining practices study of, 39
    health state comparative study by,
        36–37
    "least-worst strategy" of, 35
Netherlands
    Baby Jeremy court case, 182
    cerebral palsy rates in, 31
    EPTI outcomes in, 20
    euthanasia practiced in, 181
    Groningen protocol of, 189–190
    Kadijk court case, 181, 183
    law issues of, 181–183
    Prins court case, 181, 183
    University Medical Center of, 23
neurodevelopment disabilities, 7
New Jersey
    cerebral palsy rates in, 31
    EPTI outcomes in, 20
Newman, George, 141
Newmark v. Williams court case, 139
NHS v. D court case, 165
NICHD. *See* National Institute of Child
    Health and Human Development

NICU. *See* neonatal intensive care unit
Nigorsenga, J., 13
Nimrod, C., 13
Nishida, H., 13
non-maleficence
    beneficence and, 62–67
    Englehardt's use of, 74
    National Consultative Ethics
        Committee report on, 117–119
nurses
    disabilities rated by, 36–37
    examining practices study of, 39

obstetric management, influence of,
    16–18
obstetrician(s), antenatal data evaluation
    by, 17
O'Donnell, K., 64
Ohlsson, A., 27
Oishi, M., 13
Oman, life-support withdrawal issue of,
    40–41
Orfali, K., 191
outcomes
    of adolescence, 32–33
    assessing, 26
    EPTI's short/long-term, 26
    predicting EPTI, 23
    psychosocial/socio-economic
        influence on, 29
    school age, 29–30, 31

Panetti, N., 34–35
parens patriae
    Australia's application of, 174
    common law doctrine of, 139
    court's obligation of, 139, 168, 170
    state acting as, 142
parents
    American Academy of Pediatrics and,
        96
    anguish of, 91
    appearance concerns of, 40
    autonomy and, 59
    Child Abuse Amendments on role of,
        146
    child rearing constitutional rights of,
        139
    decision-making by, 21, 34–35, 93,
        139

disabilities rated by, 36–37
happiness of, 56
life/death choice example of, 140
limiting influence of, 156–159
neonatologist counseling of, 39–40
physician's conflicts with, 41–42,
    60
physician's deferring to, 36
physician's obligation to, 193
potential criminal charges against,
    139
right to be informed by, 150
societal trust of, 190
stress suffered by, 66
Supreme Court and consent of,
    143
testing authority of, 162–163
US courts non-override of, 148
withdrawing treatment decisions
    study of, 39
Paris, JJ, 65
Parker, M., 39
Partridge, JC, 35, 188
passive euthanasia, 72–73
patients
    duties of, 57
    self-perception of, 37
Paul, RH, 17
Percival, Thomas, 53
perinatal mortality, 11
person
    Locke's definition of, 77
    Singer's definition of, 74
personhood
    applying argument of, 78
    of disabled children, 74–79
    Englehardt on, 74
    life-support influenced by, 76
    neuropsychological standard for, 76
Peterson, S., 26
physicians
    American Academy of Pediatrics and,
        96
    continuing v. ending treatment
        choice of, 62–67
    counseling skill needed by, 87
    country variation of attitudes of,
        42
    decision-making pressures on, 61
    deference to parents, 36

duties of, 59
ecclesiastical doctrine's influence on,
    52
futility as used by, 87
Japanese expectations from, 176
life/death choice example of, 140
life-support decisions of, 34–36
litigation fears of, 36
Natural Death Act and immunity for,
    154
obligations of, 10
parent's conflicts with, 41–42, 60
parent's obligation to, 193
Percival on duties of, 53
potential criminal charges against,
    139
resuscitation decisions by, 36
rights of, 57
societal trust of, 190
treatment rights of, 136
willingness of, 138
physiologic futility, 86
Piecuch, RE, 28
Plato, writing of, 10
Poland
    Code of Medical Ethics of, 178
    law issues of, 177–178
    Medical Profession Act of, 177
preference utilitarianism, 84
premature birth, survival rates for, 7,
    195
President's Commission (US) report,
    91
    beneficial therapies described in,
        93
    criticism of adversarial nature of
        courts by, 94
    futile therapies defined in, 94
    hospital quality concerns of, 95
    information availability concerns of,
        94
    life-support withdrawal reported in,
        92
Prince v. Massachusetts (Supreme Court
    decision), 93
principilism, 58
Prins court case, 181, 183
prognosis, prediction accuracy of, 35,
    64
Psychomotor Developmental Index, 27

quality of life, and best interests, 80–85,
  86
quantitative futility, 86

R v. Arthur court case, 160–161
R v. Latimer court case, 172
re: B *(a minor)(wardship: medical
  treatment)* court case, 162–163
re: J *(a minor)(wardship: medical treatment)*
  court case, 163–165
Reagan, Ronald, 141
Rebagliato, M., 42
Rehabilitation Act of 1973, 141
  Baby Jane Doe lawsuit and, 142–143
religion, life-support issues of, 40
renaissance era, medical ethics influenced
  by, 53
Rennie, J. M., 18
report(s). *See also* President's Commission
  (US) report
  of Australia, 14
  of Canada, ,13, 18, 106–109
  Confederation of European
    Specialists in Paediatrics
    recommendations, 127–131
  of France, 116–120
  of Germany, 122
  Hastings Center report, 125–127
  international, 123–131
  International Federation of
    Gynecology and Obstetrics report,
    127
  of Italy, 121
  of UK, 18
  of United Kingdom, 110–115
  of United States, 91–105
  VLBW (Oklahoma), 18
The Republic (Plato), 9
resuscitation
  in delivery room, 18–20
  international guidelines for neonatal,
    127
  by physicians, 36
retinopathy of prematurity (ROP), 27
Rhoden, NR, 35
Ridley, A., 56
right to life, Tooley on, 75
Right to Life group, 153
right(s)

  to dignity, 165
  of physicians, 57
rights theory, 57
Rizzotti, A., 191
Robertson, John, 138
Rogers, BT, 30
ROP. *See* retinopathy of prematurity
Rosenbaum, P., 29
Royal College of Paediatrics and Child
    Health, 110–111
rule utilitarianism, 57

Saigal, S., 13, 29, 36
sanctity of life
  Glover on, 71
  principle of, 70–71
Sasaki, T., 13
Schneiderman, B., 169
school age outcomes, 29–30, 31
self-perception
  of adolescents, 32
  of patients, 37
Sherlock, R., 193
Simeoni, U., 191
Singer, P., 74
  infants defined by, 75
Skidmore, MB, 18
Smith, McCall, 161
society
  attitudes towards disabled children
    by, 9
  duty to, 53
  EPTI's economic impact on, 45–47
  law's applications in, 136
  parents/physicians trusted by, 190
  trust required of, 193
Society for Medical Law (Germany), 122
Society of Medical Law (Germany), 177
specieism, justifiability of, 77
State University of New York,
    Stonybrook, 141
Stolle v. Baylor College of Medicine court
    case, 155–156
stress, parent's experience of, 66
studies
  Australia survival rate study, 14
  Canada's ELBW study, 32–33
  Canadian comparative health states
    study, 36–37

Canadian EPTI study, 13
Chan's survival rate study, 27
Denmark physician treatment withdrawal study, 39
El-Metwally's survival rate study, 26–27
ELBW (Melbourne) follow-up study, 32
EURONIC: Staff Attitudes and Opinions study, 42–44
examining nurses/neonatologist's practices study, 39
neonatologists counseling parents study, 39–40
NICU neonatal intensive care unit international study, 28
NICU/UC San Francisco selective nontreatment study, 35
of obstetric care/EPTI survival, 16–17
parent/health professional ELBW infant attitude study, 37–38
of parents withdrawing treatment, 39
of patient's self-perception, 37
of survival rates, 12
UK population based study, 27–28
US multicenter cohort study, 27
Victorian Infant collaborative study, 29
Supreme Court (Canada), 172
Supreme Court (US)
Baby Jane Doe lawsuit and, 142
Health and Human Services Department criticized by, 143
Infant Doe case decision of, 95
parental consent issue and, 143
Prince v. Massachusetts decision of, 93
surrogates
continuing v. ending treatment choice of, 62–67
decisions of, 60
EPTIs and, 59
Feinberg on, 65
Synnes, A., 27
Szatmari, P., 29

technology, assisted reproduction, 196
Templeman, LJ, 162–163
terminal condition, definition of, 153
Texas

Hospital Corporation of America v. Miller court case, 156–159
living wills recognized by, 152
Stolle v. Baylor College of Medicine court case, 155–156
therapies
beneficial, definition of, 93
futile, 94, 119
Tooley, M., 75
treatment choices. See also inhumane treatment; life sustaining treatment; medically indicated treatment
benefit v. burden analysis, 80
continuing v. ending treatment, 62–67
doctrine of necessity and, 162
of physicians, 136
virtually futile, 145
Tucker, R., 12
Twaddle, JA, 169
Tyson, JE, 23

ultrasonograms, prepartum, 17
United Kingdom (UK)
British Medical Association of, 114–115
centralized specialist based services of, 26
Children and Young Persons Act of, 162
D v. UK court case, 165
EPTI common law of, 161
Human Rights Act of, 165
law issues of, 160–167
neonatal intensive care approach of, 26
neonatal mortality reports from, 14–16
NHS v. D court case, 165
population based study of, 27–28
R v. Arthur court case, 160–161
re: B (a minor)(wardship: medical treatment) court case, 162–163
re: J (a minor)(wardship: medical treatment) court case, 163–165
reports of, 110–115
Royal College of Paediatrics and Child Health of, 110–111

United Nations Convention on the
Rights of the Child, 187
United States (US). *See also* President's
Commission report
Baby Doe cases in, 140–143
Born Alive Protection Act of, 146
Civil Rights Commission of, 140
decision-making in NICUs of,
191–192
Department of Health and Human
Services of, 141
Durable Power of Attorney for Health
Care statute of, 153
Health Care Surrogate Act of, 148
Justice Department of, 141
law issues of, 138–159
life-support involvement by
government of, 140
Miller v. HCA court case, 188
multicenter cohort study of, 27
Natural Death Act of, 153
parents not overridden by courts in,
148
prematurity birth rates in, 195
President's Commission report, 91
Rehabilitation Act of 1973, 141
reports of, 91–105
University Medical Center of
Netherlands, 23
University of San Francisco (UCSF)
NICU study, 35
utilitarianism. *See* act utilitarianism;
preference utilitarianism; rule
utilitarianism

Van der Heide, A., 21
Van der Maas, J., 21

Van der Wal, G., 21
Veatch, RM, 58
Velez v. Bethune court case, 151, 152
Vendemmia, M., 191
ventilation
artificial, 5, 12, 62
assisted, 20, 46
need for, 3
positive pressure, 4
variance in need for, 30
Verter, J., 23
very low birth weight (VLBW) infants
Cambridge, England report on, 18
Oklahoma report on, 18
Ottawa, Canada report on, 18
viability
antepartum, 16
British Association of Perinatal
Medicine memorandum on,
111–113
limit (defined) of fetal, 14
limits of, 24
Victorian Infant collaborative study, 29
Vineland Adaptive Behaviour Scales, 30
visual disabilities, 25
VLBW infants. *See* very low birth weight
infants
Vohr, B., 12, 27

Wall, SN, 35, 188
Wilkinson, AR, 14
wills. *See* living wills
Wocial, L., 79
Woods, NS, 14
Wright, LL, 23, 27

Younes, N., 23